$2.50

DELTA LEGEND

For Debra
with gratitude
— Kelan O'Connell

Kelan O'Connell

Published by MidnightBBQ

ISBN-10: 0615778003
ISBN-13: 9780615778006
Library of Congress Control Number:
2013905436
CreateSpace Independent Publishing Platform,
North Charleston, South Carolina

For my parents,
Jacqueline and Edward O'Connell.
You've always made me feel like whatever I was doing was important
and made you proud—no matter what crazy scheme I had going
or how many times I reinvented myself.

❦ CHAPTER 1 ❦

THAT'S WHAT FRIENDS ARE FOR

Why did he let Rashawn talk him into things, Calvin asked himself as they walked toward the bus stop shortly before midnight. Probably because on some level, he felt for the guy. They'd grown up together in the same less-than-storybook neighborhood in Oakland, and while they both had absent fathers, Calvin, at least, had one stable parent at home. Rashawn's mom was, and always had been, a train wreck. These days she was more like the walking dead, still hittin' the pipe and doing whatever necessary to keep it filled.

After a twenty-minute wait that seemed like forever, they boarded the AC Transit bus that would eventually drop them near their East Oakland destination. At this hour, they were the only ones on board for most of the ride and Calvin noticed the driver frequently checking them out in his rear-view mirror. He didn't blame the man, really. It would take someone extremely vigilant and unflinching to drive a night route in Oakland.

Calvin Pierce and Rashawn Fontaine sat on opposite sides of the bus, their legs stretched out across both seats to face each other. At 16, Calvin was the more solidly built of the two, while Rashawn, who'd recently turned 17, was still on the gangly side. There was a time though, when they were just kids, that they might have been mistaken for brothers. That wasn't likely to happen these days, however; they were growing apart in most every way.

Appearance-wise, Calvin kept it considerably more real, and not just because his mother wouldn't allow anything extreme but because he didn't buy into the concept that respect came from what you wore. Sure he liked his baggies, Jordan's, and oversized tees, but Calvin didn't believe that was what made him.

Rashawn on the other hand was all about the show. His once short-cropped 'fro was replaced now with expensive shoulder-length braids. Calvin joked that a linebacker might suddenly appear out of left field and take Rashawn out since he now looked more like a wannabe NFL player than a kid from the block. And then there was the bling: fat fake diamond studs in each ear and a long thick gold chain with a gaudy rhinestone-encrusted horseshoe dangling at the end. Calvin wondered just how long it would be before Rashawn showed up with a gleaming grill.

One fashion accessory the two had in common on this night was their black oversized Raiders' jackets with hoods; uniform of the street, especially when heading out into the night to do deeds. Rashawn's jacket was the real deal, official NFL. Calvin's was a cheap flea market knock-off, which didn't matter at the moment since neither jacket could make them invisible or stop a bullet.

As they rode toward their destination, Rashawn goofed around to cover his nervousness while Calvin pulled his baseball cap low and chewed on the inside of his right cheek—a habit he'd had since childhood which became more pronounced whenever he was up to something his mother would not approve of.

When they were kids, Rashawn spent as much time as he could over at Calvin's place, soaking up the stability like a sponge. While Calvin would occasionally groan about having to do chores or homework, Rashawn would eagerly jump at the chance, hungry for the sense of order and routine Calvin took for granted. Now that they were older, things had changed. Rashawn had gradually succumbed to what many believed his inescapable fate; a perception Calvin's mom had valiantly fought to extinguish over the years. But Calvin didn't see Rashawn around school much anymore and he was hanging out with a less-than-admirable posse. The most telling difference, however, was that he no longer dropped by the apartment if there was any chance Angela was at home. He didn't hold up well under her interrogations, and on a deeper level, he couldn't bear her disapproval. So, Rashawn simply stopped coming around, and that told Angela Pierce everything she needed to know.

In certain company, Rashawn claimed to have a part-time job stocking shelves after hours at an electronics warehouse in the East-side O. While Calvin and others acknowledged Rashawn was doing something that involved a warehouse there, stocking shelves was probably not an accurate job description. More like un-stocking shelves and selling product on the street. Whether the "product" was stolen or smokeable goods, Calvin didn't know, didn't wanna know. What he knew for sure was that no minimum-wage stock clerk position came with a company car. A black Cadillac Escalade, no less. Sure it was a slightly older model, but still impressive for a 17-year-old and envied by more than a few haters.

Of course, Calvin didn't really believe Rashawn's overly complicated story of how some guy came to be in possession of said SUV. Trying to get a straight answer outta Rae Rae these days was a waste of your time and energy. The guy had a gift for swiffin' and could twist a story up to such a degree, you wouldn't know where to begin untangling it to find the nugget of truth—if there even was one.

When Rashawn first asked him to help get the Escalade back, Calvin said flat out "no" for three days straight. But Rae Rae had that goofy way of pleading which ultimately made Calvin laugh and he'd eventually cave, allowing himself to be swayed. It was only natural that Rashawn would come to him, of course—and not just because they were tight as kids. Calvin's mad skill with all things mechanical was widely known and respected in their circle. He was one of those kids who, at a very early age, took things apart just to see how they worked. Unlike most kids who attempted this, Calvin always got the things back together with every piece in the right place, every time. He had a way of making items that had stopped working start working again. He could jimmy locks, rewire almost anything electrical, and resurrect the mechanical dead. In light of these talents, his older brother Leo dubbed him MacGyver of the Ghetto. It wasn't until years later when Calvin was channel surfing one afternoon that he ran across the old show Leo had jacked the name from, at least the MacGyver part. He wanted to tell his brother he finally "got" his nickname. He couldn't, of course. Leo'd been gone four years by then.

And so, because of their history together, and the fact that Rashawn was the closest thing to a brother he had left, Calvin had a hard time saying no to him. Though in his gut, he knew he should have. If his mom hadn't taken an extra shift at the hospital that night, there was no way he would've risked sneaking out to help Rashawn ... again. Yet here he was, heading into the Deep East in the middle of the night, about to hot-wire an SUV for his childhood friend. Right about now Calvin was wishing Rashawn drove an old scraper. That would have made this mission so much easier. A scraper, however, would be a little too conspicuous for Rashawn's "warehouse" job.

Calvin reached to touch the small black leather case in his back pocket, just to make sure, then he chewed on the inside of his right cheek some more. Rashawn pulled the cord to let the driver know they wanted off at the next stop—fine by him, good riddance to hood rubbish. They exited out the rear side door and onto the sidewalk of an older neighborhood made up of run-down houses oddly intermingled with light industrial buildings.

Inner-city neighborhoods rarely go completely silent, least of all in Deep East Oakland. Sometimes the bone-rattling bass of an intense car stereo can be heard as it cruises somewhere in the vicinity. Sometimes the squealing of tires accompanied by shouts and cheers as someone pulls a sideshow. Then there are the sirens, always the sirens. Sometimes far off, sometimes nearby. At this moment, however, the urban neighborhood was eerily quiet. Nothing but the sound of a couple pitties barking in front yards as Calvin and Rashawn walked down the street exuding their best gangsta attitude; a balancing act between looking fearless and looking over their shoulders. Calvin suddenly wondered if Rashawn had a burner on him. He somehow doubted it, but then again, Rashawn had changed a lot over the last year or so. Still, he couldn't imagine his homeboy with a gun.

As they rounded a corner, Rashawn put a hand on Calvin's arm indicating they'd arrived at their destination. They stood back in the shadows at the edge of a large yard surrounded by a chain-link fence with a padlocked gate. The two-story Victorian on the property was weathered and crumbling, the front yard a sea of knee-high weeds. Bluish light from a TV flickered somewhere in the back part of the house but the front rooms were dark. A tired old sofa sat on the front porch, its floral print loud enough to see from the street—no porch light needed. Calvin envisioned a bunch of drug dealers or old men, possibly both, sitting on the battered couch choppin' it up each afternoon.

There were six cars parked two by two down the long driveway: a silver Lexus, a newer white Navigator, a much older red Mustang, and a couple of rusted-out buckets at the back that would likely never see the street again. As promised from Rashawn's earlier reconn mission, the black Escalade sat just behind the front gate. Backed in, it was parked beside the Lexus, which did little or nothing to help block the view of it from the house. The Navigator would have provided much better cover. There was maybe only twenty-five yards between the house and the Escalade, certainly not the fifty-yard buffer Rashawn had claimed. He'd also sworn up and down that the car alarm on the Escalade was disengaged. Needless to say, Calvin didn't automatically trust whatever Rashawn said. But before he even addressed hot-wiring the SUV, he would first need to deal with the padlocked gate.

Calvin signaled for Rashawn to keep an eye out as he removed his little black case. He knew instinctively which pick would be the right choice for that particular brand and model lock, and pulling it from the case, he went to work. Within a matter of seconds, Calvin had the padlock open. He then carefully and quietly removed it along with the attached chain. Rashawn rushed to open the gate but Calvin stopped him. Pulling a small can of WD-40 from his jacket pocket, he sprayed the gate's hinges to ensure it would not literally and figuratively squeal on them when opened. This was the kind of detail Rashawn would never think of, and Calvin would never miss.

As they came up on the Escalade, Rashawn retrieved the Slim Jim he'd been sporting down his pants and handed it over, knowing Calvin would be far more skilled at using it and less likely to scratch his prized whip. If Rashawn had it wrong about the alarm, they would know any second now. Calvin held his breath as he worked the Slim Jim into the driver's side door and breathed an internal sigh of relief when no alarm triggered. He had the SUV open in short order and quickly climbed inside to kill the interior light while Rashawn remained outside keeping watch as planned.

Wasting no time, Calvin got down to business. Over the last few days he'd done his homework on this specific make and model Escalade. His first task was to pop out the ignition switch. Removing a pair of wire cutters and a slide hammer from the inside pocket of his jacket, Calvin inserted the latter into the ignition, working it deep into the tumblers. This part turned out to be considerably more challenging than he'd hoped. After roughly two minutes, he was finally able to remove the ignition switch, exposing a tangle of wires—significantly more than he'd anticipated. With only the muted glow of a streetlight to work with, Calvin struggled to distinguish between the various colored wires. He retrieved a small keychain-size flashlight from his pants pocket, stuck it in his mouth, and bit down on the button to illuminate it. Now able to identify and segregate both the pink and white ignition wires, he used his cutters to snip them, then strip the plastic casing off the ends.

Standing beside the partially open passenger door, Rashawn's nervous energy ricocheted out in all directions as he split his focus between checking the compound and checking Calvin's progress. An unseen dog in the fenced back yard of the house must have caught a whiff and decided to report for duty, sounding the alarm.

"Come on, Cavi," Rashawn forcefully whispered through the passenger door.

"Not helping," Calvin sternly whispered back around the tiny flashlight in his mouth.

After a couple minutes of barking, someone inside the residence decided to take the dog seriously and have a look. The porch light popped on, illuminating the front of the house and part of the yard.

"Shit," cursed Rashawn under his breath as he ducked down, "'bout to shut it down, breh."

"I need more time," Calvin replied, but did not turn his head or stop working. Having stripped and twisted the ignition wires together, he was on to his next task; finding the starter wire that once clipped, stripped, and tapped against the ignition wires, would spark the engine to life. At least that was the plan.

Suddenly the front door of the house opened and an impressively large black man appeared in the threshold. He cautiously looked around before stepping out onto the porch to investigate.

Rashawn crouched low and carefully made his way to the rear of the Escalade, but as he went to peer around the tail light, he was abruptly stopped short with a yank. His gaudy rhinestone medallion and chain had become caught in the narrow crevice between the car and the bumper. As he tugged on the chain in an effort to free himself, the horseshoe broke off and clanked to the ground. So much for good luck.

Hearing the chunk of bling hit the cement, the man stealthily crept to the edge of the porch where he made it undeniably clear he was armed with a shotty. "Who's out there?"

Still attached to the bumper, Rashawn could not duck out of sight and was spotted.

"What the hell?!" shouted the man as he cocked his gun.

Scrambling, Rashawn managed to ditch out from under his chain, leaving it dangling from the bumper as he hurried to retrieve Calvin and abort the mission. "We gotta bounce, breh," he warned through the driver's door then headed for the street. His patna, however, did not follow.

Though he was aware of the situation, Calvin's focus was now almost trancelike. He was so close. Where others had their addictions: weed, video games, alcohol, whatever, Calvin's compulsion was found in any and all tests of his mechanical ingenuity. He could never simply walk away, make that *run* away, from this kind of challenge. While he considered the addictions of others a weakness that could prove costly, for the first time in his life, Calvin's obsession had the potential to get him killed.

The man came down the first few steps of the staircase and raised his gun, intently waiting for any moving target. Upon realizing that Calvin was refusing to flee the scene, Rashawn defaulted to his own childhood loyalty and snuck back between the cars on the driveway. He decided he would throw something into the back yard in order to distract both human and dog, but the man spotted a figure moving between cars and took aim. Rashawn knew he'd been made and dropped to the ground behind the Accord, waiting for shots to ring out. But none did. Miraculously, the gun had jammed and wouldn't fire, but the Escalade's engine did. Cursing, the man tried again to discharge his weapon without success. Furious, he hurled the shotgun aside. It landed on the stairs behind him and went off on impact, blowing a sizable hole in his front door. Now completely enraged and seeing red, the giant bull of a man was about to charge, going to handle things the old-fashioned way, with brute force.

Calvin revved the engine and pushed several buttons on the driver's door, attempting to unlock the passenger side. Every window in the Escalade rolled down before he was able to locate the correct one. He then leaned across the middle console and pushed open the passenger door. "Get in!" he commanded to wherever the hell Rashawn was hiding, which turned out to be a small space between the two buckets at the far end of the driveway.

It was now going to be a race between Raging Bull and Gangly Rashawn to see who could make it to the Escalade first. Rashawn made a break for it. Ironically, the Bull had to navigate his way around the Navigator, which gave Rashawn a split second advantage. He jumped into the Escalade, slamming the door behind him. Calvin had already dropped it into drive and was about to stomp on the gas when a large hand reached through the open passenger window and grabbed a fistful of Rashawn's braids. Calvin anxiously looked to his patna.

"Just go, breh! Drive!" Rashawn took hold of the hand grip built into the door frame and braced himself for the janky game of tug-o-war that was about to play out. Calvin romped on the gas. Tires screeched—so did Rashawn, who was nearly pulled out the window as the SUV peeled out of the driveway then fishtailed onto the street, narrowly missing a few parked cars before Calvin managed to gain control.

They sped away into the night, leaving The Bull standing in his driveway with one less vehicle, a gaping hole in his front door, and a fistful of hair extensions that he threw toward the street. "Son of a bitch!" He did, however, receive a lovely parting gift in the form of a horseshoe hunk of bling.

Driving fast while trying not to blatantly speed from the scene, Calvin repeatedly checked the rear-view mirror while Rashawn looked back over his shoulder to make sure they weren't being tailed. Calvin made several impromptu choices in direction to ensure they'd be extremely difficult to follow.

"Okay, we good," said Rashawn after a few minutes. "Iss all gravy."

As Calvin slowed to a more reasonable speed, Rashawn suddenly began to laugh.

"Nuh-uh, not funny," Calvin responded, dead serious. "That was too fuckin' close."

"Aw, I knew you could do it—you ma road dawg. Like whaaaaat!" Rashawn extended a closed fist to Calvin until he begrudgingly returned the love and knocked him back. "Way to come up, MacGyver o' the Ghet-to."

Calvin looked at him, did a double-take, then started to laugh himself. "Damn bitch, I thought that was yo' real hair."

"Shut the hell up." Rashawn rubbed his sore head, then inspected his fingers for traces of blood. There weren't any. Hitting the stereo, he cranked it up. "Man, I need a cheeseburga, fa sho!"

"No way, fool. I'm goin' straight home," Calvin shouted back over the pounding rap.

"Come on, Cavi R. We got ta celebrate getting ma whip back."

"You wanna celebrate somethin', celebrate the fact we didn't get our asses capped back there. No thanks to you."

"Best way I know to celebrate not getting' ma ass capped is with a big ol' double cheeseburger with bacon. And rings. Mm, love to have me some rings."

Calvin had to admit the adrenalin rush had given him an appetite and the thought of a burger with onion rings was hard to resist.

"I'm buuuyin'," said Rashawn, sweetening the deal.

"A'ight. But drive-through," insisted Calvin, giving in. "No way I'm gonna be seen witchew lookin' like dat."

Sadly, Rashawn's passenger-seat celebration dance was cut short by a blurp; flashing red and blue lights followed by the quick chirp of a siren.

"Aw man, I knew it!" declared Calvin, hitting his palms on the steering wheel. "I shoulda neva let you talk me into this."

Rashawn clicked off the stereo. "Be cool, a'ight? No way nigga called the po po's," he claimed, trying to convince himself as much as Calvin. "Elroys just doin' a DWB, tha's all."

But Calvin was already envisioning the hell that would rain down upon him if his mother found out anything about the night's activities. Not to mention the fact that he would likely lose his license, being that he was still a provisional driver.

The moment they pulled over, a glaring spotlight lit up the interior of the Escalade from behind. As they waited for the cops to call in the plate, Calvin attempted to push the dangling wires back into the hole where the ignition switch had once been. He thought about feeling around on the floor for the switch itself but then decided better, the boys in blue might think he was reaching for a piece.

"Ain't illegal to thug ma own ride," claimed Rashawn. "We just show 'em the registration, cousin." He then opened the glove box to find it empty—no registration, no nothing. A moment later, two male Oakland PD officers, one white, one black, approached on either side of the vehicle with flashlights shining on the occupants.

"Hey, how you doin' tonight, breh?" Rashawn asked the black officer at his window who declined to engage in street niceties, choosing instead to train his flashlight and attention on Rashawn's intriguing new 'do.

"Driver's license, registration, and proof of insurance, please," instructed the white officer standing at the driver's side. Calvin handed over his license and gave Rashawn a sideways glance, wondering how he planned to explain the absence of those all-important documents, namely the vehicle registration.

"It's ma ride," said Rashawn, leaning over to address the white officer at the exact moment the black officer shined his flashlight on the hole where the ignition switch should have been. "Look here, I lost ma keys. I don't have the registration on me, but this car's mine and I can prove it."

"Well, breh," replied the black officer with blatant sarcasm, "looks like you gonna have to do that."

And with that, Calvin and Rashawn heard those all-too-famous and dreaded words, "Please step out of the vehicle."

The black officer escorted Rashawn to the front of the cherry top and proceeded to check him for weapons. The white officer did the same with Calvin at the back of the Escalade. And as Calvin leaned on the SUV spreading his arms and legs, he looked down to see Rashawn's long gold chain dangling from the bumper.

"Yeah," said the white officer, confirming Calvin's grim realization. "We probably wouldn't have bothered," he added, removing the handcuffs from his belt, "but that chain ... well, it definitely caught our attention."

CHAPTER 2

DELTA DAWN

Suicide had just completed a six-month stint in County. Having recently turned 45, the white biker was always ready to prove he wasn't past his prime, and serving yet another aggravated assault sentence would ensure him the respect he deserved for at least another year or so. With his shaved head, prison tats, and full beard that had recently begun to gray, Suicide was the menacing middle-aged biker "extra"—only without the paying gigs. Though he still sported a considerable gut, he'd lost a few pounds on the jailhouse diet and was feeling somewhat toned. He'd been permitted to visit the weight room during the last two months of his sentence, seeing how he'd been a good boy and all; didn't assault anyone on the inside, or at least didn't get busted for it.

His first call from the crusty pay phone across the street from the Washoe County Jail was to Crow, who quickly spread the good news. Thirteen members of Satan's Posse were not currently incarcerated, working a job, or tied down by a woman and kids, so were free to join in a celebratory ride. It was decided the "club" would head down Interstate 80 to a biker bar in Sacramento, and that was about as far as any of them could plan ahead.

Crow had managed to round up a couple of younger chicks as a "welcome home" present for 'Cide, who could take his pick and Crow would entertain whichever one was left over. Since a few of the other bikers would be bringing their old ladies along, this would help prevent Suicide from messing with their women once he was good and drunk, which of course, he would be in no time. Staying clean and sober on probation was not part of the Satan's Posse creed.

The two younger women sported more ink than most Posse members, and while nothing special to look at, they were both on the skinny side. Considering nearly all the biker mamas Suicide's age were now thick in the middle, having either one of these broads on board would make for an easier ride. Crow knew Suicide didn't like to work too hard.

By 2 a.m., the bikers were partying on one of the few sandy beaches along the Sacramento-San Joaquin River Delta. With most of the shoreline throughout the Delta being nothing more than a graduated slope of large rocks strategically placed to keep the levees from eroding, a beach is a rare and coveted thing. And it was on that uncommon stretch of sand that the parole party raged on until shortly before daybreak.

As the first rays of dawn danced on the river's surface, daylight revealed a scattering of bikers passed-out on the sand. The scene resembled a tragic battlefield; the enemy being gravity mixed with alcohol and a few other substances. While some of the group had managed to stumble to their choppers parked above on the levee to retrieve a sleeping bag or poncho, most were simply sleeping where they had dropped with only the chemicals in their bloodstream to keep them warm. Luckily, it was early summer.

Awakened by his bladder, Suicide extricated himself from the young biker chick curled up next to him, undoubtedly seeking body heat rather than affection. If the bottle of Jack in his hand weren't already empty, he would have killed it in order to make the morning a little more tolerable. The aging biker struggled to his feet and staggered off through a clump of low brush bordering the beach. He didn't have to go far to find a suitable place to relieve himself. The remains of an old wooden structure stood a short distance down river. Built into the levee, it looked like a giant flood gate or perhaps the abutment to a bridge whose over-crossing had fallen into the water long ago. Now overgrown with blackberry bushes and disintegrating from years of exposure to the river and other elements, whatever the structure had once been, for the moment it would be serving as a rest-stop exit sign.

'Cide was finishing his business and zipping up when a bright light suddenly blinded him. The sun had moved just the perfect increment to hit something shiny on the weathered wood framework, throwing off a blinding glare.

Even hungover (make that still drunk) Suicide could not resist the urge to investigate. Shielding his eyes, he walked toward the decaying ruins, inexplicably drawn to the source of an intense reflective light.

❦ CHAPTER 3 ❦

DARK WATER

T imothy "Tak" Cheng rarely had nightmares. If he did, they were certainly never about his ancestral homeland of China. The 68-year-old retired pharmacist was "born and bred," after all, as American as apple pie. Apple pie made with Chinese Five Spice, that is.

While he believed each successive generation experienced a deeper sense of belonging, like many older Chinese-Americans, Tak never felt completely incorporated when it came to the Melting Pot concept of this country. Certainly not in the way his son and grandchildren appeared to seamlessly blend into the fabric of American society. Still, he was more of this place than of China, therefore it was extremely unusual that he should wake with such a start from a nightmare that had something to do with the motherland of his ancestors.

Shortly after dawn Tak found himself sitting bolt upright gasping for air, his nightshirt drenched with sweat. In the nightmare, he'd been speaking, no, screaming, in Cantonese.

And though he'd never been there, he somehow knew that in his dream he was in the Pearl River Delta region of southeast China; the place his great-grandparents had emigrated from.

As he slowly came to consciousness, Tak struggled to grasp and hold onto the shadowy details of the dream. There was a vast body of dark water, the confluence where the Pearl River spills into the China Sea. And there was an overwhelming feeling of dread. Of what, he could not name or even identify with clarity, only that his fear had something to do with the dark water. What he knew with certainty was that his nightmare was not of present-day China, but rather a time long past, perhaps even hundreds of years ago.

In the unsettling dream, several men in traditional clothing were fishing from a Chinese junk. They cast their nets into the stygian waters. Tak was on the shore frantically yelling for the fishermen to come in, to come ashore quickly. The men heard and responded. And though they tried to row the ship with long oars, they could not row fast enough, could not outdistance the thing, and then … then …

Tak woke up, struggling to catch his breath.

The nightmare triggered old feelings in him, like a scary story from childhood. The kind that seemed so real, you pulled the covers up over your head and fought to put it out of your mind each night at bedtime. That was just silly, Tak told himself. He was far too old for childish fears, or to waste any time trying to make sense of a nonsensical dream. Best to get up, put the kettle on, and let it go.

He pulled on his robe, stepped into his slippers, and went downstairs. His kitchen was situated in the back half of the old row house, while his medicinal herb shop occupied the front. As Tak lit the burner beneath the tea kettle, he remembered that a

18

shipment had arrived the previous day via UPS. Seeing as he was up early, he might as well get started unpacking it. That's probably what triggered the troubling dream in the first place—the herbs had come from China, after all.

In spite of his Western education and a successful career as a pharmacist, Tak had always harbored a passion for Eastern Medicine. He was glad he'd gotten out of the pharmaceutical racket when he did. Things had gotten more than a little out of hand in his opinion. "Ask your doctor if this, that, or the other drug is right for you." Please. The average person didn't need the plethora of prescription meds so zealously marketed to them nowadays.

Tak often wondered what his wife, Rose, would have thought of his late-in-life career as a Chinese herbalist. She probably would have just smiled and rolled her eyes the way she did when she felt he was being impetuous. He missed that. She'd been gone almost as long as he'd been retired, six years now. All the tea in China, all the chemo in America—one of the stranger things that popped into his head when recalling that deeply sad time.

The main reason Tak had never visited China was because he and Rose planned to go there together once he retired. With Rose now gone and their son off living his own life, Tak eventually sold the family home in Stockton and moved to the tiny Delta town of Locke. Though he'd never actually lived in the town before, he spent a good deal of time here while growing up nearby on his family's farm, and therefore felt a sense of connection to the place. He'd much rather be here with the ghosts of this old Chinatown than with the ghosts of his own life.

Once a thriving Chinese community, Locke was now a shadow of its former self. Tak could relate. A registered historic site, the town was built by Chinese merchants who'd emigrated from what was then known as the Heungshan District of Guangdong Province. From its humble beginnings in 1915 to its rollicking Speakeasy days during Prohibition, this eclectic little town had seen several incarnations of itself. After World War II, most of the young Chinese-American descendants of the community moved away to places that offered better jobs, education, and more integrated lives. The once bustling Chinatown began to wither and fade, falling into extreme disrepair by the seventies. But like Tak, having been through a period of mourning for its once-vibrant past, Locke was beginning to show signs of a revival. Yet another life in its old age. While neither Tak nor the town would ever be the lively versions of themselves they once were, it wasn't over yet.

So here he was, living and working in an old clapboard house whose bones creaked as much as his own. Whose walls had witnessed the struggles and small triumphs of several generations of Chinese people, followed years later by a few whites and others living on the fringe of their own society. Among Locke's eighty or so residents only a handful of Chinese lived here now. And though Tak's Cantonese was rusty, there were still a few folks in town to speak it with. As a kid growing up in the area, it was frowned upon to speak the native language of his culture anywhere but here in Locke or the safety of home. Definitely not in the white school or neighboring towns. Always caught between two worlds.

Of course, his son and daughter-in-law thought he was crazy for opening a traditional Chinese medicine shop here, especially at his age. But considering he was somewhat lost without Rose, they left him to his foolish venture, figuring it was harmless enough and would keep his hands busy and his mind sharp.

His son Kevin farmed nearby, on the land that had been in their family for generations now. Farming wasn't for Tak. Though he acted appropriately disappointed at Rose's insistence, Tak was actually delighted his son had a passion for farming and would carry on the family tradition that had skipped a generation.

Summers brought more tourists to this tiny historic town. Some would even venture to come into his shop and purchase Eastern remedies for whatever ailed them. Sometimes Tak liked to mess with the tourists a little, putting on a clipped Chinese accent and throwing in some broken English—perhaps even dispensing the occasional morsel of ancient Chinese wisdom. It amused him when people would start speaking loud broken "Engrish" back. And though he'd never set foot on a stage, Tak got a kick out of playing the part of a stereotypical Chinese character, the kind Hollywood spoon-fed America for years. His son and daughter-in-law would scold him whenever they caught him in the act, but Tak would defend his performance by claiming he was simply providing an experience. People had come to see the only town in America built by Chinese for Chinese. The fact that white people and stray cats now outnumbered the Chinese residents could be somewhat disheartening.

These out-of-towners were the predominately white pill-poppers who'd supported his first career in pharmaceuticals. They couldn't be bothered with carefully brewing a tea or dealing with a tincture, so Tak carried a few of the more palpable versions of Eastern medicines just for them. Things that cured a variety of ailments resulting from American excess: hangovers, diarrhea, sunburns, and indigestion. He also stocked up on some of the more catchy commercial remedies around this time of year; stuff tourists latched onto like He Shou Wu, which roughly translates

21

to Black Hair Mr. He. Even at his age, Tak had plenty of salt-and-mostly-pepper hair that he credited to He Shou Wu, a best seller among middle-aged white men. Many of whom, despite their beer guts, still wore Speedos when out on their cabin cruisers. If there were a Chinese herb to prevent crimes against common sense, Tak would gladly have stocked that as well.

As he worked through the morning placing bulk herbs into jars for his regular customers, and shelving herbs in pill form for the tourists, Tak was occasionally haunted by his earlier nightmare. But it was fading, melting. Not unlike the way he himself was expected to meld into American society. By afternoon, all that was left of the shadowy dream was a feeling. It felt oddly familiar, yet ancient.

❧ CHAPTER 4 ❧

COULDA, WOULDA, SHOULDA

Alameda County Juvenile Court was now in session—another packed house. Being back here again was just one more thing Angela Pierce didn't need.

Wearing scrubs beneath her jacket, the 42-year-old nurse didn't have time to go home and change. In fact, she'd made Calvin take the bus to meet her here. She had no intention of making this any easier on him. It certainly wasn't easy on her, especially since she had to find someone to cover the middle part of her shift while she tended to this "family matter." Hardly an easy task as subs generally wanted your whole shift or nothing at all. Angela hoped to make it back to the hospital for the second half of a ten-hour stint but that would depend on how things played out here. Unfortunately, she'd had some experience with the juvenile court system in the not-so-distant past, and true to its nature, things were already running an hour and a half behind schedule.

Along with the obvious anger she felt around the situation, Angela was haunted by an unnerving sense of déjà vu. This was *not*, however, supposed to be happening with Calvin. He wasn't anything like Leo. He had a mind of his own, didn't follow the pack, and didn't respond to peer pressure. So what the hell was he thinking? She'd gone over and over it in her mind the last few weeks, and it always came back to Rashawn: his downward spiral coupled with Calvin's loyalty.

Angela had done as much as she could for Rashawn but she was only a one-woman village, and in the end, he'd chosen a different path. He didn't have the strength of character her own son did, yet he'd managed to draw Calvin in this time. Well, it would be the last, she'd make damn sure of that. If only she'd moved them away from the neighborhood, they might not be sitting here today. Coulda, woulda, shoulda. She was finally making decent money but along with the paychecks came the student loan payments for her nursing education. "Movin' on up" wasn't exactly an option at the moment.

Her son looked extremely uncomfortable in the jacket and tie she'd made him wear. Images from the last time she saw him dressed in a suit began to push their way in, but Angela quickly pushed them back. Present-day Calvin fidgeted and pulled at the tight, stiff collar as he sat beside her. According to the docket his case was next to be heard by the middle-aged white judge, once he wrapped things up with the scary-looking teenager standing before him in juvie-issued sweats and T-shirt.

Over the last hour and a half, Angela and Calvin had gradually moved forward in the courtroom. They were now seated close to the front and could clearly hear the proceedings. Those juvenile defendants who were not currently incarcerated, and therefore escorted by guards, had the option of waiting outside in the hall with their guardians or attorneys until their case was called.

But Angela wanted Calvin to take in as much of this dark circus as possible, hoping it would have a negative impact. She wanted him to see the teenagers in jail attire and cuffs. But she'd been so focused on Calvin up until now, she hadn't considered her own reaction upon seeing them. Angela found herself struggling to keep her emotions in check—not see something of Leo in every black kid wearing handcuffs and juvie sweats.

Judge Mason continued to address the menacing white teenager whose shaved head was a graphic novel of racist tattoos. "I suggest, Mr. Andrews, that if you'd like to spend at least some of your adult life outside of a correctional facility, that you stop threatening your attorney with bodily harm."

"Bitch can kiss my white ass," the teen defiantly announced.

Obviously a public defender, Mr. Andrews' attorney was a young Arab-American woman who tried her best to look unfazed by her juvenile client's remark. But Angela could tell this little punk had been busy making the poor woman's life a living hell.

Angela had not retained an attorney for Calvin. She'd gone that route with Leo and it took her three years to pay off that debt. She'd been buried alive under bills for so long she wondered what daylight might look like. No, she was going to take her chances and go it alone as the sole representative of her son.

After several more R-rated outbursts from the defendant, the judge decided to move things along. "Thanks for playing, Mr. Andrews. Sorry, no parting gifts for you. Bailiff, please see that Mr. Andrews is escorted back to his preferred accommodations and we'll try this again in a few weeks."

Angela felt for the little shit's attorney, who was undoubtedly hoping the judge would recommend a more suitable replacement for her. No such luck. And as Mr. Junior White Supremacist was escorted out the side door by a large black bailiff, he flipped off the Judge with both hands cuffed in front of him. But Judge Mason simply waved bye-bye back and took up the next file handed to him. Angela felt her son stiffen beside her as they waited, watching the Judge look over his case file.

"Calvin Pierce," a Hispanic female bailiff called out to the chamber.

She didn't have to call a second time as Angela and Calvin stood and immediately took their place at the defense table before Judge Mason, who continued to pore over Calvin's file. Angela was glad to see he was carefully studying the case. She also suspected he might be doing it to make Calvin sweat a bit more, which was fine by her. Finally, the judge looked up. "Are you Mrs. Pierce?"

"I am, your honor."

"Good," was all he said before turning his attention to Calvin. "I understand you're quite skilled with engines, Mr. Pierce."

Calvin didn't know what to say. His mother was looking at him, the judge was looking at him, and he could feel other eyes in the courtroom on his back. It was a simple enough question that under any other circumstance would have been easy to answer. In this situation however, if he agreed, he might be incriminating himself. If he disagreed, he'd be lying.

Judge Mason didn't have time to wait for Calvin to cough up an answer, so he picked up the ball. "Fortunately for you, Mr. Pierce, the charge of grand theft auto has been dropped since the car you hot-wired is indeed registered to your friend, a Mr. Rashawn Fontaine. Therefore, you were doing so with the permission of the vehicle's registered owner. While your actions may not have been illegal, they were certainly unwise." The Judge took off his glasses and rubbed his eyes before continuing. "Aside from the issue of a minor driving another minor, Mr. Pierce, are you aware that while your friend's car was impounded, a canine unit discovered a rather substantial quantity of cocaine in the door panel?"

Calvin's jaw dropped slightly and Angela turned to look at him. If her glare had been irradiated, he would have been reduced to ash in an instant. Did he know? Of course not. Was he really all that surprised? Of course not.

"I take it that's a 'no'," said the Judge, drawing his own conclusion from Calvin's face. "Mr. Pierce, I could easily charge you with co-conspiracy to traffic narcotics. However, your mother has written a very persuasive letter to the court. She's convinced this is simply a case of loyalty to a childhood friend coupled with a momentary lapse in judgment on your part." He then took a dramatic pause before rendering his own opinion on the matter. "I'm inclined to believe her."

Putting his glasses back on, Judge Mason proceeded to write some notes in the file before looking up and addressing Calvin once more. "Since you have no priors, I'm going to let your mother, and not the juvenile court system, handle this one. We're all full up. Next case."

Disoriented and somewhat in shock, Calvin turned to go but Angela grabbed him by the dress jacket and yanked him backwards. She didn't have to say a word. Calvin knew what she expected and attempted to comply. "Thanks."

Angela cleared her throat, indicating that wasn't quite good enough.

"Thank you, sir ... Your Honor ... sir."

"Don't thank me," he replied, peering over his glasses. "By the looks of it, I doubt you're getting off easy."

Mother and son drove home in silence. As pissed-off and disappointed as she was, Angela felt perhaps the experience had made a lasting impression. At least she hoped so. Now that they were safely in the car and she could let her guard down, the slide-show of Leo's life, and death, began to play in her mind. The heartbreak she'd been fighting all day bubbled to the surface and tears began to run down her cheeks. Calvin knew exactly who and what she was thinking about.

"Mom ..."

"Don't talk to me right now, Calvin."

He wisely honored her request.

Hoping to crawl out of the doghouse in increments, Calvin was not playing video games or listening to music when Angela arrived home from work that night. Instead, he was making a pot of Hamburger Helper. His room wasn't exactly clean but his bed was made—sorta.

"Fixed dinner, huh?" Angela remarked as she took off her jacket and stepped out of her shoes.

"Yeah. You hungry?"

She shrugged. "I could eat."

He dished up two plates and they ate in silence at the kitchen table until Calvin dared to brave the icy waters. "So, how was your day?" Shit. He'd meant to say *work*, how was work. Too late now.

"My day? Well, lemme see. My day started out in juvenile court. Then I had to go back to work where I couldn't stop thinking, 'Oh my God, it's happening all over again.'"

"I made a stupid mistake, that's all. I'm sorry."

Angela got up from the table and put her plate in the sink; didn't have much of an appetite after all. She stood there with her back to her son, and there was nothing Calvin could do but wait for it.

"You sat beside me at his funeral. You were only 11, but you took my hand and made me a promise."

"It's not the same thing."

But the flood gates blew open and Angela turned to face him.

"You think Leo became what he did overnight? Do you? Well, let me remind you, today was not my first appearance in juvenile court. And that was not the first letter I've written to a judge saying, 'my son just made a poor choice, I'm sure it won't happen again.'"

"How was I s'posed to know what Rashawn was into?"

"Oh come on, Calvin! You're s'posed to know better. You're s'posed to *be* better."

Angela suddenly stopped herself. She was too tired and too emotionally drained to lecture Calvin on what he already knew.

"I can't go through it again," she said quietly. "I can't."

Defeated, she walked down the hall to her bedroom and shut the door behind her. Calvin dropped his fork on the plate and shoved it away.

"I'm not Leo," he said loudly toward the hall and the closed door.

Later that night, Calvin tossed and turned in his sleep. Sometime around 2 a.m., he opened his eyes to find his mother standing at his bedroom window looking out at the urban neighborhood. She heard him sit up so knew he was awake, well, sort of awake. But Angela continued to stare out the window for a time before finally speaking. "Prove it."

"What?" he asked, still groggy.

"Prove to me you're not heading down the same path."

Calvin sat there half-asleep, bewildered as to how exactly he was supposed to do that. He didn't have to ponder long of course, Angela was about to render her sentence.

"I want you to go away for a while," she said. "For the summer."

Calvin scrunched up his face and stared at his mother's back. She'd lost her damn mind.

"Your great-uncle Samuel has that place in the Delta. He's gettin' on in years and could use the help."

"Mom…"

"It's not open for discussion, Calvin."

As if on cue, and to further validate her decision, sirens began to wail in the distance and continued to grow louder until two Oakland PD black and whites raced down the street in front of their apartment complex.

"I'll feel better knowing you're safe up there. Away from all the crap that's goin' on in this city."

The sirens had faded but Angela remained at the window, staring out into the night while Calvin sat there in his bed, stunned. She wouldn't really do this, would she? She was simply overreacting to the day, he told himself; being emotional, being extreme. She'd change her mind by morning. OR maybe he was dreaming. That was it. He'd wolfed down that pile of Hamburger Helper right before going to bed and it was causing him to have this crazy dream.

Calvin punched his pillow a couple times, then lay back down and pulled up the covers. He closed his eyes and looked forward to waking up tomorrow, when he would laugh his ass off at this janky dream—if he even remembered it. Go to the Delta for the summer. Yeah, a'ight.

❧ CHAPTER 5 ❧

MARGARITA SUNSET

A rental houseboat is the epitome of getting away from it all while taking it all with you. Roughing it on vacation was not for Larry and Darlene, who hailed from Las Vegas and had fled the crushing heat of June. While the California Delta gets hot in the summer, it's nothing compared to the endless heat of a desert paved over. Unlike the countless swimming pools of Vegas that boiled under the hot sun, the waterways of the Delta were always cool and refreshing due to their depth and constant flow.

Larry and Darlene discovered a quiet slough a few days back and had anchored the rental houseboat to one of its larger islands, having no clue that such a place was commonly known as a "bedroom" in the Delta. Now that the weekend was over, the other boaters had pulled up anchor and moved on. They had the place to themselves.

An aging Italian Stallion in his mid-50s, Larry stood on the back deck of the *Casa del Agua* in a Speedo and plastic Sensi sandals. Multiple gold chains and a heavy gold watch gleamed against his leathery, over-tanned skin. It wasn't easy finding a gold waterproof watch, but Larry had his connections: fine jewelry, gaming, adult entertainment, just to name a few. Snapping his fingers and bopping his head, he flipped through the travel CD case searching for the album with *that* song, the one already playing in his head. Pulling *Tom Jones' Greatest Hits* from its sleeve, Larry slid the disc into the player. He didn't even have to scan through the tracks since his retro favorite was the very first song. Cranking up the volume on "It's Not Unusual," he started to dance, which for Larry meant adding minimal footwork to the aforementioned finger-snapping and head-bopping.

The whir of a blender erupted as Darlene whipped up a fresh batch of Margaritas at the houseboat's outdoor bar. It was late afternoon, or perhaps early evening. They didn't know which and didn't care really; they were on vacation.

A former Vegas showgirl in her mid-40s, Darlene could still pull off wearing a bikini for the most part. She'd kept herself up, and since the breasts weren't real anyway, they'd stayed in place nicely. Sure smoking and baking herself under the Vegas sun had taken its toll on her skin over the years, but that's what Botox, peels, and lifts were for. Compared to other former showgirls Darlene would occasionally run into at the casinos, she was looking pretty damn good, could still turn a head. She'd certainly turned Larry's. The two had met over a craps table at Bellagio one afternoon last year and quickly left their respective spouses.

Darlene separated the blender's plastic pitcher from its base and held forth the slushy frozen happiness. Larry suavely danced over to the bar, grabbed two plastic Margarita glasses and salted the rims for her. She then masterfully filled them to the brim with the nectar of their gods. Larry had to hand it to Darlene; not only did she make one hell of a Margarita, the woman could dance like an angel, holding a cigarette in one hand and a Margarita glass in the other while wearing platform rubber flip-flops on the deck of a rocking houseboat. God, she had talent. And a killer rack.

As "It's Not Unusual" came to an end and another Tom Jones hit ensued, Larry danced Darlene over to the side of the houseboat where an inflatable dinghy was tied alongside. "Come on, baby doll, it's sunset cruise time and you're my first mate."

"First and last mate, Captain baby," she cooed back.

Darlene momentarily returned to the bar to crush out her cigarette and top off their cocktails. Refreshments were a vital part of what had quickly become a nightly ritual since renting the houseboat; a little excursion in the red Zodiac for a change of scenery and to take in the sunset. Already aboard the dinghy, Larry stood holding the houseboat's railing to keep the inflatable steady as Darlene carefully backed down the swim ladder with a full Margarita glass in each hand. Her captain was all too happy to assist by grabbing her ass with his free hand and steering it safely aboard.

Larry got the outboard engine to fire with only a couple pulls of the cord and they were soon tendering away from the *Casa del Agua*. He hadn't bothered turning off the CD player since they'd be back soon enough and rather enjoyed the musical send off to "What's New Pussy Cat." And Tom Jones would still be serenading them upon their return since Larry had set the disc to auto replay.

The couple cruised out into the main channel of the slough where they encountered the occasional cabin cruiser. Though the captains of these vessels graciously slowed down to afford them a more manageable wake before waving and powering on, it was still difficult to navigate the rollers without spilling their drinks. So Larry piloted the dinghy into a smaller adjoining slough where there was no boat traffic whatsoever. In fact, there wasn't another soul around. He soon killed the outboard engine so they could drift a while, sip a while, and take in the scenery.

Unlike a picturesque mountain lake, a majestic stretch of coastline, or a dramatically cascading river, the California Delta possesses a subtle beauty that reveals itself more slowly. Evening is a particularly magical time on the Delta, especially in summer. Quite often the breeze dies down and the water flattens to glass. Fish jump from below, and swallows or the occasional bat swoop down from above, doing their best to keep the abundant insect population in check. Ducks might fly overhead announcing their imminent water landing before making a noisy splashdown followed by a proud flotilla. And the crickets and frogs begin tuning up in anticipation of dusk as Mt. Diablo becomes a silhouette in the distance.

Larry and Darlene sat back and took in the scene while they waited for the grand finale: sunset.

"It's just so beautiful. Isn't it the most beautiful thing you've ever seen?" Darlene asked.

"No, *those* are the most beautiful things I ever seen." His eyes fully focused on her breasts.

The couple downed the last of their cocktails and started getting frisky. While Larry harbored romantic fantasies involving the Zodiac dinghy, making love in the uncomfortable little runabout was not Darlene's idea of a good time. While she didn't mind getting worked up out here, when it came to fully rocking the boat, she preferred a larger vessel, so to speak. Darlene sat up in order to cool things down and noticed just how far from the middle of the slough they had drifted.

"Larry. Larry! We're drifting into the weeds or reeds."

"Tules. They call 'em too-leez."

"Whatever. We're drifting into 'em."

"So?"

"*So*, I don't wanna get stuck out here. I don't have my cigarettes, for God's sake!"

Larry let out with a loud sigh and went to work getting the outboard engine started before they drifted too far. Truth be told, he wasn't keen on getting stuck out here either. The dinghy didn't have running lights and even though it wouldn't be fully dark for while, he didn't want to risk having to navigate their way back to the houseboat by night. He made sure the outboard was in neutral, bumped the gas line a couple times, and yanked the pull cord. The engine caught but then immediately died. Larry tried again with the same result. He simply wasn't having the same luck with the motor he'd experienced earlier. Though he made several more attempts to get the outboard going, his efforts were in vain. The current swiftly carried the inflatable boat into the thick of a small tule island.

While wonderful to anchor to, fish beside, and admire from afar, a tule island is not a desirable destination in and of itself. These countless little islands of the Delta can be either partially submerged or completely underwater depending on the tide. With shallow muddy water, spongy decaying tule grass, clumps of floating green algae, and an overabundance of mosquitoes, these soggy islands are a crappy place to be stuck.

"Oh, great," snarked Darlene, thinking mainly of her pack of Merits sitting on the bar back at the houseboat.

"Well, I can't start it up now, the prop'll just get clogged with gunk," declared Larry, trying to think what to do next. "At least we got oars, so if worst comes to worst, we can row back."

"Row back? That'll take us all night!"

"Okay then, we'll row out to the main channel and flag someone down for a tow."

"Oh, only half the night. You better find a way to get this thing started and get us outta here, mister," Darlene demanded, her nicotine level dropping rapidly.

Larry had to improvise. "Okay, here's what we're gonna do. We'll grab hold of the tules and pull ourselves as far away from the thick of it as we can. Then I'll try the engine again."

Darlene held up her hands displaying ten flawless acrylic nails with French manicure.

"So I'll buy you a new set when we get home," he promised.

While not happy with this plan, Darlene couldn't come up with a better one. How could she have forgotten her cigarettes? Life's little annoyances were so much easier to handle with an uninterrupted flow of nicotine. She reluctantly joined Larry in grabbing the long bulrushes (aka tules) as they attempted to pull the Zodiac back toward open water. They struggled to make any headway against the current and most of the slimy reeds broke off in their hands.

"Eeew," cried Darlene, disgusted.

"Aw, for shit's sake," groused Larry, quickly giving up on Plan A. "Current's too strong anyway. I'm just gonna have to push us out."

Kicking off his sandals, Larry proceeded to lower himself over the side of the dinghy. His feet squished into the muddy bottom and the chilly water came up to his waist. "Oh jeez, frozen giblets here."

"Poor baby," replied Darlene, barely attempting to sound sympathetic.

"Don't worry, I know a way you can reconstitute 'em later."

Larry waded to the stern of the Zodiac and began to push. He made fairly decent progress, and grunting seemed to help. He managed to push the boat out past the thickest part of the tules where the water was now up to his chest. Darlene was beginning to have hope that perhaps Plan B was going to work after all and they might soon be back aboard the *Casa del Agua* where her cigarettes and more cocktails awaited. Then without warning, Larry suddenly began to thrash about in the water.

"Oh no, somethin's got me! I'm bein' pulled under," he shouted before disappearing below the surface.

"Oh my God, Larry?!"

Darlene looked over the side of the Zodiac, scanning the water's surface for any sign of him, but all she could see were the water rings rippling out from where he went under. She was about to totally freak out when Larry suddenly resurfaced on the other side of the boat and began to laugh.

"You asshole," she fumed. "That wasn't funny. Ya scared the shit outta me!"

"Aw, baby doll, I'm sorry," said Larry, repentant and treading water in more ways than one. "I thought you'd know I was just playin' witcha. What'd you think, they got a sea monster in the Delta?"

"How the hell should I know?" she replied, still pissed.

Larry hurriedly swam to the dinghy and hung onto the side in order to beg forgiveness. "Aw now baby, don't be mad. I was just tryin' to get a little adrenaline pumpin'. Hey, 'member that time I pretended you backed over me with the car?"

Darlene's recollection of the incident began to melt the ice. Who knew a potentially life-threatening accident could be such a turn-on? Seemingly ready to forgive, Darlene leaned over the side of the boat and pulled Larry's face toward hers. Inches away from a kiss, she stopped short and pointedly announced, "I need my cigarettes."

Payback was indeed a bitch.

"Alright, okay. You'll get your damn cigarettes."

Resigned to the fact that his only hope for romance relied upon his capacity to reunite this woman with her smokes, Larry moved along the side of the boat until his feet could once again touch bottom. Slogging in the mud, the occasional rock or clam shell painfully gouged the soles of his feet, which were far more accustomed to soft Italian leather. But Larry knew he would get no sympathy from Darlene, so he stoically plodded his way back to the stern where the water was now up to the middle of his chest. He suddenly regretted his "sea monster" stunt, not only due to Darlene's total lack of appreciation, but also because the dinghy had drifted and he'd lost much of the progress made earlier. Larry decided this time he would give the Zodiac one good push, sending it as far away from the tule island as possible and into the stronger current. He would then swim out to it, climb aboard and try the motor again. If he couldn't get it started in the first couple tries, it was going to be a very long evening of row, row, row your boat.

Larry gave himself a motivational count of three out loud, "One, two…"

But before he got to three, the tow rope, which was dangling in the water at the bow, suddenly went taut. The dinghy then rapidly jettisoned out into the middle of the slough before gradually drifting to a stop.

"Woohoo, baby! You're like a big strong ape," Darlene cheered, clueless as to what had just happened.

"I ... I didn't do it. I didn't even get to three," Larry called out to her, dismayed. "The tow rope, it's like it got caught on somethin'."

"What?!"

"I didn't push you, you were pulled," he shouted.

Suddenly, several yards beyond the dinghy, an enormous dorsal ridge broke the surface of the water. It was the size of a whale, but no whale had a dorsal ridge comprised of sharp reptilian-like spines. Larry's jaw dropped as he spotted the thing moving swiftly through the water. "Cheese and crackers."

Seeing his face, Darlene decried, "I'm not falling for it twice, mister, so you can just stop right now!"

The jagged dorsal ridge picked up speed, heading directly for the boat. Larry instinctively began swimming for the Zodiac. Confused, Darlene turned in time to see the lethal row of razor-sharp spines as it bore down on the dinghy with staggering force. She barely had time to scream as it powerfully hit the inflatable boat, effortlessly slicing it in two—a table saw vs. a piece of paper. Darlene was left clinging to the deflated front half of the boat, its broken wood floor now more buoyant than the once air-filled chambers.

Having witnessed the violent destruction of the Zodiac, Larry was treading water a short distance from where Darlene clung to its remains. Having ripped through the dinghy, the creature barely broke speed. It now turned and headed for Larry. Seeing this, Darlene screamed out, "Swim back to the island!"

But it was too late, there was no time to react. The massive ridge dipped below the surface and seconds later Larry was swiftly jerked backwards in the water. His face went blank and his mouth filled with blood, which flowed down his chin and neck just before he was pulled under.

Darlene immediately went into shock accompanied by survival mode. Crying and gasping, she struggled to stay afloat on what was left of the little boat. Whatever had just attacked them seemed to have vanished beneath the surface, taking Larry with it. For several seconds there was no sign of the creature. Hoping and praying the thing was gone, Darlene attempted to quiet herself in case it was still there, lurking beneath. Maybe a boat would come by and she would be rescued. Maybe any minute now she would wake up and discover this was just a terrible nightmare. She even tried telling herself to wake up. Wake up, damn it!

And it was a nightmare, just not one she would ever wake from. Large bubbles began to rise from the water just below her. She waited, trying not to whimper, trying not to breath. Fortunately for Darlene, what transpired next happened with such efficiency and speed she did not have time to process it. A giant taloned paw shot out of the water, grabbed her by the head and yanked her under. Her garbled underwater screams reached the surface in a burst of bubbles and blood. Then silence.

Moments later, the two halves of the Zodiac were struck again and again, like a killer whale playing with a water toy at Sea World. Then it was done. The waters that had been churning moments before began to settle. Shredded pieces of the inflatable boat floated along with the current, drifting back toward the tule island. Two plastic Margarita glasses, one with Savage Red lipstick on the rim, bobbed among the debris.

CHAPTER 6

NOT THE HAMBURGER HELPER AFTER ALL

The Sacramento-bound Greyhound was already idling in preparation for departure. Once there, Calvin would transfer to a second bus that would take him south to Lodi. That is, if he didn't make a run for it at the transfer point and buy a ticket to anywhere but the destination his mother had arranged. The thought had briefly crossed his mind.

Calvin and Angela stood beside the bus as the last pieces of luggage were being stowed in its underbelly. They did not look at each other or speak, choosing instead to focus their attention on anything and everything else: the ground, the sky, the traffic, the baggage handlers, the various characters wandering about the Oakland transportation terminal.

Angela had confiscated Calvin's iPod the night before, saying she would send it to him once he'd spent some quality time getting to know his great-uncle. She didn't want him checking out, the way his entire generation could so completely shut out the world.

Calvin challenged her on this, of course, swearing he would only use the iPod when he was alone. Angela wasn't buying it. She'd also taken his cell phone, claiming the odds of him finding a signal up there were slim to none. While she didn't relish being cast as the hard-ass mother, she was willing to take on the role.

Not wanting to part like this, with her son not speaking to her, Angela broke the awkward silence. "I know you think I'm bein' extreme."

"Yeah," he agreed.

"Think I'm lookin' forward to not havin' you around all summer?"

"I don't know. Maybe you met somebody."

"Damn, you figured it out. Got me a boyfriend, so I'm ditchin' the kid." She waited for Calvin to take the bait and play along but he refused. Angela forged ahead anyway, pouring it on thick. "Tyrone Gotsbank The Third, that's ma man. Ooo and rich? Honey."

"Yeah, a'ight," said Calvin, hoping to shut her down.

"Ma man's stuntin'. These scrubs ..." She briefly opened her coat like a flasher. "Just a con to keep you inna dark. I don't work at no hospital all day. Oh no child, me and Tyrell..."

"You mean, Tyrone."

"Tha's what I said, me and ma man, Tyrone. Now that yo ass is gonna be gone, we'll be spendin' all our days on his yacht. Have his skinny white butler bringin' us champagne and cracked crab."

"You don't like crab."

"Well, maybe I'm acquirin' a taste for it— 'cause we wash it down with Cristaal y'all."

"Uh-huh." Calvin shook his head but still wouldn't look at her.

"Oh, you best not disrespect me. Tyrone won't neva let you on the yacht."

"Yeah, I'm all tore up 'bout dat."

Angela grabbed her son and held him tight, determined not to cry. Or change her mind and take him home. Calvin did not hug her back.

"I love you, you know that," she said firmly.

"I better go."

Pulling away from her, Calvin joined the short line of people waiting to board the bus. He did not look back, knowing full well she would wait, and watch, until he was on board and they pulled away. Not because she thought he would bolt, but because she was that kind of mother. She watched until the kindergarten teacher eventually closed the classroom door on the first day of school. Watched, until the bus heading for sixth-grade science camp pulled out of the parking lot and disappeared down the street. Watched, until the plane carrying Junior High honor students bound for Disneyland, taxied, took off, and became a speck in the sky. She watched.

Once on board, Calvin slouched down in a window seat toward the back and attempted to look like someone you did not want to sit next to. He couldn't believe he was going to have to endure several hours on a bus without his music. This was bordering on cruel and unusual punishment: having to listen to annoying conversations, or worse yet, have people attempt to engage him in same. He decided to sleep, or at least pretend to, starting immediately.

Calvin did not look out the window as the bus pulled away from the terminal—didn't want to see her standing there. He was still pissed about the iPod and the cell phone. Not to mention the entire plan.

Due to boredom, he actually did fall asleep for much of the journey, and as Calvin slept, the Sacramento-San Joaquin Delta drew closer. Though he'd apparently been there once or twice as a kid, he had no memory of it, so didn't really know what to expect. Regardless, he was pretty damn sure it wasn't someplace he'd voluntarily choose to spend an entire summer.

He didn't know that the size of the Delta simply cannot be grasped from the ground due to the flatness of the region. That an aerial view, however, would reveal a massive labyrinth of rivers and sloughs, something like the vascular system of the human body; a thousand miles of watery veins running through an agriculturally rich body of land.

He had no idea that over a hundred years ago the Delta was nothing more than an expansive tidal marsh fed by four rivers, the two primary ones being the Sacramento and the San Joaquin. Nor did he know that the whole of it formed something of a triangle (a "Delta" in the Greek alphabet) and that both these factors contributed to its name.

This vast swampland was eventually reclaimed by the construction of an elaborate system of levees, man-made embankments that diverted the water and created more than fifty major islands ideal for farming. Where a natural island rises up and out of the water, the low-lying islands of the Delta are bowl-like tracts of land that sit below sea level, each defended from the surrounding rivers and sloughs by the levees that encircle them.

Calvin didn't know any of this, and frankly, didn't care. The sooner he got to the Delta and proved he wasn't following in his brother's footsteps, the sooner he'd be able to get the hell out. And in his mind, that was all he needed to know.

❧ CHAPTER 7 ❧

FROM OAKTOWN TO NO TOWN

When his niece first asked him about taking Calvin for the summer, his first thought was, "Oh, hell no."

At 66, Samuel Diggs wanted nothing to do with a teenager. Especially one who'd gotten himself in some trouble of late. He'd already done his stint with parenting and he wasn't all that great at it the first time. Thankfully, his ex-wife had done most of the hands-on child rearing since his job back then, as a marine parts sales rep, had him on the road most of time.

Samuel now enjoyed a pleasant, though long-distance, relationship with his own son and daughter. They came out to California to visit every other summer along with their spouses and whichever grandkids wanted to come along now that they too were grown. In the off-years when his family didn't come out West, Samuel went back to Chicago to spend Christmas with them. Otherwise, he was perfectly content with his somewhat solitary life here in the Delta. And he certainly didn't need to complicate things by taking on someone else's problem teenager.

Still, he'd always had a close relationship with Angela. Once his own kids were out of the house and he and his wife decided to go their separate ways, Samuel took a West Coast sales route and migrated back to Oakland, staying with his younger sister's family for a time until he figured out where he wanted to land. His niece, Angela, was just a little girl back then but when she gave marching orders, the other kids (and even a few adults) fell in line. Having once served in the Navy, Samuel had an appreciation for her sense of command and took a shine to his bossy little niece, nicknaming her Spitfire.

So when Spitfire called to ask him a pretty damn big favor, even though he really wanted to decline, in the end he'd said yes. Of course, Angela had delivered quite the promotional pitch, touting Calvin's knack with engines and overall mechanical abilities. Truth be told, his second career as sole proprietor of Samuel's Marine Repair was getting to be a bit much at his age, especially during the busy summer months. If Calvin was even half as mechanically gifted as his mother claimed, having him around might not be such a bad thing. Just so long as he was a hard worker and willing to learn the ropes—not just another self-absorbed teenager, the center of his own attention.

Waiting for Calvin to arrive in Lodi, the closest town with a Greyhound Terminal, Samuel began to wonder just what he'd let himself in for. Who exactly would be stepping off the bus from Oakland and into his world? Angela had sworn up and down that he was a good kid who'd simply been in the wrong place at the wrong time. But wasn't that what she said about the other one? He hadn't seen Calvin but a few times over the years and questioned if he'd even recognize him. Then again, chances were good he'd be the only black kid on the bus. Samuel still preferred the term "Black." Thought African American was a mouthful the younger generations could keep. He'd been black his whole life and wasn't interested in changing things up this late in the game.

When the bus pulled up, just a little behind schedule, Samuel scanned the passengers as they disembarked. Sure enough, Calvin was the last and only black person to exit. He didn't look like trouble, but then again, looks could be deceiving. Samuel took a deep breath and walked over to the young man. "Calvin? How you doin', son? Welcome to the Delta."

Calvin took his great uncle's outstretched hand and returned a decent handshake. A good sign. If there was one thing Samuel hated, it was a weak handshake.

"How'd you know it was me?" Calvin asked, in all seriousness.

"Well," Samuel replied with a chuckle. "I remember you from when you was just a kid. 'Sides, I seen them baggy jeans an' fancy sneakers. That's what all them Oakland kids is wearin' when they bust 'em on *COPS*."

This remark elicited a half-smile from Calvin. Hey, if the kid didn't have a sense of humor, it was gonna be a long summer.

Calvin retrieved his duffle from the baggage area and Samuel led the way to the parking lot where his older-model Chevy pickup was parked. He noticed Calvin looking the truck over as he put his bag in the bed and got in. Kid had probably never even seen a bench seat before, 'cept maybe in movies.

"How old's this thing?" asked Calvin.

"A lot older than you, that's for sure. And a hell of a lot younger than me. It's a '73."

Per usual, Samuel had to coax the Chevy into starting, but it finally did and he drove south out of the parking lot to catch Highway 12, then happily headed west out of town. Lodi had gotten too big for Samuel's taste. What were once small towns bordering the Delta were rapidly growing, encroaching faster with each passing year. He always breathed a sigh of relief once he crossed Highway 5 and got back into the Delta proper where the sloughs and farmland helped keep the urban sprawl at bay.

"I don't like comin' into town," Samuel announced, "'less I absolutely have to."

"*That* was town?" asked Calvin, incredulously.

"More like a city now. Not as congested as Sacramento or Stockton, mind you, but still too big for me. I've lived in big cities. Don't care for 'em no more."

Calvin let out a deep sigh that said everything: a teenager from the heart of Oakland stuck in the Delta for the summer, which at his age must have seemed like a life sentence. Well, all they could do was try, Samuel told himself. And if it didn't work out, or the kid got into any trouble up here, he'd simply ship his ass back on the same Greyhound he rode in on.

Leaning against the passenger door, Calvin stared out the window as the scenery shifted from suburbs to ranch and farmland. As they crossed over the South Fork of the Mokelumne, one of the four tributary rivers of the Delta, Samuel glanced over, trying to gauge the teenager's reaction to the changing landscape. He wondered if perhaps Calvin would find something unexpectedly appealing about this place, the way he himself had so many years ago. At the moment, however, "appalling" seemed a better descriptive for Calvin's opinion of the Delta.

While not one for undue small talk, Samuel figured he needed to make an attempt at conversing with the young man since they'd be living together for the next two and a half months if things worked out. "So, how was the trip?

48

"A'ight, I guess."

"You know there's people livin' right here in California who don't know anything about the Delta. Never even heard of it."

"Hm," replied Calvin with complete disinterest.

"And it's not all that far from Oakland now is it?"

Calvin shrugged. "Might as well be another planet."

His great uncle almost let this remark slide, then decided better. "Well, welcome earthling."

After that, they rode in silence.

Samuel eventually turned off the highway and drove along a raised levee road with the river on one side and farmland below on the other. Then out of the blue he excitedly asked, "You like strawberries?"

He didn't even give Calvin time to answer before veering the truck off the paved levee and bouncing down a dirt road to the farm below. Calvin grabbed the dash to steady himself until the pickup came to a stop in a cloud of dust before the farm's produce stand.

Two Asian women, Lisa Cheng, and her daughter Mei Li, waved away dust, then waved to Samuel. He'd known the Cheng family for several years now; they grew some of the best produce in California. Samuel swore that when he drove by their place the Chevy's steering wheel would start to pull, naturally gravitating toward their stand—especially during strawberry season. Samuel got out to greet his friends and mistakenly assumed Calvin would follow. He didn't of course, and instead remained in the cab, scanning the old dial radio for something other than Country or Latin music.

"Truck pull over on its own again?" Lisa chided.

"It did. I tried to fight it but it knows," replied Samuel.

Noticing a rare passenger in the truck, Lisa asked, "So what's new with you, Samuel?"

"Oh, not much. Keepin' busy," he replied, not quite ready to broach the subject of Calvin. "How's things with you ladies?"

"Good, good. You just missed Kevin. He went to help a friend with his harvest in Stockton."

"Well, you tell him I said hello."

"I sure will," she replied. Since Samuel obviously wasn't interested in acknowledging his passenger, Lisa decided to change the subject. "Hey, good news, Mei Li's decided to apply to UC Berkeley."

"Is that so?" he asked then looked to the young woman who nodded her confirmation.

"That way I can still come home sometimes and help out," said Mei Li.

"Well, I know your folks'd miss you somethin' terrible if you went to school far away."

Now Mei Li was the kind of teenager Samuel could appreciate. She was smart, funny, and easy to talk to. She spoke to you like an adult would and was always upbeat, unlike his own charge back in the truck who was too busy messin' with the radio to notice the beautiful young Chinese girl just yards away from him. His loss, and just as well. Samuel didn't want to encourage anything in that department. He didn't yet have a handle on Calvin's true character and from the looks of it, that was gonna take a while.

With the two women now blatantly splitting their focus between Samuel and the truck, waiting to see if he was going to mention his passenger, their customer decided to simply lump Calvin in with his strawberry purchase. "Would you just look at these? I'm gonna need a whole flat. Got my grand-nephew with me. He's gonna be helpin' out around the shop for the summer."

"Well, aren't you the lucky one," said Lisa.

"Yeah," replied Samuel, considerably lacking in conviction.

Since his young charge was going to have to interact with folks around here at some point, Samuel decided there was no time like the present. "Calvin," he called toward the truck. With no response, he called louder, "Calvin!"

His passenger looked up and Samuel waved for him to come meet his friends. Calvin, however, simply rolled down the window leaving Samuel no option but to proceed with the introductions from afar. "Calvin, this is Mrs. Cheng and her daughter, Mei Li."

"Nice to meet you, Calvin," called Lisa.

"Hi," said Mei Li with a wave.

"Hey," accompanied by a nod was the extent of Calvin's meet 'n' greet. He then promptly returned his attention to the radio.

Being that he was Angela's son, Samuel knew full well Calvin wasn't lacking in social skills. Therefore, he was most likely on strike. More than a little perturbed and somewhat embarrassed, Samuel was about to address his great-nephew's attitude when Mei Li intuitively stepped in to shift the focus. "Mom, why don't you go show Samuel that special row you planted for him."

"What?" asked Samuel. "You didn't."

"Of course I did," replied Lisa. "You're always asking about rhubarb, so I planted a row just for you. Now you'll have to make that famous strawberry rhubarb pie you're always bragging about. We'll judge for ourselves if it's everything you say it is."

"Gonna put me to the test, huh?"

"You better believe it," she declared.

Happy for the momentary distraction, Samuel walked with Lisa down a dirt road that cut through the middle of their farm. Fields of fragrant sweet strawberries stretched out along one side and rows of tender young corn rustled in the breeze on the other. His charge could just wait in the truck some more, since he seemed to like it there so damn much. There was rhubarb to be inspected.

❧ CHAPTER 8 ❧

FRESH FISH

Having recently finished her junior year of high school, Mei Li was doing what she'd done every summer since she was a little girl, helping her parents tend the farm and sharing the produce stand duties with her mother. Unlike many of her peers, Mei Li had worked a job since she was tall enough to reach over the counter and count back change. While she didn't mind really, she definitely appreciated it when something new, make that someone new, came along to break up the monotony.

She'd never heard Samuel talk about a grand-nephew before, but then again, their interactions generally revolved around food: his undying love for the produce of her family's farm, or his favorite menu items at the café where she waited tables part time and where Samuel ate most of his meals.

The idea of an outsider her age spending the summer in their little corner of the Delta—now that was something new. And one with an attitude, no less. Even better. Mei Li wasn't about to let this fresh fish get off the hook without a closer look. Selecting a large ripe strawberry from a basket, she walked toward the truck where Calvin continued scanning through radio stations. She could have saved him some time and offered up the number for a hip-hop station out of Sacramento, though that might have been an assumption on her part, bordering on racial stereotyping. Maybe he was searching for pop or light rock. Yeah, right.

Intently focused on the radio, Calvin didn't notice Mei Li standing at the passenger door until she thrust the strawberry before him through the open window.

"Try one."

"What the ... Man, you shouldn't sneak up on people."

"I'm sorry, did I scare you?"

"No," he flatly denied then returned his attention to the radio.

"No iPod, huh?

"Confiscated."

"Hm. Really, try it," she insisted, holding forth the berry.

"No, thanks. Not into strawberries."

"Well, then you've obviously never had one from here," she replied, continuing to showcase the ripe berry, not unlike Eve tempting Adam. "It's organic," she touted. "And free-range."

Realizing this chick was not gonna back down, Calvin begrudgingly clicked off the radio, took the strawberry and bit into it. Though he attempted to act unimpressed, Mei Li could tell from the berry's red juice running down his chin, that it was just as good as promised.

Suddenly a small round face with thick glasses materialized at the driver's side window. Mei Li's equally inquisitive little brother was about to hijack her fact-finding mission. "I'm Dent," announced the 8-year-old.

"Yeah? What kinda name's that?"

54

"Short for accident," claimed Mei Li.

"Nuh-uh! I'm going to be the first Chinese-American president," announced Dent.

"Well, considering who's cribbin' in the White House," said Calvin, "I'd say you stand a pretty good chance."

"Thank you," replied Dent with vindication. He then thrust his hand through the open driver's side window. "I appreciate your vote."

Unable to resist this kid's "never too soon to start campaigning" attitude, Calvin reached over to shake Dent's small hand.

"My real name's Lincoln. What's yours?"

"Calvin."

"Where're you from?" Dent further polled his constituent.

"Civilization."

"Oh really," said Mei Li, clearly annoyed by the arrogance of this remark. "What part of civilization exactly?"

"Oakland."

"Mei Li's going to go to college in Berkeley," her little brother volunteered.

"Hopefully," she added.

"Probably dyin' to get the hell outta here," said Calvin.

"I happen to like it here," she countered bluntly. "You better watch it, you might end up liking it here yourself."

"Doubtful," he replied with full confidence.

A dragonfly appeared and hovered near the pickup, testing the attention span of the future President Lincoln who promptly followed it into an adjacent cornfield. Now back at the farm stand, Samuel and Lisa were presently engaged in their own version of a Food Network challenge.

"I sure do appreciate you plantin' all that rhubarb."

"Pleasure's mine, seeing as you'll be returning it between two pie crusts."

"The lightest, flakiest crust you'll ever put a fork to."

"That's some pretty big talk, mister."

"Oh, it's more than talk."

Grinning like a fool, Samuel returned to the truck with a flat of perfect, ripe strawberries which he placed in the bed before climbing in and cranking the engine to life. He was in a much better mood, ready to take on whatever challenges The Summer of Calvin had in store. As Samuel waved goodbye to his friends and began to pull away, Calvin made the mistake of looking back.

Standing there with her arms crossed and her head tilted ever so slightly, Mei Li looked directly at him—an almost antagonistic smile on her face. Her little brother may have foiled her first attempt at yanking this city boy's chain, but there would be other opportunities. It was going to be a long summer, and perhaps not such a boring one after all. Game on.

❧ CHAPTER 9 ❧

NOT SO SKINNY DIPPIN'

Leaving the Cheng's farm behind, Samuel happily hummed a mindless tune as they drove along the levee road. And Calvin thought his mother did horrifically embarrassing things. Eventually tiring of his own musical entertainment, Samuel turned on the radio. A Mexican ballad lilted and crooned.

"Habla Espanol, do you?" he asked, raising his eyebrows.

But Calvin simply shook his head and slumped down on his half of the old Chevy's bench seat. As the Latin song came to an end, and a rapid-fire Spanish speaking DJ took to the airwaves, Samuel mercifully clicked off the radio. He soon pulled the truck down a short paved side road to the river's edge and killed the engine. And there they sat, facing out across the water in silence. Calvin wondered what the old boy was up to, and why they were just sitting there where the road ended so abruptly. Was Samuel gonna to give him grief for being rude to his little farm friends? Or worse yet, was he going to attempt the dreaded heart-to-heart? Calvin didn't have the patience to wait him out. "Thought we were going to your place?"

"Oh, we are. Just that my place is across the river on that island."

Then Calvin saw it: the flat, wide body of a ferry sitting directly across the river from them.

"Cable ferry. Shortest way on and off, other than boat," said Samuel.

"You gotta be kidding."

"Nope. Ol' Joe'll be here in a minute."

Across the water, the ferry's engines roared to life and the *Eddie O* soon began its slow but steady journey toward them.

"Haven't you people heard of bridges?" asked Calvin.

"Oh, we got plenty of 'em. Too many, in fact. Used to be a lot more ferries in the Delta. Only a handful left now. Damn shame, really."

"What if you're in a hurry?"

"Well, then I tell Ol' Joe to give her full throttle."

Calvin blew a puff of air between his lips expressing his opinion that "Ol' Joe" and "full throttle" did not belong in the same sentence. And he seriously doubted anything happened in a hurry around here.

With the ferry approaching, Samuel climbed out of the truck and went to stand at the water's edge where the asphalt disappeared into the river. As the vessel arrived, a large plate at its bow lowered into place becoming a ramp for cars to drive over. Samuel walked aboard and went about looping two heavy ropeties around wood pilings. The ferry could hold four cars but Samuel's Chevy would be the only vehicle on this crossing. Calvin imagined it was probably the only vehicle on most crossings.

Ol' Joe, a white, scraggly-bearded river rat, killed the ferry's engines and exited the pilothouse. Removing a bag of tobacco and papers from the pocket of his crusty Big Ben coveralls, he prepared to roll himself a smoke. Samuel greeted his friend, then called back toward the truck, "Drive her on, Calvin!"

Relieved that Samuel had one of his own to keep him company for the moment, Calvin slid behind the wheel of the old truck and turned the key in the ignition. He was only slightly surprised, yet pleased when the Chevy's engine turned over for him on the very first try. He drove the pickup on board and parked, then sat there for a minute before deciding it felt too weird to stay in the truck for the duration of the ride back across river. Climbing out, he joined the two men who were standing beside the pilothouse and Samuel made the introductions. "Joe, this here's Calvin."

Ol' Joe dispensed with the handshake since he was busy putting the final touches on his hand-rolled cigarette. "Nice to meet ya. Heard you was gonna be helping out your great uncle. Good thing, too," he said between licks of rolling paper. "That shop o' his reminds me of *Sanford and Son*—minus the son."

"Aw, now, don't you start," warned Samuel.

"Haven't seen my Merc outboard since I dropped it off there in '98," Joe taunted. "Probl'y still buried somewhere at the back o' that shop, I reckon."

His dander now up, Samuel was quick to defend himself. "That old hunk o' junk wasn't worth a plug nickel. Even if I'd fixed it, you could paddle faster. How many times I gotta tell ya? I got a clean 20-HP four-stroke just sittin' there waitin' for ya. All ya gotta do is get off your scrawny ass and come get it."

"Now why the hell would I wanna go and do that for? Then I wouldn't have nothin' to get your goat with." Mission accomplished.

A shit-eating grin plastered on his face, Ol' Joe returned the rolling kit to the pocket of his orange coveralls. "Calvin, my friend, why don't you go unhook us and we'll be on our way."

Grateful for something to do, other than listen to these two trade insults, Calvin went to untie the ferry. Producing a vintage flip-top lighter, Ol' Joe brazenly put fire to his tobacco creation under Samuel's disapproving eye. "Doc says I'm not gettin' enough tar," he quipped with a wink before stepping inside the pilothouse.

"And what the hell happened to the 'No Smoking' sign on this vessel?" Samuel called after him.

But Ol' Joe quickly fired the ferry's twin engines before hollering back, "Can't hear ya. Too loud!"

Joe put it in gear and they began to make their way back across the river. Calvin walked to what was now the bow and watched as the ferry's cable lifted from the waters ahead to feed through the mechanical pulley system on board. Leaning over the railing, he looked down at the murky green water slowly rolling by and laughed to himself recalling Samuel's comment about "full-throttle." Ol' Joe had the ferry moving at about two miles per hour—likely top speed for both man and machine. They were little more than halfway across the river when the ferry suddenly lurched, then stalled. Ol' Joe fired the engines again and dropped it in gear, but the ferry seized as the motors strained before dying once more.

"What seems to be the trouble?" Samuel asked Joe through the open window of the pilothouse.

"Aw, sometimes the old girl's just temperamental, that's all."

Calvin approached. "Doesn't sound like a problem with the engines. They're straining," he suggested. "Cable ever get snagged on stuff?"

"Does happen ever' now and then," said Joe, unfazed. Grabbing a pair of work gloves, he stepped outside the pilothouse.

Samuel and Calvin followed him to the place where the cable fed through the mechanical system. Pulling on his gloves, Joe grabbed the twisted metal line with both hands and attempted to give it a good shake, hoping to free it from whatever it might be hung up on at the bottom of the river. This turned out to be an exercise in futility as the cable was extremely taut, having little or no give.

"Snagged alright," declared Joe. Pulling off his work gloves, he turned to Samuel. "Your man here's got a good ear. Be handy to have around for the busy season."

"Well, I could certainly use a good man."

This sort of praise made Calvin uncomfortable. It'd been a while since he'd landed on anyone's good list and he wasn't quite sure how he felt about it. Luckily, the moment was short lived since Ol' Joe began peeling off his coveralls, revealing the fact that he wasn't wearing anything underneath—his shriveled white ass out there for all the world to see.

"What the hell you think you're doin'?" asked Samuel.

"Gotta go un-snag the cable," he replied.

"You're too old to be skinny dippin' in that cold water. I'll go," insisted Samuel, as he ducked out from under his suspenders and unbuttoned his pants.

"*I'm* too old?" Joe asked. "You looked in the mirror lately?"

Undeterred, Samuel dropped his pants on the deck, revealing yet another member of the Senior Commando Force. Calvin rubbed his eyes with his palms. He'd not only had enough, he'd seen enough. "A'ight, look. I seriously do not wanna see either one o' you naked," he announced. "I'll go. Just put your pants back on, both o' you. Please."

And while Ol' Joe and Samuel made a show of grousing as they climbed back into their clothes, Calvin could tell they were secretly delighted he'd volunteered for duty. He proceeded to take off his shoes and socks, then stepped out of his baggies and pulled the T-shirt off over his head. Hooking his thumbs behind the elastic waistband of his Joe Boxer's, Calvin stretched them out. "See these? Y'all might wanna think about gettin' some o' these."

"Oh, we seen 'em alright," carped Joe.

"So's ever'body else 'round here," added Samuel, "since your pants is half fallin' off."

The two senior citizens then busted up laughing accompanied by gratuitous back-slapping as they congratulated themselves on their witty repartee. They reminded Calvin of the two old geezers in the balcony from *The Muppet Movie* DVD he had as a kid.

Walking to an opening in the railing where a ladder descended to the water, Calvin surveyed the river, which was approximately three feet down. Not wanting to miss an opportunity to perhaps heckle him further, Ol' Joe and Samuel promptly followed.

"Is the water always cloudy like that?" Calvin asked them.

"Yep," replied Joe. "Lot o' silt washes through the Delta."

"From certain angles, it can be as blue as the ocean," declared Samuel. "But up close, not so much."

Not so much was right. It was more like greenish-brown.

"Still good water though. Been drinking it ma whole life," proclaimed Joe, accompanied by a tobacco-stained, gap-toothed grin that did nothing to sell the product.

Calvin continued to stare at the cloudy green water. "How'm I s'posed to see anything down there?" he asked, thinking of his mild claustrophobia.

"Well, ya aren't, really," said Ol' Joe. "Gonna be more about feelin' your way."

"Great."

"I can still go ..." said the senior, threatening to unsnap his coveralls.

"I got this," Calvin quickly insisted before Joe's wrinkly white ass made another appearance.

Descending the ladder, Calvin muttered to himself under his breath, "No damn bridge, no underwear ..." When one of his feet hit the water a new reality set in. "Whoa!" he yelped and immediately stepped back up a rung. "That shit's cold!"

"Oughta be, it's snow melt off the Sierras," stated Samuel.

"It's refreshing, alright," said Joe. "Once the really hot weather kicks in, you'll come to appreciate it."

"Not helping me right now."

Taking a deep breath, Calvin braced himself then reluctantly dropped into the river. Resurfacing a moment later, he groaned from the shock of it while treading water.

Ol' Joe leaned over the railing to impart instructions. "What ya wanna do is pull yourself down along the cable. Ya any good at holdin' your breath?"

"A'ight, I guess," he replied, flashing on the contests he and Rashawn used to have as kids, seeing who could hold their breath the longest. Calvin usually lost. Now Rashawn was sitting in jail, and here he was in the Delta (literally) about to pull himself down into the murky water and feel his way to the bottom. Definitely not the summer he'd envisioned for himself.

Calvin swam to the where the ferry's cable descended into the river and prepared himself for the feat he was about to attempt.

"We're well past the middle so it shouldn't be too far down. No worse than the deep end of a pool," assured Joe, as if this undertaking was going to be a piece o' cake.

"You be careful now," Samuel called. "Your momma'd kill me if I drowned you right off."

"I should be so lucky," Calvin grumbled to himself.

Taking in as deep a breath as possible, Calvin grabbed the cable line, dipped under the surface and began pulling himself downward, hand over hand into the river. At first, he could see about two feet ahead, but as he pulled himself deeper, the water became darker, murkier, and colder. Soon he could barely see his hands in front of him and there was an eerie silence. Calvin had to talk himself down so as not to freak out. Okay, so it was a little scary, it wasn't like a stalled elevator or a tomb, he told himself—it was wide-open water and he could swim for the surface at any time. Every few feet, he felt the space out ahead with whichever hand was free. Whatever the cable line was caught on, he didn't want to smack right into it. Calvin made it about ten feet down before the pressure in his ears and the need for air (combined with the anxiety of not being able to see) made him let go and head for daylight. Breaking the surface, he greedily filled his lungs.

"Anything?" asked Joe.

"Whatever it is," he replied, still catching his breath, "it's a lot farther down than the deep end of a pool."

Calvin pinched his nose and blew air into his aching eardrums while Samuel and Ol' Joe looked at each other, trying to decide what to do next. But before either could even voice an opinion, Calvin was already back at the cable line preparing for another descent.

"Ya sure you wanna try again? If it's too far down we can always call for assistance," suggested Joe, pulling a cell phone from his pocket.

"Wait a minute, you get cell service up here?" asked Calvin.

"Most o' the time. Why?"

But Calvin didn't bother to explain. He was suddenly envisioning the three of them stranded on the ferry for hours, waiting for help to arrive. Ol' Joe and Samuel telling stories and endlessly bickering, possibly 'til nightfall. This disturbing image filled him with a renewed sense of determination. "I think I can do it," he declared.

"Well, okay, I guess," his great-uncle hesitantly agreed. "As long as you're up for it."

Taking hold of the cable once more, Calvin took several deep breaths before the last one that would hopefully sustain him to the bottom and then some. A moment later he was back underwater, pulling himself along—only faster this time and without feeling the space out ahead, at least not for the first ten feet or so. The pressure in his ears was a little better and he was somewhat less apprehensive, better prepared for the dark depths, the silence, and the cold.

He felt the pressure in his lungs and ears at about the same place, but this time he released a small amount of air and pushed himself further down along the line. He was about to once again surrender to his bursting lungs when through the murky water he saw the bleary silhouette of a decent-size tree ahead. It was about nine feet long and roughly a foot in diameter. The cable line was hooked under one of the branches of the tree, which was subsequently wedged in the muddy river bottom. Calvin pulled himself to it and tried to jostle the thing with one hand while hanging onto the cable with the other. Budging the tree, however, was going to take more effort and air supply than he had left in him at the moment, so he headed for daylight. Only this time he brought solid information. "I saw it. It's a tree," he shouted, upon breaking the surface.

"Well, there ya have it," said Joe. "Big tree or something you can move?"

"I think I can move it."

"I don't want you doin' anything dangerous," his guardian-by-default insisted.

Calvin found this statement oddly amusing considering the incident that had landed him up here in the first place.

"I think I can handle it," he assured them.

"He's got a feel for it now, let him give it a shot," said Ol' Joe with confidence.

"Well, alright then," Samuel consented.

Calvin readied himself for what he hoped would be his last descent into the murky depths, and taking one great breath, he dipped underwater once again. Moving as rapidly as possible this time, he made his way down the cable, releasing small amounts of air along the way to pressurize his lungs and eardrums. Arriving at the bottom, he grabbed onto one of the tree's branches, counting on the weight of its whole to hold him to the bottom. He then pulled himself down to straddle the trunk, digging his feet into the soft mud on either side of it. With one great heave that released most of the remaining air in his lungs, Calvin pulled the tree as far as he could, which was only about a foot. This endeavor churned the silty river bottom, creating an underwater cloud that left him no way of knowing if his efforts had even been successful.

In the split second between moving the tree and heading to the surface, Calvin felt something strange. A surge of water pushed toward him, as if perhaps a submarine had passed nearby. There was no time, however, to give it any thought as he needed air and needed it fast. This time, his arrival from the green depths was greeted with cheers and applause from an appreciative audience of two. Obviously, his last attempt to free the line had been successful—the cable now hung appropriately slack.

"Good job!" Samuel called out to him.

"Way to get 'er done, Calvin," added Ol' Joe.

Relieved he wouldn't have to pull himself the fifteen feet or so down into the river again, Calvin relaxed. He was treading water and savoring the option of being able to take a breath whenever he wanted when something suddenly slithered against his calf.

"Shit!" Making a swimming dash for the ladder, Calvin scrambled up it, his feet barely making contact with the rungs. "Somethin' touched my leg," he declared as he arrived on deck and looked back into the water.

But Samuel and Ol' Joe just stood there, laughing their fool heads off.

"Fo'real, somethin' big and scaly swam right up against me!" Calvin insisted.

"We know. And there's your monster," replied Samuel pointing at the river.

"Big ol' carp," declared Joe.

The three of them leaned over the railing and stared down at the water.

"See, there he is. You can just make him out," said Joe, excitedly pointing out a large fish as it swam close to the surface.

"Damn, I wish I had ma pole," lamented Samuel, practically salivating. "I'd fry him up with some hush puppies for dinner."

"Naw, ya don't wanna pan-fry carp," argued Joe.

"The hell I don't!" rebutted Samuel.

"They're too bony to fry. What ya wanna do is smoke 'em 'til the meat falls off the bone."

"Since when did you become a gourmet chef?"

"Since the last time I had your bony-ass carp."

Calvin stood there, soaking wet in his boxers on the deck of the ferry while the two old boys debated the finer points of carp cuisine. It was going to be a very. long. summer.

❧ CHAPTER 10 ❧

DESPERATION SLOUGH

Terry and Neal had been friends since high school. Their mutual appreciation for fishing and beer had bonded them for life. Now in their early 30s, their fishing gear, as well as their taste in beer, had become slightly more sophisticated. But only slightly. Neal was still a bachelor, though wished he wasn't. Terry was divorced, and damn glad he was. As neither currently had girlfriends, children, or obligations past their day jobs, fishing trips were possible and sacred.

Terry had waited a full six months after the divorce to buy his coveted bass boat. He wanted to make sure his ex had her claws deep into someone else and would not be coming back to take that as well. As testament to the fact that he was over her and happily single again, he proudly named the vessel the *Nice Piece o' Bass*.

He'd had no trouble whatsoever getting full custody of the Dodge Ram with cab-over-camper because, one, contrary to what she said before they got married, his ex hated camping. And two, he had to live in it for seven months parked on Neal's driveway while she got the condo. But now that the worst was over and he had a new townhouse, the camper could once again be used exclusively for camping. Fishing and camping were Terry's chosen forms of therapy and he made sure he was in treatment as much as possible. He and Neal had been planning this trip for months. It was going to be a perfect two weeks on the Delta; good fishing, good beer, good times. Dream vacation of the single white suburban male.

It was their first day out and Terry already had a "keeper" in the basket. So far, Neal had only hooked a couple guppies and a rotted swim fin. When the river out in the main channel got a little too choppy for the kind of laid-back fishing they preferred, they cruised over to one of their favorite Delta spots, Desperation Slough. Here the water was perfectly calm and just right for slowly trolling. The day was warm, no clouds in the sky, beer and sub sandwiches in the cooler. Life was good and they were enjoying the hell outta themselves.

Neal bent over his tackle box and tried to determine which lure might do the trick. This was akin to trying to decide which shirt to wear to BJ's Brew House and possibly attract a certain waitress he had a crush on. A lure was a curious thing. True science or just dumb luck, really? Either way, Neal decided this kind of fishing was much easier, since your success or failure rate had nothing to do with the fact that you were prematurely balding, somewhat shy, and had put on a few extra pounds. Here, he stood just as good a chance of landing something as the next guy.

Choosing an especially creepy-looking lure, Neal attached it to his line and cast it into the water. It quickly disappeared into the murky depths. The two fishermen vacillated between small talk and quietly stalking their underwater prey. Then suddenly, Terry got a serious look on his face and turned to Neal. "Did you hear that?"

The only sounds Neal could identify were nothing out of the ordinary: tules rustling in the slight breeze, a couple of red-winged blackbirds trilling as they flitted among the cattails, and the river lightly slapping the hull. Still, he listened intently for a moment before answering. "I don't hear anything."

"Listen!" Terry insisted.

So, Neal strained to listen even harder. This was the moment Terry had been waiting for and he proudly ripped a resounding fart.

"Nice one," Neal conceded, having once again fallen for another of Terry's twists on pull-my-finger. "And, of course, I'm downwind of you."

"Of course. 'Cause I'm mannin' the boat!" Laughing, Terry wildly maneuvered the bass boat with his foot pedal to further demonstrate the obvious.

Neal grabbed the arm rests of his raised fishing chair and hung on for the ride. He was used to this kind of hijinks, even had a residual boyhood appreciation for them. Luckily, Terry could easily be distracted, and like throwing a stick for a dog, Neal said, "Gimme a beer, you fart hound."

Terry immediately ceased his crazy-driver antics in favor of a cold one. Still proud of himself and chuckling, he pulled two long-neck bottles from the ice chest and handed one to his fishin' buddy. "Man, I love being out in the fresh air, don't you?" he asked with a smirk.

"I'll let ya know just as soon as I catch some."

They twisted the caps off their beers and clinked the glass bottles together in a toast.

"Here's to another shitty day in Paradise," said Terry, a contented grin on his face.

"Amen to that," agreed Neal.

Lounging in the comfy mounted fishing chairs of the tricked-out bass boat, they savored their beers for a time. That is, until Neal got one of his fishing premonitions. "Hey, let's hit that bunch o' tules across the way. I got a feeling there's one big-ass fish over there with my name on it."

"Well, let's just see about that."

With that, the two men reeled in their lines and Terry guided the bass boat across the width of the slough toward the little tule island Neal believed would change his luck. Once there, he skillfully nudged the bow between two thickets of water hyacinth and slipped into a decent-sized fishing hole just beyond. The first to notice several chunks of red rubber floating on the surface of the water, Terry turned to Neal. "Check it out. Looks like somebody lost their dinghy."

"Lost more than their dinghy," replied Neal, spotting a plastic Margarita glass and a rubber flip-flop bobbing among the tules. "What is all this crap?"

"Got me. Hey, gimme the boat hook, there's something weird floatin' over here. Looks like a wig."

Grabbing the hook, Neal handed it over. "Maybe it's a mermaid," he joked, unzipping his pants.

"Or a Mer*man*."

Neal quickly zipped his pants back up.

Terry worked to fish out what appeared to be a long, blonde costume wig. He managed to snag it near the roots and proceeded to lift it, heavy and dripping, from the water. The two men remained frozen for a moment, their minds dog-paddling as they tried to process exactly what they were looking at. It resembled a cheap rubber Halloween mask with an even cheaper wig attached. Dangling from the end of the boat hook, Darlene's mangled face stared back at them. Not her whole head–just her mutilated face—framed by sopping-wet, bleached-blonde hair.

"Holy shit!" exclaimed Terry, hurling the boat hook overboard.

Tackle boxes and bait buckets overturned as the two fishermen scrambled for the back of the bass boat, attempting to put distance between themselves and the gruesome find. Neal wasn't screaming exactly, though Terry would later claim he was. But he couldn't really bust Neal for being a wuss since the two of them wound up clinging to each other at the stern of the boat, too horrified to give a damn about their un-macho display.

"That was ... human flesh, wasn't it?" asked Neal.

"Yeah. Pretty sure that was someone's face," replied Terry.

Attempting to regain their composure, the men quickly let go of each other, yet remained at the back of the boat.

"If that was her face," Neal ventured hesitantly, "where's the rest of her?"

"I don't know. I don't wanna know."

They cautiously looked around to see if there were any other body parts floating in the vicinity. Though none were clearly visible, there was plenty of other debris bobbing at the surface; all of which held the potential to reveal an equally morbid discovery if further investigated. Something Terry and Neal had zero interest in doing.

"Okay, so ... what should we do? Should we bring it to someone?" Neal asked tentatively.

The thought of dealing with a detached portion of the human body unnerved both men, who wouldn't think twice about gutting a fish or butchering a deer.

"I don't think we should mess with it. I mean, this is *CSI* shit," replied Terry, attempting to justify his reluctance to touch the piece of carnage again.

"Right," Neal eagerly agreed. "It's a crime scene, we shouldn't mess with it. That'd be like ... tampering with evidence."

"We should just leave everything the way we found it and go report it to the sheriff's."

"Exactly, we need to just back the hell outta here and go tell the sheriff's," Neal parroted.

Within a matter of minutes, the men had lowered both fishing chairs into their compartments, stowed their rods and tackle, and were headed top speed down-river toward the marina where they'd put in and taken an RV site.

Sitting in the low bucket seats designed for traveling at high speed, they bounced across the water. Terry's bass boat had a serious engine and he did not back off the throttle for wake nor wave. Neal fought hard, not only to keep his mind off the image of what they'd just found, but also to hold down the Depth Charge he'd consumed for breakfast that morning.

A Delta vacation tradition for Neal, the Depth Charge was an all-star lineup of breakfast food classics; a bed of hash browns, followed by a layer of biscuits and gravy, topped with sausage, bacon, or ham then crowned with two eggs any way you liked 'em—and Neal liked 'em over easy. All that deliciousness served up in one heaping mound. This unprecedented combo was now churning in Neal's stomach, along with half a beer. He hated the thought of getting sick on his all-time favorite breakfast. It would ruin it for him for the rest of his life. Neal was convinced he was winning the battle until he mentally relived ordering his eggs over easy. And that was all it took. He leaned over the side of the boat and the Depth Charge exploded. Chunks of vomit blew back, splattering his forehead, cheek, and hair. Not a good thing to barf at that speed.

And while disgusted, Terry didn't give Neal any grief, since his own stomach was doing gymnastics in response to what they'd just seen. Thank God he'd opted for the Cheerios.

❧ CHAPTER 11 ❧

HERON'S HARBOR

Seventeen-year-old Jess Miller attempted to keep his eyes appropriately averted as he pumped gas into a pricey new wakeboard boat occupied by two bikini-clad babes. The girls were around his same age and seemed friendly enough, but Jess was aware they'd arrived with two slightly older (and obviously arrogant) guys who were presently up at the general store renting one of the marina's houseboats. Jess found one of the girls especially attractive, a brunette who was naturally pretty; no makeup, no piercings, no tattoos. His taste was often contrary to whatever was currently popular, and these days, a non-illustrated body was extremely unusual. The other chick was the complete opposite, working short bleached-blond hair and an uninspired starter-collection of piercings and bad ink.

Jess could still be self-conscious around girls at times, especially those from the suburbs and cities. It wasn't like he thought himself an unattractive loser, he was simply aware that most girls his age could be frighteningly superficial—the stars of their own reality shows. He found this to be particularly true of tourist girls, who had a tendency to dismiss him as nothing more than a Delta bumpkin with a summer job pumping gas. He didn't have a subtle way of letting strangers know he was more than just a hired hand here. So he usually kept to himself around tourists, unless of course, someone with a curious mind engaged him in conversation.

Truth was, Heron's Harbor had been in Jess's family for over fifty years. A vintage black and white photo on the wall of the café showed the place back when it was simply a long wooden dock jutting out into the river from adjacent farmland. From those humble beginnings the marina had gradually been added to over the years, eventually becoming the Delta resort it was today. The harbor now included a boat ramp, gas dock, several covered berths, a guest dock, small general store with café, and a few RV sites.

Jess's grandparents were the proud owners of Heron's Harbor when he was growing up. He spent every summer here, fishing, swimming, boating, waterskiing, catching crawdads, and eating his grandmother's blackberry cobbler. The summer after he finished the sixth grade, his family unit of three moved from San Francisco to the Delta and took over running Heron's Harbor. At 12, Jess was learning every aspect of operating the marina alongside his parents. With the family business securely in the hands of the next generation, his grandparents retired and rambled off in a monster motorhome returning only to visit each Christmas and Fourth of July.

But two years later, the unthinkable happened. Jess's dad died suddenly from a previously undetected heart condition. He was standing on this very same gas dock swapping fish stories with a couple anglers when his heart simply gave out. Efforts to resuscitate him were unsuccessful. In an instant, he was gone.

Though his grandparents came back to help run the marina, they soon admitted it was simply too heartbreaking for them to stay. Their son had been raised here, and there was something of Scott in every corner of Heron's Harbor. His mom, Frances, felt the same way, but when she and the grandparents began to talk about selling, Jess made his stand. This place was the most important thing he had left of his dad and he had no intention of letting it go. Heron's Harbor represented the life and legacy his father had left him, and though he was only 14 at the time, he wasn't about to let anyone sell it out from under him. And in the end, Jess won out.

Of course there were times when he longed for an easier life, one like the two girls in the wakeboard boat probably enjoyed. They certainly didn't spend their summer days pumping gas, scrubbing down rental houseboats, or mucking out guest bathrooms. But then he had something they didn't; at 17, Jess was already part owner of an established business. And while he sometimes missed having things like movie theaters or fast food joints just around the corner, he still wouldn't trade his life on the Delta for that of the average urban or suburban teenager. Here, he had over a thousand miles of navigable waterways accessible just beyond his front door. Though he worked hard, he still found time to hit the water and play. These days it was usually on his new WaveRunner, and that made all the headaches, especially those of the busy season, worth it. As a kid, who only got to spend his summer vacations at Heron's Harbor, Jess used to dream of living here year-round. Now he did.

Jess and Frances continued to live in the old family farmhouse behind the levee. Having weathered a few floods in the distant past, the house had been raised at some point. They could sit on its spacious front porch in the evenings and look out over the marina. Jess felt closest to the memory of his dad when he was sitting on the old porch swing at dusk. The farmland that surrounded the house had been sold off years ago. No one in the Miller family had any desire for farming. It was boats and everything related to them that ran in their bloodstreams.

Jess finished topping off the tank of the wakeboard boat but did not ask the girls to pay. He assumed the big-shot boyfriends would be putting it on their tab since they were renting one of the harbor's houseboats for two weeks. With no other customers presently at the gas dock, Jess decided to take a chance and actually attempt a friendly conversation. "You guys want a cold water?"

"That'd be great," replied the brunette.

The blonde simply said, "Yeah, cool," without bothering to look up from the *People* Magazine that held her so captivated.

Jess snagged two bottles of water from an ice chest he kept in the kiosk and handed them off to the brunette.

"Thanks," she said, passing one to her friend. Turning back to him, she smiled and lifted her sunglasses, propping them atop her head. And that's when Jess locked onto her intense green eyes.

"No problem," he said, forcing himself to momentarily break eye contact.

"I'm Lauren, by the way. And that's Nikki."

"Jess."

"Nice to meet you," she replied, reaching out to shake his hand.

Those hazel-green eyes of hers might as well have been tractor beams. Without thinking any further down the line than that moment, Jess stepped out of his flip-flops and sat down on the dock at the nose of the wakeboard boat, letting his feet dangle in the water. Like he hoped she would, Lauren came to sit on the boat's bow where they began an easy conversation.

"So, is this your place?" she asked.

Now he was really smitten.

Out of the corner of his eye, Jess saw Samuel and his grand-nephew, Calvin, making their way down the ramp from the parking lot to the cafe. He suddenly remembered his mom expected him to be part of the welcoming committee, but considering the circumstances, that wasn't gonna happen. Instead, Jess acknowledged Samuel with a friendly wave then quickly returned his attention to Lauren of the captivating green eyes.

Calvin's wet boxers had caused his subsequently damp jeans to hang even lower than they did when dry. Since Samuel refused to introduce his grand-nephew to anyone looking like "somethin' that crawled outta Lake Merritt" they'd stopped by his place first so Calvin could drop off his duffel and change clothes.

Samuel lived aboard a seventy-foot converted barge appropriately named *The Sturgeon*. It wasn't what you'd call a handsome vessel, but it was plenty big and definitely sturdy. His floating home sat moored to its own private dock at Heron's Harbor. Though the majority of the barge's conversion had been done by its previous owner, *The Sturgeon* was a continual work-in-progress and looked every bit of it.

With his marine repair shop also located at the harbor, Samuel existed in his own little live/work microclimate. He rarely left the marina, and that's just the way he liked it. He'd leased the shop from Jess's grandparents, bought *The Sturgeon* from a retired merchant marine, and completely changed his life—all in the course of one weekend some twenty years ago. And nothing had changed much since. Until now.

Angela had confided that her son could sometimes feel claustrophobic in tight, confined spaces. Therefore, Samuel had made a concerted effort to tidy up the place and downsize the clutter so his new roommate would have a space to call his own. When Calvin looked around the front cabin and agreed it would be "a'ight", he certainly had no idea the effort required in reclaiming what had gradually become a junk room over the years.

Once Calvin changed into dry clothes, his great uncle decided it was time to introduce him to Frances and Jess, and anyone else who might be hanging around up at the café. As they walked the short distance to the marina's main hub, Samuel attempted to interview his new employee. Not that he could easily change his mind at this stage of the game.

"You ever work on an outboard motor before?" he asked Calvin.

"Nope."

"How 'bout an inboard?"

"Nuh-uh."

"Your mother says you have a way with engines, though."

He shrugged. "I do a'ight."

"Well, I'm sure you'll get the hang o' it. Your reputation precedes you."

Calvin suddenly wondered just how much Samuel and others around here knew about his recent encounter with the criminal justice system. Part of him was embarrassed, but another part of him hoped it would keep people at a distance. He didn't plan on endearing himself to anyone around here; had zero interest in becoming part of their happy little harbor.

Regardless of his intentions, Calvin was about to be hurled smack into the middle of life at a Delta resort.

The marina's small grocery and café served as a hangout for locals while catering to the seasonal tourists. It was the kind of place where you could sit at the counter, have a grilled cheese sandwich with a Coke and find out where the fish were biting. A place to buy bait and cold beer, or pick up a package of bologna and a loaf of Wonderbread. And practically everyone in the establishment fit the description of that last item, something Samuel had apparently gotten used to and no longer even thought about. Calvin, on the other hand, couldn't help but notice as they came through the front door that they were the only African Americans in the joint, possibly the only ones for miles.

The word "briquettes" suddenly popped into his head. Years ago, his mom had come up with her own spin on the saying "a cotton ball in a coal mine." Whenever she and Calvin left Oakland and found themselves in a predominately white area, she would turn to him and say, "Just a couple o' charcoal briquettes in a box o' cotton balls." Somewhere along the line, Angela's phrase had gotten whittled down to where they would simply look at each other and say, "briquettes."

A few stragglers from the small lunch crowd remained in the café, and several turned to wave or call Samuel's name as he and Calvin entered. Apparently, this was Samuel's *Cheers* and he was their "Norm." Since Frances was busy dealing with a guy at the boat rental desk, Samuel led the way to the lunch counter. He stopped by a couple tables, introducing Calvin to some fishermen and blue-collar types whose names Calvin didn't bother to retain. He figured "buddy" would pretty much cover it if they ever met again.

Calvin was sure he saw the young white dude at the rental desk do a double-take when they came in. And there was a second one just like him over at the beer cooler, loading several twelve-packs onto a store dolly. Calvin knew instinctively that these two were "buds." Both reeked of private schools, daddy's money, and a super-sized serving of self-entitlement, topped off with expensive sunglasses. And Calvin had it exactly right.

Dane and Eric were both 21 and came from the kind of money that could easily afford a Stanford education. Unfortunately, neither of them had the brains or grades to make the cut, so they were making a career out of junior college instead—if and when classes didn't interfere with their extremely full partying curriculum.

Now seated at the lunch counter, Calvin and Samuel were close enough to the rental desk to overhear the conversation between Frances and Dane, an exchange that only corroborated Calvin's wealthy-white-prick profiling.

"Lady, I've been driving boats since I was 10," Dane announced condescendingly. "So you don't have to worry about your precious houseboat, it's in good hands."

"Well now, I'm sure you're a real pro," Frances calmly replied. "But I still need you to read this brief safety handout then sign it at the bottom."

"You've gotta be kidding."

"Do I look like I'm kidding? And when you're done with that, I need you to read the rental agreement and sign here."

Any one of the locals in the place would have happily stepped in to assist Frances had she so much as raised her voice, but they all knew she could handle herself just fine. Dane's partner in slime, Eric, wheeled the now fully-loaded dolly to the front door. If he wasn't such an obvious jerk, practically anyone in the café would have gotten up out of their seat to hold the door for him. That didn't happen. After awkwardly struggling with the door, Eric finally managed to prop it open with his shoulder and called to his buddy, "Dude, let's get this show on the road."

Without even bothering to pretend he'd read the safety handout or rental contract, Dane signed two giant loopy signatures like a Hollywood star granting autographs, then snatched the keys off the counter and made for the door. Once there he turned back, "Frances, right? Be a doll and put the beer on our tab, would ya?"

The nerve. As if he were giving a 40-something cougar a thrill by calling her "doll." Truth was, if Frances wanted to be a cougar, she probably wouldn't have any trouble finding a cub or two. And it certainly wouldn't be the likes of these two.

"'The floating party is about to begin!" declared Eric. "Am I right?"

With that, Tweedle Dee and Tweedle Dick high-fived each other and headed out the door. Once outside, the sound of at least one case of beer falling off the dolly could be heard, prompting the café regulars to laugh and applaud. Frances crossed her arms, waiting to see if the jackasses would have the audacity to come back in and try to exchange any broken bottles. Apparently, they had at least some minute particle of sense and didn't dare.

Frances went behind the lunch counter and put on an apron, taking her anger out on its strings as she firmly tied them behind her. Her fair skin was flushing a shade something close to her long auburn hair as she came to stand across the counter from

Samuel. "I was this close to telling those little piss-ants they could go find some other place to rent a houseboat," she fumed. "I hate letting our boats go out with idiots like that. Got more money than sense."

"And here I am with nothin' but good sense," replied Samuel shaking his head. "Calvin, this woman with steam comin' out her ears is Frances."

"Nice to meet you," she replied and shook his hand, happy for the distraction. "Sorry you had to witness that. We really don't get that many pricks in here." She then quickly covered her mouth. "Sorry, that just slipped out."

"I'm sure he's heard the word before," laughed Samuel. "Probably met a few too."

"Ever since we heard you were coming, we've been counting the days. Isn't that right, Samuel?" she asked, attempting to regain her composure. "You hungry, can I get ya something?"

"Yeah, a'ight," agreed Calvin, realizing he hadn't eaten since that morning.

"You just make yourself at home and I'll get you gentlemen a couple cheeseburgers."

"Now Franny, I don't want you spoilin' him right off the bat," warned Samuel.

"Why not? Been spoiling you for the last five years, haven't I?"

Over at the lawn area above the rental dock, Dent Cheng sat cross-legged atop a picnic table happily working his way through a package of Red Vines. Once his farm chores were done, he often rode his bike to the ferry then over to Heron's Harbor to get his candy fix and see if any new comic books had come in. If there was nothing new in super hero world, Jess would often let him help out around the gas dock, sometimes washing boat windshields. And while not a regular service provided, people seemed to get a kick out of it, would even tip him on occasion. But things were a bit slow today, so he headed over to the adjacent rental dock where the closest thing to entertainment was watching Dane and Eric transfer gear from their Range Rover onto the rental houseboat, *Delta Destiny*.

On one of his numerous trips between the SUV and houseboat, Dane sauntered over to Dent. "Whadaya say, Jet Li? Wanna do a little Kung Fu fighting?" This was followed by several pathetic karate moves. But Dent simply stared blankly at the goofball and continued eating his licorice.

"What's the matter, kid, no speaky English?"

Dent knitted his eyebrows and continued to stare. Was this guy for real?

With no response, Dane decided to amuse the kid by performing the age-old grandpa trick. Pretending to grab Dent's nose, he then held up a fist, his thumb sandwiched between first and second fingers. "Got your nose, little Chinaman."

This time, Dent couldn't help but respond. Holding up his small fist and thumb in similar fashion, he casually replied, "Got your dick, white boy."

Witnessing this exchange, Eric doubled over with laughter. "Oh man, he gotcha good, dude!"

Dane, however, was not amused and was struggling to come up with a clever retort when a sheriff's boat pulled up at the adjacent gas dock. Dent waved to the officers on board and they waved back with familiarity. Basking in his obvious immunity, the plucky 8-year-old popped down from the picnic table, mounted his bike, and rode away.

Ramon "Ray" Cruz, a respected sheriff's sergeant in his mid-40s, jumped from the patrol boat onto the gas dock and tied the bow line to a cleat. At the helm, Deputy Burt Watson killed the engine and methodically went about the business of replacing his nicotine patch.

Sergeant Cruz had been saddled with Deputy Watson for almost a year now. A clumsy, overweight white man in his early 30s, Burt was never going to be quality law enforcement material. He was, however, somehow related to the governor, and apparently that was enough to secure him the position regardless of his capabilities, or lack thereof. Though Ray initially attempted to challenge his placement, it seemed Burt was here to stay. At least the deputy hadn't accidentally shot anyone. Yet.

Seeing the gas dock attendant was otherwise engaged, Sheriff Cruz lifted the pump nozzle. "Don't worry I got it," he teasingly called to Jess. "I can see you're busy."

And he was. Busy getting himself caught up on a girl who wasn't available.

"So, where're you guys headed?" Jess asked.

"We're not sure exactly," replied Lauren. "Where's the good water?"

Under normal circumstances, Jess would never even consider divulging his favorite place to water-ski and wakeboard—especially to a tourist. It was a place only locals and a few regulars knew about, and that's the way they liked to keep it. But it was as if this girl had somehow managed to hypnotize him, and before he knew it, Jess had a Delta map in hand and was pointing out Desperation Slough. "Hands down, this is the best," he touted.

"It's not even marked on the map. That's why it's never crowded. See all these tule islands," he explained, "they help cut down on the wind chop, so there's a lotta glass out there."

"Wow, that sounds awesome. Thanks for showing me."

Eric arrived at the gas dock and jumped aboard the wakeboard boat. Taking off his shirt, he tossed a bottle of sunscreen onto Nikki's lap, granting her the undisputed privilege of putting it on him. She grudgingly put down her magazine and smeared lotion on his back.

"Hey Eric, Jess here just told me about a place called Desperation Slough that's got killer water," Lauren informed him. "I think we should check it out."

"Oh yeah, I think I read about that. 'Pump Jockey's Guide To Wake Boarding,' right?" Eric snidely replied.

And there it was, that scorching feeling of humiliation Jess usually managed to avoid.

Over at the rental dock, Dane started the engine of the *Delta Destiny* then loudly yelled out the pilot window, "Lauren, come on!"

Mortified by Eric's comment, as well as the collective rudeness of her so-called friends, Lauren attempted to compensate for their total lack of manners. "Well, thanks again for the advice. And the bottled water."

"Burning daylight here," Dane called. "Just pay the kid and let's go already!"

Ah, insult to injury. Nice touch. But Jess got the feeling Lauren was sharing in this blister of embarrassment, and that somehow took the sting out of it. He held out his hand to help her out of the boat and she took it. Lauren paid for the gas in cash, but as she went to join her idiot boyfriend, she turned back. "It was really nice talking with you, Jess."

"Lauren!" Dane shouted possessively and laid on the horn.

Lauren, however, simply rolled her gorgeous green eyes and gave Jess a smile. "So we'll see you around, maybe."

"Maybe."

Eric fired up the wakeboard boat and revved its engine in an unbridled display of testosterone poisoning, that is until Sheriff Cruz made his presence known, prompting him to back it down several notches. Eric then gingerly pulled away from the gas dock, revealing the vessel's name on the back of the boat: *Money Talks*.

With Lauren now on board the houseboat, Dane pulled the *Delta Destiny* away from the rental dock and followed the wakeboard boat out of the marina toward the main channel.

"There's trouble looking for a place to happen," said Ray, as he and Jess watched the two vessels heading out.

"Yeah, but they're the ones who get the girls."

"Seemed like you were doin' alright to me. The one with the shrapnel in her navel, right?"

"Nah, she's more your type. Probably love your handcuffs."

"Want me to sideline the boyfriend for a while?"

"Is there some new asshole law I don't know about?"

"I'm sure I can find something. Providing alcohol to minors."

"Gonna have to build a few more holding cells if you're goin' there."

"Yeah, there's that."

"Hey, you didn't happen to see the *Casa del Agua* out there, did you?"

Ray did a quick mental recap of his day out on the water. "No, why?"

"Due back yesterday. They were a no-show."

"Huh. I'll keep an eye out."

As Jess and Ray walked past the patrol boat on their way to the café, Burt perked up from a catnap. "Hey Jess, your mom get them Otter Pops in yet?" he anxiously inquired.

"I don't know, Burt. Probably."

"I sure hope so. I seriously need somethin' to suck on."

And there were just too many comebacks in response to that statement—every one of them crude. So Jess and Ray simply let it slide and watched in dismay as Burt awkwardly climbed out of the patrol boat and waddled up the dock toward the café.

"And they let him carry a gun," said Jess.

"Yeeaah," said Ray, in a tone of utter defeat. He couldn't believe it, either.

IN THE CUTS

The last of the lunch crowd had finally cleared out and Frances was busy cleaning the grill in preparation for dinner. Having polished off their burgers and fries, Samuel and Calvin remained planted at the counter and were now making their way through obscenely large wedges of homemade chocolate cake. Calvin was quickly warming up to the idea of eating most of his meals here.

The front door to the café swung open with a bang and Deputy Watson came through it with such determination, Frances assumed he would be heading straight for the bathroom. Instead, he made a beeline for the ice-cream freezer at the back of the grocery area. Jess and Ray followed this grand entrance a moment later.

"Hey there, I want you guys to come meet Calvin," Frances called, waving them over. "This is my son Jess, and Sergeant Ray Cruz. Oh, and the one with his head in the freezer is Deputy Burt Watson." Conspicuously lowering her voice she confided, "He's got an otter on his back."

Calvin nodded in Jess and Ray's direction but remained seated. Shaking his head, Samuel stood and extended his hand to Sergeant Cruz. "How you doin,' Ray? See, Calvin, this is how we introduce ourselves to folks up here in the Delta. It's just a simple up and down motion, but I'm sure you'll get the hang of it with a little practice."

"Oh Samuel, don't be so hard on him," scolded Frances. "Stuck up here in the sticks with a bunch o' hicks."

"Speak for yourself, mom," said Jess, insulted.

Perfectly timed, Burt waddled up counting out change from his pocket, his lips already staining a freakish purple from the Otter Pop dangling from his mouth. Taking one look at him, Frances turned to her son. "I rest my case."

Suddenly, through the café's large front window, a boat caught everyone's attention as it rapidly approached the gas dock, its driver blatantly ignoring the "No Wake" zone.

"Anybody know that vessel?" asked Ray

"Looks like Terry and Neal," replied Jess. "They have an RV spot with us, come every year."

"Something must be up," added Frances, "they don't normally drive like that."

Apparently Sergeant Cruz wouldn't have to go to them to investigate. The fishermen had their vessel secured to the dock in record time and were soon jogging toward the café, bursting through the front door a moment later.

"Sheriff! You gotta come see what we found!" exclaimed Terry.

"Some woman's face, her dismembered face!" said Neal, out of breath.

"Yeah, floating in the water," Terry elaborated. "No body, no head ..."

"Just a mutilated face with hair," added Neal.

"Oh, my God," gasped Frances.

"Slow down, guys," insisted Ray, attempting to infuse his natural calm on the situation. "Where'd you see this?"

"Desperation Slough," replied Terry.

"A little tule island near Bedroom Three," Neal clarified. "There's probably more body parts out there but we didn't wanna look 'cause ... maybe it's a crime scene."

"Okay, I want you to show me the exact spot. We'll follow you out there," Ray instructed before getting on his radio. "Gladys this is Ray, X909. We're responding to a ... a possible boating accident in Desperation Slough. Over."

The voice that came back over his radio was that of a white female senior citizen. "Roger that, Sergeant. Will stand by."

Assuming somebody at the sheriff's station was messing around, Calvin let out a small laugh then quickly realized no one else found this funny. Apparently, a little old white lady really was the dispatcher.

"Terry, can I go with you guys?" Jess asked.

"Absolutely not. You're not going," declared Frances.

"Believe me, Jess, you don't wanna see this," said Terry.

"Yeah, this isn't mousse in my hair," added Neal.

Sergeant Cruz headed out the door with the two fishermen close on his heels. Deputy Watson, however, promptly returned to the ice cream freezer to secure another Otter Pop for the road. After plunking down more pocket change, he banged back out the front door the same way he'd come in.

"I wonder what the hell coulda happened," pondered Samuel. "Body parts?!"

"Guess we'll find out soon enough," replied Frances. Not wanting to focus any further on the stomach-turning details, she quickly moved to change the subject. "In the mean time, Jess, why don't you show Calvin around."

"It's a'ight. I'll check it out later," said Calvin, hoping to secure a reprieve from the Hillbilly Harbor tour.

"Go on, take a look around," urged Samuel. "Not enough day left to get any work done anyhow. I'll get ya started in the shop tomorrow."

And so, looking like reluctant field trip participants forced to buddy-up, Jess and Calvin exited the café together.

"Hope he's gonna be all right up here," remarked Samuel watching them go.

"Oh, he'll be fine," assured Frances. "Just gonna take some getting used to is all."

Jess really didn't mind giving tours of the marina, just that most people he showed around were actually interested in seeing the place. He didn't get the feeling there was anything about Heron's Harbor that was going to impress Calvin. So he decided to cut right to the chase and show him the only rental houseboat that wasn't already out. That was about as impressive as it got.

"Ever been up here before?" he asked Calvin as they walked toward the rental dock.

"When I was a kid. I don't remember, though."

"Yeah. I only spent summers here when I was a kid. Grew up in San Francisco. You?"

"Oakland."

After an awkward silence, Jess ventured a more direct question. "I take it this wasn't your idea, spending the summer up here."

"You take it right."

As they arrived at the rental dock, Jess pulled the janitor-size key ring from his belt and shuffled through it 'til he found the right one. He then boarded the one remaining houseboat and opened up the cabin so Calvin could check out the inside. "We've got six rental houseboats. Three older models and three like this one. The newer ones have pretty much everything."

Jess proceeded to walk through the interior of the forty-nine-foot vessel, pointing out its best features. "DVD, CD, flat screen, surround sound, microwave, dishwasher, two sleeper cabins, two heads…"

"What, no hot tub?"

"Oh, it's possible. My dad wouldn't go for it though. Didn't think it was worth all the hassle."

"He still around?"

Somewhat surprised by this question, Jess shook his head. "Died three years ago."

Calvin nodded and continued to look around the houseboat. He wasn't interested in bonding over family members who were gone. Didn't want to relate to a total stranger the ugly truth that he'd rather it was his absent father who was dead instead of his brother. Calvin shifted his thoughts to wondering what kind of money it would take to rent a boat like this for a week. Not that he could really see himself or any of his posse heading out for a week of fun in the sun on a houseboat. Though the image this conjured up was definitely amusing.

Jess opened the rear sliding-glass door and stepped out onto the back deck where he watched the sheriff's boat and the *Nice Piece o' Bass* making their way into the main channel before disappearing beyond the breakwater. Joining him there, Calvin noticed a fiberglass slide curving from the upper deck toward the water below. There was also an outdoor bar and plenty of places to lounge on this magical floating playland.

"We also rent out a couple ski boats," said Jess. "They're not much to look at, but they can move. You water-ski?"

"When I'm not playin' Polo or Lacrosse."

But Calvin's sarcastic remark barely grazed Jess. He was busy formulating a plan. "I think we should take a little ride."

Fine by Calvin, who assumed that meant they'd be taking this behemoth out for a spin. Instead, Jess locked up the houseboat and Calvin followed him to the end of the rental dock where a ski boat was tethered.

What the hell, thought Calvin. It'd been an interesting day so far. This morning he woke up in Oakland, then watched out the window of a Greyhound while urban civilization as he knew it disappeared, replaced by farmland and endless miles of waterways. He'd then spent the first part of his afternoon fifteen feet underwater freeing a cable ferry. Enjoyed a damn good lunch and learned one of the locals was found floating in chunks on the river. So a little joyride in a speedboat to top it all off? Why not. But if there was a tractor pull or hoedown planned for later, he was gonna have to pass.

This business of tying and untying vessels was already becoming second nature to Calvin who undid the stern line while Jess handled the bow. They climbed aboard the ski boat and Jess started the engine. As he skillfully backed the boat out of its slip, Jess made it a point to ask, "You do know how to swim, right?"

"Okay, we might not be all into the water sports," replied Calvin, "but we are into survival."

"Fair enough," replied Jess, though his original question did not contain the term "you people."

Jess made sure they were well on their way before letting his mother know about the boat tour. It was a "better to ask for forgiveness than to ask for permission" situation. Picking up the mic on the boat's marine radio, he put in a call. "This is the vessel *Hit It*, Whiskey, Yankee, Kilo 6553, to Heron's Harbor base."

Frances's voice came back a moment later, "Go ahead, Jess."

"Yeah, I need to blow this engine out so I'm gonna take Calvin for a quick ride. Over."

"Okay," Frances reluctantly agreed. "I'll watch the pumps. But don't be gone too long. Over." Then, as she often did, Frances failed to take her finger off the radio's mic button and was overheard saying to Samuel, "How much you wanna bet that ride includes a pass through Desperation Slough?"

Jess laughed. His mother could be quite entertaining, especially when she wasn't trying to be.

As they cleared the "No Wake" zone, Jess punched the throttle to full and the ski boat, which as he put it, "didn't look like much but could move," did just that. It quickly began to plane, effortlessly gliding over the water. Calvin did his best to maintain an aura of bored detachment, but truthfully, he was all about this kind of speed. Jess sat up on the back of his captain's chair, his left hand holding onto the edge of the windshield, his right hand holding the throttle to full.

"Sit like this," he shouted to Calvin over the wind barreling past them. "You get a better view."

Calvin sat up on the back of his seat and felt the intense rush of racing across water. As a kid he'd been out in paddle boats on Lake Merritt, even a charter fishing boat or two on the bay, but this was something entirely different. He could definitely get used to this.

As the ski boat approached a sailing yacht with two thirty-something white couples aboard, they all gave a friendly wave and Jess waved in return.

"Friends o' yours?" Calvin asked.

"No. People just wave to each other up here."

Yet another aspect of Delta culture Calvin would not be adopting.

Jess reduced his speed and turned the boat into a narrow side slough. They glided through a still backwater area and soon came upon a small overgrown island. A battered old rowboat sat keeled over in the mud and a decaying shack stood a short distance from shore. As they got closer, something moved at the water's edge; a disheveled, scraggly-bearded man was bent over digging for clams in the mud. He briefly looked up as the ski boat passed but did not acknowledge the intruders.

"That's Jack the Shack Man," Jess advised in a hushed voice. "Been living there for years."

"I take it he's not a waver," replied Calvin, who now grasped that he was indeed "in the cuts."

Jess gradually increased his speed, leaving Jack the hermit to his life of solitude. As they rounded a bend heading back to the main channel, a gigantic freighter appeared before them. The sight of such an enormous ship making its way up river clearly took Calvin by surprise.

"Guess you didn't know it could be that deep," remarked Jess. "It's a shipping channel. Freighters can go all the way from San Francisco to Sacramento or Stockton."

"Damn."

Jess couldn't help but laugh. Finally, something had halfway wowed this guy. And if he thought that was impressive, wait 'til he experienced the best part of a freighter passing by.

After advising his passenger to "hang on," Jess punched the throttle to full and headed straight for the massive wake left behind by the ship. The ski boat hit the wall of water and was launched, causing the engine to over-race as they became airborne. They seemed to literally hang in space for a moment before splashing down on the other side, producing a Shamu-size soaking to both occupants. Jess looked over to see if Calvin was able to recapture his air of unimpressed indifference. Simply not possible after that.

"Again?" asked Jess.

"Bring it," replied Calvin with genuine enthusiasm.

Jess brought the boat around and they hit the wake once more with similar high-adrenaline results.

Speed, machine, water. Calvin was hooked.

Having exhausted the best of the freighter's wake, Jess piloted the ski boat for the mouth of Desperation Slough and headed for the area where Terry and Neal reportedly found the human face. Rounding the bend, however, they unexpectedly came upon the *Delta Destiny* anchored off Bedroom One with the *Money Talks* tied alongside. Apparently the jerks had taken the lowly Pump Jockey's advice after all. The girls were busy getting the wake-board boat ready for a run, while the guys lounged on the back deck fueling up on beer. The houseboat's sound system was blasting white-boy rap, which made Calvin hate on them even more. "The little rich boys."

"Yeah, real charmers," replied Jess.

Clearly, these two had endeared themselves to everyone at the marina in similar fashion. As they passed near the houseboat,

Lauren looked up. Recognizing Jess, she waved, and he waved in return. Dane and Eric, however, simply glared back with contempt.

"Guess they didn't get the memo about everybody waving," quipped Calvin.

"I just don't get what she's doing with him."

Calvin had no idea which of the idiot white boys Jess's crush belonged to. From his perspective they were pathetically interchangeable. "Like the boat says, they got bank."

"She doesn't seem like that."

"Yeah, you right. Probably bein' held against her will."

Jess hit the gas and left the houseboat behind as they ventured deeper into Desperation Slough. They were about to cruise past the opening to Bedroom Two when out of the corner of his eye, Jess spotted the *Casa del Agua* anchored there alone. He quickly made a detour to see if anyone was on board, and if so, remind them that they were now overdue in returning the boat. An oversight that translated to a hefty late fee, especially since it was booked by another party starting tomorrow.

"It's one of ours," Jess explained as they came up on the vessel. "Supposed to be back yesterday." Slowing the ski boat, he idled close to the starboard side of the houseboat and called out, "Hello? Anybody on board?"

By all appearances, the occupants of the *Casa del Agua* had been there recently; the CD player was cranking out music and there was a half-filled pitcher of melted green liquid in the bar's blender.

"Is that Tom Jones?" asked Calvin.

"How should I know?" replied Jess. "How should you know, for that matter."

Calvin wasn't sure. Apparently what happens in Vegas seeps out now and then.

"They're not around, the dinghy's gone," said Jess.

"Must be coming back soon if they left the music on."

"You'd think. Looks like it's plugged in, so it's running off the main DC. Not the best use of battery power."

"Where exactly would they go around here?"

"Any number of places. Out for a cruise, fishing, maybe out to lunch. Some restaurants have guest docks."

"Lemme get this straight, people rent a boat with a full kitchen then take another boat out to lunch?"

"Sure, why not? Besides, they're from Vegas," said Jess, as if that explained everything.

"Explains the music, at least."

"Must be high rollers 'cause our daily rate gets tripled if you go past your return date."

Having satisfied his curiosity as to the whereabouts of the *Casa del Agua*, and seeing that the vessel was at least intact, Jess set a course for Bedroom Three before they missed any and all action taking place with regard to "the face." If the occupants of the rental houseboat hadn't returned to the vessel by the time he and Calvin headed back, he'd simply leave them a strongly worded note.

Arriving at Bedroom Three of Desperation Slough, Calvin and Jess could see the sheriff's boat and the *Nice Piece o' Bass* anchored off a small tule island nearby. With the tide now completely in, the little island was presently nothing more than a stand of tule grass tops surrounded by water. Jess slowed the ski boat and idled far enough back to be out of the way, though not far enough to go undetected. If Ray gave him any grief about coming out here, he now had the valid excuse that he'd been searching for the *Casa del Agua*, since he had in fact, found it.

Even from a distance, it was easy to see that Sergeant Cruz and Deputy Watson were using long pole nets to scoop things from the water. Terry and Neal were also retrieving items from the river using a couple of boat hooks.

"Guess they found more than her face," said Calvin.

Grabbing a pair of binoculars from the stow-box beneath the rear bench seat, Jess trained them on the sheriff's boat. He watched as Ray lifted his pole net from the water and placed it on a utility box at the back of the boat. Adjusting the binoculars in order to bring the contents of the shallow net into focus, it took a moment before Jess realized what he was staring at—a severed hand. A man's hand by the looks of it, a heavy gold watch still attached above the jagged, torn wrist.

"Oh, no way! You gotta check this out," he exclaimed, handing the binoculars to Calvin. "Look in the net."

After a few seconds of finding his target then focusing, Calvin was able to see what Jess was so amped-up about. "Ah naw, that ain't ..."

"Yeah, it is," confirmed Jess.

"That's messed up."

A short distance from the patrol boat, Terry and Neal were now pulling large chunks of something red on board their vessel.

"Hey, lemme see those again," said Jess reaching for the binocs. Through the lenses he was able to identify that what the fishermen were hauling aboard their boat were pieces of heavy red rubber. And suddenly it all came together: the *Casa del Agua* not returning, a red inflatable dinghy in pieces, and a gold watch. "Ho-ly shit."

"What? What part they got now?"

"The couple from Vegas," said Jess lowering the binoculars. "I think it's the couple from Vegas."

"Not Tom Jones?!"

Jess handed the binocs back to Calvin and immediately got on the marine radio. "This is the vessel *Hit It*, Whiskey, Yankee, Kilo 6553 to Sergeant Cruz, X909. Come in, Ray."

Ray was about to begin the process of photographing and bagging evidence when he heard the call come over the radio. Making his way to the pilothouse, he spotted the ski boat drifting in the distance. His voice soon came back over the radio. "I see you made it out here anyway. Over."

"Listen, Ray, I found the *Casa del Agua* anchored at Bedroom Two. No one on board and the dinghy's gone. Over."

"Okay. So what are you saying? Come back."

"The *Casa del Agua*'s dingy is a red Zodiac. Over."

"I see. Well, that's certainly something to look into. Over."

"And Ray, the guy had a pricey gold watch. Told me it wasn't easy to find a gold waterproof watch. Come back."

"I take it someone has binoculars. Over."

"That's affirmative."

"Hold for me."

Jess and Calvin watched Ray exit the wheelhouse to further inspect the grisly item resting in the net. They saw him check the time on his own less-expensive waterproof watch before returning to the wheelhouse and coming back on the radio. "Watch is working. But let's not jump to any conclusions just yet. Burt and I will stop by the *Casa del Agua* and board once we finish here. Over."

"Got it."

"Oh and Jess," Ray added, "get me all the information you have on those folks. Confirm?"

"Will do. Over."

The severed hand turned out to be the only body part Jess and Calvin were able to see. The face must have gotten bagged before they arrived on scene, and the sergeant and his deputy were more careful about concealing any additional finds.

Now late afternoon, Jess decided they'd better head back to the marina before his mom started squawking at him over the radio. They did, however, make one more pass by the *Casa del Agua*, just to be sure the couple from Las Vegas was not on board. They weren't, of course. And now the abandoned houseboat with Tom Jones still crooning away took on an eerie quality. Neither Calvin nor Jess wanted to admit just how much it creeped them out.

Heading for Heron's Harbor, Jess talked excitedly about the morbid discovery. "That's no boating accident," he declared. "It'd have to be one big-ass propeller to chop 'em up like that. And there's no way in hell a freighter could get up into Desperation Slough."

In his fascination with the concept that something violent had happened to two people he'd just met, Jess failed to consider the fact that Calvin lived with violence on a regular basis.

After Leo's death, Angela insisted they stop watching the news all together, believing that while they couldn't escape the kind of senseless brutality that had altered their lives, they didn't have to immerse themselves in it either. It didn't matter really, whether they watched the news or not; drug and gang violence had an unrelenting chokehold on Oakland. It infiltrated their neighborhood, permeated Calvin's high school, and the end-product of its handiwork rolled through the doors of the ER nightly.

For Jess, however, this kind of carnage was something new, and he was naturally fired up about it. "Maybe the guy was into something, drugs or some mob thing," he suggested. "Maybe it was a hit."

"Maybe somebody been watchin' too many *Sopranos* reruns."

"Okay, so what's your take?"

"Me? How should I know whaddup in the cuts."

"The cuts?"

Calvin couldn't believe he had to explain that one. "Boondocks."

But before Jess could respond to the obvious insult, another boat approached at considerable speed. It was the *Money Talks* with Eric at the wheel, the girls in back, and Dane being towed on a wakeboard. As they drew near, Eric veered toward them, allowing Dane to cut dangerously close and throw a sizeable spray that completely nailed both Jess and Calvin.

"That son of a bitch!" yelled Jess.

As he skied away, Dane looked back and laughed then flipped them off.

Furious, Jess immediately turned the boat around in pursuit. It wasn't about the water, hell, they were still slightly damp from wake jumping. It was the fact that this guy thought he could get away with anything. Jess decided it was time somebody taught him a lesson.

"Hold on cowboy, just whatchew think you gonna do?" Calvin asked him over the wind rushing past.

"I don't know. You don't think we could take 'em?" Jess hollered back.

"Take 'em? Oh, like we *Pirates of the Caribbean* now? Gonna board their ship and take their women? Listen up, Cracker Jack," Calvin stated loudly. "I got sent up to this mud hole as punishment. So I'm just gonna do my time and then get the hell out. I don't need no patna. And I sure as hell don't need trouble with some punk-ass white boys."

Point taken, Jess gave up the pursuit and turned the boat for home. They rode the rest of the way back to Heron's Harbor in silence.

❧ CHAPTER 13 ❧

HUESTUS, WE HAVE A PROBLEM

The front door to the Crawdaddy Club swung open and Huestus staggered out into the night. The white middle-aged former used car salesman, former delivery route driver, three-time former husband and two-time former AA member had once again over-imbibed. Huestus was thoroughly polluted.

Danny the bartender had taken his car keys again, telling him to go sleep it off in his unlocked car. And Huestus had conceded without a challenge. Handing over his keys, he gave Danny a sloppy salute before sliding off the barstool and heading out to the parking lot.

Whistling a happy tune that was more air than sound, Huestus zigzagged down the sidewalk. He fumbled for his billfold, which subsequently slipped out of his hand and fell to the ground. Though spectacularly unsteady as he bent over to retrieve it, like a Weeble, Huestus wobbled but did not fall down. Fully upright again, he rifled through his wallet which contained significantly less cash than it had three hours ago when he'd entered the bar.

"Bingo," he declared, pulling out the single spare car key he kept stashed for exactly this type of situation.

Locating his older model Buick was relatively easy. There was something to be said for driving an old tuna boat; he didn't often end up trying his key on a vehicle that didn't belong to him. Though that did still happen on occasion. Huestus opened the unlocked driver's side door of the Buick and climbed in. After buckling his seat belt—safety first—he nodded off for a moment. Coming-to a few minutes later, Huestus briefly considered honoring his promise to simply sleep it off. Then he rallied, arriving at the same ill-fated conclusion he had so many times before: he was fine.

The Buick weaved down the blessedly empty levee road, and though he wasn't driving fast, the lack of speed could not compensate for the lack of precision. Huestus had about as much control over his vehicle as the driver of a bumper car at the carnival. He decided a cigarette was in order and would help him stay awake, so he pawed for his spare pack on the passenger seat. After veering into the oncoming lane a few times, he eventually managed to grab hold of it. In an attempt to retrieve a single cigarette from the pack, several ended up on his lap, the seat, and the floorboard. But Huestus wasn't concerned; he'd probably get around to smoking most of them by the time he got home. He picked one up off his lap and stuck it in his mouth—filter end out. Looking down to push in the lighter, he simply missed a critical turn in the road and drove straight off the levee.

The Buick plunged down the rocky embankment toward the river and abruptly came to a halt. Resting at an angle, the car's front end was partially submerged while its rear axle was firmly lodged on levee rocks. Water was partway up the driver's side door and the engine was dead. As luck would have it, Huestus suffered only a broken cigarette, which was dangling from his mouth. And though he was unscathed, he was far from aware.

"Thun of a bitch."

Spitting out the broken butt, he looked out the windshield at the green waters of the river, now illuminated by his submerged headlights.

"Huestus, we have a problem."

Oblivious to the severity of the situation, he turned the key in the ignition, as if he could simply back the Buick out if it started. It didn't, of course. So he put the gear shift in "park" and tried again. Maybe that was the problem. But, no.

Huestus sat there, dumbfounded as water lapped over the hood.

"Engine must be flooded."

Sure was, just not in the way his Scotch-saturated brain had reasoned. The fact that the river was now within reach through his open window somehow failed to register. He popped the hood release, clumsily unbuckled his seat belt, and attempted to exit out the driver's side. The door, however, was firmly wedged against levee rocks and wouldn't budge.

"Now why do people have to park so god damn close?"

Scooting across the front seats, he struggled to open the passenger door. Putting all his weight into it, he eventually managed to force it open and the river swiftly spilled in, filling the interior up to the edge of the passenger seat. Unfazed, Huestus stepped out into the cold water, which did little or nothing to sober him up.

Instead of making his way up the levee bank to the road, Huestus waded unsteadily to the front of the Buick where the headlights shone into the river.

"Well, s'not the battery," he noted.

No, that was definitely s*not* the problem. It was a Sears' DieHard after all. Earlier that evening, he and Danny the bartender had discussed the merits of a DieHard versus an off-brand battery. Well, perhaps it was more like a monotonous lecture with Danny his captive audience.

With considerable effort, Huestus proceeded to open the hood, then stood there inspecting the immersed engine.

"Tha's not good."

Out in the slough, an imposing figure swam through the beam cast by the headlamps. Huestus thought he heard something ... a splash. He turned in time to see a long, spiked tail slip through the lighted waters and quickly disappear into darkness.

"What the ... Naaah."

Shaking off yet another drunken hallucination, Huestus closed the hood.

Standing waist-deep in cold water for the last few minutes had finally begun to jump-start his brain function and he grasped that he would be walking, not driving, home. As he made his way around the front end of the vehicle, the figure passed through the glow of headlights once again, this time heading in the opposite direction, and closer.

This was no hallucination.

"Holy mother."

Moving as fast as he could in soaked trousers and shoes, Huestus waded toward the partially open passenger door, but one of his saturated loafers slipped off and he fell, crashing into the door and knocking it shut. Struggling to his feet, he anxiously tried the handle but could not get the door to open.

Just offshore, the jagged dorsal ridge crested and cut through the water. It was coming straight for him. Huestus dove through the open passenger window. With his lower half still outside the car, he desperately reached for the steering wheel to pull himself the rest of the way in. But that was not to be. Terror abruptly transformed to trauma as the creature hit the lower half of his body. Huestus was being pulled out of the Buick. His fingers violently clenched at dashboard knobs, triggering the windshield wipers and turning on the radio. Then, with one final tug, he was yanked out the window.

In the green glow of the headlamps, Huestus was briefly seen being pulled along underwater, his legs firmly in the grip of some indistinguishable monster swimming just outside the beam. In an instant, he was gone, pulled into the dark depths.

The headlights continued to cast their glow into the water, and the windshield wipers kept time as the Talking Heads' "Take Me to the River" blasted from the tinny in-dash speakers of the Buick—it had a DieHard battery, after all.

❧ CHAPTER 14 ❧

LIFE'S SHORT

For the last fifteen years, the Markhams had traveled the world, some of it aboard their fifty-nine-foot yacht, *Life's Short*. Now both on the cusp of turning 70, Lou and Gloria were childhood sweethearts who'd married young. And though they never had children of their own, they were hardly without kids. For a number of years their house became something of a refugee camp for teenagers; the sons and daughters of friends and family who weren't getting along at home, yet seemed to thrive under the accepting and encouraging demeanor of the couple.

Lou was a simple guy who happened to make a fortune in mid-life off one of his simple ideas. A mechanical engineer by trade, he'd always invented gadgets in his spare time. When one of his fishing lures became a sellout hit on QVC, he quit his job and became a full-time inventor, cranking out all manner of gadgets and thingamabobs the American public snapped up and wondered how on earth they'd ever lived without. Far too reserved to pimp his own products on infomercials, Lou sold them to other companies with a decent revenue stream attached—he and Gloria didn't have to worry about money ever again. The checks just kept right on direct-depositing into their bank account no matter where in the world they happened to be.

Prior to her husband's entrepreneurial success, Gloria had been a high school geography teacher who longed to experience first-hand the many places she knew vicariously through textbooks and maps. Once the money started rolling in, Lou knew it was time to make his gal's dream come true. So they began to travel and have great adventures in far-flung places. After several years of this, however, Lou'd gotten more than his fill of flying on jets and sailing on cruise ships. Also of riding on camels, elephants, and donkeys, not to mention sleeping in hotel rooms, state rooms, and the occasional hut. Eventually, Lou worked up the courage to approach his wife with the idea of a yacht; a place to call their own, yet still be able to travel.

Turned out, Gloria didn't need much convincing and was on board in more ways than one. She too, was done with the stiff back and sore bum from sleeping in huts and riding on camels. So they purchased a home with a dock in Vancouver and continued to travel, only now they did it in the comfort of their floating second home, aptly named *Life's Short*.

They could have afforded a much bigger yacht of course, but true to their nature, they didn't need to be ostentatious and wanted something they could manage themselves without a crew. After forty-seven years of marriage, they still enjoyed each other's company on their long journeys; they complimented each other, laughed a lot, and were mates in every sense of the word.

Long before Lou struck it big, the couple lived in a simple tract home and owned a small cabin cruiser that they berthed at

Heron's Harbor back when Jess's grandparents owned the place. Though they'd been to numerous exotic locations since, they still loved the Sacramento-San Joaquin Delta. It appealed to their simple nature and held fond memories of simpler times.

The couple was presently on their way back to Heron's Harbor for a long-overdue visit. They were steadily making their way up the San Joaquin River with Lou at the helm when a large blip suddenly appeared on their new high-tech sonar screen. Gloria was below in the galley putting together a cheese platter for their impending cocktail hour when her husband called for her to come take a look.

"What do you make of that?" he asked, pointing to the sonar screen as she arrived up top.

Putting on her glasses, Gloria stared at the large blip, which appeared to be heading straight for them. "What the heck is it?"

"That's what I'd like to know."

"It's as big as a whale, for god's sake."

"Well, they have made their way into the Delta before."

"Pretty rare though. And I doubt a whale can move that fast." Tapping the screen with her fingernail Gloria declared, "This thing must be on the fritz."

"Better not be," replied Lou, who'd done his research before deciding on this particular sonar device.

Faulty equipment or not, Lou reduced his speed since they were now on a collision course with a ... blip. The couple watched the screen intently, but as the large dot approached the denser sonar waves, it abruptly reversed direction. Rapidly heading away from them, it vanished from range as quickly as it had appeared.

Having traveled the world and witnessed inexplicable marvels such as Stonehenge and the Gods of Easter Island, things of this nature, while curious, did not elicit alarm in either of them.

"Huh," shrugged Gloria. "Cocktail?"

"Absolutely," replied Lou.

♦ CHAPTER 15 ♦

SIMPLY NOT HIS DAY

Calvin had been in the Delta for nearly a week now and he was putting in some long hours at the shop. This was fine by him since it seemed to make the time go faster. He had to admit, his great-uncle was a damn fine mechanic and he'd already learned a thing or two from him. Having quickly found his way around an outboard, Calvin would soon be up for tackling some of the bigger, more challenging boat engines.

While they didn't have much to talk about, and sometimes didn't talk at all, Samuel seemed to appreciate Calvin's company and certainly his help. The two had quickly fallen into a rhythm of working together. But at age 66, Samuel had a tendency to run out of steam by early afternoon and was ready to call it a day just about the time Calvin was hitting his stride. So Calvin would stay on, working until evening when he'd meet up with Samuel for dinner, usually at the café. Samuel was a decent enough cook who could whip up a hearty breakfast and pack a respectable sack lunch, but at the end of a hard day, Calvin looked forward to partaking of Frances's dinner specials. He'd already ordered her chicken pot pie twice. After dinner, he would head back to the shop and work late into the night, a pattern that was rapidly getting them caught up on jobs and making it possible to take on even more. By the time he crashed back at *The Sturgeon* each night, Calvin was usually too tired to be bothered by the vigorous snoring emanating from Samuel's cabin.

As it turned out, Ol' Joe wasn't exaggerating with regard to the state of the shop, but if Calvin continued working at this pace, he might even have the place organized by the time he blew out of here at the end of summer.

Of course, his mother had called every day since he'd arrived until Samuel finally convinced her things were going well and she should "back off a bit and give the boy some breathing room." As far as Samuel was concerned, Calvin was keeping busy and keeping his nose clean, and she'd be the first to know if anything changed.

As far as Calvin was concerned, he wasn't having the time of his life, but he wasn't completely miserable either. He actually looked forward to his nights alone in the shop. Surprisingly, he was getting used to going old-school with no iPod, no cell phone, and no Internet. He'd found a hip-hop station out of Sacramento on the shop's vintage radio, but sometimes he'd just leave it off and work in the strange quiet of the night. No sirens, no traffic, no loud trash-talkin' on the street. Just the sound of crickets and the creaking of the shop itself, which was really just a large floating shed with a tin roof.

He saw Jess around the marina now and then, and though they acknowledged each other, their clash on the ski boat that first day had left them at a cautious standoff. Calvin told himself he wasn't here to make friends with the natives anyway. He was here to serve out the sentence imposed by his mother, a sentence he'd unfairly inherited from Leo, though there was nothing to be done about it now.

It was mid-afternoon on the first truly hot day of summer, and the old box fans in the shop were barely making a dent. Calvin had to keep wiping sweat from his brow as he finished the tune-up on a Merc 150 outboard. He hadn't gone swimming since arriving here but was seriously considering jumping in the river just to cool down. He could tell Samuel wasn't gonna last much longer. He'd been shuffling paperwork around on his cluttered desk for the last half-hour and would soon be sauntering back to *The Sturgeon* to sit under its little AC unit.

The phone jangled and his boss lifted the old-style receiver as if it weighed ten pounds. "Yellow, Samuel's," he answered at slow speed, too hot to even bother with the "Marine Repair" portion of his standard salutation.

With Samuel on the phone, Calvin took a break and walked over to one of the shop's windows that overlooked a quiet section of the marina, a small lagoon of sorts. Due to limited boat traffic, the area was ideal for swimming and there was someone presently taking advantage of that fact. A girl in a black bikini accented with deep purple flowers was floating face down on a raft, her head resting on her forearms. Her long dark hair was pulled to one side, the ends drifting on the water beside her like tendrils of a graceful jellyfish.

Calvin stared at the young woman's slender, yet pleasantly curvy body—a nice change of scenery that did little or nothing to cool him down. He was enjoying the view when his attention was suddenly drawn to something moving through the water a short distance from where the girl floated. It was a grey-colored dorsal fin that looked something like a shark. But there weren't any sharks in the Delta, were there? Calvin's mind raced as he tried to grasp what he was seeing and react. He needed to warn the girl and attempted to open the shop's old window, but the trim had been painted over countless times and wouldn't give. In the time it would take him to run out of the shop and over to the swimming area, it would be too late. Helpless, Calvin tried again to force the window with no luck. With no other options, he began pounding on the glass, hoping to get the girl's attention or at least get her to look up and see that something unnatural was heading directly for her.

In a matter of seconds, the fin reached the girl ... and smacked her right in the head. Startled, she looked up to see what the hell had interrupted her peaceful afternoon of sunbathing.

"Damn it, Jess!" Mei Li hollered.

Annoyed, she grabbed the radio-controlled fin contraption and hurled it several yards away. It splashed down then resurfaced a moment later, floating on its side.

Calvin felt like a complete idiot. There was no Creature From The Black Lagoon and no damsel in distress. Seemed the discovery of severed body parts had freaked him out more than he cared to admit and he'd let his imagination get the better of him. Even more distressing, the damsel in the black bikini turned out to be the girl from the farm, that Asian chick.

"Why ya bangin' on the window?" asked Samuel with minor irritation, his hand covering the phone's receiver.

"Uh, I was just trying to get it open, get some more air in here."

"Well, that window don't open no more."

"Figured that out."

Relieved that Mei Li hadn't heard him pounding on the glass like a fool, Calvin watched her turn over on the raft and resume sunbathing in peace.

Jess, however, was not quite done with his campaign of harassment, and Calvin watched as he crept out from his hiding place: the blackberry bushes above on the breakwater. He then carefully put down the remote control and quietly made his way to a rope swing that dangled from a tree along the embankment. Calvin would not be attempting to intervene on Mei Li's behalf this time. A moment later, Jess swung out on the rope (fully clothed) and delivered a precision cannonball that flipped Mei Li right off her raft. A frenzied splash war ensued between the two, and for a brief moment, Calvin wished he was out there goofing around and keeping cool. But his heat-induced daydream was abruptly cut short by Samuel. "Hey, guy wants to know when his Merc 150'll be done."

"This afternoon," Calvin replied without turning from the window.

"Watcha lookin' at?"

"Nothin'."

Samuel shrugged and returned to his call. "You can pick it up in the mornin' and be out fishin' just as fast as you can write me a check." Happy for his own distraction from work and the punishing heat, Samuel went on to quiz his customer. "So what's bitin' and where?"

Calvin came away from the window but wasn't exactly eager to get back to work. He'd get more done this evening anyway, once the brutal temperatures of the day had tapered off. While Samuel entertained himself with "Talk to a Live Fisherman,"

Calvin decided to poke around at the back of the shop, see what might be buried there under mounds of junk. Hopefully it wasn't any missing relatives.

In the farthest corner of the shop, the wheels of a small trailer peeked out from beneath a dusty tarp. Whatever was on the trailer had gradually become a makeshift catchall for a variety of underused shop items. Curious, Calvin began clearing off the stack of crap. With the clutter now removed, he lifted the decaying tarp to find an older-model Yamaha WaveRunner resting on the trailer. The thing was in rough condition and would clearly require some major repairs were it ever to see water again.

"Some guy unloaded that on me a few years back," said Samuel. He'd wrapped up his phone call and come to see what Calvin was up to in the "no man's land" area of the shop. "Said I could have it to fix up and sell. I thought about it, but I'm too old to be foolin' around with those things."

"Think I could mess with it?"

"You're welcome to it, long as the paying jobs come first."

That being said, Samuel decided to call it a day and mosey back to *The Sturgeon* for a cold beer and a nap. But before he ducked out the door he turned back. "You know, Jess has a real fancy shmancy one o' those," he said, pointing at the PWC. "Oughta talk to him if ya need any help or special tools."

Of course, it would be Jess. The last person on earth Calvin would want to ask a favor of.

Up at the café, Mei Li was beginning the second half of her shift with wet hair from being dunked in the river on her break. Not that she wouldn't have jumped in of her own volition in this kind of heat. The restaurant's two small AC units were cranked up to high, so the temperature inside was at least tolerable, though everyone seemed to be moving in slow motion today. Fortunately, it was a low-key kind of place. The next couple hours would be about side work and gossip until the early-bird diners started filing in. That is, if anyone had the energy to drag themselves out in this weather.

Mei Li was keeping busy refilling salt and pepper shakers—a mindless chore that gave her the opportunity to eavesdrop on Frances and Ray. The sheriff's sergeant was having a late lunch at the counter and Frances was pumping him for details about the latest Delta scuttlebutt. "So what is that, number four for Huestus?" she asked while topping off his ice tea.

"Five, if you count the delivery truck from when he had that job at the bakery," Ray replied.

"Oh yeah, I forgot about that one."

"I had a tow truck fish the Buick out this morning."

"But you still haven't found him?"

"Nope. Probably stumbled into the wrong trailer and passed out. I'm sure we'll get a call."

"You don't think he drowned?"

"Nah. Car wasn't that far under. Besides, you know Huestus, he's the drunk with nine lives."

Mei Li inserted herself into the conversation by changing the subject. "Hey, I wanna know why there wasn't anything in the paper about those people who got shredded."

Ray would have preferred to finish his lunch without discussing that particular incident, but apparently that was wishful thinking. "We're trying to keep a lid on that until we know more," he answered, attempting not to sound blatantly evasive.

"It *was* a boating accident, wasn't it?" Frances asked.

"Can't say for sure yet. There wasn't all that much evidence. We collected everything we could find, though."

"And did all the pieces make up two whole people?" Mei Li asked pointedly.

"Not exactly," he admitted.

"Maybe they'd been out there for a while and the fish had been, you know, snacking on them," suggested Mei Li. She then made little snapping fishes with her hands accompanied by sound effects.

"Mei Li!" cried Frances.

"Hey, I'm just sayin'." Pleading innocent, she shrugged and headed for the storage closet to get more salt.

Calvin entered the café wiping sweat from his brow and walked directly to the cold drink case in the grocery area.

"Hey there," called Frances, forever trying to make him feel welcome.

"Hey," he replied with a nod en route to the beverage case.

Standing there enjoying the cold blast from the refrigerated unit, Calvin didn't realize Mei Li had materialized behind the cooler door. As he reached for a couple Cokes, she pounced. "So how's it goin', Oaktown?"

Startled, he fumbled the drinks and both cans hit the floor.

"Oops, sorry. Didn't mean to scare ya ... again."

"You didn't," he flatly denied. "My hands are sweaty, that's all."

She wasn't really sorry, of course, though she did feel a little bad upon seeing him down on all fours struggling to locate the second can, which must have rolled under a display rack.

Taking pity on him, Mei Li got down to help look for the elusive soda, and as she bent close, her pony tail fell to one side.

Calvin noticed her hair was still damp, and it smelled intoxicating; a combination of spicy incense and tropical flowers. Though she was now dressed in a casual uniform of khaki pants and a Heron's Harbor T-shirt, Calvin couldn't help but picture the black bikini with the deep purple flowers. Fortunately, Mei Li quickly located the missing soda can wedged beneath a potato chip rack.

As they both stood up, Calvin attempted to regain his composure. "Thanks." Taking the can from her, he made a beeline for the counter to pay for the Cokes and make his escape.

But Mei Li wasn't quite through with him. "Guess you heard about those people getting chopped up," she called after him.

"Yeah," he replied, barely turning around.

"We try to have a little carnage now and then. You know, something to impress the big city folk."

"Mei Li!" Frances scolded, while Ray rolled his eyes and shook his head.

Fleeing out into the heat, Calvin tried to shake off the awkward encounter. He seriously needed to get the image of her bikini and the scent of her hair out of his head. He made his way over to the rental dock where Jess was busy scrubbing black fingerprint dust off the *Casa del Agua*. Walking to the bow of the boat, Calvin placed one of the cold Cokes on the deck near Jess—a peace offering of sorts. "Listen, about the other day," he said, gingerly broaching the subject.

"What about it?" asked Jess, without looking up or interrupting his work.

"I was just ... I don't know, mouthing off."

"You don't want to be friends, that's cool. I've got friends."

"Yeah."

Having momentarily forgotten what just happened at the café, Calvin popped the top on his soda, which subsequently sprayed all over him. Jess couldn't help but laugh. And Calvin took it. Apparently, this was his day to act a fool, and there wasn't a damn thing he could do about it.

A moment later, a boat horn sounded repeatedly. The Markhams' yacht was approaching and the couple waved enthusiastically from the bridge. Tossing his sponge in the bucket, Jess headed for the guest dock to greet them. On his way, he bent down and snagged the Coke. "I should probably tap on this before opening it, huh?"

"True that."

Halfway up the rental dock, Jess turned back. "I'll catch up with you later, a'ight?"

"Yeah, a'ight."

With the dinner crowd virtually nonexistent due to the heat, Frances closed up shop in favor of a barbecue on the lawn to celebrate the Markhams' return to Heron's Harbor—one of the perks of being the boss of a casual joint. Should anyone come by looking for a meal, they were welcome to join the party. Ray even offered to give Frances a break by manning the barbecue, a gesture she gladly accepted.

The sun was finally on its way to other parts of the world and people were beginning to perk up. Gloria Markham stood at the head of a picnic table excitedly doling out gifts from their world travels. Mei Li was already sporting an elaborate Hmong tribal hat and Jess was the proud owner of a rain stick from Thailand. Reaching into her bag of goodies, Gloria brought forth a wooden carving of a native woman with enormous breasts that she handed to Ol' Joe. "Now Joe, this is a sacred piece from the tribe's spiritual advisor."

"Witch doctor," Lou clarified.

"Oh, he was such a fascinating man," his wife gushed.

"I'll bet he was," replied Joe, inspecting the piece.

Digging into her bag again, Gloria retrieved another wooden statue, this time a male with a considerable phallic appendage. "Now this is a fertility god from a small village in New Guinea."

Those who had not yet received a gift held their breath, fearing they might be the one for whom Gloria had chosen this particular item. Samuel turned out to be the lucky winner.

"Oh, it's not just about fertility," she explained, handing it to him, "it's about good luck. So put your lottery tickets under it and see what happens."

"I'll do that," he replied, trying his best to act nonchalant about holding the figure.

Ol' Joe turned to Samuel and pointedly announced, "I don't think you should bring your doll over to play with my doll," thus prompting laughs all around.

"And this is a love potion from Ecuador," said Gloria, holding up a bottle.

"Anyone notice a theme here?" asked Lou.

Gloria proceeded to liberally sprinkle the potion on Frances and Ray.

"Aw now, Gloria, you went and got some o' that on me," cried Samuel. After a suggestive wink from Ray he warned, "You stay away from me now. I don't care if you are the sheriff."

Passing the love potion to Mei Li, Gloria advised, "Be careful with that, it's extremely powerful stuff."

Having gotten wind of the barbecue, Calvin quickly wolfed down a sandwich at *The Sturgeon* and attempted to go unnoticed as he made his way back to the shop. Considering how his day had gone so far, the last thing he needed was to be trapped in a social situation with the Hillbilly Harbor Gang. He was doing his best to circumvent the gathering on the lawn by casually walking behind a row of parked cars. And just when he thought he was in the clear, he heard Samuel call out, "Hey Calvin, come on over here. I want you to meet some folks."

Damn. So close.

Calvin reluctantly walked back to the picnic area and tried not to make eye contact with Mei Li. Thankfully, her crazy-ass hat with strands of dangling beads helped considerably in this regard. He was still struggling with the fact that he'd been staring at her earlier, thinking the chick in the black bikini was a seriously bangin' package. It was the heat, he told himself, like when people in the desert think they see water.

"Gloria, Lou, this is my grand-nephew, Calvin."

"Pleasure to meet you Calvin," said Lou, standing to shake his hand.

"Oh, I have just the thing for you," announced Gloria as she excitedly began rummaging in her bag to retrieve an item. "I must have had a premonition about you. I was so taken with this piece but I didn't know who it was right for." She then walked over to Calvin with a primitive-looking medallion necklace in her hand. He froze as she slipped it around his neck. "This is given to the boys in a certain New Guinea tribe when they become men. It protects the wearer against evil spirits and mythical monsters."

"Uh, thanks," he said, wishing it would simply protect him from all of them.

"Grab a seat," urged Frances. "Ray does a mean hot dog."

"Nah, I'm good. Got some stuff to do in the shop. But thanks for the ... this," he said holding the medallion away from his chest.

Calvin then slowly backed away from the group, as if they were zombies who might try and grab him, turn him into one of them—a weenie-roasting, s'mores-eating, campfire-sing-a-long zombie. And once he felt sure they would not be coming after him, he turned and walked purposely toward the safety of the shop. He planned to spend the rest of the evening in blessed solitude, fully focused on his passionate new relationship; the one with the old WaveRunner. He was already envisioning his Dr. Frankenstein moment when he would see his creation brought back to life. Having savored his first taste of speeding across water, he wanted more and longed to get back out there as soon as possible. Only next time, it would be on his own, and the rebuilt PWC was going to be his ticket.

He'd found an owner's manual in the seat compartment of the 9-year-old WaveRunner, which provided some insight into what was what. It was not, however, a service manual. With no Internet access, Calvin was going to have to figure out most of this on his own, a hitch that would undoubtedly slow his progress. Unless of course, he was willing to break down and ask Jess for help. But that would be a last resort. At least he'd made a goodwill gesture today, albeit a very small olive branch.

The crickets were in full form on this warm still night, and they loudly serenaded Calvin as he stood under the glow of a single work light, staring down into the PWC's open engine compartment. So absorbed in taking his first real look at the engine, Calvin didn't notice that Jess had walked up and was standing at the open shop door.

"Hey."

Calvin jumped, hitting his head on the PWC's engine compartment lid, causing it to slam shut. "Why does everybody do that up here?" he asked accusingly.

"Do what?"

"Sneak up on people."

"Sorry. Maybe we should all wear whistle tips."

There was an awkward moment, then, Calvin actually laughed. Shaking his head, he lifted the engine cover once more and began attaching several extensions to a standard socket wrench.

Jess came closer and watched, but did not offer to assist. "You really think you can do something with this old bucket?"

"Maybe. Might need some help."

"I'm no miracle mechanic."

"Probably got the right tools, though."

"Probably. You realize, if you do get it running, you're gonna be hooked.

"So?"

"Well, it is a water sport. They might not let you back in the hood."

"Funny," he replied and continued poking around the engine before nonchalantly asking, "So, what's with that girl from the café?"

"What girl?"

"Asian chick."

"Mei Li? She works here part time in the summer. Her family owns the farm down the road. Why?"

"Just askin'. Thought maybe you guys were hooked up."

Making a face, Jess quickly clarified. "We grew up together. She's more like a sister. You interested?"

"No," he insisted. "She's too… I don't know."

"Feisty?"

"Maybe. Not interested in a feisty female, thanks."

"I hear that. So, you're off tomorrow, right?"

"I don't know."

"Come on, it's Sunday, you need to take a break. I've got coverage on the gas dock and you're gonna learn to water-ski."

"Like hell."

"Perfect. I'll see ya tomorrow then, 'round 11." Jess started to leave, then turned back at the shop door. "By the way, a super-extended socket wrench ain't gonna cut it. You can borrow my drive shaft tool. I'll have it for ya tomorrow."

And with that, Jess disappeared into the night.

Calvin continued to struggle with his adapted wrench. He wasn't quite ready to admit Jess was right—that he would, in fact, be needing a specialized drive shaft tool. After several more minutes of fumbling, Calvin finally gave up and tossed the oversized socket wrench onto a workbench. Only it kept going, crashing into a metal tool cabinet before loudly clanking down on the cement floor, causing the crickets to momentarily cease chirping.

This was simply not his day.

❦ CHAPTER 16 ❦

PIECE O' MEAT

The Delta summer sun feels good on old bones, and Joe wasn't gonna let that morning's rays go to waste. His stretch of river at the ferry crossing was calm, the water barely lapping against the hull. There was a slight breeze too, just enough to make it downright pleasant—perfect conditions for a midmorning snooze. Later would be too hot.

Hunkered down in his captain's chair on the deck of the cable ferry, Ol' Joe slumped over and nodded off. If anyone called him on it, he would simply deliver his standard line, "just restin' my eyes." Hell, it was a slow Sunday morning, and if anyone wanted a crossing they could simply honk and he'd be there momentarily. No sense being cooped up in the pilothouse reading the paper when a nap in the sun could be had. And it was a good nap too, until that damn horsefly decided to pester him.

Half asleep, Ol' Joe swatted the annoying insect away without even opening his eyes. He didn't need to come to full consciousness to recognize the buzz of a Delta horsefly, they were the size of B52 Bombers this time of year. It landed on his nose. Swat. It landed on his ear. Swat. It did a buzzy little jig in his beard. Swat, swat. But Joe held firm, determined to outlast this bothersome pest. Hopefully the dang thing would soon find some other piece o' meat and leave him to nap in peace. It didn't take long, however, for the persistent fly to break the old boy's determination. Joe abruptly rose to his feet, waving his arms like a lunatic.

"Dag nabbit, shove off!" he shouted. "Ruined ma damn nap, ya damn fly!"

Now fully awake and mad about it, something a few yards up river caught Joe's eye and instantly irked him; a man in an inflatable fishing tube floating at the river's edge. Even from a distance, Joe could tell this was another dumb tourist who had all the latest gear but couldn't be bothered with the rules and regulations. Another out-of-towner peeled from the cover of Cabela's catalogue and pasted onto a Delta postcard. Well, time to give Mr. Fancy Pants Fisherman a reality check.

Joe marched over to the side of the ferry. Since the guy wasn't facing in his direction, he'd have to holler to get his attention. Cupping his hands around his mouth Joe called out, "Hey, Buddy! Ya gotta move on. There's no fishin' near a cable crossing."

But the angler didn't even bother acknowledging him. Was this city slicker blowing him off? Still facing away, the fisherman was gradually drifting closer and Joe got a better look at all his highfalutin gear, which only made him wanna run the guy off more.

"Didja hear me, mister? Ya gotta clear out. Can't be fishin' around a ferry. It's dangerous!"

Again, no response from the fisherman. Joe decided the guy probably had one of those iPod thingies stuck in his ears. Damn foolish thing to not be aware of your surroundings, especially in water. In short order, the fisherman drifted up against the side of the *Eddie O* with a soft thud.

"Well, I'll be," said Joe, scratching his beard.

He noticed the fisherman's line was slack, and though the man's face was obscured by his pricey fishing hat, Joe concluded the guy musta fallen asleep. Fishing and napping went hand-in-hand after all, and Joe wished he was doing either or both, rather than dealing with this idiot.

Walking to the pilothouse, Ol' Joe returned with a boat hook a moment later. He leaned over the railing and attempted to rouse this knucklehead by poking at the guy's inflatable fishing tube with the hook.

"Hey pal, time to wake up. Not gonna catch anything with a slack line anyway."

Nothing. So he poked a bit harder.

"Come on, buddy. Rise and shine!"

Joe jostled the inflatable tube but good this time, causing the fisherman to tip over backwards thus revealing the reason this guy was so damn unresponsive—both of his legs had been severed, mid-thigh.

"Ho-ly cripes! Aw, jeez."

The man's fishing pole remained clenched in his rigor mortis grip. His face, now partially underwater, a frozen, shocked death mask. Poor amateur bastard, musta gotten himself too close to a spinning prop. It happened now and then.

Several horseflies began to buzz around the mangled, fleshy stumps where the man's legs had once been, and chances were good Joe's nap-destroyer was among them. Found another piece o' meat after all. But what really struck Joe was how the guy's fancy fishing hat had stayed in place. Was still on, in fact. Now that was a quality piece of outdoor wear.

Joe got on the horn to Gladys at the Sheriff's Office, then threw a cargo net over "stumpy" and secured it, ensuring he wouldn't drift away. And while he waited for Sheriff Cruz to arrive, Ol' Joe dug through the accumulated piles of newspapers and magazines in the pilothouse. Where *was* his Cabela's catalogue?

❧ CHAPTER 17 ❧

WALK THE PLANK

Jess was lounging on the rear bench seat of the ski boat with his legs outstretched when Calvin arrived on the rental dock. Without looking up or removing his sunglasses, Jess casually said, "Couldn't cut it with standard tools, huh?"

"But you knew that."

"Got what ya need right here," he said, pointing toward the long drive shaft tool laying beside the seat. "Loan it to ya once we get back from a ski run. I'll even throw in a service manual download."

But before Calvin could reply, another set of footsteps made their way down the dock. He turned to find Mei Li approaching and promptly shot Jess an accusatory look.

"Gotta have a spotter if you're gonna ski," said Jess, pleading innocent.

"I didn't say I was gonna ski," replied Calvin.

Mei Li arrived and placed a small cooler on the edge of the dock. If she was wearing that bikini, it was safely concealed under her shorts and halter top.

"Hey, Oaktown," she chirped before jumping on board.

"Calvin. It's Calvin."

"Okay, Calvin. So, you ready?"

"Tell you what, you guys can ski and I'll spot."

"Oh come on, we've taught lots of people to ski," she assured him. "It'll be fun."

Behind her, Jess held up the coveted tool for added incentive.

"I'll pass just the same."

"What's the matter, scared to try something new?" she baited. "Afraid you might not look street?"

"I really don't need this," he replied and turned to go.

But Mei Li wasn't going to let him off that easy. "It must be exhausting, really," she said loudly, "exuding that much 'tude on a daily basis." She then climbed out of the boat and stormed past him down the dock.

"Hey," Calvin called after her. As she turned around, he picked up her cooler and held it forth. "You forgot this."

Miffed, Mei Li marched back. But as she went to take the cooler, he moved it out of reach. "I'll try," he said, relenting. "A'ight?"

Crossing her arms, Mei Li took a moment before accepting this belated offer. "Fine."

A tentative agreement in place, the two returned to the ski boat, climbed in, and sat down. Both pulled sunglasses down over their eyes and refused to look at each other.

Smiling to himself, Jess climbed behind the wheel and started the engine. "Alrighty then. Guess the captain won't be performing any marriages on this cruise."

Calvin didn't think getting up on a water ski was going to be easy, but he also didn't think it was going to be this hard. He'd either tumbled head over ski or fallen backwards on his ass on all previous attempts, and was about to try—for the eighth time— at getting up on the damn thing. His mounting frustration, however, only served to make him more determined to conquer this screwball sport. His last wipeout had separated him from the ski, and he was awkwardly struggling to get his foot back in the boot as Jess and Mei Li circled nearby in the boat, working to get the tow rope to him.

"You were close," Mei Li called out. "But you've gotta remember to keep that ski up and stay tucked at first. Let the boat do all the work. Once you feel the ski start to plane, *then* stand up."

"How come I don't get to start with two skis?" Calvin called back. "I thought that's how everybody started."

"You don't need to mess with two," she replied. "I've seen the way you move, you can handle a single."

"Ooo, she's seen the way he moves," Jess teasingly remarked, though only loud enough for Mei Li to hear. She responded by repeatedly whacking him with the ski flag.

"Hey, don't distract the driver," he protested, batting her away.

Mei Li returned her attention to their student, who was now bobbing in the correct position with ski on and tow rope in hand. Jess then carefully eased the boat forward until the rope was straight.

"Ready?" she asked Calvin.

"Ready as I'll ever be," he groused.

"Say when," she urged.

Weary of saying "hit it" only to end up hitting the surface of the water with his body, Calvin attempted to change his luck by changing his words. "Go!" he yelled.

Jess punched the throttle and Calvin once again struggled to get up. And he did for a brief moment, then quickly lost control, his body skipping like a stone across the surface of the river before sinking to a stop. Another epic fail.

"Oh, that was so close," declared Jess, having witnessed the tumble in his rear view mirror. "He's almost there."

"I know!" agreed Mei Li. She then encouragingly called out to Calvin, "You're almost there. This next time is it for sure."

Calvin was floundering in the water, trying to shake off his latest spill when another boat approached. Mei Li held the bright orange ski flag high, alerting them to a skier in the water.

"Oh great," said Jess upon realizing that the boat was, in fact, the *Money Talks*.

At the wheel, Dane reduced his speed and circled nearby before loudly announcing, "So this is where the U.N. Ski Team practices."

"Ya know, there's a whole lot o' river out here," replied Jess. "Why don't you go find some other place to play?"

"Aw now that's not very nice," Dane yelled back. "We just wanna take in some of the local color."

Hoping to dissuade Dane from starting something, Lauren attempted to intervene. "Come on you guys, let's just go."

But Eric quickly shut her down. "Relax. We're not gonna hurt your little boyfriend. We're just havin' some fun."

Ignoring the boatload of gawkers, Calvin continued to ready himself for yet another attempt at getting up on the ski.

"Hey," Dane called over to Jess, "you know what they call teachin' a black guy to water-ski don't ya?"

"You're fucking hysterical," replied Jess, who typically only swore under extreme circumstances. He was finding, however, that the mere sight of these two instantly brought him to that level.

Not being the brightest or most aware individual, Nikki naïvely asked, "What do they call it?"

Lauren cringed, knowing Eric would be all too happy to enlighten his dim girlfriend to the racist punch line. And he did. "Trollin' for alligators! Get it?"

She didn't, really. But judging from Dane and Eric's laughter, this was one of their all-time favorites in what was undoubtedly a stellar repertoire of racist humor.

"You'd think we were trolling for dickheads," Jess shouted back.

"Hey, it's just a joke," insisted Dane before soliciting Calvin, "You can take a joke can't ya bro?"

Having gotten her first taste of these two, Mei Li decided it wasn't something she wanted to stick around and savor. "Come on in, Calvin," she called to him. "You should probably take a break."

"Yeah, better give it up, buddy," Dane yelled. "Wouldn't want you to hurt yourself."

But Calvin's stubborn streak had already kicked in, and it had little or nothing to do with the idiot white boys circling nearby like vultures. "One more time," he insisted.

Jess and Mei Li looked at each other, and while they didn't like it, they weren't about to challenge him. Especially since Calvin was ready to go with ski on and tow bar in hand. He was also making a concerted effort to stay in the correct position while Jess kept the tow rope taut.

Accepting his decision, Mei Li imparted her final instructions. "Okay, think about what I told you."

Roughly thirty yards beyond where Calvin floated in the river, something odd broke the surface. A graduated row of three horns crested and cut through the water. A split second later, the jagged dorsal hump appeared directly behind. As quickly as they surfaced, however, they dipped back under without detection since all eyes were locked on Calvin.

"This should be good," Dane informed his boat mates before ratcheting up his heckling. "Don't worry about everybody watching you, dude," he called to Calvin. "Just pretend like we're not even here."

Dane obviously had no idea just how skilled the target of his harassment was at doing just that. Calvin had already engaged the same singular focus he did when tackling any mechanical challenge.

Unbeknownst to everyone, the events taking place above the water line were only half the drama being played out. Below the surface some twenty yards behind Calvin, four large amphibian-like webbed paws with sharp talons pushed aggressively through the murky water. With predatory precision, they propelled a long reptilian body toward the bright yellow ski vest and its contents.

"Hit it!" yelled Calvin.

Jess did.

For several seconds, it looked as though Calvin's latest attempt at water-skiing was going to end the same as all his previous ones. But just when it seemed that he was about to crash and burn, Calvin somehow managed to pull it out and stood up on the ski. This small but important victory had Mei Li cheering wildly while Jess pumped a defiant fist in the air. Lauren and Nikki cheered as well, or at least they did until they got the stink eye from Dane and Eric. Meanwhile, the target of their tormenting skied away.

Calvin fought hard to stay up on the ski, and while not the picture of grace, he was doing it, he was water-skiing. He worked to stay directly behind the boat, not wanting to attempt crossing the wake just yet. Surprisingly, he was able to ski a considerable distance. That is, until Mei Li decided she was too warm, and in between her encouraging claps and cheers, she took off her halter top, revealing a bikini underneath. For a second, Calvin thought he was going to be okay; not let this distraction throw him. Besides, it wasn't the black bikini with purple flowers, it was a solid red one, which didn't have the same effect. At least that's what he told himself, right before he drifted over the wake and executed a stunningly nasty wipeout.

He was floating on his back with the ski several feet away when Jess maneuvered the boat to him. Leaning over the side, Mei Li cautiously asked, "You okay?"

"Yeah. It's all good."

"Ready to go again?" Jess asked.

"Not that good."

Reaching out a hand, Jess helped pull Calvin to the swim platform of the ski boat. Once back in the boat and out of his vest, Jess tossed him a towel and Mei Li handed him a beer: the secret cargo of her cooler. She cheerfully raised her bottle in a toast. "Way to go, Oaktown. Told ya you could do it."

"And showed those pricks up at the same time," added Jess with delight, as he twisted the cap off his beer and clinked his bottle to theirs.

"Probably still laughing their asses off," said Calvin.

"It wasn't a thing of beauty but I've seen worse," said Jess.

"You got the last laugh anyway," insisted Mei Li.

"That shit's hard! I didn't think I was gonna make it."

"But you did," she replied. "Guess you'll have to come to the One Plank with us now."

"What the hell's a One Plank?"

"Old-school term for a single ski, and now wakeboards," said Jess. "There's an annual party for that crowd. You should come."

"Yeah, it's out on Buzzard Island. Promise you'll come," insisted Mei Li.

And there they were again, the Delta zombies, ever eager to turn him into one of them. Wasn't it enough that he'd just tried one of the whitest sports on earth next to NASCAR?

"Holy crap," Jess suddenly exclaimed while wiping down the ski. Holding it up, he pointed to a long, deep gouge at the back. "Damn, are you ever hard on a ski."

The three spent the next several hours out on the water. Jess taught Calvin how to tow a skier with Mei Li as the unwitting, though non-protesting volunteer. He proved to be a natural driver of course, which gave Jess the confidence to take a few runs with Calvin at the wheel. An excellent driver herself, Mei Li suspected Calvin's ego had taken a bit of a bruising, so she let him tow Jess while she spotted.

By early afternoon they'd all had enough and began making their way back to Heron's Harbor. But as they neared the ferry crossing, it quickly became apparent something serious had happened. Not only was the sheriff's boat tied alongside the *Eddie O*, the Sheriff's patrol car, as well as the coroner's wagon, were parked on board the ferry.

"Wonder what's going on," said Mei Li. "Hope nothing's happened to Ol' Joe."

"No, he's right there," assured Jess, pointing.

Sure enough, Ol' Joe was standing beside the pilothouse rolling a cigarette while Ray and Burt assisted the coroner in lifting what was left of the mangled fisherman out of the river.

"Oh my God!" shrieked Mei Li, and covering her face, she turned away.

But Calvin and Jess continued to watch in disbelief as the legless remains were brought on board and placed in a body bag.

Jess turned to Calvin. "What the hell?"

But Calvin had nothing, other than to state the obvious. "Y'all got some crazy-ass shit goin' down in the cuts."

❦ CHAPTER 18 ❦

DELTA MUD BUGS

Standing over a pot of boiling water in the galley of *The Sturgeon*, Samuel added a generous amount of Tabasco to the Zatarain's Seasonings that were already permeating the entire boat. Calvin sat at the table and watched his great-uncle tend to his potent concoction as they hashed over the latest find: Stumpy the Fisherman.

"Another boating accident?" Calvin asked with blatant skepticism. "You can't seriously be buying that."

"Well, we do get our share 'round here," replied Samuel. "Maybe some hotdog boater went whizzin' too close to shore and didn't see the guy. Lopped his legs right off."

"Come on. And the couple from Vegas too?"

"Well, if it ain't boatin' accidents, then what is it? A serial killer?"

"They usually white. Take a look around."

Samuel chuckled and inspected his bubbling pot with child-like anticipation. "So, I hear you're a big time water-skier now."

Calvin blew a puff of air between his lips. "Barely able to get up on that thing."

"Still pretty damn good."

"You ever try it?"

"Oh, hell no. I like my behind in the boat, with a fishin' pole in ma hands and a beer between ma knees." Samuel then ventured to ask, "So's this mean you'll be goin' to the big bash?"

"No," Calvin unequivocally denied.

Snagging two hot pads, Samuel poured the boiling pot into a strainer in the sink then allowed cold water from the tap to run over its precious contents before turning back to Calvin. "I think ya oughta go. Oughta get out some, socialize."

"Yeah? How many black kids you think'll be there?"

"Well now, lemme see. There's you, and then there's ... prob'ly just you."

"That's what I thought."

"Now if it was a catfishin' derby, that'd be whole 'nother story. But a water-ski party," he admitted, "not a lot o' brothers on that circuit."

Samuel scattered the contents of the strainer onto a platter and brought it to the table with fanfare. "Hooeey! You ready for a real treat? Delta mud bugs!"

Calvin stared at the mound of crawdads with blatant disgust. And the crawdads stared back, their beady little black eyes daring him.

"Well, dig in," urged Samuel who grabbed a crawdad and eagerly ripped the tail from its body causing thick yellow innards to ooze out. Tossing the head and torso section onto a side plate, he enthusiastically dunked the crustacean's tail in melted butter then loudly sucked the meat into his mouth. "Mm, mmm."

"Think I'll pass," said Calvin preparing to head up to the café. "Get me somethin' to eat that won't be starin' at me while I do it. 'Sides, I know what those things dine on," he added, "and I *don't* eat bottom feeders."

"Suit yourself. More for me," declared Samuel, the pile of discarded crawdad carcasses steadily growing beside him.

❧ CHAPTER 19 ❧

REVENGE OF THE BOTTOM FEEDERS

Though exhausted from yet another long day of running the café and store, Frances didn't feel like she could sleep just yet, so she grabbed a cold beer from the fridge and parked herself on the front porch swing of the old farmhouse. She left a light on in the kitchen but kept the porch light off—liked to sit in the dark on nights like this and see if she could feel Scott's presence—something that was becoming harder with each passing year. It'd now been three since he died, and he seemed so far away.

But she and Jess were managing and that was the important thing. Frances considered herself lucky to have such a mature son who didn't give her any grief, well at least nothing major. And while the marina was never going to be a gold mine, it brought in enough to pay the bills—they were doing alright. Though she never could have imagined she'd be widowed at 40. Sure, she had Jess, but a child could never fill the void left by an absent partner.

As it turned out, keeping Heron's Harbor had probably saved her from losing her mind. She rarely had time to sit around and feel sorry for herself. At the moment, however, Frances was struggling to keep from doing just that. Attempting to avoid a pity party, she tried shifting her thoughts to something else. Unfortunately, the first thing that came to mind was the dismembered fisherman Ol' Joe had discovered earlier that day. And while she hadn't seen the body herself, she might as well have, since Jess insisted on giving her all the gory details. Jesus, what a gruesome thing to have happened.

She was trying once again to think of something more positive when Sergeant Cruz came walking up her front path. Still in his uniform, Ray looked as if he needed a distraction just as much as she did.

"Hey," she called out, happy for the unexpected company.

"Hey yourself. Saw your light on."

"You just *now* off duty?"

"Yep. Been a long day."

"Ready for a cold one?"

"I was hoping you'd ask."

Frances stepped inside to grab another beer while Ray lowered himself onto the porch swing with a considerable sigh.

Ray and Frances had known each other for about two years now, ever since he transferred to the Delta, becoming sergeant of the Marine Patrol. Ray grew up in Stockton and had worked various posts as a sheriff's deputy, and later sergeant, throughout the state. When the Marine Patrol position came up and he got it, he was more than ready. The chance to spent most of his shifts out on the water was exactly the change he needed after his divorce. Sure, the economic cutbacks and downsizing of personnel (not to mention being saddled with Deputy Watson) had put a damper on the gig. Still, a bad day out on the water was better than a good day in a patrol car.

Ray found himself attracted to Frances from the start, though did his best to keep it under wraps. He knew how much she'd loved her husband and wasn't sure she was ready for anything more than friends. But after the day he'd just had, he could definitely use a friend, so took a chance and swung by Heron's Harbor on his way home. When Frances came back through the screen door and handed him a beer, his day suddenly got better.

"Okay if I leave the light off?" she asked.

"God, please."

She joined him on the porch swing and they rocked for a while, sipping their beers and looking out at the lights of the marina.

"So what's going on around here, Ray? Two freak accidents just days apart?"

Ray sighed and rubbed his tired eyes. "Wish I knew what to tell ya. Been dealing with the coroner and that fisherman's family all day."

"Last thing you need is me bringing it up again. Sorry"

"It's okay. Though I wouldn't mind talking about something else for half a minute."

It only took Frances a moment to come up with a change of subject. "Well, the One Plank's coming up."

A reminiscent smile appeared on Ray's face. "Hard to believe that thing still goes on."

"I trust you guys'll be keeping an eye out."

"Oh yeah, same as when we were teenagers. The sheriff's boat'll just happen to be in the area checking channel markers," he assured her. "I take it Jess is going."

"I couldn't exactly say no, now could I?

"I still remember the last year I went—summer before I left for the academy. There was this girl there. I didn't know her name, never even seen her before. But man, I was completely smitten."

"You never told me about a girl."

"Nothing to tell really. I didn't have the nerve to ask her to dance. She ended up leaving with some guy whose family owned a marina. This marina."

"Ray Cruz, you were at the One Plank and you didn't ask me to dance?"

"Just as well. Think if you'd ended up married to a sheriff."

"A horrible fate, huh?"

"Depends on who you ask, my ex-wife for example. Besides, you would have missed out on all this."

"Oh yeah ... all this."

Perhaps it was exhaustion that finally broke down the self-imposed barrier Ray had been able to maintain until now, but he found himself leaning in to kiss her. And she didn't lean away.

Ray and Frances were about to make the connection they'd been moving toward over the last two years when they were stopped short by a woman's blood-curdling screams coming from somewhere down in the marina. Ray hung his head for a split-second, then dutifully shifted into response mode.

Over at the shop, Calvin was fully engrossed in tinkering with the WaveRunner, while Jess was equally engrossed in one of Samuel's old *Players* magazines. As screams broke the night quiet they both dropped what they were doing and went to investigate.

After another full day of fishing and beer, Terry and Neal were already in their bunks when they heard the same screams and stumbled from the camper; Neal in trout-themed pajamas and

Terry in boxer shorts. Ray and Frances soon ran past them, followed a moment later by Calvin and Jess. The fishermen looked at each other, shrugged, and quickly joined the party, following the shrieks to their source.

With Ray leading the pack, the entourage soon arrived at the guest dock where a rotund man and his equally rotund wife stood on the back deck of their cabin cruiser. Though the woman had momentarily ceased her screaming, she continued to blubber with her head buried in her husband's chest. Berthed nearby, Lou and Gloria were already on scene in matching sweat suits and Lou pulled Ray aside. "Whatever's happened, she seems to have gone into shock. Fairly incoherent at this point."

"Yeah, I can see that," replied Ray. He then approached the side of the cabin cruiser and asked the husband, "May I come aboard?"

Relieved at the sight of a sheriff, the man eagerly nodded "yes."

Ray climbed over the side of the vessel and calmly waited for an explanation while the woman continued caterwauling.

Samuel soon arrived in his robe and slippers. Rubbing sleep from his eyes, he asked, "What's all the hubbub?"

"We're 'bout to find out," replied Calvin.

Finally, the big fella spoke. "We was just checkin' our crawdad trap," he told Ray, "and when I pulled it up there was a ..." Pausing, the man gulped, but before he could finish his story, the wife became hysterical once more.

"No! I can't even hear about it. I can't!" Crying and flailing her chubby arms, she fled below into the boat's cabin.

"You better see for yourself." The man then handed Ray a supersize flashlight that matched the supersize couple. "I'd hold it for ya," he said sheepishly, "but I better go check on my wife." Then he too, retreated below.

Frances climbed onto the swim platform at the rear of the boat and reached to take the flashlight from Ray. "Here, I'll hold it."

Suddenly protective, he was hesitant to relinquish it. "There's no telling what's hung up on this thing."

"I'm a big girl," she assured him.

Ray raised his eyebrows in a manner that said he wasn't completely convinced, but he handed it over just the same.

Frances turned on the flashlight and shined its intense beam on the area where the trap's line disappeared into the still green waters. Those gathered leaned over in anticipation as Ray began to pull on the line, a chore that required considerable effort. Whatever was caught in the trap was causing it to be unnaturally heavy.

A large metal homemade crawdad trap soon arrived at the surface with more than just crawdads on board. A section of Huestus lay wedged in the basket; his head, neck, right shoulder and arm were intact, though freakishly separated from the rest of him. Half a dozen crawdads clung to his waterlogged skin, picking from the spongy flesh. One of his eyes was a squishy milky-grey, but the other was perfectly flawless and stared back at his finders with glassy intent. The group erupted in horrified gasps, immediately followed by utterances the likes of "Oh, shit" and "Holy crap."

When a rogue crawdad crawled out from between Huestus's blue lips, the light beam got shaky then radically shifted upward as the flashlight dropped into the drink. It quickly sank to the bottom where it became an eerie muted beacon casting upward through the murky water.

"Sorry," Frances uttered, weakly.

In the dim glow of the guest dock's overhead lights, Ray placed the crawdad trap with its horrific cargo on the boat's swim platform. "Frances, go call Burt at home and tell him I need him here," he directed. "Lou, I need you to stay as a witness until he gets here, if you're okay with that."

"Not a problem," agreed Lou. "Whatever you need, Ray."

"Everyone else should go," announced the sergeant. "You don't need to see any more of this than you already have."

Frances bolted to make her call as the rest of the group slowly dispersed. Calvin and Samuel brought up the rear and therefore saw Ray pull on a pair of latex gloves retrieved from his pocket before beginning the morbid task of removing crawdads from Huestus. He then carefully placed the crustaceans in a bait bucket borrowed from the cabin cruiser—bizarre evidence indeed.

Leaving the dock, Calvin shook his head and admonished his great-uncle. "What'd I tell ya 'bout eatin' those things?"

Samuel instinctively wiped his mouth with the back of his sleeve.

CHAPTER 20

THINGS THAT GO BUMP IN THE NIGHT

Too unnerved to simply call it a night, those who'd had the misfortune of witnessing the latest catch of the day, aka Huestus, were gathered under the muted lights of the café after hours.

Frances had shifted into Red Cross mode and was serving boxed donuts and coffee to the shell-shocked troops. Having stopped by the camper, Terry now had on jeans and a sweatshirt, while Neal had simply added a fishing hat and vest to his trout-themed pajamas. Samuel decided to stick with the robe and slippers ensemble he'd arrived on scene in.

Half-sitting, half-leaning against a counter stool with his legs outstretched and his arms crossed over his chest, Calvin surveyed this wacked group of characters he was now thrown in with. How the hell did this happen again?

Ray didn't have the heart to store the segment of Huestus in the harbor's bait cooler 'til morning. So he'd sent Deputy Watson to deliver the body part to the nearest morgue, once he'd finished tagging and photographing the evidence—some of which was still crawling around in a bait bucket wondering where the delicious buffet had gone. Though it took a superhuman level of patience, Ray was eventually able to get statements from the couple who'd made the grisly discovery. Lou's calm demeanor helped considerably in this effort. Shortly before they rejoined the others at the café, Lou pulled Ray aside and told him about the strange sighting he and Gloria had witnessed on their radar screen that morning. They agreed, however, to keep this piece of information to themselves for the time being.

"Are you absolutely sure it's him?" Frances anxiously asked as they entered the café and came to sit at the counter.

"I'm certain of it," replied Ray. "He had a glass eye."

"My God, poor Huestus," she sadly replied. Frances struggled to keep her hand from shaking as she poured coffee for the newcomers. She'd been holding out hope that everyone's favorite local drunk hadn't met his demise in such a ghastly manner.

"I called Danny over at the Crawdaddy Club," said Ray. "Apparently Huestus was good and liquored up the last time anybody saw him. Probably didn't even know what hit him."

"That's the million-dollar question," said Terry. "What the hell *did* hit him?"

No one had an answer.

"Well, I know *I* won't be able to sleep," said Frances, stepping behind the counter to put on an apron. "Anybody want something more substantial than donuts?"

"I could use a little somethin'," said Samuel. "Got a funny taste in ma mouth."

Gloria joined Frances in the kitchen and they began pulling staples from the refrigerator. Frances thought perhaps a big batch of scrambled eggs was in order; that is until she cracked the first one and it reminded her of Huestus's gooey one eye. She then promptly changed the menu to grilled cheese sandwiches.

"Think we should invite that poor couple to join us?" Gloria asked Ray.

"I wouldn't bother," he replied. "The wife took a Valium and the husband had a double scotch while I was taking their statements. They're probably on another planet by now."

"Wish I was," said Neal.

"Aren't you going to issue some kind of a warning?" Terry asked the sheriff's sergeant.

"Be happy to. If I had a clear idea what I was warning people about."

A face suddenly smashed against the glass of the front door and everyone jumped. It was Burt, who'd simply assumed the door was unlocked but got a jarring reality check that it wasn't.

"I think you should issue a warning about your deputy," said Calvin as he went to open the door for Burt. "Yo, you scared the crap outta us!"

"Why's the door locked? Ya got a sheriff in here for Christ's sake," Burt replied with agitation as he brushed past Calvin and headed straight for the coffee station. The deputy poured himself half a cup, filled it the rest of the way with creamer, and added five packets of sugar. He desperately needed something to help calm his nicotine craving. Driving to the morgue with a plastic-wrapped chunk of Huestus in the back seat had seriously weakened his resolve to quit. If he hadn't been in uniform, he would have bummed a butt off the first smoker he found, wrecking a two-week smoke-free run.

Burt gulped down half the milky-sweet coffee before remembering the plastic baggy in his jacket pocket. "Hey Ray, guy at the morgue wanted me to give you this." Tossing him the baggy, he added, "Said it was clenched in Huestus's fist."

Everyone gathered around Ray as he held the baggy up to the light to inspect its contents.

"What is it?" asked Jess.

"Knob from a car radio," said Calvin, prompting everyone to look at him as if he was a seasoned car stereo thief. "Don't worry," he assured them, "your eight-track players are safe."

"That's what it is, alright," said Ray. "There was a knob missing from the Buick's radio."

"I'll bet Huestus was scanning stations when he was attacked," said Terry.

"Maybe the killer was in the backseat," added Samuel.

"Maybe it was a vampire," suggested Neal.

"What?!" exclaimed Ray.

"It's always vampires these days," replied Neal with a shrug.

"True. I just signed up for the vampire channel," announced Burt in all seriousness.

"Really?" Terry asked with genuine interest. "How much that run ya?"

"It's not vampires, alright?!" exclaimed Ray, determined to squelch this ridiculous line of thinking—especially since his own deputy now was part of the crazy-making.

"Oh, I wouldn't be so certain. It fits their pattern," said Neal with conviction. "Vampires can move at that incredible speed and just shred people to pieces."

"Teen novels, Neal? Really?" asked Jess.

Undaunted, Neal continued to lay out his case for a vampire by reenacting the scene as he envisioned it. "So Huestus was driving down the road after a few too many. He's scanning the radio dial looking for smooth jazz when he's suddenly grabbed from behind. The vampire's in the backseat, he bites him, and starts draining him. Huestus struggles, he swerves and drives off the levee. The vamp then finishes him off, shredding him and tossing his parts out the window where they're carried down river."

"There wasn't any blood in the car," Ray flatly countered.

"'Cause he drank it all," replied Neal, as if this was a no-brainer.

Trying to lighten things up, Jess suggested, "Well, if Huestus was tanked, maybe we should ask around, see if anybody saw a really wasted vampire that night."

But Ray's sense of humor had run out several hours ago. "We're not looking for vampires, werewolves, or zombies, folks," he stated bluntly. "It's not trolls who live under bridges, evil leprechauns, or aliens. And as a Latino, I can say with one hundred percent certainty, it's not a chupacabra."

"What about that Shack dude?" asked Calvin.

"Jack?" replied Jess. "No way, he's harmless."

"Yeah? Well, maybe he snapped," suggested Calvin.

"Could be in the water," said Burt, causing Ray to cringe. He didn't want them to go there just yet, but it was too late.

Standing over the open ice cream freezer holding an empty Otter Pop box, Burt decided to present his own theory. "Back in the sixth grade, there was this kid, Marty Snodgrass. He set his pet piranha free in the Delta."

"A Piranha couldn't survive in the Delta," offered Lou in his ever-calm, ever-logical manner. "They need more tropical waters like the Amazon."

"Maybe it's adapted," Burt insisted. "Grown bigger, stronger, more deadly."

Calvin began to laugh. "Y'all can just chill, a'ight? 'Cause the deputy here's cracked the case. It's the Snodgrass piranha."

"I'm not ruling it out," said Burt, stepping toward Calvin in a challenging manner.

Calvin responded by getting up in the deputy's face, "Yo, I think you need to cut back on the Otter Pops. They startin' to freeze your damn brain."

"Alright, listen up everyone," announced Ray as he moved between the two, forcing them to back up off each other. The sergeant was now done letting the inmates run the asylum and he firmly asserted his authority. "Tomorrow I will open an investigation to see if, and how, the three incidents are linked. If they are, we'll figure out who or what we're dealing with. Until then, I want everyone to stop speculating. We all need to just calm down and call it a night before our imaginations get the best of us. Although in some cases, it might be too late."

In spite of the all the excitement, Calvin had no trouble whatsoever falling asleep that night. He'd consumed two grilled cheese sandwiches along with a generous side of potato salad, three donuts, and two glasses of milk. Since most of the group could barely eat after witnessing the grisly discovery, he and Jess had selflessly unleashed their teenage appetites on the spread.

An hour later Calvin was fast asleep in his bunk having a dream about visiting Rashawn in juvie. They were outside the correctional facility, standing on opposite sides of a chain-link fence with razor wire at the top. Rashawn's side was a basketball court and he was dribbling a ball, something Rashawn could barely do in real life.

"I'm just glad I'm in here. Not out there witchew, breh," Rashawn told him.

"Yeah? Why's that?" Calvin asked.

"'Cause it can't get me up in here."

But before Calvin could ask him what "it" was, Rashawn turned and passed the ball to … Deputy Watson?! Burt took the ball down court and stuffed it, then swung from the hoop, glaring back at Calvin antagonistically. Calvin tried to get Rashawn's attention once more but he was now immersed in the world's oddest one-on-one game ever—with Burt Watson, of all people.

Without warning, Calvin was abruptly yanked from his dream as something forcefully hit the hull of *The Sturgeon*. He sat bolt upright and looked around. The vessel certainly seemed to be swaying, but was it moving any more than it normally did when the tide was coming in or going out? He couldn't say. Other than Samuel's uninterrupted snoring and the sound of water lapping against the barge, the night was quiet, still.

Calvin reached over to the nightstand, and retrieving the medallion Gloria had given him, he slipped it over his head. Couldn't hurt. He then lay back down on his bunk, waiting, listening. Nothing. Nothing but snoring and the usual creaking of *The Sturgeon* as it moved against its moorings. Calvin soon dismissed the loud thud against the hull as nothing more than a piece of driftwood. But he still couldn't fall back to sleep. His mind was busy rehashing the dream: Rashawn and Deputy Watson shootin' hoops in juvie?

And what exactly was "it"?

𝅥 CHAPTER 21 𝅥

THE BEAUTY OF THE BEAST

Not wanting to miss any of the debate taking place between Jess and Frances, Mei Li quickly seated a tourist couple who'd wandered into the café. After practically tossing menus at them, she speed-recited the Daily Specials before hurrying back to station herself beside the lunch counter. Seated on a counter stool watching his mom prep the grill for lunch, Jess was busy thinking up his next irrefutable talking point in hopes of swaying the argument his way.

"I don't like it," said Frances, picking up where they'd left off while trying to keep her voice out of customer range.

"Mom, you heard Ray," Jess countered in an equally hushed voice. "He's not even going to issue a warning."

"Yet," she replied.

"Even if it *is* a serial killer, do you really think he's gonna take a boat out to Buzzard Island and massacre a hundred teenagers?"

"Maybe. I don't know! Look, I just don't feel comfortable letting you go now, that's all."

"That's all?" he asked, clearly annoyed. "That's not rational. And it's not fair."

"It might not be fair but it's more than rational," she replied.

"Mom, whatever's going on is happening in isolated areas when there's no one else around. There's going to be tons of people all together in one place. I can't think of a safer scenario."

"I can," his mother replied. "You two not going. Mei Li, what does your mom think?"

"Well, she said ..." Imitating her mother, Mei Li proceeded to rattle off a tirade in Cantonese.

The moment she finished, Jess and Frances simultaneously said, "See!" each claiming a point in their favor. When the service bell for the gas dock rang, Jess made for the door, but not before informing his mom, "We're not done talking about this."

"Oh, I think we are," Frances volleyed back without taking her eyes off the grill.

As soon as the lunch shift ended, Mei Li headed down to the gas dock for a pow wow. Leaning against a pump while Jess took meter readings, her resolve began to waver. "I don't know, maybe it's better if we don't go," she said with resignation.

"Oh, I'm going to the One Plank, and so are you," he insisted. "Calvin's right, we do live in the cuts. That party's as exciting as it gets around here. So we're going."

"Well, my mom's so busy with the farm, she falls dead asleep by 8. It's not like she'll notice if I slip out. What about Calvin, think he'll go?"

"I doubt it. In case you haven't noticed, he isn't exactly lovin' life in the Delta."

Mei Li was about to say something more about Calvin when a harsh grinding sound drew their attention to the marine repair shop across the water. One of the shop's lesser-used garage doors was being opened for the first time in years and it loudly groaned its complaint. Behind the door, lay a water berth where boats could be driven or towed in then hoisted up for repairs. Shielding their eyes from the bright sunlight, Jess and Mei Li tried to make out who was working on what in the darkly shaded berth. When an engine fired to life and revved, Jess knew instantly it was not that of an outboard, but rather, a jet. A moment later, Calvin emerged driving the resurrected WaveRunner.

"Oh, no way," Jess uttered, his mouth agape.

Not only did the thing sound solid, Calvin had even managed a fairly decent paint job on it. The once crusty PWC now sported a fresh coat of black marine paint with the name *The Beast* artfully stenciled on both sides in purple. The artist himself had no conscious explanation as to why he'd chosen this particular color theme. Sporting board shorts and an older-style ski vest he'd found in the shop, Calvin casually guided the WaveRunner toward the gas dock at a slow idle, acting as if he'd done it a thousand times and it was no big deal.

Mei Li couldn't fight the smile spreading across her face and she turned to Jess. "Um, about what you were saying a minute ago—from the looks of it, I'd say he's assimilated. Not sure if that's a good thing, but hey."

Calvin arrived at the dock and killed the engine. "Gonna need some gas. I've got the oil," he stated matter-of-factly.

Rather than snap to and lift the gas nozzle, the dock attendant got down on his haunches to thoroughly inspect the resurrected watercraft. And there he stayed, taking it all in.

"So, I was thinking," said Calvin. "I'd like to put this baby to the test. Know anyone who might wanna race me?"

Less than an hour later, Mei Li stood at the water's edge with a ski flag in hand. Out in the river, the two competitors anxiously idled at an imaginary and somewhat fluid starting line; Calvin on *The Beast*, a restored GP 1300R, and Jess aboard his new Yamaha WaveRunner VXR. To the unsuspecting observer, it might have appeared as though an old Toyota Celica with a new paint job was about to take on a much newer Porsche.

"This baby can do close to seventy miles per hour," warned Jess.

"Bring it," replied Calvin, confidently.

Jess laughed, and for a split second, he thought about taking it easy on him. But by now he knew that wasn't something Calvin would want or appreciate, so decided to give him the challenge he'd asked for. "Alright, let's do this," he said, putting on a pair of racing goggles.

Calvin, in turn, put on an old snorkel mask, which only made Jess laugh harder. His challenger, however, was impervious to his amusement with him; he'd already engaged his notoriously single-minded focus as they waited for the signal from Mei Li. The straightaway they'd chosen was momentarily clear of all other vessels, so they would be free to race approximately one mile upriver without distractions or obstacles. The swing bridge ahead was their designated finish line.

Mei Li raised the orange ski flag. "On your marks, get set … go!"

They hit it, and for the first half of the stretch, they were virtually neck and neck. Then, shortly past the halfway mark, and much to Jess's dismay, Calvin pulled ahead … and not just a little. *The Beast* flew across the water reaching speeds well above seventy miles per hour. Leaving Jess in his spray, Calvin crossed under the bridge well ahead of his opponent. Releasing the throttle, he let *The Beast* settle in the water and removed his snorkel mask. He was casually idling in a circle when Jess pulled up a moment later.

"What the hell did you do to that thing?!"

"Musta been that drive shaft tool, bruh," he replied, with a shrug. Quite pleased with himself, Calvin began to laugh, leaving Jess to simply shake his head in amazement.

Having watched the entire race through binoculars, Mei Li found herself doing a private little victory dance at Calvin's underdog win. As she continued to observe him through the lenses, laughing and joking around with Jess, she quietly admitted to herself, "I think I might be in trouble."

❧ CHAPTER 22 ❧

ISLAND FEVER

After a few more debates with Frances, who in turn got Lisa Cheng involved, Jess and Mei Li conspicuously relented, agreeing to go to the movies on the night of the One Plank rather than attend the party. Considering the nearest town with a theater was roughly twenty miles away, this would afford them a fairly wide window of opportunity. Mei Li met Jess at the farmhouse, appropriately dressed for a casual night at the movies, and after telling Frances which film they'd decided on, the two headed off in Jess's truck shortly after dark.

Approximately a half-mile from Heron's Harbor, Jess pulled off the levee and drove along a dirt road beside farmland. After stashing the truck behind a long-abandoned grainery, they scrambled up the levee to the road and began making their way back to the marina on foot. Jess carried Mei Li's backpack, which contained more suitable party clothes and supplies. The night was warm and clear with a full moon so bright it rendered flashlights unnecessary.

"So he said 'no' for sure?" Mei Li asked as she half-jogged to keep up with Jess's long strides.

"Pretty much. I didn't push him on it."

"Well, maybe you should have."

"Hey, we put it out there. If he wanted to come, he'd be here. Besides, I think maybe you ..." Jess balked at completing this sentence.

"What? You think maybe I what?"

"I think you make him nervous."

"Me?! Why?" she asked, doing her best to sound innocent.

"Oh please, you know why."

But before she could protest further, he turned and held a finger to his lips. They were approaching the outskirts of the marina and would need to be quiet in order to pull off this caper without getting busted. Jess hoped they wouldn't run into any harbor tenants who might unintentionally rat them out to his mom. Luckily, due to the ideal weather, almost everyone who was up for the weekend had already taken their boats out. Therefore, Heron's Harbor was remarkably quiet.

Not taking any chances, Jess and Mei Li cautiously crept down the rental dock to quietly board the *Hit It*. Once untied, they carefully pushed the ski boat away from the slip, then used oars to paddle toward the main channel where it would be much safer to start the engine; far from the ever-vigilant ears of Frances the Harbor Master. Paddling a boat designed for horse power was ploddingly slow and awkward, but Jess and Mei Li were determined to make their escape undetected.

As they made their way under the overhanging tree boughs along the breakwater, a body suddenly dropped from a limb above, landing squarely in the boat—only this body was alive.

Mei Li started to scream but quickly stopped herself upon realizing the body belonged to Calvin, who was now standing upright in the back of the boat.

"Son of a bitch!" exclaimed Jess, trying not to yell. "What the hell, Calvin?"

"You scared the living crap out of us!" scolded Mei Li in a forced whisper.

"Sorry," said Calvin, laughing, and not sorry at all.

"Don't ever do that again," Mei Li reprimanded him, a hand over her still-pounding heart.

"I don't think I could do that again, even if I tried," he replied. "But man, you shoulda seen your faces."

"Our faces?!" said Jess, "you should see my underwear."

Stifling his laughter, Calvin took the oar from Mei Li and began to paddle. "Come on, let's get this pontoon out to the real water."

Mei Li responded by socking him in the arm for good measure.

"Ow. A'ight, I get it. No more drop-ins."

Once they were far enough into the main channel, Jess started the engine and hit the running lights. He brought the ski boat up to a reasonable speed, though nothing close to what he would have in the light of day. Even with the full moon illuminating the river's surface, as an extra precaution, Calvin stood between Jess in the driver's seat and Mei Li in the passenger seat, skillfully training a spot light on the waters ahead. This would give Jess a visual on any potential hazards like floating driftwood, shallow sandbars … or bodies.

Having successfully snuck out, and heading to a party they weren't supposed to attend, put them all in a good mood. Jess and Mei Li soon forgave Calvin for scaring the hell out of them, especially since he had them busting up with laughter, imitating their startled faces as he reenacted the moment of his drop-in. Though Calvin originally had Samuel's blessing to attend the One Plank, considering the latest developments, that would've undoubtedly been rescinded had Samuel thought for one minute Calvin might actually go. This meant all three were essentially out on the lam. The night was theirs, with a full moon, a sky full of stars, and a party on a remote island awaiting them.

Before long, a line of tiki torches flickered on the horizon ahead and music drifted across the water toward them as they approached Buzzard Island. Located at the farthest edge of Desperation Slough, the secluded island was roughly a half-mile in diameter. Unlike the countless tule islands of the Delta, Buzzard Island featured plenty of solid land with trees and lush vegetation, making it a choice spot to party and play. An assortment of small boats were already tethered to its large main dock, but a few spaces remained and Jess eased the ski boat into one of them. With the *Hit It* secure, the three made their way onto land then followed a path carved through the underbrush, heading for the source of the music. They soon arrived at the heart of the island, a large open area where roughly a hundred teenagers, give or take a few, were already partying and dancing. The loud music easily won out over the noisy gas generators that were supplying power to the party, most importantly to a makeshift DJ booth manned by a white kid with his hat cocked right.

Colored spotlights illuminated the tree canopies overhead, and strings of clear bulbs ran from bough to bough. The island had been transformed into the real-life version of what cheesy proms attempted, but failed miserably, to achieve.

Spotting some friends across the way, Jess broke off from Mei Li and Calvin. "I'll catch up with you guys at the clubhouse," he called back before being swallowed up by the crowd.

Prior to arriving, Mei Li had made Calvin and Jess keep their eyes ahead on the river as she changed into a slinky summer party dress and sandals, an outfit that wasn't lost on Calvin, though he tried not to let it show. Apparently, it wasn't lost on several other guys either, and more than a few heads turned as they walked past. Or maybe it was him, being that he was the only black guy on Fantasy Island. No, it was definitely her.

An awkwardly goofy dude in a Hawaiian shirt with matching board shorts frantically worked his way across the party toward them. "Hey, Mei Li," he called out, waving wildly as he approached.

"Oh, hey, Stanley."

"Wow, I'm so glad you're here. We gotta dance," he eagerly suggested.

"Yeah, ah, how 'bout later," Mei Li replied, trying to be polite.

"Okay, you're on. Oh whoa, is that some of your famous Chow Fun?" he asked thumping the plastic storage container she now carried.

"Yep, sure is."

"Awesomeness! I can't wait to hit some o' that."

"Stanley, this is Calvin."

"Oh, hey. Nice to meet you," Stan replied and earnestly attempted a bro handshake.

"Yeah," said Calvin, going with it as best he could. Saving this guy from himself, however, wasn't really possible.

"Well listen, I'm gonna go show Calvin the clubhouse," Mei Li told her would-be suitor.

"Yeah okay, cool. And hey," Stanley added with a wink, "I'll hook up with you later for that dance."

"You betcha," she agreed with a forced smile before grabbing Calvin by the hand and yanking him down a new path leading away from the dance floor.

"A clubhouse, huh?" Calvin asked with a laugh. "Was that the secret handshake?"

"Funny," she sternly replied.

Truth be told, he was enjoying holding her hand, but decided to downplay it. "Girl, I think Stan the Man wants to get in your Chow Fun."

Dropping his hand, Mei Li delivered another firm sock to his shoulder.

"Ow, Damn! That's two."

"Don't make me go to three," she warned before walking ahead.

Emerging from the path, they arrived at the small clubhouse. The shack looked as if it'd been around for years—and it had. A throwback to the original Tiki craze of the fifties, a large bamboo bar with a thatched roof of dried palm leaves held center stage. The original clubhouse décor of vintage wood water skis, Tiki gods, and hula girls remained but had been added to by each subsequent generation. Rock posters, aliens, and skulls were now part of the mix, making the place a retrospective of pop culture throughout the years.

A small crowd hovered around the bar staffed by two self-appointed bartenders presently engaged in dueling blenders. Having taken a different path across the island, Jess had managed to beat Calvin and Mei Li there and was already bellied up to the bar. Waving them over he introduced them to the dreadlocked white surf dude working one of the blenders, "Guys, this is our new best friend, Board."

"You're just in time," announced Board. Killing the blender, he filled several plastic cups from the fresh pitcher of Pina Coladas. After topping each one off with a paper umbrella and straw, he doled them out—reserving one for himself, of course. "So ma dudes, what's with all the carnage?" he asked. "It's freakin' people out, man."

"So much for Ray keeping a lid on it," said Jess.

"It does seem like kind of a small turnout," Mei Li noted, assessing the crowd.

"Total bummer, man. Oh well, more beverages for us," the bartender declared then raised his cup in a toast. "Righteous waves!" Board didn't let the fact that they were nowhere near the ocean cramp his style.

As they clunked plastic cups together and savored their first sip, Calvin spotted Dane and Eric across the way helping themselves to several bottles of water from an ice chest. "Check that," he said, nodding in their direction.

"Ah great, the brothers dickhead," replied Jess. "What the hell are they doing here?"

"Stockpiling water, so I'd say they came to rave," replied Calvin, before remembering Jess had a thing for the brunette. "Doesn't mean she's into it," he quickly added, a little too late.

This latest development instantly put a damper on Jess's party mood.

"Let's just ignore the Rave Slaves and have fun," Mei Li insisted before taking a healthy pull on the straw in her drink. "Hey, these are really good," she proclaimed. "Like a coconut Slurpee. I could drink these all night."

And she did. Or at least she tried. Roughly two hours later, Mei Li was hanging on Calvin in the middle of the dance floor, making him slow dance with her to a fast song.

Sensing he'd be the one piloting the ski boat back to Heron's Harbor, Calvin had stopped at one drink. Spotting Dane and Eric at the party only reinforced his decision to stay straight. While not personally familiar with Ecstasy, he knew it supposedly made its users happy and euphoric. Calvin sincerely hoped that was the case, since he didn't trust those two as far as he could throw them. Being an asshole was one thing. Being an asshole under the influence was something else entirely.

At the moment, however, he was rather enjoying Mei Li's non-combative attention, though he was keenly aware that she herself was under the influence of several Pina Coladas. If there was one thing that reverberated in his mind with his mother's voice sternly narrating, it was "Never take advantage of a girl. And I mean, *never.*"

Mei Li suddenly pulled away. Significantly unsteady on her feet she announced, "I don't feel so good."

"Mm hmm." Taking her by the hand, Calvin led her off the dance floor. "Come on Sideways, it's reverse gravity time. What goes down, must come up." Hoping to find someplace private, and quickly, before the inevitable happened, Calvin headed for the dock with his charge in tow.

Back at the heart of the party, Dane and Lauren took a break from the dance floor, gravitating to the edge where they could catch some air. Eric and Nikki soon followed. Sweating profusely, Dane grabbed a bottle of water and splashed a handful on his face before drinking some. Eric did the same, then handed the bottle to Nikki. "Keep sipping," he advised her, "but not too much. You need to stay hydrated, just don't overdo it."

Dane pulled a small baggy of colored tablets from his pocket. "Who's ready for more party favors?"

"You really think that's a good idea?" asked Lauren disapprovingly.

"Hey, you're the one who wanted to dance," he replied.

"And you can't dance without it?" she countered.

"Sure I can, but why?"

Eric laughed then condescendingly informed her, "This would be a boring white-trash pot luck without Candy. We're having a blast. You should try it."

Dane pulled two colored tablets from the baggy and handed one each to Eric and Nikki, who didn't hesitate to down them with water. He then picked out a pretty purple one, and showcasing it between his thumb and forefinger, he moved it toward Lauren's lips. When she declined with a shake of her head, Dane simply shrugged, put the tablet on his own tongue and swallowed it. "It's not like some big bad drug," he assured her. "It just makes whatever you're feeling more intense."

"Exactly, it's like a mood enhancer," added Eric.

"I'll pass just the same," said Lauren.

"But you should be with us," cooed Nikki, hugging her. "We're having the best time."

"I thought I *was* with you."

"You know what I mean," she said, petting Lauren's hair.

"Come on Cuddle Puddle," said Eric, prying Nikki away, "let's go rave our asses off." Pulling her onto the teeming dance floor, they quickly disappeared in the lively crowd.

After taking another hit of water, Dane grabbed Lauren's hand, "You ready?"

"Actually, I'm gonna sit this one out," she said pulling her hand away.

"What?! Come on baby, I'm starting to feel so right," he said, stroking her cheek. "I want you with me."

"We're just not on the same plane."

"We could be," he replied patting the baggy in his pants pocket. But again, Lauren refused with a shake of her head.

"Okay look, I'm gonna go dance," he bluntly told her. "I'll come find you after a while."

Before she could even reply, Dane left her standing there and walked over to a group of girls dancing together. He soon had one of them in tow and led her into the thick of the dance floor.

Angry, yet strangely relieved, Lauren stood there for a moment trying to decide what to do. What she didn't realize was that Jess had witnessed the entire exchange from a short distance away. Without hesitating, he walked over to her.

"Hey," he said loudly over the music.

"Oh, hey. How are you?"

"Good. Enjoying the party?"

"Honestly? Not so much."

"You're not here on your own, are you?" he asked, trying his best to sound like he didn't already know the answer to that.

"Technically, no. Emotionally, yes."

"Oh, I see. I think."

"Yeah."

Jess took a moment. Not to work up his courage, but rather to rein it in. Something that simply wasn't possible. "Do you want to go for a walk or something?"

"Yeah, I do. And ... I wouldn't mind just the teeniest sip off your beer."

"I think I can swing that," he agreed, then with feigned reluctance added, "You don't backwash do you?"

"No," she replied with a laugh.

"Okay then," he consented and handed over his bottle. "But honestly, I wouldn't mind, even if you did."

Taking a sip, she handed it back and he eagerly took a hit after her, hoping to taste her lip gloss.

With Jess leading the way, they escaped the intensity of the dance floor on one of the many trails that cut across the island. At one point, the path narrowed and was so overgrown with thick foliage that it blocked out the moonlight, making it difficult to navigate. Jess reached his hand back to Lauren, and she took it.

Out at the end of the boat dock, Calvin and Mei Li were having an altogether different experience of getting to know each other more intimately. Mei Li was laying on her stomach with her hands gripping the edge of the dock as the Pina Coladas made their reentry into the atmosphere. Calvin did his best to hold her hair back while trying to stay out of smell and splatter range. Eventually, there was a break in the action, although Mei Li remained prone on the dock, her cheek resting on a boat cleat. While this didn't look terribly comfortable, Calvin wasn't about to question her on it. So, he simply sat down beside her as she attempted to recover.

Looking around, Calvin noticed most of the boats were already gone and though he didn't have a watch, he guessed it was now well after midnight. Since news of the killings had gotten out, curfews were likely being enforced with severity. Calvin looked up at the full moon in a sky filled with stars. Coming from a large city, this kind of night sky was not something he was used to, but was definitely coming to appreciate. He suddenly wished he'd been a better monitor of Mei Li's Pina Colada intake. Her plaintive groans, however, quickly brought him back to the reality of the situation.

"Never felt this bad in my entire life," she moaned.

"Been there," he replied. "Don't worry, you'll live."

"Not sure I want to. Water. I need water," she pleaded.

Calvin was torn. He didn't want to leave her here, but there was no way she was going to make it back to the main part of the island in her condition.

"Okay, I'm gonna go get you some water," he said giving in, "but don't move. I mean it."

"Uhhh. Don't worry. Can't move," she whined, adjusting her head as if it were somehow possible to find a comfortable position on a metal cleat.

Leaving her there on her chrome pillow, Calvin made his way back to the clubhouse bar to round up some bottled water. Jogging along the path, he amused himself by imitating Mei Li in a high-pitched voice, "Mmm, like a coconut Slurpee." Laughing, he then added in his own voice, "A coconut Slurpee that'll kick your ass."

He soon arrived back at the clubhouse to find Board passed out face down on a vintage long board atop the bar.

"Wipeout," he declared and reached over the unconscious surfer to grab a couple waters. Since he was now close to the heart of what remained of the party, Calvin decided to take a look around to see if he could find Jess and possibly persuade him to call it a night, considering Mei Li was toast.

177

But the night's spectacular sky was not going to waste on Jess and Lauren, who'd found a good-size chunk of driftwood at the river's edge and were sitting close, taking turns identifying constellations. While they could still hear the music from the party, it was nowhere near the decibel it was on the dance floor, so they could actually hear each other speak without yelling.

"And those three right next to it make up Orion's Belt," said Jess, pointing up at the sky.

"Wow, you do know a lot of them. No App needed."

"My dad was big into astronomy. I still have his telescope."

"Very cool."

"Yeah," he replied, before falling quiet. Jess seriously wanted to kiss her but held back. He wasn't convinced that was something she'd welcome, and he definitely didn't want to risk ruining the moment by getting shot down. She'd come here with another guy, after all. Hell, was staying on a houseboat with him for god's sake. She probably just needed a friend, and even though he'd settle for that, he desperately wanted to kiss her.

Sensing what was going on with him, Lauren broached the subject. "I don't even know what I'm doing with Dane. Part of me knew it wasn't right from the start, but I went with it anyway. What a mistake."

"So, what are you gonna do?"

"Correct my mistake."

"I vote for that. When?"

"As much as I'd like to say tonight, considering who we're talking about, it's probably best if I wait 'til after the trip."

"I don't like the idea of you being out there with him, not even for one more night. I don't think it's safe. And to be perfectly honest, it makes me crazy."

"I'll be okay, I promise. And for the record, I would have broken up with him anyway. But meeting you reminded me what it feels like to be around a really nice guy."

"And this is the part where you tell me what a great guy I am and how we'll be the best of friends."

"No, this is the part where I tell you to shut up and kiss me."

So he did.

Kissing Lauren was everything Jess thought it would be from the moment he first looked into those green eyes. In fact, it was even better than he imagined, which promptly caused him to lose perspective. He suddenly broke off the kiss but stayed holding Lauren's face in his hands, their foreheads touching. "I can't let you go back to him."

"We don't have a choice, really."

"Sure, we do. Come home with me. My mom would be thrilled if you left that jerk. We have a guest room you can stay in and…"

"Jess, stop." Sitting up straight, Lauren looked directly into his eyes to stress her point. "Dane's not someone you just walk away from. His ego's far too big. Even though he's already bored with me, he has to be the one to end it. And trust me, he will. 'Cause I intend to be an even bigger uptight bitch than he already thinks I am. Hell, he'll probably end up throwing me overboard."

"Better not, I'll kill his ass."

"He's not even worth the trouble," she said, before quickly kissing him once more. Taking the silk flower lei from around her neck, she put it on him. "The sooner I get back to that party, the sooner my vacation from hell will be over. And the sooner you and I can start seeing each other for real."

179

Jess stood up and pulled her toward him for one last kiss. "Why do you have to be so damn logical? I can't argue with that." Putting his arm around her, they began walking back to the party. "I hope you know this goes against everything I am."

"I know. That's why I like you."

They then made their way back through the tangle of shrubbery along the path. But as they stepped into the clearing near the dance floor, Jess was reluctant to let go of her hand. In an instant, they ran smack into Dane, who was frantically searching for his missing possession. A possession he now found in the custody of someone else.

"Son of a bitch!" Dane shouted, and charging Jess, he shoved him up against a tree.

"Dane, stop it!" Lauren yelled, attempting to intervene. "You're being paranoid."

"No, he's not," said Jess, looking Dane squarely in the eye, egging him on. "He has every right to be threatened by me. He should be."

"Shut up! You shut the fuck up!"

Jess managed to push Dane off and he stumbled back.

"You wanna fight me? Fine. Let's take it out to the beach," said Jess.

"We're not taking it anywhere, prick. I'm gonna kick your ass right here in front of all your little friends."

A small crowd quickly gathered. Jess took off the lei Lauren had given him and stuffed it into his pocket as the two began to circle. Dane rushed to throw the first punch, which connected, and the fight was on.

Somewhere at the edge of the thinned-out dance floor, Calvin heard someone yell, "Fight! There's a fight!" And as several people ran past to get a ring-side seat, something told him he'd better check it out. Sure enough, when Calvin pushed his way to the front of the spectators, there was Jess mixing it up with the punk-ass white boy. "So much for the love drug," he remarked to himself.

Seeing Calvin, Lauren ran up to him, pleading, "You've gotta stop them."

A part of him thought about doing just that, but the rest of him knew this'd been coming and he told her the deal. "Can't. Gotta let it play out."

Across the gathering, Eric and Nikki forced their way to the front of the crowd and Calvin waited to see what Eric would do. The unwritten rule regarding rival males bashing each other's brains out was that it was a one-on-one affair. That rule, however, was sometimes ignored. Calvin quickly sized Eric up and knew Eric was doing the same. Though the guy was taller, Calvin figured he could probably take him. If Eric jumped in, he would then have the right to join in the melee. And while he wasn't a fighter under most circumstances, the idea of whaling on one or both of these jerks definitely had its appeal.

With the fight now the main attraction, even the DJ decided to shut it down in favor of watching the action. Fortunately for Jess, astronomy and boats weren't the only things his dad had taught him; he was more than holding his own. Though Dane came out of the gates with an impressive initial burst of aggression, he was rapidly losing steam. Perhaps that last little purple pill wasn't such a good idea after all; might even have been cut with something more than MDMA.

With his stamina and focus considerably compromised, Dane began to falter and Jess soon gained the upper hand, delivering several solid punches. The last and most effective of which landed just below Dane's sternum, causing him to double over and fall to his knees. Jess then grabbed him by the crew collar and held him upright as the blood-lusting spectators urged him to deliver the crowning blow. He didn't, however. He knew this wasn't the way Lauren wanted things to go down, and he felt her watching. Much to the disappointment of the crowd, Jess simply let go and backed away, leaving Dane to crumble and fall forward, barely able to catch himself before face-planting on the ground. When Eric and Nikki rushed to Dane's aid, Jess stepped away.

Calvin walked over to the undisputed winner who was now bent over with his hands on his knees spitting out blood from a split lip and bitten tongue. Twisting the top off a bottle of water, Calvin handed it to him. "And to think, I almost didn't come tonight."

Still catching his breath, Jess took a stinging swig of water and spit out a pink stream. "Well, it wasn't a drive-by, but I didn't want you to be bored."

"Ah, but you missed the opening act. Little Miss Chinatown outta control and losing her lunch."

"No way."

"Truth. I only caught your fight club 'cause I came back get her some water."

They watched as Dane's entourage of two picked him up off the ground. When Lauren moved in to assist them, Dane spewed the last of his venom at her, "Get the fuck away from me, bitch."

Eric and Nikki headed for the dock with their defeated comrade between them, his arms slung over their shoulders. But before they disappeared into the night, Eric turned his head, hurling one last threat in Jess's direction, "This isn't over, prick."

But Jess did not take the bait or respond. His attention was now fully on Lauren, waiting to see what she would do. Stay or go.

She turned and walked away ... from her so-called friends, and into Jess's arms.

"Party o' four," proclaimed Calvin.

❦ CHAPTER 23 ❦

MARCO ...

On the far side of Buzzard Island, three teenagers, a girl and two guys, sat on the shore of a secluded man-made cove, passing a bottle of rum and chasing it with an energy drink. Immersed in their own private party, they were blissfully unaware that there had been a fight, or even what time it was.

The girl suddenly stood up, kicked off her flip-flops, and began making her way toward the water, shedding her dress as she went. Down to just a thong, Lady Godiva of the Delta walked into the cove up to her waist before turning back and beckoning the guys to join her. "Come on! It feels great!"

They didn't need to be asked twice. The boys, one stocky and one lanky, were practically tripping over themselves as they ran toward the water, tugging off their shoes, shirts, and pants as they went. Their white butts glowed in the dark before they dove in and hurried to catch up with the girl who was heading for a swim platform anchored in the middle of the cove.

Arriving at the platform first, the stockier guy scrambled up onto it then quickly ran to the edge yelling, "Naked cannonball!"

before jumping in the air, tucking tightly, and plunging into the water. Upon resurfacing, he received high marks from the two judges in the form of cheers and applause. The uninhibited trio began taking turns climbing out of the water then jumping or diving off the platform for the entertainment of the other two—a daring version of show and tell. Skin diving beneath a full moon was making for a night they would not soon forget. Unless, of course, they continued drinking and forgot.

Having quickly exhausted this thrill, Lady Godiva suggested they try a new game. "I've always wanted to play nude Marco Polo."

"I'm in," said Stocky, without hesitation.

"Me too," agreed Lanky.

Both guys immediately volunteered to be "it," realizing the position would allow them to pursue a half-naked girl and perhaps innocently cop a feel in the process. A Ro Sham Bo was held to determine which of them would be the lucky first "Marco." Lanky Guy's Paper-Over-Rock won the coveted title.

As it turned out, Lanky was possibly the only person on the planet who took the rules of Marco Polo seriously and didn't cheat by peeking. Only someone a tad short on brain cells would actually hurl themselves about blindly in a large body of water. And apparently, this guy was "it" in more ways than one.

As quietly as humanly possible in water, Stocky Guy and Lady Godiva swam in opposite directions away from Lanky, who soon called out, "Maaarco," as the game began.

CHAPTER 24

NIGHT GAME

Just as Ray had promised Frances, the sheriff's patrol boat was in the vicinity of Buzzard Island on the night of the One Plank. Though to the best of his knowledge, Jess and Mei Li were not in attendance, Ray knew plenty of other local teenagers were. Therefore, he made sure he was close enough to respond if necessary, yet far enough away to be unobtrusive. Just because he was a sheriff's sergeant now didn't mean he hadn't enjoyed some wild times in his younger days. Ray was keenly aware what the One Plank was all about and was willing to turn a blind eye, as long as things didn't get out of hand. He thought about pulling this night shift alone then decided he'd better have Burt along as backup, just in case. Not that Burt could really be called "backup" with a straight face. More like a warm body with a badge.

They'd spent the bulk of the evening patrolling the waterways near the party, taking the opportunity to look for anything unusual that might provide a lead into the deaths of the Vegas couple, the fisherman, and now Huestus. But nothing out of the ordinary presented itself. So far it'd been a fairly routine shift. They'd given out one citation for water-skiing after sunset, another for being out after dark in a vessel with no running lights, and had issued one warning to a rental houseboat of smokin' hot lesbians who were playing their music too loud. Ray was convinced the neighboring vessel of fragile-ego fishermen would not have called in the complaint had the women so much as looked at them or waved. Other than that, the night had been about patrolling the area and killing time with relatively few incidents to respond to.

The patrol boat was presently tied to a lighted channel marker in the middle of the river, the tiki torches of Buzzard Island flickering in the distance. Ray was up above on the marker with a flashlight making sure everything was in order, while Burt was content to remain below on the boat's back deck, listening to a Giant's night game on his portable radio. Since it wasn't his idea to put in voluntary overtime to babysit the One Plankers, there was no way Burt was going to completely miss a game he could be watching from the comfort of his La-Z-Boy with a bowl of kettle corn in his lap.

Technically, the upkeep and maintenance of channel markers fell under the jurisdiction of the Coast Guard, so checking them was simply an excuse for the sheriffs to be in the area. It also gave Ray a break from being cooped up in the patrol boat with Burt.

Being that this was the night of the One Plank, Ray found himself in a reminiscent mood. He was thinking about how close he'd come to kissing Frances, a woman he'd first seen all those years ago at the One Plank when they were both just teenagers themselves. Seemed their lives had come full circle. They'd each married other people, moved away, and had a child. His own daughter was heading off to college in the fall. Now here they were, back in the Delta, single, and attracted to each other—at least he hoped the feeling was mutual.

Below on the radio, a home run was hit and the sports announcer, as well as the stadium crowd, went bonkers. So did Burt, who cranked up the volume and did a painfully awkward celebration dance on the back deck of the patrol boat.

Above on the channel marker, Ray suddenly got a sharp pain in his left earlobe. Whenever his abuela wanted him to pay attention when he was a kid, she'd pinch his left earlobe but good. A practice she vowed to continue from the afterlife and had somehow managed to pull off. To this day, whenever Ray's left earlobe stung, he dutifully paid attention.

Leaning over the side of the channel marker, he called down to Burt, "Hey, turn that thing down for a minute, will ya?" With no response, Ray hung even further over the side and yelled, "Burt!"

Startled, the deputy jumped and turned down the radio. "What?!"

"I need quiet for a minute," Ray insisted.

Burt grudgingly clicked off the radio so Ray could listen to the sounds of the Delta by night. But as with the rest of the shift, nothing out of the ordinary presented itself. Perhaps he'd mistaken a mosquito bite for his dead grandmother. Thankfully, no one outside of his immediate family knew that story; he'd be the laughing stock of the Sheriff's Office.

❧ CHAPTER 25 ❧

DEADLY GAME

With the most exciting event of the party (the fight) now over, what remained of the One Plank quickly sputtered out and people began to disperse, heading for their boats and home.

The naked trio in the cove, however, were still going strong. Lady Godiva and Stocky had managed to out-maneuver Lanky for quite some time, which wasn't all that difficult really, considering the guy's puritanical approach to the game.

Eager to have his chance at being "it" and pursue the girl himself, Stocky decided to speed things up by putting himself directly in the path of Marco. He stealthily snuck up onto the swim platform and prepared to deliver another of his famous cannonball dives. Only this time he'd make sure he landed so close to the dweeb, there'd be no way the guy could miss tagging him. Seeing what Stocky was up to, Lady Godiva struggled to stifle her laughter. There he was, standing buck naked on the platform trying to cover his member with one hand while shushing her with the other—a visual which only made her laugh harder.

Upon hearing the girl's giggles, Lanky called out suspiciously, "Maaarco?"

Go time.

"Polo!" shouted Stocky as he flew into action.

At the exact moment Stocky Guy ran to the edge of the platform and launched himself into the air, the head of an enormous creature emerged from the water: a dragon. Its massive jaws snapped open exposing razor-sharp teeth that glistened in the moonlight, and like a dog catching a Frisbee, the dragon effortlessly nabbed Stocky mid-air and retreated below surface.

Having witnessed the dragon's snatch and grab, the girl immediately went into shock. Unable to even scream, she whimpered softly while frantically looking around for any sign of the creature.

The now deadly game of Marco Polo continued for Lanky, who hadn't seen a thing. But having heard the dramatic movement of water, Marco hastily drew his own conclusion as to what was happening and adamantly registered his protest. "Hey, no fish outta water, remember?!"

Determined not to let his opponents out smart him, Lanky swam toward the sound of ripples, the spot where the dragon had submerged. Once there, he quietly treaded water, listening closely for the sound of another body moving nearby. Slowly, the upper portion of the dragon's tremendous head surfaced before him. Lanky could hear breathing and sensed he was closing in on his prey, a grave miscalculation of his role in this new game.

"Maaarcooo," he beckoned confidently, to which the dragon responded with a snort. Lanky laughed at the impressive sound effects and a victorious grin quickly spread across his face.

"Gotcha now!" he proclaimed, and lunging forward, he smacked the dragon directly on the snout. "You're it!"

Lanky opened his eyes to find himself face to face with an implausible creature. The dragon's black eyes shone like crystal balls in which the teenager could see his own terrified reflection. And though his mouth dropped open, no further reaction was possible. The dragon took Lanky before he could even make a sound, then slipped beneath with its prize.

The girl was now faced with a critical decision; how to save her own life. She desperately wanted to swim for shore, but the platform was closer. The twelve by twelve wooden dock anchored in the middle of the cove would now be her life raft, and she swam the fastest heat of her swim team career to reach it. Thankfully, she made it, and quickly scrambled up the swim ladder. She then huddled in the middle and tried to remain silent, her body shivering from shock, her mind racing, trying to figure out how to survive until someone came to her rescue.

Having given Dane & Company a wide berth to get gone, Calvin, Jess, and Lauren were on their way to collect Mei Li and head for home when a series of blood-curdling screams arose from the cove. Of the twenty or so remaining party-goers, a few took off running in the direction of the screams to investigate. The rest simply took off running.

"Come on," said Jess, and taking Lauren's hand, they too, headed for the cove. But Calvin didn't immediately follow. He had a nagging feeling he should get back to Mei Li, though in all likelihood she was still passed out with her head on a cleat. When a second series of screams erupted, Calvin gave in to his own curiosity and followed Jess and Lauren, running along the path toward the cove. They soon caught up with the others on a small beach, everyone trying to figure out exactly what was going on.

At first, all they could see was a panicked half-naked girl crouched in the middle of a swim platform out in the cove. The water, however, was unusually choppy for a protected cove on a calm night. A beefy guy on the beach decided to swim out to the girl and help her back to shore, but as he waded in she cried out to him, "Don't! It's in the water!" No sooner had she issued this warning, when the top part of the dragon's head broke the surface just yards from the platform, its jagged dorsal ridge appearing a moment later. Beefy guy quickly retreated to the safety of shore amid screams and gasps from those gathered there.

Now it was clear, some sort of creature was aggressively cutting through the water, circling the swim platform and causing it to rock dramatically in the wakes. The platform wasn't going to be the girl's life raft after all, rather she was a delectable morsel bobbing on a paper plate.

"Holy shit," exclaimed Jess.

"A'ight, this is not good," said Calvin.

"What the hell is it?" Jess asked.

But no one had an answer.

"Help! Someone please help me!" the girl begged.

"Oh my God, what are we gonna do?" Lauren anxiously asked.

Jess suddenly let go of her hand. "Stay here with Calvin. I'm gonna get the boat." He then took off running, heading for the main dock.

Those on the beach continued to watch helplessly as some kind of sea serpent continued circling the platform with determined force while the girl pleaded for a rescue. "Please don't let it get me! It already got the two guys I was with."

Calvin went to the edge of the water and called out to her, "Hang on, help is on the way. We got a plan, so you gotta hang on, a'ight?"

"What's the plan?" the guy standing next to him asked.

"Damn if I know."

Arriving at the ski boat, Jess quickly untied it and jumped aboard. So focused on getting back to the cove in time, he didn't notice Mei Li pathetically sprawled out at the end of the dock. Firing up the boat, Jess sped away, leaving behind a substantial wake that seriously rocked Mei Li. She'd already been jostled about by several other wakes as people took off in their boats, including the massive roller left behind as Eric angrily tore out in the *Money Talks*.

"Hell ..." Mei Li declared weakly. "I'm in hell."

Jess sped back to the other side of the island. Once inside the cove, he slowed down and scanned the waters, trying to determine the location of the creature. At the moment there was no sign of it, so he headed straight for the platform. Coming up alongside he extended his hand to the girl, but as she reached to take it, a massive spiked tail rose up out of the cove behind her and violently knocked her off the platform into the water. She resurfaced several yards away, disoriented and bleeding from a head wound.

"Help me. Please," she implored, while struggling to stay afloat.

Jess powered the boat toward her, but it was a race he would not win. The dragon easily got there first, its enormous head and jaws briefly rising out of the water before powerfully hitting its prey. Forced to veer the boat away at the last second in order to avoid colliding with the creature, Jess looked back in time to see the dragon dive below with its latest trophy. Those on shore reacted with horror, not only at the girl's demise, but at their first comprehensive glimpse of the dragon—a sight that prompted most to run for the interior of the island.

Devastated that he could not save the girl, Jess idled the ski boat and anxiously waited to see if and where the dragon would resurface as he tried to determine his best course of action. Considering the sheer force and speed of the creature, he doubted he could outrun it. Calvin sensed what Jess was grappling with. And though he wasn't absolutely sure he had the right answer, something in his gut told him Jess should not attempt to flee, that doing so would only draw the dragon to him.

Stepping to the edge of the shore, Calvin called out to Jess, "I think you should cut your engine!"

With someone he trusted now validating his own thoughts, Jess turned the ignition switch to "off" and began to drift silently in the cove, certain the pounding of his heart would be enough to attract the creature. Those left on shore nervously scanned the surface of the water and held their breath. So did Jess. His eyes soon found Lauren on shore, her face an anxious open book. Still, seeing her there somehow made him feel calmer. If he wasn't gonna make it and this turned out to be his last night on earth, it had been a damn good one. Tonight, he'd gotten the girl.

After several tense moments of watching and waiting, the dragon finally reappeared, surfacing just beyond the opening to the cove. This would buy Jess the time he needed to get the ski boat to shore and he quickly turned the key in the ignition. But the engine wouldn't catch. He tried it again, same result. When those on shore began yelling and pointing, he was too afraid to look, convinced the dragon was coming back for him.

Then someone yelled, "It's heading for the main dock!" And while this was a welcome turn of events for Jess, the reality of the dragon's new direction quickly registered with Calvin. Bolting from the beach he raced back across the island, vaulting driftwood logs, hurdling large rocks, and tearing through dense shrubbery along the way. Winded and gasping for air, Calvin made it to the main dock in time to find the dragon on a direct course for Mei Li who was still sprawled out at the end exactly where he'd left her. Sprinting down the dock, he grabbed her hand and attempted to pull her to her feet. "Come on girl, we gotta bounce!"

But she was dead weight.

"Nooo," she moaned. "I think I'm gonna be sick again."

"Gonna be worse than sick if we don't get your ass up outta here!"

He next grabbed her 'round the waist and tried again to pull her up, but Mei Li had taken hold of the cleat, ensuring she wasn't going anywhere. With desperate determination, Calvin frantically worked to unhinge her fingers. Finally managing to pry her off, they stumbled back together as the enormous head and upper body of the dragon rose out of the water before them. Calvin seized Mei Li by the hand and tried to make her run up the dock with him, but she promptly sat down at his feet, becoming an anchor. Neither fight nor flight was possible in this moment. And there they remained, just steps from the edge of the dock, a mighty dragon towering over them.

Calvin bent down and pulled Mei Li to her feet. For a second he considered dragging her backwards up the dock, but in struggling to even prop her up, he quickly realized that wasn't an option. Perhaps if they remained frozen, he thought, played opossum, the dragon would lose interest. That wasn't gonna happen either since Mei Li had become a comical rag doll. Fighting the spins, she kept her eyes tightly shut. With her head slumped over and hair falling in her face, Mei Li remained completely oblivious to the fact that the living incarnation of a mythical creature was about to make them its next meal—a unique combo plate of Chinese and Soul Food.

Then the creature screeched out an ungodly noise.

The brain does crazy things in life-threatening situations, and Calvin's mind was suddenly busy trying to decipher what the dragon's screech reminded him of—a cross between a lion's roar and a bad fan belt, he decided.

Mei Li, on the other hand, upon hearing the demonic sound, pressed the palms of her hands to her temples and lifted her head to sternly admonish the source of such an irritating noise. "Please, I'm begging you. My head is splitting here."

As the hair fell away from her face, the dragon abruptly stopped its hellish screeching and focused on her with an intense curiosity bordering on recognition. Mei Li opened her eyes and struggled to focus. Girl and dragon stared at one another for a long moment, then the dragon slowly and carefully backed down into the water and disappeared.

"Never gonna drink Pina Coladas ever again." Mei Li's last words before passing out and crumpling in a heap. Calvin barely managed to catch her before she hit the deck.

Still adrift in the cove, Jess was about to try yet again to coax the ski boat's engine to life. There'd been several failed attempts already and he feared his frantic efforts might have flooded it. He lifted the engine cover in the hope that airing it out might be the fix he so urgently needed. He was lucky the dragon had momentarily left the cove, but Jess had a sinking feeling he'd used up more than one night's allotment of good fortune. He'd won the heart of Lauren, and won the fight with Dane. Now it appeared his luck was tapping out. Turning the key in the ignition once more, the engine cranked but would not catch. Defeated, he picked up the radio mic. "Ray, if you're out there, this is Jess. We have an emergency situation on Buzzard Island. Mayday, mayday. Request assistance."

And Ray *was* out there. After a second undeniable pinching of his earlobe, he'd climbed down off the channel marker and made Burt turn the game off for good. A moment later Jess's transmission came over the marine radio. The distress in his voice was alarming and Ray grabbed for the mic. "Jess, it's Ray. Talk to me, what's going on?"

Jess was about to answer when he heard shouting from the shore. Lauren and those remaining on the beach were screaming and pointing to the entrance of the cove. The dragon was returning. Dropping the radio mic, he reached for the key in the ignition. Those on shore began to panic, but Jess resisted. Instead, he took a deep breath and looked up to the sky. "Dad, I'm either gonna get outta this, or I'm gonna be seein' you real soon ... like in a few minutes." He then bravely turned the key. The engine caught immediately.

Though his first impulse was to punch the throttle to full, Jess was mindful not to do anything drastic that might kill the engine, so he carefully brought the ski boat up to speed. He turned to find the dragon closing in on him. Realizing he didn't have the time or space to out-maneuver the creature, he decided to head straight onto shore and pray the thing wouldn't follow.

As the boat headed directly for the beach, Jess pulled the flower lei Lauren had given him from his pocket and quickly broke it in one place. He then wrapped one end around the throttle and tied the other end to the steering wheel, thereby locking the throttle in "full." With the dragon now just feet from the stern, Jess made his way to the bow of the boat and braced for impact.

Carrying an unconscious Mei Li, Calvin arrived back at the cove in time to witness the spectacle that was about to unfold.

"Get outta the way!" Jess yelled to those on the beach as he prepared to hit the shore. A moment later, the ski boat violently made land. Jess was launched into the air upon impact and landed several yards up on the beach. The boat itself traveled a considerable distance out of water before its prop became lodged in sand, killing the engine.

The dragon unwittingly followed the ski boat onto shore. Beaching itself, it screeched out its displeasure. The small handful of people who hadn't fled the scene were now granted an unprecedented view of the dragon in its entirety—no 3D glasses required.

The thing was enormous; at least fifty feet long from snout to tail's end. Its massive serpentine body was covered in giant plated scales that were inherently green, yet shimmered with an iridescent luster in the moonlight. Other creature-features included a deadly sharp dorsal ridge, webbed talon claws, three horns along the top of its head with lizard-like flares on either side.

The humans scrambled back in case this thing could operate on land. It quickly became apparent, however, that it couldn't. Visibly distraught at being out of water, the dragon soon switched its ungodly screeching to a threatened, though equally annoying hiss. It defensively raised the flares at the side of its head and began to squirm its way backwards toward the water. Once sufficiently submerged, the dragon turned and headed out of the cove, its head and dorsal ridge moving rapidly away from shore until it dove under and vanished completely.

Lauren ran to where Jess was laying on the sand, holding his side. "Oh my God, are you alright?"

"Yeah," he lied and grimaced. "Think I might've busted a couple ribs, though."

Calvin walked up and deposited a still unconscious Mei Li on the sand beside Jess. "I take it back. You people in the cuts really know how to party. Ya'ight, bruh?"

"Well, I'm alive. What about Mei Li, she okay?"

"Other than a nasty hangover, she'll live. But I'm tellin' you man, that thing could've nailed us and it didn't. Took one look at Mei Li and bounced."

"Maybe barf is a dragon repellant," said Lauren, catching a whiff.

Mei Li began to come to. Still groggy, she uttered a phrase in Cantonese.

"She speakin' Chinese?" asked Calvin.

Mei Li sat up and reiterated the phrase, only this time in English. "Someone has awakened the dragon."

Just then, the sheriff's patrol boat came blazing into the cove with lights flashing and siren wailing.

"Better late than never," said Calvin.

"Not his fault. I should have radioed him sooner," said Jess.

"Looks like you're both busted for hittin' this party."

"Feels more like the party hit us," replied Jess, his face contorted in pain.

Half an hour later, those who had witnessed the attack were gathered at the clubhouse as Ray tried his best to instill a sense of calm, something that simply wasn't possible. The sergeant considered calling for backup from his own agency, or perhaps the Coast Guard, but ultimately decided to hold off until he had a chance to fully assess the situation. He didn't like the idea that the witnesses (and probably the victims themselves) had been under the influence of at least one clarity-hampering chemical. A bunch of partying teenagers did not reliable witnesses make.

Burt got busy taking statements while Ray put his EMT skills to work stabilizing Jess's ribs until they could get him to a doctor. Jess was grateful Burt was interviewing Lauren several yards away. He didn't want her to see him this close to passing out, his fingers clenching the edge of the bar in agony as Ray taped him up.

Totally bummed that he'd blacked out and missed the whole damn thing, Board fumbled around behind the bar, sheepishly cleaning up the excessive evidence of under-age drinking.

Elbows on the bar and head in hands, Mei Li sat hunched over beside Jess while Calvin did his best to ply her with water. He'd managed to round up some ibuprofen for her aching head, along with Jess's aching everything.

"Look, it's not that I don't believe you," said Ray, applying the last strip of tape to Jess's ribcage. "It's just that I ..."

"Don't believe us," said Jess through clenched teeth.

"You have to understand my position. We responded to a party where three teenagers have supposedly been killed. And the witnesses, who just happen to be under the influence of alcohol and God only knows what other substances, all claim it was a dragon."

"I only had one drink," said Calvin, "and I'm tellin' you straight up, that's what it was."

"Okay, but put yourself in my shoes."

"Ray, you know me," said Jess, finally able to breathe. "Do you seriously think I could make this shit up?"

"Other than a wrecked ski boat and two large drag marks in the sand, I've got no physical evidence of a crime," replied Ray. "Couple that with the fact that no one present seems to know the three people who were supposedly killed. So, even if I believe you, I'm gonna have one hell of a time selling this to law enforcement. Not to mention the general public."

"If this keeps up, not gonna be a general public," said Calvin.

Lauren came to stand beside Jess and he linked his arms around her waist, prompting Ray to ask, "So, the black eye and split lip, those from the boat crash as well?"

"Yep," was all Jess was willing to give up. "I have a black eye?" he asked Lauren, who nodded and gently kissed it.

Witnessing this blatant display of affection, Mei Li turned to Calvin, "How long was I unconscious?"

"Long enough," he replied.

"Anything else happen I should know about?"

"Like what?" he asked, incredulous. "Oh, there was this dragon that ate some people, but you caught part o' that show, right?"

Mei Li continued to give him the stink eye to which he responded, "Seriously? You think maybe we hooked up in between your barf sessions?"

"I hate to ruin this beautiful moment between the two of you," said Jess, "but I think Mei Li should tell Ray about the Chinese fairy tale."

"It's not a fairy tale," she replied indignantly. "It's a legend."

Jess gave her a look that implied, "What's the difference"?

"Well, can't be any more bizarre than what I've already heard," said Ray. "What's the story, Mei Li?"

"Something my grandfather told me when I was little. It's the legend of Gong Luhng—the river dragon. It has something to do with a dragon being brought to life for revenge, but I can't remember the details. You'll need to ask my grandfather."

"And the thing was afraid of Mei Li," said Calvin. "Seriously, it took one look at her and bounced."

Burt approached, informing Ray, "Same story all around, Sarge. Some kind of a ... dragon."

"Looks like your piranha theory is officially dead," noted Calvin.

But the deputy kept his cool and didn't react to the snide remark. Burt's crime drama, lead-detective alter ego had already kicked into high gear. Putting his hands on his hips, the deputy gazed out toward the cove and declared, "Whatever it is, we'll get to the bottom of it."

"Good luck with that," said Calvin. "I haven't seen the bottom of it, but judging from the parts I have, I'd say you got your work cut out for ya."

Momentarily brought back to reality, Burt turned to Ray and gruffly asked, "How do you wanna handle this? They're all scared to take their boats home. Nobody wants to go anywhere near the water."

Ray heaved a heavy sigh. "Can't say as I blame 'em. Alright, so what do we know? It seems this..." he hesitated, "dragon, or whatever it is, is attacking at night." He then looked to Mei Li for confirmation. "Does that fit with the legend?"

"You're asking me?! Like I said, I was a little kid when I heard it."

"Right," he replied with resignation. "I'm chasing down leads from a children's story." The sheriff's sergeant looked at his watch then announced in a voice loud enough for all to hear, "Listen up, everyone. Daylight's only a couple hours away, so we'll all stay here 'til morning then head back to the marina as a group."

Ray hoped his hunch was right, that the thing was only attacking between dusk and dawn. At least his left earlobe didn't feel pinched, so there was that.

❧ CHAPTER 26 ❧

REFLEX ACTION

Morning light shimmered on the tranquil waters an hour after dawn. Startled, a pair of ducks took flight as a kayaker gently paddled into their quiet neck of the slough. It was the kind of morning an outdoorsman lives for: solitude, nature, beauty.

Then, without warning, the kayak was aggressively bumped from below and overturned. It remained upside down for only a moment, however, as the seasoned kayaker promptly managed to right his vessel—an impressive feat since he was now headless. His arms made one last reflex-action attempt at paddling before he went limp and his decapitated body slumped over. Blood gushed from the meaty wound of a neck stump and mixed with river water as it flowed down over his life vest, then spilled onto the front of the boat.

The kayak, with its horrific cargo, continued to slowly drift through the water—a sportier, though less animated version of the Headless Horseman of Sleepy Hollow.

❧ CHAPTER 27 ❧

UNLOCKE-ING A MYSTERY

Calvin wasn't exactly sure why he'd been summoned to go along on Ray's fact-finding mission, other than the *fact* that he and Mei Li had been granted an up close and personal audience with the dragon. But now for the second time in his life, Calvin found himself in the rear seat of a patrol car. Fortunately, this time his hands were free and he was considerably less concerned about the final destination.

Mei Li had offered to ride in back but it didn't seem right to let her. She probably suspected this wouldn't be his first back-seat patrol-car-ride, and it suddenly mattered to him what she thought. So, Calvin acted like it was no big deal and casually climbed in back, leaving Mei Li to ride shotgun beside the shotgun as Ray drove them north along the levee road. No one had gotten more than a few hours of sleep upon returning from Buzzard Island earlier that morning. Between Mei Li nursing a hangover and Ray grappling with the realities of an increasingly dicey situation, conversation was limited.

Ray soon turned right at the "Welcome to Locke" sign and proceeded to drive down the narrow main street. Calvin looked out the window at the strange little town with its turn-of-the-century-style row houses standing smack up against one another. Several of the old wooden buildings were in serious disrepair. A few even leaned precariously against a neighboring building or slumped forward toward the street. Calvin had never seen a town like this before. His initial impression was that it looked more like the Old West section of an abandoned theme park, rather than a place where people actually lived. "Is this place for real?" he asked.

Ray chuckled. It'd been a while since he'd seen Locke through the eyes of a newcomer. His mind had been so preoccupied with the events of the last few days, he'd forgotten that this unique little town could be something of a curiosity to outsiders. "It's real, alright," he replied. "It's the only rural town in America built entirely by Chinese."

"My grandfather's one of the last Chinese-Americans living here," added Mei Li.

Ray pulled over and parked outside one of several storefronts lining the short, one-way Main Street.

"Like a damn ghost town," said Calvin, as he got out and looked around.

"It is not," countered Mei Li.

Sensing he'd touched a nerve, Calvin shut the hell up and followed Mei Li and Ray to a small storefront. A string of bells on the front door announced their arrival as they entered Cheng's Chinese Herb Shop, which seemed curiously dark for business hours. As his eyes adjusted, Calvin took in the vast array of jars, bottles, and bins crowding the space, the air a sticky-sweet mixture of their mysterious contents.

Mei Li called out for her grandfather, "Yeh-yeh?"

But there was no reply, just the sound of wind chimes drifting through an unseen window or open door somewhere at the rear of the building.

"Ghost town," Calvin reiterated under his breath.

"He said he'd be here," she assured Ray before calling again. "Yeh-yeh, where are you?"

Mei Li was about to take her search to the living quarters in back when a prolonged, guttural growl came from behind the front counter and everyone froze in their tracks. A second later, what looked like two giant gnarled claws flipped up onto the glass counter top. Already on edge, Ray had his finger on the snap of his holster, and Calvin was halfway to the door when Tak Cheng popped up from behind the counter waving two large ginseng roots and howling like a hokey Halloween ghost. "Ooo. Ooooooo."

Quite used to her grandfather's antics, Mei Li hadn't fallen for his prank, but scolded him as if she had. "Yeh-yeh! You scared us half to death!"

"Aw, I'm sorry, suen-neui. Did you think I was some kind of monster?" he asked with glee.

"Yeeah!" replied Calvin, coming away from the door.

This notion only served to delight Tak more and he proudly proclaimed himself, "The Ginseng Monster of Locke!"

His granddaughter simply shook her head and quickly moved on with the business at hand. "Yeh-yeh, you remember Sergeant Cruz?"

"Of course, nice to see you again." Tak put down the roots to shake Ray's hand.

"And this is my friend Calvin."

"You're very skittish," declared Tak, pointing a finger. "I have something for that." Scrambling up a nearby library ladder, he began rummaging through glass bottles on an upper shelf.

"Yeh-yeh, I need to ask you something," Mei Li called up to her grandfather who'd suddenly become a helium balloon bouncing around above them. "Have you heard about the killings?"

"Oh yes, very disturbing news." Tak shook his head, yet continued to busy himself among the bottles. "Do you have any suspects yet, Sergeant Cruz?"

"There's a creature of interest," offered Calvin.

Ray cleared his throat and went to stand beside the ladder. Looking up at the older gentleman, he stated, "Mr. Cheng, your granddaughter seems to think these killings have something to do with a Chinese legend you're familiar with."

Tak instantly stopped what he was doing and looked down at Ray. He then looked to his granddaughter for confirmation of what the sheriff was implying.

"Three more people were killed last night," said Mei Li. "I was there and I saw what did it. It was Gong Luhng."

Tak came down the ladder and sat on a lower rung, suddenly looking as though he'd had the wind knocked out of him. Mei Li went to her grandfather and put a hand on his shoulder. "Yeh-yeh, are you alright?"

He nodded "yes" but took a few moments to compose himself. Removing his studious glasses, Tak rubbed his weary eyes. He then took a handkerchief from his pocket and wiped the small round lenses before placing them back on the bridge of his nose, as if this ritual would somehow make what he was about to say seem rational. "When I first heard of the killings, I didn't want to believe what came to mind," he admitted. "So I denied it, hoping it wasn't true, hoping these deaths were simply accidents. Or at the very worst, of human origin. But now, I'm afraid my darkest nightmare has come to fruition." Tak looked up at Ray and confirmed his granddaughter's hunch. "Someone has awakened the dragon."

❧ CHAPTER 28 ☙

THE DREAM OF GOLD MOUNTAIN

Calvin, Ray, and Tak sat at the kitchen table as Mei Li poured Oolong from her grandfather's antique teapot, which ironically featured a gold dragon wrapped around its middle. The tiny tea-cups looked more like shot glasses to Calvin, who waited to see if there was some specific ritual to drinking tea from thimbles. Placing the teapot in the center of the table, Mei Li sat down opposite Calvin. And as he watched her arrange her long, onyx-black hair over one shoulder, a rush of electricity surged through his body. Apparently, this wasn't exclusively a bikini or party-dress-induced sensation.

The hot tea seemed to revive Tak and after several sips from his small cup, he began to speak. "The last time the dragon was summoned was 1915. It happened right here in the Delta and was witnessed by my great-grandfather and his son, my grandfa-ther. It was the first time Gong Luhng was called forth in Gum Saan, which means Gold Mountain."

"That's what the Chinese immigrants called California," added Mei Li.

"The story of the dragon's incarnation was passed down from generation to generation," said Tak. "It was told to me by my father when I was young, just as I told my own son when he was young."

"And you told me too, Yeh-yeh, when I was a little girl."

"I did. Because your father wouldn't. He wanted it to end, this ritual of passing down what was now considered merely legend. He worried it might cause you to have nightmares, the way it had for him. And for me."

"I just thought it was a bedtime story," said Mei Li. "A pretty scary one for a little kid, but I never believed it was real or true."

"It's both. As I grew older, I too came to think of it as purely legend," acknowledged Tak. "Because that's what I wanted it to be."

"Why didn't you come to me after the first two incidents?" Ray asked him.

"And what would you have thought, sergeant, if I'd walked into your office and told you I believed a dragon had attacked that couple from Las Vegas, as well as the fisherman?"

Ray pursed his lips then admitted, "I would have thought you'd lost your marbles."

"Exactly. And keep in mind, the story of Gong Luhng is a well guarded secret, one that was never to be shared with outsiders. The family lines of those who witnessed the dragon's last appearance have mostly died out now, or moved away. Or, like my own son, the later generations think of it as simply Chinese folklore. But considering what has happened, and what will undoubtedly continue to happen, the time has come to break our code of silence and tell the story. It'll help you understand what you're up against, what we're all up against. And what we may have to do to stop it."

Everyone was quiet as they waited for Tak to go on, and in that hushed moment, Calvin felt a chill roll up his spine. Only this time, it had nothing whatsoever to do with Mei Li. This was a feeling of ominous foreboding unlike anything he'd ever felt before.

"Tell us the story, Yeh-yeh, from the beginning," urged Mei Li.

And so, Tak began. "Well, as you probably know, the first major wave of Chinese immigrants came to California in the early 1850s around the time of the Gold Rush. The oppressive political and economic turmoil in China after the Opium War and the Taiping Revolution forced many to leave their homeland in search of a better life in other parts of the world. Most people don't realize that word of gold being discovered in California reached southern China before it even reached the east coast of America. To those suffering in China, the dream of striking it rich in Gold Mountain was a powerful lure, and many desperate souls made the journey. But the long voyage by ship was a perilous one, and once on board, the Chinese emigrants were subjected to horrific conditions of overcrowding and disease. Countless numbers died at sea before ever setting foot in this country.

"For those who did manage to survive, the dream of a better life in Gold Mountain was soon replaced by the ugly realities of racism and prejudice. The white, mostly American-born miners of the Gold Rush quickly came to resent the Chinese. Their resourcefulness and tireless work ethic were seen as a threat. So it wasn't long before exclusionary laws and excessive taxes were put into place; making it not only dangerous for the Chinese to pursue mining, but virtually impossible for them to succeed if they tried. Only a small percentage of Chinese miners actually struck it rich and returned home wealthy. The rest remained here in America, scraping out a meager existence any way they could.

"But Chinese are the ultimate survivors, thanks in part to our ability to adapt. The former miners soon began taking positions as domestic servants, laborers, and sharecroppers. The truly shrewd, however, went into the business of selling goods and services to the very miners and communities who'd shut them out. That's how some of the first Chinese-owned mercantiles, laundries, and restaurants came into existence here."

"Reminds me a little of today's Indian Casinos," suggested Ray. "Ingenious retribution."

"Yeah, payback's a bitch," added Calvin.

"So it would seem, though I doubt the Chinese were thinking any further down the line than survival," said Tak.

In requesting her grandfather tell them the back story, Mei Li had miscalculated just how far back he might go. Not only was Tak a history buff, he rarely had this kind of captive audience. "Okay Yeh-yeh, thanks for the Chinese-in-America history lesson," she interjected, "but can we cut to the dragon?"

"You said to tell the story from the beginning, suen-neui. And our history in America is a key part of it."

"I happen to like history," said Ray.

"Yeah, I was gettin' into it," added Calvin.

"Guys, remember, we're here to find out about the dragon," Mei Li insisted.

"And we'll get there," replied Ray, who was rather enjoying sitting down, drinking tea, and listening to Tak.

"Besides, the sooner we know everything," said Calvin, "the sooner we might have to do somethin' about it."

"Precisely," agreed Ray.

So, as much as she wanted to move things along, Mei Li defaulted to her long-instilled sense of respect for elders and backed down. Obviously her grandfather had captured the attention of his guests, who seemed genuinely interested in the history lesson. "Well, at least he didn't start at the Ming Dynasty," she said with resignation.

"Go on, Yeh-yeh, tell us some more," urged Calvin, garnering himself an exaggerated eye roll from Mei Li.

With his granddaughter voted down and his new fan club of two hanging on his every word, Tak felt obliged to give the people what they wanted. "Very well. Now, where was I? Oh, yes. While the Gold Rush might not have panned out for the Chinese, so to speak, the notion that a better life could be found in Gold Mountain continued to persist. Soon thousands more came from China as cheap labor to build the Transcontinental Railroad.

"In spite of the ongoing Civil War, the U.S. Government was determined to connect the East and West coasts by rail. And though the Central Pacific Railroad offered decent wages to white men in California to build the eastbound segment, few had any interest in the backbreaking work, especially since mining was still an option for them.

"So, faced with a labor strike along with a manpower shortage, the Central Pacific decided to capitalize on the abundance of cheap labor in the Chinese who'd been effectively forced out of mining. The railroad initially hired fifty Chinese, paying them a third less than white laborers while making them pay for their own food and board. Well, of course, the first fifty proved a formidable work force. So they quickly hired fifty more. And fifty more after that, and so on, until the number of Chinese railroad workers reached into the thousands. The Chinese workers of the Central Pacific easily out-built all other rail workers. It was said they could put down ten miles of track in a day, trouncing the mostly Irish workers of the Union Pacific who could barely lay one mile of track in a week. Naturally, the railroad recruited even more laborers directly from China, until at one point, the number of Chinese working on the eastbound segment of the Transcontinental reached over ten thousand."

"Holy smokes," said Ray. "How come you're still a minority?"

Tak laughed and replied, "Because it takes women to make a population explosion, and there simply weren't many. Due to the stringent laws against Chinese women immigrating to America, there was maybe one Chinese woman for every thirty men back then. Also the fact that thousands of Chinese died building the railroad. It was extremely dangerous work. When the crews of the Central Pacific hit the solid granite of the Sierras, it was decided the only way to make real progress was to blast through with nitroglycerine. Guess which workers got that job."

"Aw nah, that's messed up," said Calvin.

"Well," Tak shrugged, "we do love our fireworks. But seriously, the Chinese were the only ones brave enough, or perhaps desperate enough, to work with the volatile explosive. Even with all these hardships, life here was still more desirable than the impoverished life most were suffering back in China. And the money the laborers sent home made it possible for their families to survive. So young Chinese men continued coming to this country. First risking their lives to get here, then risking their lives again to make the Transcontinental a reality. And my great-grandfather, Cheng Wei Han, was among them."

"Okay, now we're gettin' somewhere," declared Mei Li.

"With his parents' blessings and hope for a better life, Cheng Wei Han left his village in the Guangdong Province of Southeast China in 1865 and sailed for Gold Mountain. He was only 14. Once he arrived in San Francisco, he was immediately hired by the Central Pacific Railroad and spent the next four years of his life blasting granite and laying track.

"It's believed that my Great-grandfather Cheng was present on the day the eastbound tracks of the Central Pacific met the westbound tracks of the Union Pacific. There's a very famous photograph taken May 10th, 1869 in Promontory Point, Utah. It captures the moment a final gold spike was driven into the ground connecting the two railroads. Ironically, there doesn't appear to be any Chinese faces in that photograph."

"What?!" exclaimed Calvin. "After everything they did, they don't even get to be in the dang picture?!"

"The photo's quite grainy, so it's to hard to say definitively. Some believe the Chinese had assimilated, so didn't stand out. Still others believe the Chinese were intentionally excluded from the staged photograph."

"I'm thinking they were dissed," said Calvin.

"Considering the sentiment of the time ... I'm thinking you're right," agreed Tak.

"Ah, the American Dream," said Ray. "More like a pipe dream for a lot of our ancestors."

"Huge injustice. And a valuable history lesson," stated Mei Li, once again hoping to move things along. "But we're still not getting to how a dragon wound up in the Delta."

"Ah, but we are," said Tak. "With the railroad complete, the Central Pacific retained only a few Chinese as maintenance workers and left the rest to fend for themselves in Utah. Didn't even make good on their promise of a return train trip back to California. So, thousands of newly unemployed Chinese men fanned out across America looking for work. A good percentage of them made their way back to San Francisco, while others ended up in remote places taking whatever work they could find. There was, however, a massive reclamation project underway in a vast swampland of California known as the Sacramento River Delta. And Cheng Wei Han made his way here and found work building levees."

"So it's possible your great-grandfather built some of the levees that exist today," suggested Ray.

"Absolutely," replied Tak. "Though they've been reinforced over the years, many of the levees we know today were built a long time ago by Chinese laborers—and by hand, I might add."

"That musta taken forever," said Calvin.

"Initially it did. But things went considerably faster once the Chinese signed on. They even invented a special horseshoe so horses could walk in the mud and haul in materials. Once the steam-driven clamshell dredge was introduced, the number of Chinese needed in levee construction declined. So many of them simply moved into the thriving farming and canning industries—the result of all this rich new land. A few private landowners, however, continued to use Chinese laborers because they not only built strong levees, they could simultaneously cultivate the farmland the levees created. Great-grandfather Cheng worked for one such landowner, a man by the name of William Parsons.

"Parsons was a decent enough man and a fair employer who relied heavily upon Cheng Wei Han. Having worked hard to teach himself English, Wei Han earned the coveted position of crew foreman. He ended up spending the next fourteen years of his life here in the Delta, building levees and farming for Parsons. But great-grandfather longed to marry and start a family. With so few Chinese women here at the time, if a man wanted to find a wife, he had to return to China. Unfortunately, not many could afford it. By the time Great-grandfather Cheng saved up enough money to return home, he was already 32. And by then there was a new obstacle facing anyone who returned to China yet wished to come back to Gold Mountain. A little something known as The Chinese Exclusion Act of 1882."

"That name says it all," quipped Calvin. "They didn't bother to sugar-coat it."

"No, they didn't," replied Tak. "And even if you'd been in this country for years, once you left, it was next to impossible to return unless you held merchant status or were somehow sponsored. Fortunately for Cheng Wei Han, he had an ally in William Parsons. His sponsorship of great-grandfather helped secure his return in spite of The Chinese Exclusion Act.

"So, Cheng Wei Han returned to his village in Guangdong Province and married. Unfortunately, his young wife had several miscarriages and bore no children. After twelve years, Wei Han decided to return to America, bringing his wife with him. This was rare indeed. But he also brought with him a young nephew whom he claimed as his son. Long Yuen Shun was the only son of great-grandfather's sister, who'd been married off into the Long family. Since Wei Han and his wife had no children, his sister begged them to take her young son back to Gold Mountain with them, hoping to spare him the shame and poverty that had befallen the once-great Long family. Against his better judgment great-grandfather agreed, bringing 6-year-old Long Yuen Shun to America."

"Traditional Chinese put their family name first," Mei Li informed Ray and Calvin. "And 'Long' means dragon."

"As Chinese people, we all consider ourselves descendants of the dragon," added Tak. "However, this particular line of the Long family was said to possess the power to call upon the River Dragon, Gong Luhng, in matters of justice and vengeance."

"Finally, we're getting to the part I kinda remember," said Mei Li.

"How a dragon came to be in the Delta," acknowledged Tak. "A few years after Cheng Wei Han returned to America, his wife finally gave birth to a boy, my grandfather Wah Ming. Great-grandfather was once again working for William Parsons and life was getting a bit better. At least it was until Parsons passed away unexpectedly and his only son, Richard, took over the family business of farming and ranching. Richard Parsons was nothing like his father. He didn't share his father's respect for the Chinese laborers who worked his land. He was also notoriously greedy.

"Having long-coveted a neighbor's property, one of the most desirable tracts in the Delta, it was believed Richard Parsons bribed the Chinese laborers working his neighbor's land, getting them to build inferior levees. Then he simply waited for the inevitable to happen. Once a levee gave way and his neighbor couldn't afford to rebuild, Parsons snapped up the land for a song. Apparently, he did this on more than one occasion. And though great-grandfather knew what the younger Parsons had done, with a wife and family depending on him, he had no choice but to keep his mouth shut, and keep his job."

"This Richard Parsons sounds like trouble," said Ray.

"He was that, alright. But the real trouble began as trouble often does," said Tak. "When a boy meets a girl."

Calvin and Mei Li exchanged a fleeting glance before averting their guilty eyes. She studied the tea leaves in the bottom of her cup, while he looked up at the ceiling fan as it slowly rotated the intoxicating air seeping in from the herb shop.

❧ CHAPTER 29 ❧

INFERNO

Richard Parsons, a balding white man in his early 40s, sat on his horse in the shade of a lone sycamore tree and watched as a dozen Chinese men toiled under the hot Delta sun. The labor crew was hard at work rebuilding a failed levee on the landowner's latest property acquisition.

A few of the laborers still wore traditional Chinese clothing and coolie hats, a single black braid trailing down the middle of their backs. Most, however, had cut off their customary queue and adopted the Western-style clothing born of the Gold Rush: denim Levi's, cotton shirts, and leather work boots. Other than two plow horses used to drag large rocks to the site, the men relied solely upon their body strength and simple hand tools to maneuver the heavy stones into place then move mounds of earth in around them.

Some thirty years prior, Parsons had come West with his father, who purchased their first piece of Delta marshland with East Coast family money. Reclaiming it with levees, he'd transformed the tract into rich, profitable farm and ranch land. After his father's death, Richard took over and went about steadily increasing his land holdings—often by less than honorable means.

Cheng Wei Han, the 44-year-old foreman of the crew, had been a laborer for most of his life. Arriving in America at the age of 14, he'd already worked on two of this country's most ambitious undertakings: the Transcontinental Railroad and now the Sacramento-San Joaquin Delta. Though he'd returned to China in his 30s to marry, he eventually made his way back to California and the Delta, thanks in part to the sponsorship of Parsons' father. Transferring his loyalty, Cheng Wei Han remained in the employ of the son, building levees and tending the fields of the wealthy landowner's ever-expanding holdings.

Like he himself once had, Wei Han's 15-year-old son, Wah Ming, was already laboring alongside the adult men of the crew, as was his nephew, Long Yuen Shun, who was now 24. Though he'd claimed Yuen Shun as his son in order to bring him to this country, it was obvious to everyone but the gwai lo that Wei Han and Yuen Shun were not cut from the same cloth.

Long Yuen Shun had grown to be a tall and strikingly handsome, though willful, young man. In spite of Wei Han's efforts to reign in his hot-headed nephew, Yuen Shun would never accept a position of servitude. He deeply resented being bossed by any man—especially a white man. This prideful demeanor often invited trouble and there were times when Wei Han regretted bringing his nephew to Gold Mountain. Life here was hard enough without attracting the attention of those who had it in for the Chinese, and Richard Parsons was just such an individual.

The oppressive heat coupled with the choking dust was making Parsons even more short-tempered than usual. Wiping dusty sweat from his brow with a handkerchief, the landowner looked around for someone to take his ill humor out on. He quickly found his favorite target: Yuen Shun. Parsons sensed something prideful in the young Chinese man, and it irked him. How dare a lowly Chinaman act as if he was as good as any other man, more specifically, a white man.

"Tell that big ugly one to stop stirring up the dust," Parsons yelled to Wei Han while pointing at Yuen Shun.

Though it was obvious the plow horses were the primary source of the thick dust, Wei Han had no choice but to give his nephew the order in Cantonese. After which, Yuen Shun briefly glared up at Parsons before resuming his job of pushing loose soil over newly placed levee rocks—only now he stirred up even more dust. Hoping to diffuse the situation, Wei Han asked for a midday break for his crew. Fortunately, the landowner consented before catching on to Yuen Shun's obvious rebuttal.

Taking their break beneath a stand of young cottonwood trees, the crew shared a simple meal of rice with vegetables and bits of cooked fish. Having quickly devoured his lunch, Yuen Shun joined two others who were gathered around the folding game table of a chubby traveling merchant, Wang Feng Ying. Wang peddled small sundries like soap and lotus candies to Chinese laborers, but he was really just a sleazy con artist who frequented the workplaces of bored and restless young men, hoping to dupe some out of what little money they made.

Wang's con of the day was a sleight-of-hand shell game and Yuen Shun was steadily losing his temper along with his money. When the pudgy merchant gleefully revealed that the young gambler had once again failed to find the pea beneath the correct shell, Yuen Shun went for his throat. Wei Han quickly intervened.

After pulling his nephew off the blubbering con man, he advised Wang to gather his bag of tricks and leave, or he might just let Yuen Shun finish what he'd started. Wang Feng Ying begrudgingly packed up his case and left, but not before hurling a number of threats in Cantonese—from a safe distance, of course.

Relieved that Parsons hadn't witnessed the altercation, the foreman reprimanded his nephew before returning to his meal. Having survived years of working with nitroglycerine on the Central Pacific Railroad, Wei Han found it frustrating that he now had to deal with the human version of Black Powder; his volatile and explosive young nephew.

The crew was back to work under a scorching afternoon sun, when like a mirage through the heat waves, a beautiful young Chinese girl appeared on the levee and walked toward them. Pulling a hand cart behind her, she made her way along the embankment until she reached the sycamore tree where Parsons was again supervising from atop his horse. Once there, the girl removed a small folding table and chair from the cart and set them up at the base of the tree. She then spread a cloth and laid out lunch from a basket.

Wisely, the laborers continued their work, keeping their eyes averted. Or at least didn't let Parsons catch them if they stole a fleeting glance at the beautiful girl. With so few Chinese women in Gold Mountain, to see one as young and lovely as Hoi Yin was like a sip of cool water to men dying of thirst.

Yuen Shun, however, found it impossible not to gaze at her with intensity. This was not the first time he'd seen the beautiful Hoi Yin. Her parents worked as caretakers for Parsons and her family lived in a tiny one-room outbuilding near his large Victorian main house. Her father tended the livestock and did various odd jobs while her mother did the cooking and cleaning. Fifteen-year-old Hoi Yin and her younger brother performed a variety of chores for the bachelor landowner. Hoi Yin was never allowed in town, and Richard Parsons would not permit what would have undoubtedly been an endless line of suitors to come onto his property. Parsons himself had taken an unsavory interest in the teenage girl of late, giving her more and more tasks that required her to spend time with him alone.

Once his lunch was ready, Parsons made Hoi Yin stand and wait for several minutes before finally dismounting and permitting her to serve him while the men continued laboring nearby. Standing beside the table, she dutifully kept her head down and her eyes on the ground while Parsons ate his meal. But feeling the stare of the handsome Yuen Shun, Hoi Yin looked up, and as she did their eyes met. Witnessing this, Parsons flew into a rage and rose from the table, nearly knocking it over. "Make that stupid Chinaman quit gawking and get back to work or I'll can him," he screamed at Wei Han. "He's not to look at her ever! You understand?"

The foreman nodded and again sternly addressed his nephew in Cantonese. Yuen Shun reluctantly did as he was told, but Parsons continued to watch him like a hawk throughout the remainder of his meal. Once he'd finished eating, Hoi Yin packed up the cart and pulled it back along the levee in the direction of the farmhouse. While mounting his horse, Parsons was momentarily distracted, and Hoi Yin looked back to find Yuen Shun defiantly watching her. Their eyes met again and her heart skipped a beat.

With the levee crew done for the day and Parsons in the main house being served supper by her mother, Hoi Yin took advantage of a rare moment of freedom and walked out into the cool of the evening with an apron full of scraps for the chickens. As she stood in the pen feeding the hens happily clucking at her feet, she suddenly heard a loud turkey gobble. But there were no turkeys in this enclosure. She turned to find Yuen Shun peering around a tree trunk just outside the pen. He gestured for her to come to him. Looking around to make sure neither her parents nor Parsons were in sight, Hoi Yin shook the remaining scraps from her apron and stepped outside the pen. Yuen Shun reached for her hand and together they ran toward the levee bank.

The young couple began to steal away whenever possible. Sometimes they walked along the river in the evenings and Yuen Shun would gather wild flowers or pick berries for Hoi Yin. The beautiful young woman was the only person who would come to know the gentle, more humble side of Long Yuen Shun. Soon, they began to talk of running away together; to start a new life in San Francisco. They had no way of knowing, however, that their fate had already been sealed by the actions of two others.

Hoi Yin's father was a notorious gambler who'd gotten himself deeply in debt at several of the Chinese gambling parlors in the area. He was continually harassed and threatened by those attempting to collect on his outstanding loans. What little money the family made in the employ of Parsons was already spoken for before it even came to them. Her father's shameful habit had condemned them to a life of perpetual servitude to a heartless landowner. There seemed no way out of their hopeless situation, that is until Richard Parsons approached Hoi Yin's father with an unseemly proposal.

Upon her pending 16th birthday, Hoi Yin would take over the duties of her mother, becoming Parsons' primary house servant. She would also move out of her parents' small shack and come to live in the main house with the bachelor landowner. In return, Richard Parsons would pay off all of the father's outstanding gambling debts, as well as give the family a generous monthly stipend. The beautiful Hoi Yin would be her father's winning lottery ticket, and sadly, he took little or no time in accepting Parsons' sordid offer.

With her 16th birthday but a week away, Hoi Yin's father decided it was time to break the news of this deplorable agreement to his daughter. He feebly attempted to promote the arrangement as a positive opportunity for all, telling Hoi Yin she should feel honored to be chosen by such a wealthy and respected white landowner. But Hoi Yin was repulsed and devastated. How could her own father do this; sell her to Parsons as if she were no better than a hog? And though Hoi Yin's mother hated him for what he'd done, like her daughter, she had little or no say in this world, having herself been married off to her pathetic husband when she was only 15.

Hoi Yin's shock soon evolved to fury, and she lashed out at her father, chastising him for having plunged the family into destitution with his reckless gambling. She vowed that she would not allow herself to be the concubine servant to Parsons, for her heart belonged to Long Yuen Shun, and he would never stand by and let her be sold off like a piece of livestock. Incensed that his daughter dare confront him with the ugly truth, Hoi Yin's father flew into a rage, striking her repeatedly until her mother intervened. And though he wanted to beat her further for disrespecting him, he forced himself to stop. Not because he had remorse, but because he feared damaging the merchandise Parsons was so interested in securing.

Her spirit broken, Hoi Yin lay face down on her bed sobbing as her mother tried to comfort her. Unwavering in his decision to give his only daughter to a man with less than honorable intentions, her father sat down at the table and began composing a note.

Later that night, Hoi Yin's little brother hurried along the wooden sidewalks of Walnut Grove's Chinese quarter, carrying with him a lantern and a note. He was charged with delivering the written warning to Yuen Shun stating that he was never to see Hoi Yin again, for she was now the property of Richard Parsons.

After visiting several places where young Chinese laborers gathered and inquiring as to the whereabouts of Yuen Shun, the brother was directed to a gambling parlor down an alley at the rear of a boarding house. Approaching the first person he saw at a gaming table, who just so happened to be Wang Feng Ying, the boy asked him in Cantonese, "Do you know which one is Long Yuen Shun?"

"I might. Why?" replied the chubby con man.

"I'm to give him this."

"Let me see." Snatching the note from the boy, Feng Ying opened it. An evil smile soon spread across his face as he read the message contained within. Returning the paper to the boy, Feng Ying was all too happy to point out Yuen Shun at a back table. But as the little brother turned to go, the slimy con man stopped him and clumsily performed the age-old grandpa trick. "Got your nose!" he announced, his fat thumb wiggling between two fingers.

Holding forth his little fist and thumb in similar fashion, the young man delivered an insulting comeback in Cantonese.

Offended, the con man raised a hand as if to strike, but the boy ran to Yuen Shun, and after quickly delivering the note, he fled.

As Long Yuen Shun read the devastating words on the page, Wang Feng Ying began to laugh with cruel delight.

The thought of his beloved Hoi Yin being given to the hated Parsons ignited the deep-seated bitterness that lived within Yuen Shun. His famous temper was about to erupt. And there would be no stopping it this time. Enraged, he violently turned over the gaming table, causing an oil lamp to smash to the ground. Fire rapidly spread across the wood floor and the gambling house was quickly engulfed in flames. Patrons attempted to fight the blaze but were soon forced to retreat, overwhelmed by the intense smoke and flames.

Amidst the chaos, Yuen Shun walked out of the gambling parlor as if in a trance. He made his way to the small living quarters he shared with his aunt, uncle, and cousin. After retrieving an item from beneath his sleeping cot, he rousted the family from their beds, telling them to gather what they could in case the fire spread. As they scrambled to collect their belongings, Yuen Shun uncharacteristically hugged his aunt and cousin. He then made a fist with his right hand, and holding it in the palm of his left at chest level, he bowed respectfully to his uncle before disappearing into the night.

And the fire did spread, becoming an inferno that ravenously consumed the Chinese Quarter of Walnut Grove. Though the residents tried in vain to save their homes and businesses, in the end they were forced to flee with whatever possessions they could carry.

With the flames of the fire raging in the distance, Long Yuen Shun stood barefoot at the end of a pier—in his hands, *Luhng dik Gu-Sih*, the family Book of Dragon. Unbeknownst to Yuen Shun's father, his mother had secreted the book away, placing it in her 6-year-old son's arms as he boarded the ship bound for Gold Mountain. Over the years, Yuen Shun had read the book numerous times, and through it, came to understand the special power his family possessed; the power to call upon Gong Luhng in acts of retribution. He also understood that this extraordinary power came at a cost, for the one who calls upon the dragon must pay the ultimate price before vengeance can be exacted. Having started the blaze that was rapidly destroying the Chinese Quarter, and facing life without his beloved Hoi Yin, Long Yuen Shun had no reason to live.

Opening the Book of Dragon, he began to read the calling-forth incantation aloud in Cantonese, his voice strong and unwavering. He then closed the book and carefully placed it behind him before stepping onto a tall piling at the end of the pier. With his hands outstretched to the river, Yuen Shun shouted out the final phrase of the incantation, "Vengeance of the dragon shall be mine!"

A moment later, Gong Luhng rose out of the water before him. Showing no fear, Yuen Shun laughed with the insane delight of a madman. He then lowered his head in deference to the dragon and Gong Luhng took him with one powerful snap of its massive jaws.

By morning, there was nothing left of Walnut Grove's Chinese Section but the smoldering frames of buildings. A few women, children, and merchants picked through the remains of their town, salvaging what little they could find.

Exhausted and still covered in soot from fighting the flames, the levee crew, minus one, was once again laboring at the river's edge on Parsons' land. With their homes reduced to ash, there was nothing left to do but start over, and that would require money.

Driving a horse and buggy along the levee, Parsons approached—a tragic Hoi Yin at his side, a rifle across his lap. Reining the horse to a stop beside Wei Han, he angrily asked, "Where is he?! Where's Yuen Shun?"

"He would not be so foolish as to show his face here," Wei Han answered. "Not after what he has done."

"You better make sure he never comes around here again," warned Parsons. "If he does, I'll kill him."

Parsons whipped the horse and began to pull away, when out in the river, a great wave developed and pushed toward the levee. The crew stopped working and stared. As the tremendous wave reached the shore and crashed on the rocks, Gong Luhng rose up from behind it. Dropping their tools, the men scattered, running down from the levee into the field below. Parsons' horse spooked and reared in its harness as the landowner grabbed for his rifle and took aim. Somehow sensing the dragon was to be her savior, a guardian sent to deliver her from a cruel fate, Hoi Yin did not panic or scream.

After repeatedly pumping and firing several shots at the creature, which did nothing more than anger it, Parsons attempted to flee by whipping an already traumatized horse. In the pandemonium, Hoi Yin jumped from the carriage and ran down the levee as Gong Luhng closed in. Seizing the entire buggy in its mouth, the dragon lifted it off the ground, easily crushing it with its massive jaws. Suspended in the air, the horse struggled until it broke free of its harness. Falling into the river, it swam for shore. Parsons cried out, begging the men to help him as he dangled by one hand from the mangled carriage. But the laborers knew this was his fate, and none came to his aid. Unable to hold on, Parsons fell into the river. He too, tried to swim for the levee, but the dragon snatched him up in its powerful jaws and shook him like a rag doll. Parsons screamed in agony until finally, Gong Luhng swallowed him whole.

The creature then turned and stared down at the workers who stood frozen in the field. Stepping forward, Wei Han spoke to the great dragon in Cantonese. "Guardian of the river, you have defended the honor of your family and brought vengeance upon the enemy of Long Yuen Shun. Cease now. There are no enemies among these men."

The dragon surveyed the frightened workers below until its stormy black eyes found Hoi Yin standing among them. Fixated, it stared at her for a long moment, and the young woman returned its gaze, tears of gratitude glistening in her own eyes. Hoi Yin then respectfully lowered her head before Gong Luhng, and the dragon appeared to nod in return before slowly retreating into the river and disappearing.

Gong Luhng would now have to be contained. The levee crew went to work building the tomb to the exact specifications as detailed in The Book of Dragon left behind by Long Yuen Shun.

Working among the charred remains of his shop, a Chinese blacksmith melted down a collection of salvaged trinkets and treasures, even a few gold nuggets, in order to forge the large gold seal as depicted in the ancient book. Within a matter of days, the seal, as well as the tomb, were ready.

Embedded in a levee, the tomb was a massive log-lined chamber open to the river with three sturdy support rafters stretching across the top—one at each end and one in the middle. A solid wood gate hung suspended above the entrance, ready to be dropped into place like a guillotine. Two stacks of logs, each held back with three ropes, stood at the ready on either side of the watery trench. These would ultimately become the ceiling of the tomb. With all the elements in place there was only one thing left to do: bait the trap.

The obvious choice, Wang Feng Ying, soon dangled above the water-filled tomb in a crudely constructed cage and angrily shouted curses at the men who sat below on the levee, waiting. They didn't have to wait long. Wah Ming soon pointed out to the river and called to the others in Cantonese, "It's coming!"

As the men took cover behind the log piles, Gong Luhng rose up out of the water and stood at the opening of the chamber. Above in his cage, Feng Ying erupted in a spectacular fit of hysterics, which worked like a charm. Gong Luhng slipped under the first rafter and entered the watery trench in pursuit of the highly animated morsel dangling at the far end of the tomb.

Maneuvering under the middle rafter, the dragon was now fully inside the chamber and closing in on Feng Ying, who was now screaming like a little girl. As the dragon rose up out of the trench, about to snap its massive jaws around the cage, Wah Ming wielded a machete and severed the thick rope that held the gate suspended. The heavy piece fell into place with a mighty splash and the dragon spun 'round to attempt an escape, only to discover its exit had effectively been cut off. Trapped, Gong Luhng began to screech and thrash about in the watery trench.

The moment had come to complete the entombment and the men cut the ropes on both log piles, sending them powerfully tumbling over the rafters, encasing the tomb. They then quickly pushed mounds of earth over the logs as the muffled sounds of the dragon echoed from within.

Standing atop the earthen roof of the tomb, which was now a seamless part of the levee, Wei Han began reading the calling-off incantation from The Book of Dragon. With two men holding onto his legs, Wah Ming hung over the front of the gate in order to hammer the gold seal into place. The noises emanating from inside the tomb began to subside, barely audible over the blubbering of Feng Ying who was swinging back and forth in the cage above, whimpering like a baby. As the crew lowered the bamboo chamber containing the demoralized con man, they caught a whiff of something foul. Apparently, coming that close to being eaten by a dragon scared more than just the smugness out of Wang Feng Ying.

Soon, all was quiet in the tomb as Wei Han spoke the last line from The Book of Dragon. "That which has been awakened is now returned to sleep. Rest peacefully, defender of the Long family and guardian of the rivers, until you are once again called forth."

❧ CHAPTER 30 ❦

THAT WHICH HAS BEEN AWAKENED ...

"**W**hy didn't they just kill the thing?" asked Calvin.

Half an hour had slipped by while they sat listening to Tak tell the story of Yuen Shun, Hoi Yin, and the dragon who was now back among them.

"You cannot kill Gong Luhng," explained Tak. "You can only entomb it. The seal on the tomb ensures the dragon will rest peacefully until the next time it's called forth, or the seal is broken."

"Do you think someone ... perhaps a descendant of the family, has summoned the dragon?" Ray asked.

Tak shook his head no. "That line of the Long family was believed to have ended with Yuen Shun. And there's another reason I don't believe Gong Luhng was deliberately called forth."

Rising from the table, Tak walked into a small sunroom off the kitchen. With sleight-of-hand skill, he produced a key from some secret hiding place and used it to open an antique Chinese trunk that now served as a window seat. Removing a large flat object wrapped in red silk, he brought it to the kitchen table. Tak carefully folded back the cloth to reveal an extremely old book with an intricately carved wood cover. "This is *Luhng dik Gu-Sih*—the Long Family Book of Dragon."

Ray, Mei Li, and Calvin moved in to get a closer look at the detailed carvings on the cover, the most elaborate of which was a glimmering gold relief of Gong Luhng.

"After the self-sacrificial death of Yuen Shun, the book became my great grandfather's responsibility to guard," Tak informed them. "It's been passed down from generation to generation until it became mine. It's never left my possession."

Mei Li could not resist the urge to run her fingers over the ornate dragon, and as she did, Calvin thought for sure he saw the lights flicker. "Yeh-yeh, it's so beautiful. You should have it on display," she suggested.

"That would only be inviting trouble," replied Tak. "Remember, no one but our family was supposed to know anything about Gong Luhng *or* The Book of Dragon."

"Well, that cat's outta the bag," said Calvin. "And it's one nasty-ass cat."

"So if nobody but you knows about the book," said Ray, "that means the seal's been broken."

"Yes. Either deliberately or accidentally," confirmed Tak.

"And now this thing's on the loose, attacking at random," Ray furthered.

"I'm afraid so," replied Tak. "The reason it's killing indiscriminately is because it has no clear marching orders or directive."

"So why didn't it attack us when it had the chance?" Calvin asked.

"Because my granddaughter's related to the Long family by marriage."

"Lucky for her the dragon recognizes extended family members," said Ray. Turning to Calvin he added, "And lucky for you she was there."

Calvin gave Mei Li a sideways glance. "You're related to a dragon."

"Apparently," she replied with a shrug.

Calvin was trying to decide whether this new development was a turn-off or a turn-on when Mei Li opened the ancient book without hesitation, causing him to flinch. "Hey be careful with that thing," he warned, waiting for some Harry Potter shit to go down. Though none did, Calvin wasn't entirely convinced it wouldn't. "Just don't unleash something else, a'ight?"

Ignoring him, Mei Li carefully leafed through the rice paper pages, each one filled with beautifully handwritten Chinese characters. Though she could speak fairly good Cantonese, Mei Li had yet to master the elaborate sinography of written Chinese. "Yeh-yeh, what does this say right here?"

Tak looked at the Chinese characters she was pointing to and read them aloud. "That which has been awakened, must be returned to sleep."

"So how many Scooby snacks does this thing need before it's ready for nap time again?" asked Calvin.

"Unfortunately it's not about feeding. Keep in mind, the dragon itself is not evil. Gong Luhng is considered the guardian of rivers and defender of its people. However, lacking a specific adversary upon which to exact retribution, I'm afraid this could go on indefinitely." Tak paused then hesitantly added, "Unless of course ..."

"Unless of course, what?" Ray reluctantly asked.

"Unless we can re-entomb it."

"You're swiffin, right?" said Calvin.

"I'm almost certain I'm not," replied Tak, who then turned to Ray. "Sergeant, your thoughts?"

Ray took a moment before responding. Actually, he was waiting to see if a television crew was going to pop out from behind a door and tell him he'd been "punked." But no camera crew materialized and everyone was waiting to see what the person in charge of law enforcement had to say about the whole re-entombment concept. "Alright, I'll bite. Suppose I take a huge leap in suspended disbelief and say, 'Okay, we'll just re-entomb it.' How *exactly* would we do that?"

"Well, the easiest course would be to find the seal, then find the original tomb, make sure it's in good condition and lure the dragon back into it."

"Did you really just say, 'easiest course'?" asked Calvin.

Tak was about to expound on this idea when his granddaughter interrupted. "I wanna know what happened to Hoi Yin."

"Ah, sweet Hoi Yin. Well, since her father was afraid she and Yuen Shun would try to run away together, he quickly finalized his deal with Parsons the morning after the fire. With his extensive gambling debts paid off, her father fled the area with the first monthly stipend, essentially placing his only daughter into slavery and abandoning his wife and son."

"What a piece o'...," declared Calvin.

"Agreed," said Tak. "But in the end, they were all better off without him. And *everyone* was better off without Richard Parsons. Those who'd witnessed the landowner's demise and helped entomb Gong Luhng, made a pact to pretend as if Parsons was still alive. They divided his property equally among them, farming and managing it like a secret co-op. Great-grandfather Cheng handled all the business transactions. If anyone came looking for Parsons, Wei Han simply told them he was back East attending to business matters. Richard Parsons wasn't someone anyone in the Delta would miss. And even though the loss of Walnut Grove's Chinese section was tragic, it inspired a group of Zhongshan merchants to lease land from a man named George Locke and build their own town. This town."

"But did Hoi Yin ever fall in love again?" asked Mei Li.

"No, she never did. Long Yuen Shun was her one and only true love. It was said that she could often be seen throwing wild flowers into the river from the pier where Yuen Shun met his fate. I knew her as a middle-aged lady, living in a little house on her share of Parsons' land. Chinese people couldn't legally own land in California until 1952 when the Alien Land Laws were finally overturned. Sadly, Hoi Yin died at the age of 54 before ever getting her name on the deed to her parcel of land."

"Her story is just so ... tragic," said Mei Li.

"Yes, but her life could have been so much worse had Yuen Shun not done what he did in summoning the dragon," replied Tak.

"Which brings us back to our current predicament," said Ray. "By any chance does The Book of Dragon give the exact location of the tomb?"

"Unfortunately, no. The book was written several centuries ago and contains only the Long family history and the ritual incantations for calling forth and calling off the dragon. The details of Gong Luhng's incarnation in the Delta were intentionally passed down as oral history only. The men who last entombed the dragon swore never to reveal where it slept."

"Of course they did," said Ray.

"But you said the tomb was embedded in a levee on Parsons' land," said Calvin, "which became your family's land, right?"

"Our farm is only a fraction of what Parsons owned back then. Before he was killed, Richard Parsons had amassed several tracts of Delta land, which translates to literally hundreds of acres."

"That's a lot of territory to cover," said Ray. "I held off 'til now, but maybe it's time to bring some other agencies in on this."

"Do what you feel you must, Sergeant Cruz," said Tak, "but I would recommend that you think very carefully before calling in the cavalry. With no tangible evidence they can relate to, they'll probably think you've lost your mind. Might even relieve you of your post. And ...," he added, "bringing more people to the Delta right now, would simply be bringing more bait."

Ray heaved a heavy sigh. "I'll take that under advisement. But at the end of the day, it's my responsibility to ensure public safety."

"Yes, but you also don't want to incite mass hysteria," replied Tak.

This concept of mass hysteria in the Delta gave Calvin something to think about. Part of him wanted to stay and see how it all played out, even with this new development about Mei Li being cousins with a scaly murderous dragon. Yet another part of him hoped Ray would call in the cavalry and possibly ignite a media frenzy that would have him on a Greyhound back to Oakland the second his mom got wind of it.

The crackly voice of Gladys the dispatcher suddenly broke in over Ray's radio. Apparently a kayaker had gone missing, and though it was still too early to file a missing persons report, Gladys decided to pass this latest development onto Ray just the same.

"Guy's wife said he put in at Cork's Marina at dawn," Gladys informed him over the radio. "And he's usually home by 10 a.m. at the latest."

It was now 2 p.m. and the kayaker's wife was worried. As well she should be.

❧ CHAPTER 31 ❧

LOST AND FOUND

Determined not to turn tail and run like little girls, Terry and Neal decided they wouldn't completely pull the plug on their Delta vacation, but rather limit their fishing to the safety of shore. Once Ray gave them the "all clear" they'd put the *Nice Piece o' Bass* back in the water and resume their fishing trip as planned.

Seated in folding chairs with lines in the water and beers in hand, the anglers were making the best of the afternoon by fishing from a dock a few miles up river from their RV site.

"So we're not out in the boat," said Neal, "this is still good."

"Oh, hell yeah," agreed Terry. "Not gonna let some freaky shit ruin our fishing trip."

Behind them, the headless kayaker drifted up against the dock with a dull thud.

❧ CHAPTER 32 ❧

THE CAVALRY

No one knew for sure exactly how old Gladys Couch was, but apparently retirement was not a concept she was familiar with. Her primary duties at the Sheriff's Office consisted of answering phones, manning the radio, consuming an unprecedented amount of baked goods, and keeping everyone abreast of the most implausible stories printed in the tabloids. Oh, and quashing any and all accusations of ageism against the Office of Sheriffs.

With Tak's permission, Ray brought The Book of Dragon back to the office where he scanned the ancient illustration of the gold seal; the prototype for the one likely removed from Gong Luhng's tomb. Luckily, he still had Mei Li and Calvin in tow so put them to work creating a flyer, giving them specific (though intentionally vague) wording to go along with the image. "Historical Chinese artifact missing from private collection. Anyone with information regarding this piece should contact the local Sheriff's Office."

Technically, Ray should have put Gladys on the flyer project, but like Burt, Ray'd inherited the senior citizen along with his sergeant's position, and her computer proficiency was about as sharp as Burt's law enforcement skills.

Ray'd been mulling over what Tak said with regard to calling in other agencies. But as he looked around his office, the choice seemed obvious. His dispatcher was eating a jelly donut while reading the *National Enquirer*, his deputy was struggling to tear into a fresh nicotine patch, and two teenage civilians were performing the bulk of the work. Ray stepped into his office, closed the door behind him, and picked up the phone. His first call was to his commanding officer at the state level.

Out in the main office, an outside call came in and Gladys put down her tabloid, barely managing to get her headset on to answer before it rolled to the message center.

"Sheriff's Office, Gladys speaking." After that, there was a series of "Uh-huh's" along with some note-taking until she signed off with, "Alright, we'll handle it from here. Thanks for the call." Removing her headset, she announced, "Looks like that missing kayaker's been found."

"Well, that's good news," said Mei Li, hoping it was.

"Not exactly," replied Gladys.

Ten minutes had passed and Ray was still barricaded in his office, about to place his third, and decidedly *last* phone call, especially when considering the way the two previous ones had gone.

During the first call, Ray's commanding officer at the Head Office laughed so hard he had to put the phone down in order to wipe tears from his eyes. The more Ray insisted he was not "pulling his leg," the harder his boss laughed. Upon picking up the receiver again, his commanding officer had to confess; Ray really had him going for a minute there, especially since he never pegged the sergeant for a practical joker. And before hanging up, Ray's boss thanked him profusely for making his day—he hadn't laughed that hard in years.

His second call, to the head of the Coast Guard Station Rio Vista, had gone even worse. Ray knew it wouldn't be easy convincing the stern female commanding officer in charge that there really was a dragon on the loose in the Delta. But when she suggested he might consider putting in for "personal time" to enter a drug and alcohol program, he immediately passed the whole thing off as a prank and promptly hung up.

Running out of options, Ray decided his third and final call needed to be to the governor. Since Burt was somehow related to the man, he could bring the deputy in to corroborate his story—and vouch for his sobriety if need be. Ray felt a glimmer of hope when his call was swiftly put through to the governor, perhaps he would finally be getting the cooperation he urgently needed.

The governor listened intently while Ray detailed the events as they'd unfolded, beginning with the couple from Las Vegas and leading up to the most recent incident on Buzzard Island.

"So that's the situation," said Ray. "Believe me, I know how crazy this sounds, but the fact is, people are being killed by a dragon in the waters of the Delta."

There was a moment of silence as the governor digested this implausible scenario. "Have you seen this thing for yourself, Ray?" he asked.

"No sir, I haven't, but we have several eyewitnesses who have."

"The kids who were under the influence at the party."

"There was moderate drinking, yes," admitted Ray, "but the witnesses all gave identical descriptions of the dragon."

"I see. Ah, Ray, can you hold on a second?" This was followed by the familiar click of a call being switched to speaker phone. "Sorry about that, Sergeant Cruz. Now, tell me again what it is you believe is viciously killing people in the Delta."

"As I explained, it's a very large water dragon."

"From a Chinese legend," the governor clarified.

Ray could hear snickering in the background. Apparently, a couple cronies from the governor's staff had been invited in to eavesdrop. His last glimmer of hope suddenly began to fade.

"Now is that anything like the Loch Ness monster?" the governor inquired with thinly veiled sarcasm.

"No," Ray emphatically denied, which only made him sound desperate. "Unlike the Loch Ness monster, we have victims. Not to mention witnesses who can testify to the existence of this thing."

"You know, they've got a picture of that Loch Ness monster. Do you have a picture of this thing?"

"No sir, I don't. Like I said, I've just got eye witnesses along with a growing body count. Sir, I understand that you and Deputy Burt Watson are related. If you don't believe me, why don't you let me put Burt on the line and he can validate what's going on here and what we're up against."

"No need to put Burt on the line, sergeant. There's a reason I stuck him down there with you. I'd heard good things and was hoping perhaps you'd have some influence on him. But judging from this conversation, I'd say it's the other way 'round."

The comment elicited more snickers from the governor's cronies.

"Look, all I'm asking for is some additional backup, maybe some National Guard troops, just until we know for sure what we're dealing with."

"Tell ya what, sergeant, you just keep an eye on the situation and keep me posted. And hey, if ya get a picture of that dragon, you've got my number."

And just like that, Ray's final hope phone call ended with a click, then a moment of dead air followed shortly thereafter by a rapidly pulsing busy signal.

So that was it, he was officially on his own.

As he hung up the receiver, Ray tried to convince himself he was relieved. Now he wouldn't have to deal with the bureaucratic bullshit that would have undoubtedly ensued had multiple agencies gotten involved. Then he began to wonder just how long it would be before they sent someone to evaluate his competency. Hopefully when they showed up, there'd be a giant dragon here to greet them. Ray was suddenly wishing he'd listened to Tak and not attempted to solicit outside help at this point. But too late now. And until the men in white coats came to take him away, the burden of keeping the local population safe rested squarely on his shoulders.

Accepting his Lone Lawman position, Ray went back to work. As he exited his office he noticed Burt was preparing to head out on a call while Mei Li and Calvin looked as though they'd seen a ghost. Holding up a red pushpin, Gladys walked past him to a large Delta wall map that already had seven pushpins stuck in it.

"What's that for?" he asked hesitantly.

"That missing kayaker," she replied matter-of-factly. "Turned up right here," she added, jamming the pin into the map. "Body was still in the kayak, but his head's MIA."

The color had drained from Mei Li's face and it looked as though the hangover she'd finally managed to vanquish was making a come back.

"Who found him?" Ray asked.

"Same unlucky bastards who found the broad from Las Vegas," Gladys replied.

"Terry and Neal?" he guessed.

"Yep," confirmed Burt. "I'm about to head over there now. Already called the coroner for a pickup. I'm not personally delivering any more dismembered bodies."

Turning to Ray, Gladys pointedly inquired, "I take it your phone calls didn't go so well."

"How'd you know?"

"Wasn't born yesterday, ya know."

And though everyone wanted to say, "Yeah, we know!" they all kept their mouths shut.

Ray hung his head and fessed up, "I basically made a fool of myself on every level of law enforcement—local, state, and federal."

"Coast Guard?" asked Gladys.

"Suggested I take some personal time and check myself into rehab. Which is looking kinda good right now."

"What about my cousin? Did you try him?" asked Burt.

"I did. He wants an eight-by-ten glossy of the dragon before he'll get on board."

"He's a prick," said Burt. "Always was."

"I don't know why people are having such a hard time with this," declared Gladys. Now back at her desk, she held up a copy of the *Weekly World News*—her version of a PowerPoint presentation. "Says right here they got a forty-foot squid living in the sewers of London."

"So now what?" asked Calvin, his hopes of heading back to Oakland on the next Greyhound rapidly evaporating.

"Well, until we have some hard evidence to prove this thing exists," replied Ray, "we're basically on our own."

Trying to regain her composure, Mei Li stood by the water cooler taking small sips from a paper cup while studying the wall map. "So the first attack happened in Desperation Slough," she observed. "But the fisherman was found at the ferry crossing and Huestus was found at Heron's Harbor."

Ray joined her at the map and pointed to one of the pins. "Huestus drove off the levee here, at the western edge of Desperation Slough."

"And Buzzard Island is at the eastern edge," offered Mei Li.

"That fisherman was in a floating tube," Calvin pointed out as he too came to stand before the large map. "So he could've been attacked there then drifted with the tide. Same with the kayaker."

"Exactly," agreed Ray. Under normal circumstances, he would never discuss crime scene details with Calvin and Mei Li, but they were already in deep and there really wasn't any "normal" left to cling to.

"And the kayaker was attacked after dawn," added Calvin. "So your theory about it only happening at night just got trampled."

"I realize that," replied Ray. "I seriously need to figure out a way to keep people away from the water but without causing mass hysteria."

As they stared at the map, behind them Gladys loudly exclaimed, "Shit!" When they all turned around to see what the problem was, she elaborated. "Poop. People don't like to swim, ski, fish, or put their boats in crap. So, start a rumor there's a sewage leak somewhere up river of Desperation Slough. Maybe one of those large pipelines that runs along the levee sprang a leak. Could happen. That oughta keep 'em away from the water for a while."

"That's brilliant," said Ray.

"And it won't freak people out as much," added Mei Li.

"Oh, it'll freak 'em out alright, just in a more manageable way," replied Gladys.

"It's perfect. Gladys, crank up the rumor mill," ordered Ray.

"I can do it with one phone call to my friend Darla," the feisty senior declared before taking a healthy bite out of her bear claw. "Half an hour from now," she added, sharing a mouthful of masticated pastry, "pretty much everyone in the Delta will have heard about it—especially if I tell old blabbermouth not to say anything."

"And after that, I need you to call a meeting at Heron's Harbor for this afternoon," instructed Ray. "I only want those who know the real situation to be there. We need to keep this circle extremely tight for the moment."

"Gotcha."

"Burt, I want you to drop Mei Li and Calvin back at Heron's Harbor en route to the location where the kayaker was found," Ray directed as he prepared to head out himself. "I need you to secure that scene and keep people away from the water. Use the raw sewage story if necessary. I'm counting on you."

"But ... what about you?" asked Burt, obviously nervous at finally being entrusted to handle something big on his own.

"I'll be out in the patrol boat looking for the tomb."

"Wait a minute," said Calvin, "I thought we just agreed nobody goes near the water."

"We have to find two very important things: the seal and the tomb. I'm a peace officer, it's my job to risk my own safety for the safety of others. And I can cover a lot more ground in the boat."

"Yeah? And if anything happens to you, *then* who's in charge?" asked Calvin, rolling his eyes toward Burt, who was fumbling to secure his gun belt.

"Don't worry, nothing's going to happen to me," Ray assured him. Heading out the door, the sergeant turned back. "Thanks for all the good work, you guys, I really appreciate it." Which in spite of what he'd just said a moment ago, sounded suspiciously like someone who knew there was a possibility he might not be coming back.

❧ CHAPTER 33 ❧

KING OF THE CASTLE

Ray had to laugh. While Gladys might not be worth a crap when it came to modern technology, her idea about the sewage spill rumor was sheer genius. It seemed like there were already fewer vessels out on the water, and though the sheriff in him seriously wanted to chase off the occasional boater he did encounter, Ray resisted. The governor, as well as the head of the Coast Guard already thought he was a head case; he didn't need any civilian reports bolstering that opinion.

Since Desperation Slough stood out as the dragon's preferred hunting grounds, that was exactly where Ray was headed. He figured the tomb must be located somewhere in the clandestine slough. Seemed Gong Luhng was hanging out there, killing time and killing people while it waited for an assignment with regard to exacting revenge in the name of the Long family.

Arriving at the mouth of the slough, Ray slowed down and scanned the waters for any sign of the suspect. With no indication that the dragon was lurking in the immediate vicinity, he began a methodical search of the area. At the moment, Ray was especially grateful that Desperation Slough wasn't widely known to outsiders. Year after year, the coveted spot went intentionally unmarked on Delta maps as a favor to the locals. If a murderous dragon absolutely had to materialize in the Delta, from a law enforcement standpoint, this was the best possible scenario in terms of limiting prey, and therefore, body count.

Cutting away from the main artery of the slough, Ray cruised into the channel of Bedroom One where the rental houseboat, *Delta Destiny*, was anchored nose-in to the tule island. With no one on board and the *Money Talks* gone, Ray got the feeling the group was simply spending the day wakeboarding someplace else—hadn't become the dragon's latest victims.

Continuing on, he scoured the waters, and more specifically the shoreline along the levees, searching for anything that looked remotely like the tomb as Tak had described it. He'd certainly patrolled this area plenty over the last two years, so how was it that something big enough to contain a dragon could have gone unnoticed? The Chinese levee crew who build it must have done something ingenious to disguise it, Ray reasoned. And something had to have changed recently to unearth it. But what? There hadn't been any dramatic levee failures of late. So maybe it wasn't anything dramatic at all. Perhaps it was simply a matter of time and the elements chipping away at whatever had been put in place to hide the tomb.

It was common knowledge that the levees of the Delta had been steadily eroding away for years, placing not only the region but the entire state in an extremely precarious position. What to do about the situation was endlessly under debate by farmers, lawmakers, environmentalists, and fishermen—anyone and everyone who depended on the waters of the Delta. It was pathetic really, how few Californians even knew where the Delta was, or how screwed they'd be without it. But it seemed everyone wanted its water, regardless of the cost to the resource itself.

As Ray neared a rare stretch of beach that bordered Preacher's Tract, he spotted something that equally irked him: a considerable amount of trash left behind by people partying there. He secretly hoped that the dragon had eaten whoever left their garbage strewn all over the beach. But more than just trash, Ray soon spotted several large logs the size of telephone poles scattered along the shore and floating at the water's edge. He assumed a lumber barge must have lost part of its load out in the main channel, until he realized the logs were extremely old and appeared to be hand-hewn. Up ahead and just beyond the beach, his eyes found the ruins of an old bridge that had once spanned this part of the slough. He'd seen the weathered abutment countless times. This time, however, something was different. Cruising closer, Ray realized the front wall was gone—he was looking straight into a massive log-lined trench built into the levee.

"Of course," he said out loud.

After imbedding the tomb in the levee, the Chinese laborers had disguised it by building a bridge right over it. The roof of the chamber seemed to have collapsed, or was perhaps damaged by the dragon as it came back to life. Otherwise, the interior structure was in surprisingly good condition. It appeared to be built out of old-growth redwood, making it impervious to practically any environmental challenge.

Equally old and weathered, a second abutment stood directly across the way and was still intact. A dragon hadn't recently burst out of that one, and hopefully never would. The bridge's over-crossing was likely built out of a lesser material and had therefore disintegrated, falling into the slough years ago, leaving only the timeworn support structures as sentinels. How many times had Ray cruised past these weathered abutments and never given them a second thought.

The levee bordering this side of Preacher's Tract was built unusually wide to accommodate the tomb, which was roughly seventy feet deep and thirty feet wide. An old pear orchard now occupied the farmland that lay behind it. Currently up for sale, it would likely be replaced with vineyards, since the new agricultural landscape of the Delta was steadily turning over to America's favorite fruit juice: wine.

It suddenly struck Ray as funny that there was a time, back before the bridge collapsed, when farm vehicles drove right over a sleeping Gong Luhng. And until just recently, boaters cruised past the tomb's entrance, oblivious to the fact that a dragon slept within.

Calvin, Mei Li, Jess, Lauren, Samuel, Ol' Joe, Terry, Neal, Tak, and Burt all filed in, taking over the café once the meager lunch crowd cleared out. The rumor mill had definitely put a damper on business and Frances found herself serving the gang the bulk of what she'd prepared for that day's paying customers. At least it kept her busy; knowing Ray was out patrolling the waters of Desperation Slough had put her on edge. When he finally came sweeping through the front door, she had to keep herself in check and not run over to throw her arms around him. But when he looked right at her and winked, she practically melted. This exchange did not go unnoticed by Jess, who was genuinely glad to see his mom acting happy again, even in the midst of all this craziness.

"First the good news," announced Ray, as he came to stand at the counter to address the troops. "I've located the tomb."

"Where?" Tak excitedly asked. "Were you right, is it in Desperation Slough?"

"I don't suppose you remember an old wooden bridge that used to span from Preacher's Tract to Blackberry Island?" Ray asked him.

"That thing was already history when I was a kid," replied Tak. "We used to play King of the Castle on what was left of the Preacher's Tract side."

"Really. Did you ever pretend there was a dragon in your castle?"

Tak's mouth dropped open, causing Calvin and a few others to laugh.

"Apparently your great-grandfather and company decided to use the tomb as an abutment, then built the bridge right over it."

"Hidden in plain sight," said Tak. "Ingenious."

"So, that's the good news," Ol' Joe piped up. "Let's have it, what's the bad news?"

"We have to somehow lure the dragon back into it," Ray stated unapologetically.

"That's what I was afraid you were gonna say," grumbled Joe.

"How the hell are we gonna do that?!" asked Samuel with a mouthful of potato salad.

"I'm working on that," replied Ray, "but before we even start down that path, we have to first find the seal."

"Talk about your high-stakes scavenger hunt," said Jess.

"What's the prize?" asked Neal.

"We get to live," quipped Calvin.

"Sounds good to me," said Terry.

"Looks like there was a false front on the tomb's gate. Once it eroded away, the seal was exposed and ripe for the taking," said Ray. "Hopefully, whoever took it is still in the area and has it in their possession."

"Not if they figured out it's *not* brass," warned Tak.

"Don't tell me that thing's solid gold," said Frances.

"No, but it's certainly got enough in it to be valuable," replied Tak.

"That's why I've got Gladys checking with pawn shops in the surrounding cities," said Ray.

"What if we can't find it?" asked Burt. "Can't we just make a new one?"

"Possible but not practical," said Tak. "According to The Book of Dragon ..."

"The book of what?!" asked Terry.

"Dragon," Ray, Calvin, and Mei Li simultaneously replied.

"According to the book, the seal must be forged at the hands of a Chinese craftsman," Tak dutifully explained. Upon realizing everyone was staring at him, he clarified. "A Chinese blacksmith, to be precise. I'm the herb guy, remember? You need Dong Quai, no problem. Seal of Dragon—sorry, gotta send out."

"That's why I'm hoping we can find this thing," said Ray, holding up a flyer. "And we need to do it quickly without inciting widespread panic in the process. With minimal restoration, the tomb should be ready in a day or so. I've rented a BobCat but I could use some additional manpower since Burt has to stay on duty."

"Neal and I used to work some construction gigs back in the day," offered Terry.

"I guess we could help," said Neal with hesitation. "As long as we don't have to go in the water."

"No," Ray assured him. "Nobody goes anywhere near the water. Understood?" Good," he said, off their fervent nods. "Now, I need the rest of you out distributing flyers and asking around."

And with that, the members of this new and disturbing version of Delta Force filed up to receive their stack of flyers and an assigned area to cover. The last in line, Frances reached to take a stack of the one-sheets, but Ray grabbed her hand. "Everyone but you."

"What? Why?!" she demanded.

"Because Heron's Harbor is gossip central, and I need you here keeping your finger on the pulse and acting like everything is normal."

"Normal," she stated. "Really?"

As if that were somehow possible.

❧ CHAPTER 34 ❧

SEALED WITH A ...

Jack the Shack Man knew things about the Delta no one else did: backwater sloughs where catfish the size of bowling pins could be caught by hand, the exact location of sunken cabin cruisers that could still be harvested for supplies, and countless other hidden gems that only someone who lived as he did could know.

So when Ol' Joe saw the hermit making a rare appearance in town, he believed he'd hit pay dirt. Hell, it wasn't out the question for Jack to have discovered the seal himself and taken it for a scavenger's trophy. The thing might even be stashed away in his shack right now, being used as a trivet or some such nonsense.

Jack was busy feeding aluminum cans into an automated recycling center in a parking lot when Ol' Joe cornered him.

"This mean anything to you?" Joe accusingly asked while holding up a flyer.

The scruffy hermit glanced at the image of the Chinese seal and shook his head.

"You absolutely sure 'bout that?"

A man of few words, Jack had already said "no" in his own way and ignoring Ol' Joe, he moved on to the business of depositing his stockpile of plastic bottles.

"Well, that's a shame, 'cause there's a prize for whoever finds this thing and turns it into the sheriff," announced Joe.

But Jack was already bored with the old river rat's blathering. Or at least he was until Ol' Joe unwittingly spoke the words that piqued his interest. "It's like a big scavenger hunt, see."

Being that Jack was the ultimate scavenger, participating in a large-scale scavenger hunt was tantamount to competing in the Dumpster-Diving Olympics. "What do I get?" he asked, suddenly engaged.

"You mean if you find it? Well ..." Ol' Joe took a moment to think. He knew money didn't hold all that much value for Jack. Rumor had it he'd once been a big muckety-muck on Wall Street, suffered a meltdown, and walked away from it all. Then again, it was also rumored that he'd been a famous sportscaster, a disgraced evangelical minister, and a male model. Whatever his former life, Jack had been living in a falling-down shack on a tiny Delta island for several years now. He lived off the land, scavenging supplies as needed and cashing in on people's laziness to recycle. So what would be a coveted prize in Jack's world?

"A can o' pork and beans," Joe said at last. Realizing the hermit was not fully on board yet, Joe upped the ante. "The really big CostCo-size can."

And that was all it took. Snatching the flyer from Ol' Joe, Jack nodded and declared, "I will find this. And I will win."

With that, Jack the Shack Man joined in the search for the ancient Chinese seal.

Calvin and Mei Li were assigned to cover the small nearby town of Isleton and were expected to keep at it until they ran out of flyers or until Burt came back to pick them up.

It was shaping up to be another brutally hot afternoon and Calvin was steadily losing steam for a scavenger hunt he seriously doubted would yield any results. Hot and annoyed, he sat down on a curb in the shade. Behind him, the double doors of a bar were propped open allowing the cool air conditioning to wastefully spill out onto the street, some of it reaching his sweat-drenched back. Inside, a group of bikers were shooting pool and drinking cold beer, blissfully unaware that a dragon was terrorizing the Delta. As Calvin stared at their motorcycles parked across the street, he wished he could simply jump on one and make for Oakland.

He began trying to convince himself these feelings for Mei Li were simply a fluke; natural response to being isolated from his own pack and the girls back home. Probably best if he snuffed it out in the early stages and didn't start anything. He was only here for the summer anyway, and it would be way too complicated with the different hometowns, different cultures ... different everything. Not to mention the whole related-to-a-dragon thing.

"What the hell?!" scolded Mei Li upon discovering him slacking off and daydreaming on the curb.

And then there was her bossy side.

"Seriously?" he replied. "You really think we stand a chance of finding this thing? Damn needle in a hay stack."

"Well, we're definitely not going to find it sitting on our asses."

"Here," he said holding forth his remaining flyers. "You go ahead and hand out the rest of these. I'm hot, I'm tired, and I'm done."

"So that's it? You're just giving up."

"Might as well pack it in and get the hell outta Dodge. But you can keep lookin' as long as you like. Thing ain't gonna eat you anyway."

Fed up, Mei Li shook her head and walked away from him down the sidewalk. But Calvin didn't even notice. His focus had suddenly been drawn to a blinding light bouncing off something across the way. As he stood and went to investigate, Mei Li stormed back to let him have it.

"You know what?" she yelled at his back as he walked across the street to where seven motorcycles were parked. "I'm done too," she declared. "I'm done with your whole bullshit attitude."

While Mei Li continued to berate him from the sidewalk, Calvin got down on his haunches beside one of the bikes and reached out to touch ... the seal.

Lashed to the extended forks of a chopper with leather cord, the gleaming gold seal made for an especially gaudy motorcycle accessory.

"You wanna give up?" Mei Li yelled. "Fine. I don't need you. *We* don't need you. In fact, why don't you just go back to the hood where the only thing you have to worry about is your own sorry ass."

Taking out his pocketknife, Calvin began cutting away the leather cord while Mei Li continued her tirade, only now she was coming across the street to drive home her point at point blank range. "You know what you are?!"

At that very moment, Calvin stood and held forth the seal. Mei Li's mouth dropped open with a gasp. "You're … amazing," she uttered, then threw her arms around his neck. "Oh my God, you did it. You found it!"

Laughing, Calvin lifted her off the ground and whirled her around. The next thing they knew, they were kissing. And they probably would have continued making out for a good long while had it not been for the audience of seven angry bikers who'd materialized with pool cues in hand.

"What the fuck?" said Suicide, who was flanked by Crow, Panhead, Maggot, Skull, Mongrel, and Crank—altar boys, one and all.

"Bounce!" directed Calvin, and grabbing Mei Li's hand, they took off running down the main street of town with bikers in hot pursuit. Miraculously, the sheriff's patrol car pulled around the corner in the next block. Calvin waved and whistled for a rescue while holding up the gold seal. "Yo, Burt!"

Grasping the situation, Burt stopped the car and stepped out with his gun drawn, a fresh Louie-Bloo Raspberry Otter Pop dangling from his mouth. As Calvin and Mei Li took cover behind the patrol car, the middle-aged bikers came to a halt just yards in front of Burt. And though winded, they were more than ready for a confrontation.

"Fucker stole that off my bike," said Suicide, pointing at Calvin, "and I want it back."

When Burt didn't immediately respond, Calvin and Mei Li thought for sure he was choking under the pressure, would maybe even pass out. But that was not the case this time. No, this was the Clint Eastwood scenario Burt had played out in his mind countless times, had waited his entire life for, in fact. Deputy Burt Watson was simply savoring the moment.

Standing his ground with service pistol squarely trained on the bikers, Burt reached up to remove the Otter Pop from his mouth, and turning ever so slightly, he spat a perfect blue stream onto the ground. "The way I see it," he stated, cool and collected, "this young man simply recovered a piece of stolen property."

"Stolen my ass. I found that. It's mine and I want it back," countered Suicide, who took a step closer and the other Posse members followed.

But Burt didn't even flinch. "You boys might wanna reconsider," he said calmly. "See, I'm trying to quit smoking' right now, and well, that makes me more than a little edgy. Downright jumpy, if ya know what I mean."

The bikers looked at one another. Was this guy for real?

"Any o' you boys ever tried quittin'..." Burt continued, "then you know what I'm talkin' about. Makes ya just wanna up an' kill somebody."

After another tense moment (and much to the surprise of the other bikers) it was Suicide who backed down. He'd tried quitting again on his 45th birthday and nearly lost his mind. And what he wanted more than anything at this moment, was a cigarette. That, and the fresh pitcher of beer and combo pizza they'd just ordered back at the bar. The middle-aged biker had zero interest in going back to the slammer. Hell, maybe he wasn't all that attached to the big gold circle with the dragon on it after all. Raising his hands, Suicide began slowly backing away. Dumbfounded, the rest of the gang quickly followed suit.

Returning the melty blue pop to his mouth, Burt talked around it. "That's right. Nice an' easy and nobody gets run through the system." He then turned and told Calvin and Mei Li to "Get in. We've got a seal to deliver."

After walking backwards halfway down the block, the Posse members turned and headed for the bar. Maggot slapped 'Cide on the back. "You didn't want that thing on your bike anyway. Looked totally gay."

Suicide expressed his thoughts on the matter by breaking his pool cue across Maggot's lower spine.

❦ CHAPTER 35 ❦

SEEING IS BELIEVING

In spite of the mysterious events unfolding, Lou and Gloria decided to stay in the Delta, remaining aboard the *Life's Short*. Though Frances tried her best to persuade them to temporarily forsake their yacht in favor of her guest room, true to their independent nature, they steadfastly refused. Setting a course for Desperation Slough, the couple had departed the guest dock the morning after a hunk of Huestus showed up in a crawdad trap. Fearful was one thing they were not. They were, however, completely unaware of the latest developments, including the carnage on Buzzard Island and the revelation that the perpetrator was, in fact, a dragon. A dragon who was stalking the waterways of their favorite slough.

Knowing the Markhams were anchored out in Desperation Slough, Jess and Frances had been frantically trying to reach them by cell phone and marine radio. With no answer, they were beginning to worry. They had no way of knowing that Lou and Gloria were simply taking advantage of being the only ones anchored at Bedroom Two and were enjoying their extensive jazz music library cranked up on the yacht's killer sound system. Any and all attempts to contact them were easily drowned out by the likes of John Coltrane, Miles Davis, and Thelonious Monk.

It was day two of the sewage spill rumor and business at the Heron's Harbor gas dock was virtually nonexistent. By late afternoon, Jess was done with sitting around and decided to take matters into his own hands. The Markhams were like another set of grandparents to him, and the only way to make sure they were okay was to go and get them. Despite the determined attempts by Lauren and Mei Li to dissuade him, Jess was preparing to head for Desperation Slough on his WaveRunner to do just that.

"This is a really bad idea," said Mei Li, "your ribs are broken."

"They're bruised, not broken," he replied. "And I can't just sit around not knowing. I have to make sure they're alright. They have no idea what's going on."

"Then I'm going with you," said Lauren.

"Not a chance. And if either one of you even thinks about telling my mom ...," he warned.

"I still say we should let Ray handle it," insisted Mei Li.

"He can't. He's got his hands full rebuilding the tomb," Jess replied.

"Well, what about Burt?" Mei Li suggested.

"He's got the whole territory to patrol on his own. Who knows when he could even get around to it. Look, I'm just gonna take a quick trip out there, find the Markhams, and come right back," he assured them. "I'll even do a pass through Bedroom One," he told Lauren, "and if the jerks are still there, I'll give them a head's up as well."

"They won't listen to you," she replied.

"Then that's their problem and it's out of our hands." In putting on his ski vest, Jess winced in pain, thus triggering a new round of clucking from the two nervous hens.

"Don't do this," begged Lauren.

"Yeah, don't be stupid. I'm serious, Jess," said Mei Li.

"So am I," he replied.

"Jess, please," Lauren pleaded, "I'm really scared."

"Just stay here with Mei Li and I'll be back before you know it."

The gas dock swayed slightly and Jess looked up to see Calvin coming down the ramp. He was suited up, prepared to go out on *The Beast*. It suddenly made sense why the girls were working so hard to delay his departure.

"Can't let ya go alone, bruh," said Calvin.

"I don't think you have any say in the matter," Jess replied.

"You'd be so easy to stop right now, it's not even funny."

And Jess knew he was right.

"It's all of us, or none of us," declared Calvin as he handed Mei Li and Lauren the ski vests he'd borrowed from the *Hit It*. Pulling Mei Li into him, he added, "And I ain't goin' nowhere without dragon repellant."

When the repeated beeps of a delivery truck backing up to the rear door of the café sounded, the foursome knew their window of opportunity had arrived, and they took it. With Frances distracted, they climbed aboard the WaveRunners and slipped out of the harbor undetected.

Mei Li linked her arms around Calvin's waist and held tight. Lauren did the same with Jess as the two PWC's flew top speed over the water—all eyes intently scanning the river for any signs of the dragon as they raced toward Desperation Slough. Arriving at the mouth of the slough, they swiftly made their way to

Bedroom One. Rounding the bend, they found the *Delta Destiny* anchored in the same spot it had been previously with the *Money Talks* anchored several yards behind.

Slowing to an idle, Calvin and Jess circled a ways off. They could see Dane and Eric lounging on the back deck drinking beer.

"You two hang back," said Calvin, "let us handle this one."

Jess nodded his agreement and he and Lauren remained behind as Calvin and Mei Li drove toward the houseboat.

Seeing them approaching, Dane turned to Eric. "I don't fucking believe this."

"Probably coming to get Lauren's stuff."

"Hope they brought scuba gear!"

Laughing like jackals, the two high-fived each another.

Calvin circled several yards from the houseboat's starboard stern, prompting Dane and Eric to come stand at the railing.

"Nice ride," Eric sarcastically commented. "Is that a Wave Scraper?"

Ignoring him, Calvin cut to the chase. "Listen, we came to warn you. There's something in the water. It's attacking people."

"Something in the water ...," Dane replied incredulously.

Nikki got up from where she was sunbathing on the roof and came to stand at the edge. "What are you talking about?" she called down.

Calvin steered *The Beast* a little closer to the houseboat and turning to Mei Li, he nodded for her to give it a shot.

"Look," she said, "we know this sounds crazy, but there's a creature in this slough. And it's killing people."

"Straight up," confirmed Calvin. "It nailed three people at the party that night—after you left."

"No shit?" said Eric, smirking. "So what's this thing look like?"

"Don't worry, you'll know it when you see it," replied Calvin.

Dane quickly decided to not only play along, but to hijack their little game— altering it to one of his own design. He gave Eric a look that told him to follow his lead. "Okay. Wow, we really appreciate you coming out to warn us. And hey, I just want to apologize. I been kinda outta line. So, tell your friend ...," he added, nodding toward Jess out on the WaveRunner, "I'm really sorry about the other night."

"Whatever," replied Calvin.

Having drifted closer, *The Beast* was now just feet from the houseboat and Calvin looked up to issue a final warning. "Just be careful. No joke, this thing is shreddin' people. I'd get the hell outta here if I was you."

"Yeah, we'll do that. And hey, no hard feelings, right?" Dane reached over the railing and extended his hand to shake on it. "We good?"

Calvin hesitated, then against his better judgment, reached out and returned the handshake. Only Dane locked onto his wrist and wouldn't let go. "Grab her!" he yelled to Eric, who snatched an unsuspecting Mei Li by the shoulders of the ski vest. Lifting her off *The Beast*, he pulled her over the railing onto the houseboat.

"Let go, you asshole!" she demanded, struggling to break free.

But Eric had her in a stronghold and Mei Li wasn't going anywhere. "Take it easy wild thing," he laughed.

Standing up on *The Beast*, Calvin took hold of the houseboat's railing and attempted to board. But Dane was there in an instant, and planting a foot squarely in his chest, he forcefully kicked

Calvin off into the slough where he treaded water, trying to figure out what to do next.

Jess and Lauren pulled up a moment later. "Let her go!" Jess yelled. "I'm the one you're pissed at."

"I'm not pissed," he replied. "In fact, I like this one better. I definitely got the better end of the trade."

"Dane, listen," Lauren called to him. "No matter what you think of me, they're not joking about the dragon. It's real. I've seen it."

"Oh, a dragon is it?" he replied, followed by a forced laugh. "That is rich. You kids musta stayed up all night thinking that one up."

Grabbing his beer, Dane tried to force some into Mei Li's mouth. "Here honey, have a drink. You and me are gonna have some fun."

"That's enough, Dane," said Nikki, "Just let her go."

"Aw come on, Nik, don't be a party pooper," he replied.

Hoping to go undetected, Calvin made his way to the stern and managed to grab hold of the edge of the back deck. He was pulling himself up when Dane spotted him and ran over, stomping on his hands until he dropped back into the water.

Furious and amped on adrenalin, Calvin threatened, "I swear to God, I'm gonna kill you if you don't let her go."

"Yeah, you look real tough treading water," laughed Dane.

Then out of the blue, Nikki began to scream bloody murder.

"What the hell is your problem?!" Dane yelled up to her.

Continuing to scream, she pointed to the port side of the vessel. From their vantage point, Dane and Eric were unable to see what it was that had Nikki's bikini bottoms in a bunch. Taking Mei Li with them, they made for the back deck where they quickly bound her hands and feet with the rope of an extra anchor to ensure their hostage wouldn't take advantage of the moment and escape. They then rounded the corner of the houseboat to investigate and were treated to an IMax view of Gong Luhng. Their mouths dropped open at the sight of the enormous creature now half out of the water and towering above them.

While Dane and Eric were busy getting acquainted with the dragon, Calvin swam after *The Beast*, which was rapidly drifting away with the current. Suspecting Gong Luhng had arrived at the party, Mei Li struggled to free herself from the thick rope and attached anchor. Unable to Houdini her way out of the convoluted tangle, she simply scooted across the back deck, dragging the whole shebang with her. And as she peered around the corner of the houseboat, there he was in all his glory; the hell-raising defender of the Long family staring down at Dane and Eric, who were suddenly cardboard cutouts of the tough guys they'd been moments ago. They stood frozen, trying to process what they were seeing, while Nikki continued to scream and Gong Luhng began to screech.

"Stop screaming!' Mei Li advised her. "You'll only attract it to you."

Clapping a hand over her mouth, Nikki shut the hell up.

Eric suddenly bolted, running for the bow where he threw open the storage locker in search of a weapon, any weapon. Finding a flare gun, he struggled to load it, but his hands were shaking uncontrollably. Giving up, he stuffed a handful of shells into his pocket and made for the ladder that led to the roof, the dragon's glassy black eyes tracking his every move.

Circling at the starboard side of the vessel, Jess and Lauren could now see the top of the dragon's head as it loomed above Nikki, who stood paralyzed.

"Jump!" Jess yelled to her. "We'll get you!"

"Just do it, Nikki," urged Lauren. "For God's sake, jump!"

Immobilized by fear, Nikki was unable to comply.

Once on the roof, Eric managed to load a cartridge into the flare gun. "Gonna show this mofo who's boss," he yelled down to Dane.

His buddy, however, had fled inside the houseboat and was madly searching for the keys to the *Money Talks* with the intention of making his escape alone. Above, Eric took aim and fired a flare directly at the dragon, which did little more than piss it off and it screeched out its annoyance.

Downriver, Calvin managed to catch up with *The Beast* and scrambled aboard, only to be rewarded with a temperamental engine that refused to start. "Come on baby, where's the love?"

Dane bounded out the back door of the houseboat, but Mei Li was there, blocking his escape route. "Going somewhere?"

"Screw you," he replied and pushed past her to open the gate in the railing. Realizing he was about to jump in and swim for the *Money Talks*, Mei Li struggled against her bindings and managed to grab hold of his arm. "Hey, at least get me outta this before you bail," she demanded.

"Get off me, you crazy bitch."

Still holding onto to Dane's arm as he suddenly jumped for the water, Mei Li lost her balance and fell in after him, her hands and feet firmly bound with the rope and anchor.

Drifting downriver on *The Beast*, Calvin looked up at the moment of Dane and Mei Li's tussle and watched in what seemed like slow motion as they went overboard together. Dane quickly surfaced and swam for the wakeboard boat. Mei Li, however, did not reappear. Calvin immediately stripped off his ski vest, and abandoning *The Beast,* he jumped in, swimming for the place where he saw her go under. Once there, he took in a deep breath and dove under.

In a flashback to his first day in the Delta when he'd pulled himself down into the river to free the cable line, Calvin frantically searched the murky waters for Mei Li. He soon found her about five feet under, held fast to the bottom and struggling to free herself from the tight anchor rope, her air supply rapidly escaping her lungs. Grabbing her face, Calvin pulled her mouth to his and blew air into her lungs. He then went to work trying to free her. Frustrated that he couldn't manage it on the first attempt, Calvin tried not to look panicked as he held up his index finger, assuring her he would be right back.

Continuing to circle at the starboard side of the houseboat, Jess and Lauren saw Calvin briefly appear at the back of the vessel, but with the chaos playing out above the surface, they remained oblivious to the drama unfolding at the bottom of the river.

Having been alerted by Frances that the foursome were missing, Ray soon arrived on scene and got his first real look at the dragon—impressive, to say the least. But there was no time to focus on just one aspect of the pandemonium. The sheriff's sergeant had to quickly triage the chaotic scene to determine who and what to deal with first.

Now aboard the wakeboard boat, Dane was frantically tearing through its interior searching for the spare key, since the original was inconveniently located in the shorts pocket of Eric who was busy launching another flare at Gong Luhng. This time, however, the dragon fired back. Its enormous tail rose up out of the water, and like a lethal version of a porcupine, several giant quills shot from the end. Two hit their mark, piercing Eric through the chest. A third struck a gas can stored on the roof, causing fuel to flow across the deck. Nikki watched in horror as Eric's blood mixed with gasoline and Gong Luhng looked down upon its handiwork.

In the waters behind the houseboat, Calvin was now on his third round of rescue breathing for Mei Li while still struggling to untangle her from the thick rope and heavy anchor. He'd managed to free her hands on his second trip down, but her feet remained firmly shackled. Now at least, when he went up for air, she was able to continue working on the knots at her feet herself until he returned with more air supply.

Above on the houseboat's roof, mortally wounded and bleeding out, Eric looked up at the dragon. "You're not real," he weakly uttered. "You're not even real." As Gong Luhng screeched out its deafening rebuttal, Eric attempted to get one last shot off. But he was barely able to raise his arm. He was, however, able to pull the trigger and a live flare hit the deck, igniting the gas puddle he now stood in. Impaled and engulfed in flames, Eric stumbled across the roof and fell from the starboard side of the houseboat into the slough.

With the vessel ablaze, Nikki was forced to do what she should have done in the first place and finally jumped overboard. Swimming for the surface she came face to face with the scorched body of her boyfriend floating above. Screaming underwater, Nikki pushed him away and headed for daylight.

Ray's voice came over the patrol boat's PA. "Get away!" he called to Jess and Lauren. "I'll get the girl. Just get the hell outta there!"

Jess complied, and punching it, he powered away from the houseboat while Ray moved in to collect a traumatized Nikki.

Below the surface, Calvin delivered his fifth round of rescue breathing to Mei Li, but it was simply not providing the quality of oxygen she so desperately needed. Fading fast, she could no longer help to untangle herself. Complicating matters was the fact that their frantic efforts had churned up the muddy river bottom; it was now virtually impossible for her rescuer to see what he was doing in the cloudy water. His mind racing, Calvin suddenly heard Ol' Joe's voice in his head, "Gonna be more about feelin' your way."

His very next thought was of his mother's jewelry. Whenever one of Angela's necklaces became hopelessly tangled, she would quickly give up and hand the impossible chain off to Calvin. Not surprisingly, he welcomed the challenge and often timed himself to see how fast he could get the thing unknotted. It's just like a chain, he told himself now. He didn't even have to untangle the whole thing, just needed to loosen the focal point knot and shift the stress. Finding the largest knot with his hands, he began to manipulate it back and forth until he could wedge his thumb into the middle and create some give. He then pushed the whole convoluted tangle counter clockwise until the snare that threatened to drown Mei Li finally relinquished its death-grip. There was now sufficient give, and grabbing Mei Li around the waist, he pulled her free. Breaking the surface a moment later, they gasped for air. And though she was coughing and choking, Mei Li was alive.

Dane swiftly freed the now-idling *Money Talks* from its last tie line, and punching the throttle, he left Calvin and Mei Li to contend with an insulting blast of prop wash.

"I'm gonna kill him," Calvin vowed while trying to keep Mei Li's head above this latest liquid assault.

"Take a number," she replied between coughing fits.

Calvin helped Mei Li swim with him away from the burning houseboat toward the middle of the slough where Jess and Lauren now waited. They'd managed to catch up with *The Beast* adrift downriver and Jess was on board with the engine running.

Speeding from the scene, Dane briefly looked back at the houseboat ablaze and the destruction he left behind. Missing from the equation, however, was Gong Luhng. Turning to face forward again, Dane was instantly confronted with the reason the dragon wasn't visible back at the houseboat. Having stealthily made its way up the slough's main artery underwater, the dragon had over-taken the *Money Talks* and was now rising from the waters ahead. Cutting sharply, Dane pulled a 180, barely managing to avoid a collision with the creature before speeding full-throttle back in the direction he'd just come.

En route to pluck Nikki from the water near the flaming houseboat, Ray realized the *Money Talks* was returning at a high rate of speed, so he held back, waiting to see what Dane was up to.

In the middle of the slough, Calvin took possession of *The Beast* and after climbing aboard, he pulled a shaky Mei Li side-saddle onto the seat in front of him. They were about to get the hell out of Bedroom One when the *Money Talks* came flying back into the area. Holding their positions, everyone watched, cautiously waiting to see what the loose cannon known as Dane was going to do next.

When the dragon shot out of the water directly in the path of the wakeboard boat, it became clear that a deadly game of cat and mouse was being played out—and Dane was on the losing rodent side. He tried once again to veer the boat away and escape, but the dragon was quick to cut him off. This time Gong Luhng lunged, its deadly jaws snatching the driver right out of his seat. Dane screamed in agony as the dragon savagely shook him like a chew toy. Unmanned, the *Money Talks* continued on, crashing into the levee where it burst into flames. Gong Luhng then tossed Dane into the air and swallowed him down like a Gold Fish Cracker as everyone stared in disbelief.

"Told him not to mess with the Chinese girl," said Calvin.

A second later, the houseboat exploded.

With Mei Li and Lauren holding on tight, Calvin and Jess raced away full-throttle, fleeing the deluge of debris raining down over the slough. With Nikki now safely aboard the patrol boat, Ray followed the PWC's out of the area. Behind them, Gong Luhng briefly resurfaced to claim Eric's charred, shish-kabobbed body.

The only thing left of the *Delta Destiny* was a smoldering hull softly burning above the water line. Piled up on the rocks and fully engulfed in flames, the *Money Talks* would undoubtedly be the next to explode.

Dane and Eric had been schooled the hard way, that one, there really was a dragon lurking in the Delta. And two, not a good idea to screw with anyone even remotely related to the Long family. Unfortunately for these two, there would be no future opportunity to apply the lessons learned.

Its work here done, the teacher retreated into the slough and vanished.

❧ CHAPTER 36 ❦

GOODBYE SIRENA

Though their awesome sound system effectively drowned out marine radio and cell phone calls, Lou and Gloria had no trouble whatsoever hearing the rental houseboat explode a bedroom island away.

Having just settled onto the back deck to enjoy a bottle of champagne, the moment Lou released the cork, the *Delta Destiny* exploded nearby. Climbing to the upper deck with binoculars, they could see a large plume of black smoke rising, however, the tall bamboo that inhabited Bedroom Two completely blocked their view of the action taking place at the surface of the water. Gloria was preparing to put in an emergency radio call when the two WaveRunners and the sheriff's boat rounded the bend heading their way.

Coming up alongside, Jess called out to them, "Man, are we ever glad to see you guys!"

Once everyone was safely aboard the yacht, Ray found himself on the opposite side of the fence; he was now the one relating a fantastical story about a dragon. And though they would have dearly loved to savor Ray's "shoe on the other foot" moment, Calvin, Mei Li, and Jess excitedly chimed in to validate his story.

Fortunately for Ray, Lou and Gloria were uniquely open-minded individuals who had no trouble whatsoever accepting things that defied the ability of science to explain them. They took in this sensational information without even batting an eye and appeared far more intrigued by the dragon than concerned about the havoc it was currently wreaking.

"Well, this is quite a development," said Lou with genuine fascination.

"And Mei Li, that's some family secret," added Gloria.

"Yeah, a deadly one," she replied.

A moment later, the *Money Talks* detonated with a deafening boom.

As Nikki began to shake, Gloria wrapped her in a blanket and made her sip on some brandy before putting her to bed in a guest cabin. Since she was obviously still in shock, Lauren remained below to keep an eye on her.

It was decided they would head back to Heron's Harbor with everyone on board the *Life's Short*, save for Ray who would follow in the patrol boat. The next order of business was to winch the two PWC's on board.

Once *The Beast* and Jess's WaveRunner were safely situated on the back deck, it was time to move out. Calvin retrieved the tule hook anchor at the bow, while Jess helped Lou hoist the main anchor at the stern. Manning the helm, Gloria skillfully backed the yacht away from the tule island of Bedroom Two.

In keeping with their eccentric nature, the Markhams had always used a large inflatable mermaid for their anchor line marker. But as Jess and Lou pulled in the anchor, the whimsical pool toy came loose and was carried off down river in a steady breeze.

"Oh no," said Jess, "there goes Sirena."

"Yep. Looks like I'll have to break it to Gloria that our gal's abandoned ship," lamented Lou.

"But she loves that thing."

"Well, no sense crying over lost mermaids," reasoned Lou before calling "all clear" into his walkie-talkie.

Gloria put one engine in forward and the other in reverse, causing the yacht to gracefully pivot in place. The *Life's Short* and the sheriff's boat then headed for Heron's Harbor and the safety of land.

Passing the opening to Bedroom One, they quietly took in the eerie scene. On their port side, the scorched remnants of the *Delta Destiny* remained anchored off the tule island. Burned to the water line, white smoke now rose from its blackened hull. On their starboard side, what remained of the wakeboard boat— the charred engine block— sat isolated on levee rocks as though it had crash-landed there from outer space. Pieces from the two vessels littered the surface of the water, prompting both captains to reduce their speed in order to carefully navigate the floating debris field. There were, however, no bodies or body parts to collect this time, Gong Luhng had made sure of that.

A particularly large chunk of wreckage drifted by and caught everyone's attention. It was the fully intact transom of the wakeboard boat, hauntingly boasting the concept that "money talks."

Once fully under way, Gloria recalled the strange occurrence of their first day back in the Delta and picked up the radio mic. "Ray, do you read me?"

"Loud and clear."

"This may sound crazy, but I think the dragon might have an aversion to sonar waves. Over."

Ray's voice came back a moment later. "Gloria, at this point, nothing sounds crazy."

Well behind them in the heart of Desperation Slough, Sirena the unfettered inflatable mermaid bobbed across the surface of the water. That is, until Gong Luhng chomped into her, popping her like bubble wrap before taking her under.

❧ CHAPTER 37 ❧

HISTORY IN THE MAKING

Little more than a week ago, they were gathered in the café after hours, guessing as to who (or what) might have done Huestus in. Never in their wildest dreams could they have imagined it would turn out to be a dragon. More unbelievable still: the task of stopping it now fell to them. Yet here they were, some still half-asleep, gathered in the café once again. This time it was early morning, before Frances even opened for breakfast.

While the troops fueled up on coffee and donuts, Jess and Frances pushed four tables together so Ray could spread out the oversized wall map he'd brought from the Sheriff's Office. Calvin, Mei Li, Lauren, Samuel, Old Joe, Terry, Neal, Tak, Lou, Gloria, and Burt soon huddled around the map as Ray prepared to lay out his strategy. He'd gathered up salt & pepper shakers along with ketchup and mustard bottles to be used like pieces of a war game.

"Okay," said Ray, calling the meeting to order. "First of all, I want to make it perfectly clear that no one should feel obligated to participate in this undertaking. But since you've all been involved up to this point, I hope you'll stay."

They all looked from face to face to see if anyone would excuse themselves. When no one did, Ray nodded his gratitude. "Next, I'd like to thank Calvin for pulling off the impossible by finding the seal. Not to mention some pretty heroic life guard duties."

When the group erupted in cheers and applause, Calvin shook his head and waved them off. "I mighta found the seal, but Burt's the real hero. The man out-thugged a bunch o' gangstas, y'all. So give it up for Burt," said Calvin, leading the next round of applause. He then held forth knuckles to the deputy, who came as close to looking hip as he ever would when he knocked Calvin back.

"Alright," said Ray, getting back to the task at hand. "Assuming the dragon has an aversion to sonar waves, we're going to use that to herd it into the tomb." Grabbing a yellow mustard squirt bottle, he stuck it on the map at one end of Desperation Slough saying, "Sheriff's boat." He then picked up a red ketchup bottle and identified it as the "*Life's Short*" before placing it on the map at the other end of the slough. "Lou, I hope you'll be amenable to letting Terry and Neal pilot the yacht."

"I'd have no problem with that, but truthfully, you'll need the younger and stronger men with you. Besides, I know my instruments and I know my ship."

"We're perfectly capable of herding a dragon into a tomb," his wife added.

"Actually Gloria, I'd prefer it if you stayed here with Frances, Mei Li, and Lauren," the sergeant suggested.

"Ray Cruz, don't tell me you're a closet sexist!" she countered.

"No," he denied. "I simply want them to keep the marina open and act like nothing unusual is happening."

"And I'm sure they're perfectly capable of handling that without me, since I will be aboard my vessel," Gloria steadfastly declared.

Lou looked at Ray and shrugged. "We've been shipmates for forty-seven years. Take it from me, you're not gonna win this one."

"Okay," said Ray, giving in.

Adjusting his game plan, he lifted up the ketchup bottle and placed it back down. "To clarify, Lou and Gloria will start here at the mouth of Desperation Slough in the *Life's Short*. And Burt," he said, pointing to the mustard bottle, "will start at the other end of the slough in the patrol boat. There are plenty of side channels the dragon can slip down to evade you, so I don't want you to use your sonar until you have a confirmed visual sighting."

Grabbing six salt & pepper shakers, Ray placed them around an X he'd marked on the map. "The rest of the team will be waiting here at the tomb where I'll oversee and coordinate along with Tak. Terry, Samuel, and Joe will be manning one log stack," he said, pointing to three pepper shakers. "Calvin, Jess, and Neal—you'll handle the other," he added, pointing to three salt shakers. "If everything goes as planned and we're able to herd the dragon in and trap it, Tak will then perform the entombment ritual."

"But the last time they entombed the dragon, they used bait. Remember?" said Calvin.

"No bait," stressed Ray. "I can't let anyone take that risk."

"Besides, they didn't have sonar last time, and we do," said Tak. "We'll drive the dragon into the tomb, rather than lure it."

"Exactly," confirmed Ray. "Once it's in, we'll need to work quickly to entomb it. I realize this plan isn't fool-proof, but it's all we've got. And remember, if anything goes wrong, we abort the mission and regroup. Understood?"

Off their nods of agreement, Ray issued the charge. "Let's move out."

As everyone began to file out, Calvin lagged behind staring at the map. When no one was looking, he picked up the salt shaker Ray had used to represent him and replaced it with a pepper shaker before heading out the door. He just couldn't let that one go.

Terry and Neal were the first to depart for the tomb, and as they pulled away from their campsite, a small round face with thick glasses appeared in the camper's window directly above the cab.

Unbeknownst to the fishermen, a certain stowaway had slipped into the camper just moments before their departure, even though his mother had strictly forbidden him from going. The re-entombment of Gong Luhng was history in the making and the soon-to-be fourth-grader was determined not only to witness it, but to document it for the next Science Fair. Dent was still peeved about that poser Blake winning it again last year, even though it was blatantly obvious his research scientist father (who didn't even live in the area) had done his entire exhibit and FedExed it to him. Well, not this time, Blake the Fake. No, this was going to be Dent's year—the year of the dragon.

Down at the gas dock, the two vessels responsible for handling the water side of the dragon round-up, the *Life's Short* and the patrol boat, were being readied for departure. Lou was at the helm of the *Life's Short* checking his instruments while Gloria was busy stowing extraneous deck items. After smacking her knee on *The Beast* for a second time, she was sincerely wishing the boys had offloaded their PWC's. But it was too late now, so she turned her attention to more important matters, like securing the wine cellar—just in case things got hairy out there.

Burt fired up the engine on the patrol boat while Ray undid the tie lines for him. Arriving on the gas dock, Frances held a small cooler out to the deputy. "For the road."

Taking the cooler from her, Burt opened it to find a pirate's bounty of Otter Pops.

"Much obliged, ma'am," he said, tipping his sheriff's cap before happily taking the stash on board.

Frances smiled and walked on to the end of the dock, giving the sergeant a moment with his deputy.

"You gonna be alright on your own?" Ray asked him.

"I handled those bikers didn't I? I can handle this."

"I know you can." For the first time, Ray genuinely believed Burt was morphing into an actual deputy sheriff and would rise to the challenge. "Once you get a visual on the dragon and I give the signal, put that sonar on and keep it on unless I say otherwise."

"Will do."

"Stay safe out there," Ray's last words of advice before he pushed the patrol boat away from the dock and watched Burt head for the main channel.

Gloria approached, and putting her hands on her hips, she nodded toward the end of the gas dock where Frances stood alone. "I think maybe you'd better go talk to her."

"Yeaaah," he sighed. Ray dutifully walked to where Frances stood with her arms protectively crossed as she watched the sheriff's boat move past the breakwater and disappear.

Though she refused to look at him, Frances soon spoke. "You know, when Scott died, I just wanted to get us the hell outta here. Just pack up and move back to San Francisco. But Jess begged me not to sell this place."

"I know," he replied. "And for what it's worth, I'm really glad you stayed."

"Right now, I'm wishing we hadn't." Still not looking at him, she added, "I can't lose another member of my family, Ray."

"You're not going to, I promise. Look, I know he's your son, but he's also a man now. And I need him."

"So do I," she quickly countered.

"If you tell Jess he can't be a part of this, he'll blow you off and do it anyway. You know that's true."

Reluctantly, Frances nodded her acknowledgment of this fact.

"I guarantee you he'll be safely away from the water," Ray promised. "I won't let anything happen to him."

"There are no guarantees in life, Ray. We both know that by now."

"Okay then, how 'bout if I give you my word? That's gotta count for something."

Resigned, though still upset, Frances radically changed the subject. "I'm just happy nothing got started between us."

"Yeah, you look real happy," he replied with a laugh. "I'm coming back. We're all coming back. I promise."

"Good. Fine."

Taking her by the shoulders, Ray turned her toward him. "And when this is over, we *are* going to get something started. You hear me?" Though she tried to turn away from him, Ray took her face in his hands and kissed her.

Witnessing the passionate exchange as they pulled away from the dock, Gloria nudged Lou. "And you said that love potion was a bunch o' malarkey."

"I stand corrected."

Up at the marina's parking lot, the geriatric division of dragon trappers, Samuel, Ol' Joe, and Tak, piled into Samuel's truck and prepared to head for the tomb site. Joe was sandwiched in the middle with Tak firmly wedged against the passenger door cradling the seal and The Book of Dragon on his lap.

Repeatedly cranking the engine, Samuel pleaded for the Chevy to start. "Come on now, baby. Don't do me like this."

"Oh, for the love of God," groused Joe.

"Maybe you should try kissing it," suggested Tak.

Calvin, Mei Li, and Jess arrived and took stock of the trio of seniors stuffed into the old pickup as Samuel struggled to get it started.

"If this is the cavalry, we're in a world o' hurt," declared Jess.

"And what the hell's with all the engine's not starting?" asked Calvin.

"It's called suspense," replied Mei Li. "How ya likin' it?"

"Not so much."

Mei Li walked to the passenger side and leaned in to her grandfather. "Please be careful, Yeh-yeh."

"Not to worry, suen-neui. This dragon-trapping thing runs in the family."

As Samuel continued cranking the starter, Calvin and Jess climbed into the back of the pickup in anticipation of departing ... any day now. Left standing beside the truck, Mei Li crossed her arms and glared at Calvin until he sheepishly climbed out to say a proper goodbye. Self-conscious at having an audience, he attempted to simply give her a platonic hug.

"Yeah, right," she said, before putting a serious lip lock on him.

A second later the engine caught with a loud backfire. Samuel promptly threw the truck in drive and began pulling away, forcing Calvin to run in order to catch up. Jess reached out a hand and pulled him safely into the truck bed before the Chevy shambled off down the road.

"Thought you said she was too feisty," Jess teased him.

"She is," insisted Calvin. "Only way I can shut her up."

Ray jogged for the patrol car parked above the gas dock only to discover Gladys sitting in the passenger seat looking at her watch.

"Good thing you're not the fire chief," she stated as he opened the door.

"I take it you're going along," he said, getting in.

"Damn right I'm going. Been readin' about this kinda crap for years. Think I'm gonna miss an opportunity to see the real thing?"

"Then buckle up. I don't have time to argue."

"Goodie!" she chirped, clapping her hands like a preschooler. "This'll gimme somethin' to rant about when they put me in the home. I'll be screamin' about the dragon every time I fill my Depends."

And with that, Team Dragon set out on their mission, leaving Frances, Mei Li, and Lauren to hold down Heron's Harbor and act like nothing out of the ordinary was taking place in the Delta. Nothing at all.

❦ CHAPTER 38 ❦

WOMEN AND CHILDREN LAST

Ray's insistence that the women remain behind and put on show of normalcy turned out to be a complete joke, as there was simply no audience to perform for. Word that there was a serial killer on the loose, coupled with the rumored sewage spill, had rendered Heron's Harbor a veritable ghost town.

With not a soul in the joint, Frances leaned on the lunch counter anxiously drumming her fingernails on its formica. Mei Li paced back and forth in front of the large plate glass window, staring out at a virtually dead gas dock. Jess had given Lauren a crash course in gas dock attendance, but she'd only had one customer all morning: a tourist couple in a patio boat who simply needed to use the restroom. Otherwise, the place was deadsville.

"This is just bullshit," declared Frances.

"Totally," agreed Mei Li. "I should be there. I'm related to the dragon by marriage for God's sake."

"That's right. And why should we stay here pretending nothing's happening when there's no one to pretend to."

"I say we lock it up and go," suggested Mei Li.

Frances hesitated for only a moment before whipping off her apron and tossing it on the counter. "They could probably use our help and don't even know it."

"Absolutely!"

Frances quickly scribbled a note stating they were "Closed for Repairs" and taped it to the front door. She then wrote a second note that read, "Out of Gas, Come Back Tomorrow." She'd have Lauren post it on the gas dock's kiosk.

While Frances grabbed her keys and hit the lights, Mei Li flipped the "Open" sign to "Closed". But as they defiantly stepped out the door, they ran smack into Angela.

"Hello. I'm Angela Pierce."

Caught off guard, the two stared at her with their mouths agape.

"Samuel's niece," she clarified. "Calvin's mother ...," she added in hopes of getting some response. Any response.

"Yes, of course. Calvin's mother," Frances finally coughed up.

"Listen, I was just over at the shop but nobody's there. It's all locked up," Angela related. "So I went down to *The Sturgeon* and they're not there either."

But before Frances or Mei Li could respond, Lisa Cheng came running up and frantically asked her daughter, "Have you seen Dent?!"

"No, I thought he was with you."

"He was, but he disappeared. I was hoping he was with you."

"Oh no," said Mei Li

"Oh my God," uttered Lisa, realizing they were thinking the exact same thing.

"What? What's going on?" asked Angela.

"We'll fill you in on the way," Frances told her.

"On the way where?"

❧ CHAPTER 39 ❧

THE HUNTED

Arriving at the mouth of Desperation Slough in the *Life's Short*, Lou and Gloria reduced their speed and began winding their way through its channels in search of Gong Luhng. Three and a half miles to the east, Burt piloted the patrol boat around Buzzard Island and slipped into the narrow eastern entrance of the slough, beginning his own hunt for The Delta's Most Wanted. Since neither vessel would be relying on their sonar until it was to be used as a herding device, this was going to be an old-school visual search, with the two vessels slowly snaking their way towards each other and the newly restored tomb.

Out here alone on this crazy dragon hunt, Burt suddenly wished he hadn't tossed the emergency pack of cigarettes he used to keep stashed on board the patrol boat. Remembering the Otter Pops from Frances, he reached for the cooler at his feet. Sir Isaac Lime was going to have to suffice. Burt's lips were soon staining an alien green as he piloted the patrol boat and scanned the waters ahead.

Gathered at the tomb site, the shore team took up their positions under Ray's direction. Calvin, Jess, and Neal stationed themselves at the log stack on the right, while Samuel, Old Joe, and Terry manned the one on the left. Ray and Tak stood above on the levee; director and assistant director of an event that might well rival a Super Bowl half-time show.

A short distance away, Gladys set up her folding chair under a sycamore tree and settled in. With binoculars hanging around her neck and a foam visor stuck on her head, she looked like an early bird spectator for the Rose Parade.

The shore team in place, it was now a matter of hurry up and wait. They braced themselves to sweat it out, both physically and psychologically, on the warm, breezeless Delta afternoon. Ray walked to the water's edge and stood beside the suspended wood gate, scanning the waters of the slough. "We're set on this end," he reported into his radio. "You guys have anything?"

"That's a negative," Burt came back.

"Nothing here either," reported Lou.

A mischievous crow landed atop the tomb's gate and proceeded to march back and forth, stopping occasionally to scold the dragon trappers who waited below in the hot midday sun. It wasn't long before Gladys was slumped over in her folding chair, struggling to keep from nodding off.

Below the levee in the old pear orchard, the temperature inside Terry's parked camper continued to rise and Dent figured he'd waited long enough. Opening the door a crack, he peeked around to make sure he was in the clear before slipping out—a camera dangling around his neck. With everyone's attention fully focused on the waters of the slough, Dent easily went undetected as he scurried to the levee, then scrambled halfway up the back side to hunker down and wait for the action.

Lou continued to guide the *Life's Short* through their half of the slough while he and Gloria kept a sharp eye on the waters ahead.

Then it crested.

The jagged dorsal ridge broke the surface several yards off and was swiftly moving toward them.

"There he is! There's our boy!" Gloria excitedly announced.

Lou quickly got on the horn. "Ray, we've got a visual, it's coming straight for us."

"Roger that," the sergeant replied. "Turn on your sonar and let's see if it reacts."

"Sonar on," confirmed Lou, flipping the switch. He and Gloria then split their focus between the image on the screen and the real deal heading directly for them. In an instant, they watched the dragon pull a hasty U-turn at the surface and rapidly move in the opposite direction.

"It's responding, Ray. Moving away fast," Lou reported.

"You copy that Burt? They've got it on the run, it's heading your way."

"That's a big ten four, am standing by. Nothing here yet but I'll ... holy moly! Thing just crested!"

"Put your sonar on and let's pin him," instructed Ray.

Once Burt hit the switch, it was only a matter of seconds before there was an obvious response. Repelled by the sonar, the dragon moved away from the patrol boat, determinedly moving in the opposite direction until it encountered the sound waves emanating from the *Life's Short*. It then immediately turned and began to double back.

"You should have a visual on each other any minute now. Once you do, start herding it toward us," Ray advised the water team. He then called up to his shore team, "Stand by!"

Craning their necks and shielding their eyes, the land crew anxiously waited and watched for any sign of the boats and their captive.

"I just wanted to catch some fish and drink some beer," Neal nervously lamented.

"Hold on, bruh," Calvin advised him, "'cause the catch o' the day is headin' this way."

"Neal, this is gonna be the biggest fish story of your life," added Jess.

With the dragon ping-pong-ing between them as it tried to evade the irritating sonar waves, the two vessels came into visual range of each other and those on shore. Gong Luhng suddenly rose up out of the water, thrashing and screeching before plunging back into the slough. Those who had yet to lay eyes on the creature were simultaneously awestruck and scared shitless. Terry and Jess both whipped out their cell phones and began shooting pics and video.

"You've got it cornered," Ray excitedly called into his radio. "Now bring it on in."

Intently focused on the dragon rodeo, no one noticed Dent belly-crawling up the mound of loose earth stationed at the back edge of the tomb.

Half a mile away, Frances pulled her Jeep over to the side of the levee road in order to get her bearings. Though she had a fairly good idea of the tomb's location, finding it by land was not the same as finding it by water, especially since it was situated on a remote tract of private property.

Grabbing her binoculars, Frances stepped out of the vehicle—her four anxious female passengers hot on her heels. Scanning the levee banks through the lenses, she eventually spied Gladys slumped over beneath a tree. This quickly led her to the tomb site, where her eyes found Ray pacing and talking excitedly into his radio, and where Terry, Samuel, and Ol' Joe stood beside a stack of logs as they looked out toward the water. Frances then spotted the boats out in the slough, and just as she was about to put down the binoculars and return to the Jeep, the dragon breached. "Oh my God."

"What?! What is it?" the other four demanded.

Angela immediately snatched the binoculars, practically choking Frances with the strap as she held the lenses up to her own eyes. With Frances's head pulled flush against her own, Angela soon saw for herself what was "Oh my God" worthy when the dragon burst out of the water writhing before splashing back down. Panning to shore, she quickly found Calvin standing with two others at the left side of the tomb. "Please tell me this is not happening. I did not send my son up here so he could be in even more danger!"

A sudden movement at the periphery caught her attention and Angela panned to find Dent struggling to position himself on the mound of unstable earth above the tomb. "Oh Lord," she blurted out.

"What?!" the other women asked in unison.

"Do you have some way to radio that sheriff?" Angela asked Frances.

"No. But I can call his cell."

"I seriously doubt he's gonna answer his phone right now. Get in the car!" she yelled. "Just get in the car!"

The women all ran for the Jeep.

The two vessels of the water team were now positioned behind the dragon, working in unison to push Gong Luhng toward the opening of the tomb. Though initially agitated, their captive now seemed surprisingly resigned to its fate and was steadily moving toward the entrance of the tomb.

The shore team held their breath as the dragon headed their way.

"That's right, get back in your crib," said Calvin, under his breath.

"Come on, just a little further," implored Ray.

It appeared as though Gong Luhng was actually complying, as it agreeably entered the tomb. Ducking under the first two rafters, it was now halfway in with its massive head out of the water and its eyes focused straight ahead on ... Dent. Perched atop of the dirt mound above, the gutsy 8-year-old raised his camera and prepared to make history.

"Blake the Fake's not gonna take it this year," he proclaimed. "Say cheese!"

Evidently, even mythical creatures have an extreme aversion to paparazzi, and as Dent took several flash photos, the dragon went ballistic. Screeching and rising up out of the tomb, it smashed into the middle rafter, snapping it like a twig. Unaware that Dent was even in the mix, Terry dropped his phone, whipped out his buoy knife and frantically began severing his rope.

"Hold off!" Ray yelled to him. "Do not release your logs!"

With Terry's rope now compromised, Samuel and Ol' Joe grabbed hold ahead of him in an effort to stabilize their stack of logs, which had shifted ever so slightly.

Frances's Jeep came barreling into the pear orchard below. Braking to a stop in a cloud of dust, the five women jumped out and ran for the levee, some of them screaming out Dent's name. At the head of the pack, Mei Li arrived at the edge of the tomb as the loose soil beneath Dent's feet became a dirt avalanche, steadily flowing toward the open trench. She tried to run up the side of the moving earth to catch her little brother, but he slid right past her, just out of reach.

"Dent!" Mei Li screamed helplessly as he slipped over the edge and down into the tomb.

Seeing the situation, Ray immediately got on his radio. "Cut your sonar! We need to abort!" He then shouted to the shore crew, "Hold your positions! We'll handle this."

Ray and Tak joined the women at the edge of the tomb who were beside themselves with worry as they looked down into the watery trench. Dent was laying face-down on the rear rafter, roughly six feet below the top edge of the tomb. He'd landed squarely on the thick railroad tie, an arm and leg slung over each side as if resting on a horse. With his head off to one side, Dent was looking directly into the glassy black eyes of the dragon, who was now hunkered down in the water staring up at him.

On her stomach at the edge of the tomb, Mei Li called to her little brother, "You okay, buddy?"

"Yeeaah."

"The dragon won't harm him," Tak assured everyone.

"Okay, but does he want to spend eternity entombed with it?" asked Ray.

"Nooo," Dent's adamant response echoed up from below. "I have to start fourth grade in September."

Cocking its head, the dragon looked up at the boy with fascination.

"Just keep talking to him, Dent," urged Mei Li. "He likes it."

"Sooo ...," said Dent, trying to come up with dragon-appropriate topics. "Do you have a favorite super hero? I have three. I also like Xbox. I'm getting really good at it. I don't play any of the dragon slaying games, though. Just so you know ...."

While Dent continued to jabber away to a captivated dragon, Ray began devising the most effective way to extract the 8-year-old while still keeping the dragon in the tomb.

Though holding their positions as ordered, Calvin could not stop himself from wanting to help Mei Li. "I can't take this," he said finally, and began walking for the edge of the tomb.

"You can't," insisted Jess, stopping him. "Ray said to hold our positions. We've gotta let them handle this."

And while he didn't like it, for the moment, Calvin stayed put.

Meanwhile, Terry, Old Joe, and Samuel struggled to hold onto the threadbare rope of their log pile, especially now that they knew what had transpired and what would happen if they failed. Though the two log teams could not see each other, Terry called across the tomb to his fishing buddy. "Ah, Neal?"

"Yeah?"

"Can I see you over here for a minute?" he requested through clenched teeth.

"You heard Ray, we're s'posed to hold our positions," Neal called back.

"Neal?!"

"Yeah?"

"Get your ass over here or I'll make sure you're the one spending eternity with the damn dragon."

Noting the tone of Terry's threat, Neal walked up and around the drama taking place at the edge of the tomb. Upon seeing the situation, he quickly took up a position on Terry's compromised rope.

Jogging from the patrol car, Ray arrived back at the tomb with a rappelling rope and harness.

"You can't be the one to go," Tak advised him, "the dragon will surely attack. It has to be me."

"No, Yeh-yeh," said Mei Li. "I'm younger. I'll go." Off her grandfather's slightly wounded look she added, "I'm used to hauling Dent around. Besides, you have to be ready to perform the ritual."

"She's right," said Ray, backing her up. "And I'm gonna need the rest of you to help me pull them back up."

As Ray began helping Mei Li into the harness, Angela stood beside Lisa trying to keep her calm while trying to keep from totally freaking out herself.

Offshore, Lou watched through binoculars as Mei Li was lowered down to the rafter, and once there, began securing her little brother.

"What's happening?!" Gloria demanded.

"Slight change of plans," he replied, handing the lenses to his wife.

Nearby in the patrol boat, Burt watched the scene through his own pair of binoculars while sucking on a fresh Otter Pop. When a splat of orange goo hit the console, the deputy unconsciously wiped it away with the back of his sleeve, but in doing so he inadvertently bumped the sonar switch to "on."

For no reason that was immediately apparent, the dragon suddenly went berserk prompting Tak to yell, "Pull them up!" Ray, Frances, Angela, Lisa, and Lauren hauled them up with lightning speed. As Mei Li and Dent arrived safely on top, Gong Luhng reared up and whipped around. Smashing through the front rafter, it blazed out of the tomb.

"Put your sonar back on," Ray yelled into his radio. "Don't let it get by you!"

But as Burt went to flip the switch on the patrol boat's sonar unit, he realized it was already on. "Oh, shit."

Though Lou flipped their sonar device back on, he and Gloria watched helplessly as the dragon's dorsal ridge blazed past them and headed off down the main artery of the slough.

"Too late," Lou reported over the radio, "he slipped by us."

As Ray stood defeated at the edge of the tomb, Samuel called to him, "Ah Ray, now that you have a moment, we could use a little assistance over here."

Meanwhile, on the other side of the watery trench, Calvin stood looking in the direction the dragon had fled while chewing on the inside of his right cheek. He promptly sat down and began taking off his shoes.

"What are you doing?" Jess asked him suspiciously.

"We might not have needed bait before," Calvin replied, pulling off his T-shirt. "But we hella need it now."

"Oh, no way man, don't be crazy."

"Thing ain't gonna catch me on *The Beast*."

"Maybe not, but ..."

"Hey," said Calvin, cutting him off. "You know what they call a black guy on a WaveRunner, don't ya?"

"Trollin' for dragons?" Jess guessed.

"You know it," he replied, holding forth knuckles.

Realizing there wasn't a damn thing he could do to change Calvin's mind, Jess knocked him back. "Go get its scaly ass."

Down to board shorts, Calvin walked into the water up to his waist, then turned and called back to Jess. "And tell 'em to get the damn roof fixed. 'Cause when I come back, I won't be alone." With his mother and the others temporarily distracted, Calvin dove in and began swimming for the *Life's Short*.

Over on the compromised log pile, Ray finished tying off a new rope, replacing the one nearly severed by Terry. When he finally said, "Okay, that oughta hold it," the four men collapsed with relief.

The women approached with Dent in tow and Samuel looked up to find his niece glaring at him with hands on her hips.

"Angela!" he blurted out, as if he was happy to see her, when in fact he was scared out of his mind at what she might do. But before Spitfire had a chance to lay into him for letting Calvin be a part this escapade, Lisa had her own disciplinary agenda to carry out.

"Dent, don't you have something to say to everyone?" his mother asked sternly.

"I'm sorry," he mumbled with his head hung low.

Though frustrated and discouraged, Ray couldn't stay mad at the kid. "It's alright, Dent," he assured him. "The important thing is, no one got hurt."

When Jess approached looking like the cat who swallowed the canary, Mei Li was quick to ask, "Where's Calvin?"

"Ah, he had to go," he cryptically replied.

"Had to go? Go where?!" demanded Angela.

"Fishing?" Jess sheepishly suggested.

"Oh no," said Ray.

"Yeeaah," confirmed Jess.

"Oh no, what?!" asked Angela, ready to wring someone's neck to get a straight answer.

"He mentioned that we should probably get the roof fixed before he gets back," Jess informed Ray.

The sergeant immediately got on his radio. "Lou, Gloria. You've gotta stop him. I don't care if you have to lock him in the head, do not let Calvin go after the dragon."

But it was too late. Calvin had swum out to the *Life's Short* where he was greeted by a surprised Lou and Gloria, who wondered to what did they owe the pleasure of his company. Calvin convinced them that since the dragon had escaped and there was gonna be some down time while Ray regrouped, he thought he'd take the opportunity to use their facilities since he urgently needed to after all the excitement.

Being gracious hosts, the couple directed Calvin to the nearest head on board, where he stayed for only a few moments before requesting they show him how the "complicated" marine toilet worked. And that should have been their first clue. Once Calvin had lured them both inside, he proceeded to slip out, locking them in the head with a chair wedged under the handle. He then swiftly secured an anchor line off the bow to make sure the *Life's Short* wouldn't drift and run aground. By the time Calvin heard Ray's voice come over the radio up top, he'd already shoved *The Beast* overboard and quickly fired the engine.

Pulling up alongside the yacht, Calvin could see Lou and Gloria's faces smooshed together as they looked out the porthole window of their head. Holding up the medallion hanging around his neck, he called out to them. "Yo, thanks for the necklace. I think it might come in handy."

Pulling a donut, Calvin then tore off down the slough, singularly focused on his mission to find and lure the dragon back to the tomb. He did not acknowledge his mother standing at the water's edge. Nor did he respond to her as she yelled for him to, "Come back here this instant! You hear me?! Calvin!"

After agonizing for several minutes and feeling horrible about what he'd accidently done, Burt broke formation and powered the patrol boat in the direction Calvin had gone.

Witnessing his plan unraveling even further, an exasperated Ray got on his radio to the deputy. "Burt what are you doing?"

"I gotta help Calvin," he came back. "It's my fault the dragon went nuts. I accidently hit the sonar switch."

Ray released his mic button so Burt wouldn't hear him say, "Shit." A moment later he was back on radio trying to keep yet another member of his team from going AWOL. "Burt, listen to me, it's not your fault. It was an accident," Ray insisted. "You hear me? I'm ordering you to return to your position."

But Burt was determined to correct his mistake, even if it meant disobeying a direct command. Clicking off his radio, the deputy sped off in the patrol boat, resolved to round up both Calvin and the dragon.

❧ CHAPTER 40 ❧

THE ROUND-UP

Having successfully evaded entombment, Gong Luhng fled the irritating sonar waves and escaped the confines of Desperation Slough, slipping into the deep water channel of the San Joaquin River. Now the entire Delta was its oyster with unlimited choices in direction complimented by an unprecedented selection of prey.

Speeding across the water in pursuit of the fugitive dragon, Calvin soon arrived at the confluence of Desperation Slough and the San Joaquin River where he was forced to take a shot-in-the-dark guess as to which direction the dragon might have gone. Up river or down? And there would be countless fork-in-the-road decisions ahead, considering the vast number of sloughs and cuts that branched off the San Joaquin River. For whatever reason, Calvin chose downriver and simply hoped for the best.

As he raced along, scouring the surface of the water with no sign of the dragon, Calvin began to realize just how daunting the task he'd undertaken truly was. Tracking down Gong Luhng now that it had ventured into the greater maze of the Delta was going to be the ultimate challenge. But he'd found the seal, albeit by dumb luck, and he was determined to not only find the dragon, but lure it back to the tomb.

In a matter of seconds, there was another directional choice to be made and Calvin simply made it without hesitation—agonizing would be a dangerous waste of time at this point. Splitting off from the San Joaquin, he drove *The Beast* into yet another side slough with still no sign of the escapee. He soon came upon a resort with a small beach and swim area. As he slowed to observe the 5 Mile Per Hour Zone posted at the water's edge, he noticed a second sign announcing the name of the resort: Jaybird's Naturist Retreat. Calvin assumed this was a place for nerdy bird watchers to vacation and swap boring field notes. But as he drew closer and surveyed the scene, he quickly got the picture that "naturalist" and "naturist" are two completely different things.

Dozens of blindingly-white naked bodies sunbathed and frolicked on the beach, and in his opinion, none of them fell into the category of show-worthy.

"Aw naw," he uttered, out loud. "That's just wrong."

And there were even more naked bodies, floating on rafts and swimming off shore. A man with no hair on his head and way too much hair on his body floated in the middle of the slough, his butterball butt stuffed into a large inner tube. Hairy guy took a momentary break from feeding chips and beer into his pie hole to wave to Calvin, who pretended he didn't see that. When the newcomer's bewildered eyes landed on two elderly couples playing badminton on the beach, he'd seen enough.

Calvin was about to leave NakieLand behind and head back to the main river when his conscience tapped him on the shoulder. With so many people in the water, he really should try to warn them somehow. If the dragon stumbled upon this place, it was going to be like HomeTown Buffet—and the shrimp were already peeled.

As Calvin sat idling on *The Beast*, pondering what to say and how to say it, a middle-aged woman swam toward him. And of course, she was doing the breast stroke.

"Hey there," she called. "Looking for someone?"

"Uh, you could say that," he replied, trying not to look at her.

"Well, if you don't find them, maybe you'd be interested in someone a little more experienced?"

Calvin made a face but didn't need to come up with a response since the special "someone" he was looking for shot straight up out of the water in front of them with hairy fat guy and his inner tube squarely in its jaws. The all-you-can-eat buffet was now open and Gong Luhng was helping itself to the first course. People on the beach screamed hysterically while those in the water made a swimming dash for shore. As Gong Luhng powerfully chomped down on its catch, the inner tube exploded with a deafening bang, causing the dragon to forcefully spit it out while somehow managing to retain the soft chewy center. Calvin ducked as the deflated rubber tube became a trajectory flying overhead. "Only likes the donut holes."

Terrified, the woman who'd approached him moments before grabbed onto the side of *The Beast* and pleaded, "Take me with you!"

"No can do, Cougar Town. Already got a date for this dance." With that, he squeezed the throttle and left her behind.

Calvin raced directly at Gong Luhng, who tried to nab him by snapping its fierce jaws like a dog after a fly. But he skillfully maneuvered the WaveRunner just out of reach and the dragon came up empty. Turning around, Calvin idled and stood up on *The Beast* to issue a challenge. "You want a piece o' me?" Gonna have to do better than that!" He then zoomed dangerously close once more, and again managed to pull off a death-defying feat.

Calvin knew his ability to handle *The Beast* had improved greatly, but he also sensed the dragon was wearing down. It seemed just a tad slower than it had during previous attacks. Maybe it was in need of an energy-boosting feeding frenzy, or perhaps there was a time limit on its incarnation that Tak was not aware of. Whatever the reasons for the dragon's slowed response time, Calvin was grateful. His ploy had worked; Gong Luhng's focus remained exclusively on him, giving those in the water enough time to make it safely to shore.

The moment had come to lead dragon-breath back to Desperation Slough and the fate that awaited it there. To make sure he retained the dragon's undivided attention, Calvin pulled a series of tight 360's, then idled several yards away.

"Whatsa matter big boy, you poopin' out?" he brazenly called to Gong Luhng. "Well, follow me, cousin—'cause I know the way to nighty-night land. I'll even tuck yo ass in."

Suddenly lunging with renewed energy, the dragon barely missed Calvin who'd already hit the gas and was speeding out of the slough the same way he'd come in. Only this time he had a seriously pissed-off dragon in tow.

Flying up the San Joaquin River with the throttle wide open, Calvin prayed his mechanical skills were solid enough to once again save his hide. So far, so good. *The Beast* was barreling across the water at speeds close to seventy-five miles per hour without a hitch. Every few seconds, Calvin turned to check on his tail-gater, and most times, he caught sight of the jagged dorsal ridge cutting through the water after him. There were roughly four boat lengths between *The Beast* and the other beast, and Calvin planned to keep it that way. He'd seen Gong Luhng overtake the wakeboard boat and knew anything was possible. What he would do if and when the dragon got the upper hand, he couldn't say. Though he seriously doubted claiming to be a close personal friend of Mei Li's was going to fly, and he was suddenly wishing he had his Dragon Lady along for this wild ride.

"Sure, go on up to the Delta for the summer," Calvin sarcastically said to himself. "Can't get in any trouble up there!"

And what the hell was his mom doing here?! Talk about crappy timing for a surprise visit. Right now she was probably freaking out on everyone back at the tomb site. Nobody could do furious and scared out of her mind quite the way his mom could.

But back to the scary at hand, having made his way up the San Joaquin River, Calvin would soon be approaching the mouth of Desperation Slough. As he turned around to check on his charge, the dragon was suddenly absentee—nowhere to be seen. Calvin repeatedly glanced back but no dorsal ridge crested. Dammit.

Circling back, he scoured the waters of the river. "Here kitty, kitty, kitty."

Nothing. No sign of the thing and the river was eerily calm. At least it was, until Gong Luhng shot out of the water beneath him, rocketing *The Beast* skyward. Calvin and his trusty steed parted company mid-air and came splashing down as two separate entities. Resurfacing, Calvin saw *The Beast* floating upside down several yards away. His first thought: PWC's weren't supposed to do that. Then again, they weren't supposed to be launched fifty feet into the air to free fall and submarine back into the water. Next thought: the dragon was going to be on him in an instant. Calvin wouldn't let himself look to see just how close the dragon was. Instead, he immediately began swimming for *The Beast*—his only choice really, given the circumstances. Making it to the WaveRunner, Calvin used the excessive adrenaline pumping through his body to flip it over and climb aboard.

Gong Luhng had gone undercover, probably taking its revenge by toying with him. The phrase "It's not nice to play with your food" reverberated in Calvin's mind as everything became surreal and disconnected. It was as if he was watching someone else's hand violently shaking as they tried to attach the lanyard to the starter. Someone else's thumb, repeatedly depressing the starter button of a hopelessly waterlogged engine.

Slowly and defiantly, Gong Luhng emerged from the waters before him. Calvin looked up into the victorious eyes of his adversary. So this was it. This was how he was going to die. His assailant was clearly savoring its moment of triumph, and rearing its head back with instinctual precision, the dragon prepared to strike. Calvin heard himself call out Leo's name, the way he had when he was a little kid in need of a rescue from street thugs on their block. Unfortunately, Leo would not be able to save his little brother this time.

But someone else could.

Calvin heard a siren wail and turned to see Burt powering the patrol boat directly for Gong Luhng. Cutting away at the last second, the deputy managed to distract the dragon—pulling its focus from Calvin and putting it on himself. Abruptly yanked back to reality and real time, Calvin immediately began coaxing *The Beast* to life as it drifted further down river. "Come on baby, show me some love. I saved your ass from the junkyard, now you gotta save mine."

Meanwhile, Burt kept the dragon busy by circling it in the patrol boat. Incensed at being pulled off its kill and harassed, Gong Luhng swiped at the boat with its deadly taloned paws. Removing his handgun, Burt leaned out of the wheelhouse and began firing shots at Gong Luhng, who responded in turn. Raising its enormous tail, the dragon brought down the hammer. The giant tail of armored scales came crashing down on the vessel with violent force. Burt barely managed to jump overboard as the patrol boat was efficiently smashed in two.

Down river, *The Beast* finally returned the love and sparked to life.

"Hang on man, I'm coming!" Calvin yelled to Burt.

What remained of the patrol boat's wheelhouse floated between Burt and the dragon. As Calvin raced to the rescue, he saw the deputy dive under. Seconds later, Burt's terrified face briefly appeared in the shattered window of the wheelhouse the moment before Gong Luhng forcefully hit it, taking it below.

"Nooo!" Calvin screamed. "Burt!"

Holding out hope that the deputy had somehow managed to survive the brutal attack, Calvin desperately searched the waters. "Burt!" But Gong Luhng soon burst from the river to proclaim its victory.

"You son of a bitch!" Standing up on *The Beast*, Calvin called out his challenger. "That's it, you are goin' down. Nobody eats my friend and gets away with it. Get ready, 'cause yo ass ... is 'bout to be entombed." Punching it, he pulled a fast sliding turn just out of reach of the dragon's deadly swipes before speeding up river once more. Gong Luhng immediately took up the chase.

Calvin raced into the mouth of Desperation Slough with the dragon hot on his tail. He soon flew past two black men fishing from the levee bank—the upper part of the creature's head and its deadly dorsal ridge clearly visible as it cut through the water after him.

Astounded, the younger fisherman elbowed his senior companion. "You catch that?!"

"I sure did," confirmed the elder. "Black kid on one o' them wave mobiles. Don't see that too often."

In Calvin's absence, the land crew had worked feverishly to replace the two smashed rafters. Ray was feeding an emergency fire escape ladder into the tomb when *The Beast's* engine could be heard approaching. In a matter of seconds, Calvin rounded the bend with the dragon close on his heels.

"Comin' in hot!" yelled Jess.

"Everybody in position!" called Ray.

Flying past the shore team, Calvin turned around then pulled a jump off the partially exposed dorsal ridge of the dragon. Gong Luhng immediately rose up screeching.

"You better be ready," Calvin called to those on shore, "'cause this mofo is pissed off!"

"Well yeah, it's pissed off," remarked Jess.

Reducing his speed, Calvin circled before the entrance of the tomb. Suddenly reluctant to do what he knew he must, Calvin looked down into the narrow confinement of the tomb, then back at the dragon.

"*Now* what the hell's he doin'?" Joe demanded, "Having second thoughts about sacrificing *The Beast*?!"

"Maybe," said Samuel. "Or maybe the tomb's looking a little ... confining."

"That's the idea!" replied Joe.

Above on the levee, an exasperated Ray shook his head. "This kid's gonna be the death of me."

"You?!" exclaimed Angela.

Though the dragon was breathing hard, it was still in the game and perfectly capable of mayhem. Calvin knew he couldn't afford to agonize even one moment longer. Pointing *The Beast* into the tomb, he accelerated and drove to the back wall where the rope ladder was waiting.

"We've had one hell of a ride," he said, patting the engine compartment of his trusty steed, "but it's time to say g'bye."

Above, Ray and the women waited anxiously for Calvin to climb onto the ladder. Overdosed on adrenaline, they were prepared to swiftly haul him up if need be.

"Get Ready!" Ray yelled to the rest of the crew. "On my signal ..."

The moment Calvin took hold of the ladder, Gong Luhng lunged into the tomb, its obsidian eyes locked on him.

"Cut the Gate!" called Ray.

Wielding an axe, Neal severed the rope and the massive gate fell into place with a mighty splash. The dragon turned to find its exit effectively cut off. Enraged, it snatched *The Beast* up in its jaws and hurled it toward the back wall of the tomb where it crashed just feet from where Calvin was climbing. Breaking apart on impact, the WaveRunner fell in fractured chunks to the water below.

"Really?!" Calvin yelled at the dragon. "You just had to do that?"

Apparently so. Gong Luhng wasn't going down without a fight this time. It also wasn't going down alone. The dragon suddenly slashed at Calvin with its taloned paws, and though he managed to escape being eviscerated by ducking, its razor-sharp claws easily sliced through the ladder and he plunged to the water below. The moment Calvin came to the surface, the dragon was upon him, towering above as he treaded water. He heard his mother scream out his name, but couldn't bear to look up at her. His eyes remained firmly locked with Gong Luhng's.

"Just cut the ropes, Ray," Calvin instructed, his voice frighteningly void of emotion. "It got Burt. It's not gonna stop unless you do it."

Calvin heard his mother scream, "Nooo!" as someone pulled her back from the edge of the tomb. Ray was struggling to make the call he knew he had to, when a figure suddenly fell from above, splashing into the watery trench beside Calvin. A second later, Mei Li surfaced.

"What the hell you think you're doin'?!" he exclaimed.

"I think I'm saving your ass," she replied, pushing her long wet hair away from her face.

While those above nervously looked down at Mei Li and Calvin treading water in the trench, Gong Luhng belted out one of its famously annoying screeches. Only this time, it sounded more like the plaintive cry of a lost bear cub, rather than a powerful dragon. Obviously confounded by the sudden appearance of Mei Li, it wailed out its consternation.

"Hold that thought," Mei Li addressed the dragon. She then turned to Calvin and yelled over the loud pathetic screeching "Now, if you really don't need my help ..."

"Did I say that?" he yelled back.

Satisfied, Mei Li returned her attention to the dragon and began speaking to it in Cantonese. Gong Luhng soon ceased its caterwauling and stared down at her, captivated.

"What'd you say?" Calvin asked.

"I said, Poor dragon, you must be very tired from your big adventure. Wouldn't you like to close your eyes and take a nap?"

"Poor Dragon?!"

Gong Luhng snorted loudly and glared at Calvin.

"It's good, it's all good," he assured. "You want her to sing you a lullaby?"

"I don't know any lullabies," Mei Li insisted through clenched teeth.

The dragon began screeching again.

"Fake it!" urged Calvin.

Mei Li thought for a moment, then started to sing a familiar song—only in Cantonese. As her voice echoed sweetly through the tomb, Gong Luhng began to settle down into the water.

"Puff the Magic Dragon? Really?"

"Hey, I'm under a little pressure here."

When the dragon picked its head back up, she quickly launched into another verse. A heavy rope was lowered along the back wall and they gingerly swam toward it and grabbed hold. Mei Li's gentle singing reverberated through the tomb as she and Calvin were efficiently pulled up.

Once they arrived safely up top, Ray called to the crew in a hushed voice, "Get ready."

"Wait!" Mei Li implored Ray. "Do we have to do it so violently? I mean, look at him."

Those above peered down into the tomb at a dragon who was now peacefully reclining in the water, practically snoring.

"Since when did *it* become *he*?" Calvin pointedly asked.

"Since I found out *we* have a personal connection," she replied.

"*It* ate my deputy," Ray sternly reminded her.

"But Gong Luhng is like family," she pleaded. "And look, he's completely harmless now."

Seeing Ray's face, and knowing there was absolutely no flexibility in the matter, Calvin took Mei Li by the hand and pulled her aside. "Could I see you over here for a minute?"

And as he walked her away from the tomb, Ray gave the signal.

Ropes were released and logs thundered over rafters. Eventually, there was silence as a cloud of dust slowly rose from the newly encased tomb. Everyone stood frozen, listening. But all was quiet within.

Jess came to stand beside Lauren, who promptly turned her face away from him.

"Are you crying?!" he asked.

"It's that song," she nodded. "It gets me every time. First, little Jackie Paper doesn't come back ... and now ... this."

Laughing, Jess hugged her to him.

Terry fired up the BobCat and began moving loose soil from the mound, depositing it on top of the logs. Others grabbed rakes and hoes to help distribute the dirt over the roof. Once completely covered, the tomb once again looked like a seamless part of the levee and the dirt road that ran along it. Ready to perform the ritual, Ray and Tak walked to the edge of the tomb. The sergeant hung over the front and hammered the seal onto the gate as Tak read from The Book of Dragon in Cantonese.

"That which has been awakened is now returned to sleep. Rest peacefully, defender of your people and guardian of the rivers, until you are once again called forth."

Still somewhat in shock, Angela walked over to stand beside her son. "Thought I'd just stop by, see how things were going up here."

"Goin' a'ight," he nonchalantly replied.

"Anything you wanna tell me about?"

Calvin shrugged. Then putting an arm around Mei Li, he casually mentioned, "Oh, I met this girl. She's got some crazy-ass relatives but I think you're gonna like her."

"I think I already do," his mother replied.

❧ CHAPTER 41 ❧

SCOUT'S HONOR

With the final element of the entombment complete, the dragon-trappers gathered in the shade of the pear orchard, everyone shaking hands, hugging, and slapping each other on the back in celebration of their monumental achievement.

Ray called for their attention. "Everyone, I'd like us all to observe a moment of silence for Deputy Burt Watson." As they bowed their heads, Ray eulogized the deputy in a few simple words. "He was a good man. A brave man. May he rest in peace." The ultimate compliment from his commanding officer. Trying not to get choked up, Ray ended the moment by clearing his throat. "Tak has something he wants to ask you all."

Stepping forward, Tak spoke. "The last time Gong Luhng was brought forth, the people who ultimately entombed him, some of whom were my ancestors, swore an oath: never to divulge where the dragon slept. Out of respect for them, and for the good of all people, I ask that each of you now do the same."

"But what about the Science Fair?" Dent asked, seeing his chance for victory slipping away.

"I'll help you come up with something even better," Mei Li assured her little brother. "Something that will blow them away. I promise."

Tak held forth The Book of Dragon and asked them all to place their right hand upon it. As they did, a lone cloud moved in front of the sun, darkening the sky. A gust of wind suddenly pushed through the pear orchard and out across the slough. Tak posed a question in Cantonese, and though they didn't comprehend its exact meaning, each replied, "I do." Then as quickly as it happened, the sun returned and the air was once again still.

Looking around, Frances suddenly realized two people were missing. "So who's gonna swim out and let the Markhams outta their head?"

"Oh crap," said Calvin, feeling guilty. "I totally forgot."

"I'll go," said Jess.

"Me too," said Lauren, and hand-in-hand they made their way to the water's edge and waded in.

Ray looked to those remaining and asked, "So, how are we gonna keep this from happening again?"

"The seal must be hidden from view," said Tak.

"I guess I could build a false front out of reclaimed wood so it matches," said Ray, "but that's gonna take a while."

"Well, in the mean time I've got an old Highway sign that says, 'Danger, Keep Off,'" Joe offered. "It's big enough to cover the seal."

"Sounds like a plan," agreed Ray. "I don't know about the rest of you but I'm starving." Putting his arm around Frances, he added, "I could sure use one o' those killer burgers at Heron's Harbor."

"Come on, everybody," said Frances, "Burgers are on me."

As the team began to scatter, Angela turned to find Calvin and Mei Li lagging behind. "I take it you two will be joining us a little later."

"Here," called Frances, tossing Calvin her keys. "We'll catch a ride with the sheriff. Maybe he'll even let me ride up front."

"Yeah, up front's much better," confirmed Calvin.

Bringing up the rear and quite proud of themselves, the geriatric division of dragon-trappers piled back into the old Chevy.

"Gentlemen, I believe this calls for a beer," declared Joe.

"But what about that road sign?" Tak asked. "We should cover the seal ASAP."

"Aw, nobody's gonna mess with it in the next hour. It was a total fluke anybody even found it in the first place," replied Ol' Joe.

"I'd still feel better if it was concealed," insisted Tak.

"And it will be," vowed Joe, "shortly after we have a nice cold beer. The Crawdaddy Club's right on the way to my place."

"I am kinda parched," admitted Samuel. "It should be fine for a bit," he assured Tak.

"Okay, but don't forget." Tak wagged a finger at Joe.

"Scout's Honor," he promised with a military salute.

"You were obviously never a Boy Scout," said Samuel.

"I coulda been but I joined the merchant marines instead."

"Maybe we could grab a quick bite, too," hinted Samuel. "I been eatin' way too many burgers lately. Anybody else got a hankerin' for Chinese food?"

"I could go for some Mexican," said Tak.

Samuel turned the key in the ignition but as usual the Chevy insisted on being temperamental about starting. "Come on now baby, daddy wants a beer and some grub."

"Here we go again," groused Joe. "Good thing your business is boat engines. Drivin' this truck is like shtuppin' your grandma."

"Oh, I didn't shtup my grandma," retorted Samuel, "I shtupped yours."

"Gentleman, please," said Tak, "my sensitive Asian ears."

The Chevy's engine suddenly sparked to life, silencing its doubters with a deafening backfire.

"Alrighty then," said Samuel smugly, and turning to his passengers he held a vote. "Show of hands, who wants Chinese?"

Tak raised a hand and cast his vote for "Mexican."

Knowing full well he held the deciding vote, Ol' Joe threw a wrench in the works by nominating "Soul Food."

With the sun about to make its exit stage west, Calvin and Mei Li stood at the water's edge, looking one last time upon the ancient seal that would soon be hidden from view—hopefully for a very long time.

"Sleep tight, Gong Luhng," said Mei Li.

"Yeah, do me a favor, stay asleep for the rest of my damn life."

Calvin took Mei Li's hand and together they climbed the rocky embankment. Standing atop the dragon's tomb, they looked out at the now tranquil waters of Desperation Slough. When a gentle breeze arrived and moved through Mei Li's hair, Calvin pulled her into him. Finally, they were able to experience an unhurried kiss—no bikers chasing them, no dragon breathing down their necks, just the two of them learning each other.

And as the last rays of the afternoon shimmered on the gleaming gold seal below, a gentle snoring could be heard. Only it wasn't Gong Luhng, but Gladys. Sound asleep in her folding chair beneath the sycamore tree, she'd missed the whole damn thing.

❧ CHAPTER 42 ❧

Я должен курить

A Russian freighter was lumbering its way along the deep water channel of the Sacramento River at dusk when a sailor on deck spotted something in the water and yelled to his shipmates.

A short while later, the merchant marine and two of his comrades were huddled around a table in a small cabin enjoying an evening of vodka, cigarettes, and song. Nearby, a robust female sailor watched over a man in a bunk who was somehow managing to sleep in spite of his loud cabin mates. Eventually, the obnoxious singing pulled the man from his deep slumber and he turned over. Burt opened his eyes and sat up, taking in his surroundings.

The husky Russian woman smiled, and removing a hand-rolled filterless cigarette from her mouth, she held it to Burt's lips. Inhaling deeply, his face melted in nicotine bliss. The sailors cheered wildly as Burt ceremoniously ripped the tattered nicotine patch from his arm and defiantly tossed it aside. This called for another round of watka, including one for their newest shipmate.

Later that night, as the five drunken comrades hung on each other and wailed Russian love songs, the freighter sailed under the Golden Gate Bridge and out to sea.

❧ CHAPTER 43 ❧

SENTENCE COMMUTED

Angela found Calvin already back at work in the shop the following morning. She watched him confidently working on the engine of a ski boat for a moment before conspicuously placing his cell phone and iPod on a nearby workbench.

"I take it you'll be spending the rest of the summer here," she said.

"That was the sentence. Remember?"

"I suppose that could be reduced to time served, considering the circumstances."

"Yeah?" he replied, pondering the option. "What about Tyrone Gotsbank?"

She shrugged. "I dumped his rich ass. The luxe life is so overrated."

"Mm hmm."

"Up to you. I'll be headin' home this morning, so lemme know what you wanna do."

Calvin looked around the shop. "We got a lot o' jobs stacked up. And Samuel could really use the help, you know, gettin' through the busy season."

"Uh-huh," she replied knowingly.

"And there's this guy Ray knows—has an old WaveRunner he wants to unload. Says I can have it for free since it doesn't run."

"Oh, it'll run," she said proudly. "Then there's that feisty Chinese girl. Not to mention a lot o' people around here who seem like they'd be pretty tore up to see you go."

Realizing his mind was already made up, Calvin nodded. "You be okay if I stay?"

"Oh, hell yes. Might even go out on a date. Find me a real boyfriend. We can double date when you get home."

"No," he said plainly.

"No?!"

Calvin simply shook his head.

"I don't suppose you'd climb up outta that boat and show me some love before I go."

He did, of course. And as she hugged him, his mother said, "I'm proud o' you. You know that." Letting him go she added, "I'm never gonna forgive your ass for scaring the bejesus outta me, but ... you did what you thought was right."

Calvin walked his mother to the door and opened it to find Mei Li, Frances, Ray, Jess, Lauren, Lou, and Gloria—all waiting to see what he would choose and bracing themselves for a possible goodbye.

"Oh, you can all relax," Angela informed them. "He's stayin'."

As the group heaved a collective sigh of relief, a handsome black sheriff's deputy in uniform approached.

"Sergeant Cruz?" he asked, reaching to shake Ray's hand. "Gladys told me I'd probably find you here. I'm Deputy Jackson, the interim replacement you requested."

Seeing Angela's reaction to the age-appropriate new deputy, Frances and Gloria quickly jumped on it.

"Are you absolutely sure you have to get back?" Gloria asked her.

"You really must stay," insisted Frances. "We're having a 'Welcome to the Delta' barbecue on the lawn this evening for Deputy ..." she turned to the newcomer for a name assist.

"Jackson."

"We are?" asked Ray.

"Of course, we are," said Frances. "It was your brilliant idea, remember?"

"Oh, yeah. I have so many of 'em, it's hard to keep track sometimes."

"Well ...," said Angela, looking to Calvin who nodded his approval, "I suppose I could stay for a barbecue."

"So, I take it this is a fairly quiet assignment," the new deputy asked Ray. "I can't imagine anything too crazy happens up here in the Delta."

When everyone laughed nervously, he looked at them suspiciously.

"Nah, nothin' much happens up here in the cuts, bruh," said Calvin, covering. "And if we're lucky, you'll be bored outta your damn mind."

LOVE AND INFLATION

With the *Nice Piece o' Bass* back in the water, Terry and Neal eagerly resumed their fishing trip where they'd left off after being rudely sidelined by a dragon. Still too superstitious to return to their favorite spot in Desperation Slough, they took Samuel and Ol' Joe's tip about a lucky fishing hole they favored in Potato Slough. This turned out to be a great recommendation and both fishermen had sizable "keepers" in their baskets within the first hour.

There was only one down side to this splendiferous new spot: it came with Samuel and Ol' Joe. What started out as a blissful morning of fishing soon hit the skids when the tipsters themselves showed up in old aluminum boat—the first clue that these two fishing parties had dramatically different styles when it came to their beloved sport. The two seniors noisily settled in just yards from the bass boat and not only conversed loudly, they never shut up.

"You can't retire," announced Ol' Joe, indignantly.

"The hell I can't," countered Samuel.

"Well, if you retire, then people'll wonder why I don't retire."

"That ain't my problem," claimed Samuel. "Once Calvin graduates, I'm giving the whole shootin' match to him."

"What makes you think he wants that junky old shop?"

"I'll have you know that junky old shop is a respectable money-makin' business."

And on and on it, went until Neal finally turned to Terry and voiced what they were both thinking. "Time to find a new spot."

"Absafrickenlutely," agreed Terry.

"Gentleman," Neal called over to them, "we hereby relinquish this fishing hole to you."

"You leavin' already?" asked Samuel.

"But we just got here," said Joe.

"Very kind of you to share, but we don't wanna overstay our welcome," replied Neal.

"And four on a fishing hole is bad luck," claimed Terry, pulling that one out of his ass.

"I never heard o' that," replied Samuel.

"Me neither," said Joe.

"Well, now ya have," declared Terry.

As the boys of the bass boat began reeling in their lines, Neal noticed a substantial weight on his and it quickly became apparent something other than a fish was rising to the surface attached to his lure.

"What the hell is that?" asked Terry with unmitigated paranoia.

Neal immediately stopped reeling and all four fishermen anxiously leaned in for a closer look. Approximately a foot below the surface, what appeared to be a woman's hand with bright red nail polish was clinging to the end of Neal's line.

"Oh please, not again," said Terry.

"I can't even look," blurted Neal, turning his head.

Grabbing the boat hook, Terry cautiously poked at the thing before pulling it to the surface. The limp hand was attached to the equally limp body of Sirena the Mermaid. Once the others began to laugh with relief, Neal turned and opened his eyes.

"Here ya go, buddy," said Terry holding forth Sirena. "A girlfriend at last."

Taking the deflated mermaid, Neal carefully unhooked her from his fishing lure. "She's kinda cute," he declared. "Just needs some patch work."

"They usually do," Terry flatly announced. "They usually do."

❦ THE FINAL CHAPTER? ❦

WE HAVE A WINNER

Humming a mindless tune, Jack the Shack Man was happily rowing along in his battered skiff when something onshore caught his eye. Letting go of the oars, he stood up in the boat— one hand scratching his ass, the other shielding his eyes from an intense glare.

Retrieving a crumpled piece of paper from his back pocket, Jack carefully studied the image on the flier, then gazed back up at the gleaming gold seal.

Laughing like a lunatic, he threw his hands in the air.

"I win!"

A NOTE FROM
THE AUTHOR

Though the 1915 fire that destroyed the Chinese Quarter of Walnut Grove was very real, its true cause remains unknown. I'm pretty sure, however, that it wasn't started by someone with the power to call forth Gong Luhng. But then again ...

For more information about the history and experiences of the Chinese in Gold Mountain and the California Delta, please seek out the books listed on the Recommended Reading and Resources page, all of which proved invaluable when researching and writing *Delta Legend*.

The Sacramento-San Joaquin Delta is a fragile ecosystem in critical need of preservation and protection. For more information about the Delta and how you can help, visit the places and websites listed.

If you visit the Delta in person, please tread lightly. And wherever you live, find out where your water comes from and what you can do to conserve it.

Kelan O'Connell

RECOMMENDED READING AND RESOURCES

Books:

The Chinese in America, A Narrative History, by Iris Chang (Penguin Books, 2003)

Canton Footprints, Sacramento's Chinese Legacy, by Philip P. Choy (The Chinese American Council of Sacramento, 2007)

Bitter Melon, Inside America's Last Rural Chinese Town, by Jeff Gillenkirk & James Motlow, introduction by Sucheng Chan (HeyDay Books, 1993)

One Day, One Dollar: Locke, California and the Chinese Farming Experience in the Sacramento River Delta, by Peter C. Y. Leung (Chinese American History Project, 1984)

The California Delta, Images of America Series, by Carol A. Jensen, Hal Schell Archives and the East Contra Costa Historical Society (Arcadia Publishing, 2007)

Places to visit in person and on the web:

Delta Farmer's Market and future home of the Delta Discovery Center, 2510 State Highway 12, Isleton, California. www.discoverthedelta.org

The historic town and shops of Locke, California, starting with the Locke Boarding House Visitor's Center. www.LockeCa.com and www.Locketown.com

California Railroad Museum in historic Old Town Sacramento, California. www.csrmf.org

California Delta Chambers & Visitors Bureau: www.californiadelta.org

MY HEARTFELT THANKS AND GRATITUDE GO OUT TO ...

My parents, Jackie and Ed, for that old houseboat on the Delta, among other happy childhood memories. Extra credit to my valiant mom, a life-long reader who proofed the earliest and roughest versions of this work.

My three older brothers, Terry, Pat, and Mike, who endured my endless questions about boats, engines, fishing, watersports, law enforcement, and more. Special thanks to Panhead Pat for proofing.

Tom Size, my past, present, and future partner in crime, for encouraging me to self-publish and for handling so many of the technical aspects this entailed (especially e-publishing). There's just no way I could have done this without you.

Cody and Kelsey O'Connell, for keeping me at least plausible with regard to ever-evolving Hip-Hop culture and slang—though I would've had to change the manuscript daily were I to keep up fo'real.

Michael Bertram, for midnight barbecues on the Delta and his support of a much earlier incarnation of this work and its author.

Dr. Carolyn Vaughn and Jane Hall who encouraged me to bring *Delta Legend* into the classroom, and all the students whose enthusiasm for this story helped carry me through in the face of rejections. Special thanks to Z, for his love of this book and for being one of the first to bring Calvin to life in a reading, even though he really wanted the story to be about Rashawn.

Gina Dallara and Lonnie Hoyt for always providing sanctuary in the redwoods. G for early proofing and allowing me to talk my way through it on hikes along our beloved West County trails. My apologies to anyone who overheard us and worried they'd stumbled upon something truly sinister:

> G: Did you kill them yet?
>
> K: No, not yet. I'm working on it, though. It's hard, I'm getting sort of attached.
>
> G: But you have to kill them right?
>
> K: Absolutely, and I will. By this time next week, they'll be dead.

The ever-supportive chick posse: Connie English, Carolyn Vaughan, Becky Thatcher, Laura Miles, Katie Ciocca, Cathy Kane, and Karla Rasmussen.

Author and editor, Gabriella West, for working her magic on the manuscript and making me look like I know what I'm doing.

Dave Williams, for his brilliant cover art and design.

Debra Unger of the Delta Farmer's Market who welcomed me back to the Delta after too long away. And Nick Catanio for keeping Delta oral history alive from his post at the Farmer's Market.

Ken Scheidegger, for letting me pester him. But more importantly, for his steadfast guardianship of the California Delta through Discover The Delta Foundation, along with Wendy Martin and Laura Gregory Lea.

Mok Tze San (aka Kathy) for her assistance with Chinese names and for patiently trying to get me to understand the subtle and not-so-subtle nuances of Cantonese. Though she did not succeed, she kept me from completely failing.

Joyce and Alex Eng of the Chinese American Council of Sacramento (just to name one of their many affiliations) for their suggestions regarding the real history, especially since I stuck it in the blender to whip up this fantasy cocktail.

Clarence Chu and the board of directors, members, and docents of the Locke Foundation, for their stewardship and preservation of Locke, California and its rich history.

Alice McLeish, realtor and proofer extraordinaire.

Norman Wimer, for putting his educator's eye on the first physical copy and for making me laugh during a time when it was desperately needed.

Jeff McThorn of Delta Watercraft, who has his own PWC action story to tell.

Friends and colleagues too numerous to name here, who graciously laughed when it wasn't funny, smiled and nodded enthusiastically when it stunk, and cheered me on every time I stalled out. You know who you are and how much I love you.

And those on the other side who continue to inspire me: my spitfire sister-in-law, Sandy O'Connell, and my dear friend, Miriam Wright. Though you never got to read the final product, you're there in its pages.

Though she's been writing in one form or another since the age of 20, *Delta Legend* is Kelan O'Connell's first solo novel. She began writing in college, creating character monologues as a way to stand out in auditions and later went on to write sketch comedy, one-act plays, and

Photo by Tom Size

more specs for screen than she cares to admit.

Kelan holds a degree in Theatre Arts from San Francisco State University and has worked in the Film and Television Industry in Northern California and Los Angeles—among her many other day jobs. She currently lives in Northern California with her partner, Sound Engineer/Producer, Tom Size, and the incredibly spoiled pets of Camp RunAmuck. You can find her blog about writing, cooking, art, and life at www.kelanoconnell.blogspot. com.